I0742262

ILLUSTRATING LIFE AND OTHER STORIES

SEAN PLATT

Copyright © 2026 by Sterling & Stone

All rights reserved.

No part of this book may be reproduced in any form or by any electronic or mechanical means, including information storage and retrieval systems, without written permission from the author, except for the use of brief quotations in a book review.

The authors greatly appreciate you taking the time to read our work. Please consider leaving a review wherever you bought the book, or telling your friends about it, to help us spread the word.

Thank you for supporting our work.

Foreword

Seventeen years ago, I sat down to write a story and accidentally created a new life.

Like most authors, I started with short stories: quick bursts of imagination that demanded to be written before I really understood what writing even was. Over the years, as I built a career on novels, those shorts became experiments, explorations, side quests to the main narrative of my creative existence … until something shifted.

I realized I'd been treating shorts like sketches in a notebook: practice for the "real" work. But shorts aren't preparation for something else. They're their own art form, demanding their own attention, their own craft, their own respect. And I had hundreds of ideas, writhing in my mind and piling up like unopened mail. Ideas too strange, too specific, too urgent to wait for a novel-length exploration.

Ideas begging for breath.

This collection is the result of that shift.

Illustrating Life and Other Stories assembles narratives that wrestle with what it means to be human in a world increasingly mediated by technology, altered by loss, and complicated by our own desires for perfection, connection, and meaning. You'll meet alien artifacts that offer impossible choices, AIs threatening to erase human creativity, vampires confronting the mathematics of eternity, and artists so consumed by creation they forget how to live.

What connects them isn't genre — it's obsession. Transformation. The fragile alchemy between loss and discovery.

The aftershocks after each story matter. Not just for context; they're reflections on the creative process itself, on what these narratives mean to me and why they exist. Some anthologies present stories as artifacts awaiting discovery. This one invites you into my workshop, shows you the tools, lets you see the sawdust on my floor.

As an artist, my job has always been to illustrate life, to capture those paradoxical truths fiction reveals better than fact ever could: the ways we break ourselves chasing perfection, the price of ambition, the terror and beauty of love, and the uneasy hope that our creations might outlive us.

This is the first in what I hope will become a long library of such collections: snapshots of where my mind wandered, what questions I couldn't stop asking, which shadows I felt compelled to follow.

The stories here stand alone, but together they form a constellation, mapping what we're willing to sacrifice, what we can't afford to lose, and what still glows when everything else fades.

Thank you for opening this book. Whether you've been walking with me for years or just joined the journey, I hope something here stirs, unsettles, or illuminates.

The canvas is ready.

Happy reading.

Sean Platt

ONE

Amethyst Smash

I COULDN'T KEEP my eyes off of Kimi, and like usual, she didn't want me to.

We'd been out behind Brunson's barn for forty-five minutes already, and I figured we were a few minutes from kissing, then maybe some under-the-shirt stuff before Kimi took off her top.

Patience was getting harder, and so was I. But Kimi didn't like it when I was too eager, so I was mentally reciting the *Pledge of Allegiance* to seem like I wasn't.

Not exactly the easiest thing in the world, with Kimi in her little skirt and no bra. She liked to tease me, and I liked to be teased, but today the game was a little too long.

"Did you try the slaw?" Her eyes rolled to the back of her head as she swallowed.

"Yeah. It was delicious."

I'd been done eating for a while. We could have done that at home. Instead, we were having a picnic all the way over at Brunson's place because the bank had owned the land for more than a year. Everything was overgrown, no one ever came by, and it was a good thirteen miles from anything else.

The perfect place for a romantic early evening interlude without fear of interruption.

Neither my dad nor my brother was around to give me any shit. I could tell Kimi I loved her all I wanted to, and without worrying about all their *oohs* or *aahs* that were always a lot uglier than they sounded. Acting like they were playing when they were really trying to hurt me.

I was a year older than Kimi. She was just seventeen, but we'd been in love ever since she was in the seventh grade and I was in eighth. We had one class together, but that's all it took. I needed to see her twice and talk to her once.

We'd been dating ever since the spring fever took us both four years ago. Everyone knew we were gonna get married one day, and they all liked to say it. Except for Kimi's parents. They hated the idea, for sure. Liked to pretend I didn't exist. But I knew it by freshman year, and Kimi started believing it by the time she was in high school. Neither of us was dumb enough to say anything and take the ridicule. Until this year, when I was sneaking up on graduation, and it was finally time to start making plans.

Most of the time, it was all I could think about. What would life be like for us once I was out of school and could take care of Kimi full-time?

I was good at building websites and was already making enough on the side to prove that college was stupid, at least for me. I didn't want to be a doctor or lawyer or anything else that would keep me in school when I could start earning good money now. Kimi thought she probably still wanted to go and was doing all the homework to make college a possibility.

Still, it didn't matter if we were gonna get married eventually or not, Kimi's parents saw us both as young, and me as irresponsible, so we had to pretend like we weren't doing it and always had to find the most far-off, secluded places before she would agree to so much as lock lips. Once we got down to the good stuff today, it would be our third time rounding home.

"You really should try this coleslaw."

"I don't think I can," I said. "I think you took care of that for us."

Kimi looked down at the empty container of coleslaw and started laughing. Then she turned to the half-empty bottle of wine and started laughing harder. I thought about pouring her some more, but didn't want to go too far. That happened once, and it wasn't fun for either of us.

"Well, I'm still hungry, and the meat's all gone."

I shook my head and gave Kimi a grin. "Not all of it."

She looked away, blushing, but was in no way uninviting.

I scooted closer. Put a hand on her shoulder, then slipped a finger under the strap of her tank top and lowered it. "I love you."

"I love you too, Vic."

Her words were slurred, but not too bad. She didn't bother lowering the other strap herself. Instead, Kimi peeled off her shirt. Then, while staring into my eyes, she began to take off her bra.

It was unclasped, but still hugging her swollen breasts when she paused, eyes widening at something behind me.

I turned around and looked up just as an amethyst flash ripped through the dusk and exploded into the ground with a deafening crash, maybe about a mile away.

"What was that?" Kimi asked, surely tipsy and maybe scared.

"I don't know. We can go check it out. After. If you want."

But Kimi's bra was already back on, and now she was reaching for her shirt.

"What are you doing?"

"I want to know what that thing was."

"*Now?* Don't you wanna finish?"

"We'll finish later. I promise. Even if it's in the truck. But I wanna go see, okay?"

I didn't know how to refuse Kimi, and she said she'd even do it in the truck, which she'd always refused before. "Okay. Then let's pack it up."

I'd never tidied an area faster, gathering all of our picnic supplies into the basket, then rolling the blanket under my arm and tossing it all into the back of the cabin before opening Kimi's door. It was all a little uncomfortable, seeing as she'd made me harder than Trigonometry, and now I had to ignore it. "M'lady."

Kimi climbed inside Bessie, then I slammed her door. Less than a minute later, we were barreling through an overgrown field, on our way to find something that fell from the sky.

"Think we'll be able to find it?" she asked.

Kimi was buckled in, leaning forward to clutch the dashboard and smiling wide. I tried not to have my feelings too hurt that she was so much more interested in whatever fell from the sky than she was in the picnic I'd driven twenty-six miles to prepare.

"I don't think it'll be hard," I said, stepping on the gas, the F150 still heading for the line of lilac smoke pluming into the sky.

Despite the lack of a road, it only took a few minutes to get there. I parked ten feet from the crater and told Kimi to stay in the car while I went to check it out.

Kimi jumped out of the car. "Like hell I will!"

She scurried over to the hole, beating me there by a couple of seconds. She was already peering down by the time I got there.

Kimi gasped.

"What is it?"

"I have no idea." She shook her head. "I've never seen anything like it."

Me neither. The hole was about the size of an inflatable swimming pool, and maybe twice as deep. A strange little violet artifact sat in its center, glowing. Small and odd. Metal, but maybe not. It still shimmered with heat from its journey through the atmosphere, the finer details sharp and unmelted in a way that seemed entirely alien. Not necessarily from another planet, but from nowhere near western Texas.

"What do you think we should do?" Kimi took out her phone.

I closed my hand gently around her wrist. "Well, I don't think we should take a picture."

"Why not?"

"I don't know," I admitted.

It might have been five minutes we spent staring into the crater, or it might have been more like an hour. The sky did get darker, but it was hard to tell with the hole glowing so bright in every shade of purple.

Lavender, lilac, and mauve. Periwinkle, plum, and violet. They were all there. Amethyst, especially.

"I want to touch it," Kimi said.

"Me, too. But I don't think we should."

"Why not?"

"I don't know."

And again, we stared.

Eventually, Kimi started down into the crater. It was

now dark, but I was afraid to check the time. I didn't even want to take out my phone. I was horrified that Kimi was moving, especially in the direction she was.

"Wait! Don't go down there."

"Too late," she said, halfway into the crater.

I scrambled down behind her.

She gasped. "It's the most beautiful thing I've ever seen."

I couldn't argue. It was a lovely piece of metal, though it also looked like a rock. Reminded me of one of the three pieces of jewelry my mom left behind before she ran off with Mr. Parker, but of course, this one was different. And a million times more beautiful. The metal gleamed more than anything I'd ever seen. And it was so very purple.

But there was something not right about it, and both of us knew it.

"What's that feeling?" Kimi asked.

"I don't know. It's like … there's someone else there."

She turned and looked at me curiously.

My eyebrows arched. "You don't feel that?"

"I feel something, but no. It isn't that."

"Explain it." I was practically begging; that's how bad I needed to know.

"I need to touch it." Her body lurched a few inches forward, almost involuntarily. "But I'm also …" She swallowed, almost couldn't say it. "… repulsed by it."

Kimi took a step.

I grabbed her by the arm, harder this time.

She shrugged me away, took another step.

I had to stop her. She was too close to that thing. "Please!"

She looked back.

"Wait."

"For what?" Her face was rinsed in purple. Orchid forehead. Violet eyes.

"Let's go."

"After I touch it." Kimi took another step.

"Please, baby. I'm begging you. Don't touch that thing."

I didn't know what to do. Kimi looked like she was going to make a leap for the strange object. It was almost within her reach, and even though I hated to admit it, right now that stupid glowing metal whatever was more important to Kimi than I was.

It didn't help that she couldn't feel the menace there, looming around us.

What was so clearly a threat, Kimi accepted as an invitation.

"There's nothing to worry about. What are the odds that we would be out here to see this, Vic? We were *supposed* to be here. This is for *us*." Kimi took her final step and picked it up. "It feels as beautiful as it looks."

Her saying that filled me with chills.

But it must've stopped feeling beautiful. Kimi dropped the thing and cried, "OW!" She looked at me, her face twisted in pain. "That thing just stabbed me!"

I looked down at the glowing metal rock. "I don't think it stabbed you."

"It stabbed me, Vic. There were, like, these tiny little metal claws. They *grabbed* my finger and *stabbed* me."

"Okay." I wasn't going to argue. "Wait! What are you doing?"

"I dropped it. And now I'm going to get it."

Kimi bent down.

I scurried two steps behind, then grabbed her by the arm. "We don't know what that thing is."

"Exactly. Aren't you curious?"

"Sure, of course, but not enough to go out and touch the thing. You just said it burned you."

"I said it *stabbed* me."

"Right."

She bent down and picked it up again. "OW!"

And again, she dropped it into the dirt.

"That thing fell from space. It's probably still burning. It could be radioactive or something. You have to—"

"I told you it stabbed me, Vic." She gave me a dirty look, then — impossibly — went to pick it up again.

"Kimi ..."

"What?" She turned around and looked at me, kneeling, her hand hovering an inch from the rock.

"Let me get it for you."

Kimi stepped aside. I took off my shirt, remembering how fifteen minutes ago she was taking off hers, and then used it to gather the rock or whatever it was.

But I didn't feel any heat.

Curious, I unwrapped my shirt and picked up the rock. It felt smoother than I imagined, especially considering the thing definitely had its edges. I'd never felt anything like it, though it did make me think about squeezing Kimi's breasts. She let me do that all the time, even in the truck. Not that the feeling was the same, it was just alluring like that.

I laughed. "I guess it doesn't want to stab me."

"Shut up," Kimi said, though she was laughing, too. "Are you going to make me a piece of jewelry?"

"With this?" I held up the rock. "I wouldn't even know how."

"I bet your dad would be happy to help."

"Like I'd ask *him*. How about I drill a hole through the top and stick a piece of string through it? Then we can call it a necklace."

Kimi shook her head, smiling.

"How about if I get you a Ring Pop at Lotty's and I'll rubber band this thing to the top."

She shook her head again, a second away from laughing.

"Okay, I got it. How about I use it as a hood ornament? Then we can share it. Not like I go anywhere without you unless I have to."

And there it was. She shoved me while laughing. "Give it here."

I handed it over. Kimi dropped the rock into her purse before the thing could burn her or stab her or whatever again.

"You really think you should take that?"

"What do you want me to do with it?" She looked at me like I was crazy. "Leave it here?"

"Why not?"

"It's a space rock, Vic! How many times in your life do you expect something to fall from the sky? And right when we were about to do it. I think that's special."

"*Were* about to do it," I mumbled, pouting.

"We can still do it." Kimi nodded to nowhere a few feet away. "Then I'll have my special sky rock to remember it by."

I still felt uncertain and must have looked it.

"Come on, Vic. Give me one good reason why I can't take it with me."

"Because we're not supposed to be out here."

"You drove me out here because you wanted to fuck me." She laughed and slapped me on the arm. "So fuck me."

Then she took off her shirt and looked down at my crotch.

Four minutes later, we were back in the F150 and on our way home.

"What are you gonna do with that thing?"

Kimi shrugged. "Why do you care?"

"I don't."

"You do. This thing has you all worked up. I haven't seen you this agitated since—"

"I'm not agitated."

And I wasn't. There was just something creepy about that rock and how much Kimi wanted to keep it. Seemed a bit obsessive to me.

But then again, that's how Kimi was about everything. Including me.

I walked her to the door like always, once again ignoring the creepy figurines lining the front steps. I promised to come by tomorrow after church. Her parents always took a nap after service, and sometimes I liked to sneak into her room. Kimi was even acting like she wanted me to sneak in tonight, teasing me like a dare. Said she needed me to keep her safe from the scary rock.

Before I could work up the nerve, Kimi laughed and slapped me on the shoulder again.

But the next day, she turned me away after service. It took her more than ten minutes to answer my pebbles on the glass. Long enough that I seriously considered splitting.

She didn't look happy to see me when she finally came to the window. "What are you doing here?"

"I told you I was gonna come over."

"Well, you can't stay." Kimi was practically wagging a finger. That wasn't like her at all.

"You're not happy to see me?" I felt stupid standing there, grinning up at my girlfriend like an idiot.

"I'll be happier when I'm not worried that my parents

are gonna see you and then kill me." Kimi closed the window, then opened it again real fast and flashed me a smile to let me know she wasn't pissed. "I'll see you tomorrow, okay?"

"Okay," I said to the closed window.

Monday was better. Kimi's parents took her to school like always, but I drove her home, which I got to do every so often, and that was nice. She was chatty, even more so than usual, and telling me all sorts of stories. Even though she seemed extra happy, I couldn't get her to do anything dirty in the truck. By the time I dropped her off, she seemed almost irritated with me.

I must have messed up, because Tuesday was worse. I didn't see her before school, and it felt like she was avoiding me at lunch. My Kimi seemed to want to talk to everyone but me. But she was standing in front of the flagpole after school. I started to walk over and even called out "Kimi!" on my way.

All I got was a goodbye with her hand as she climbed into her parents' car.

I got to see Kimi both before and after school on Wednesday, and she seemed excited to see me both times. Got a long, wet kiss during the second one. Like she wanted to be mine again. But then I couldn't find her at lunch, and she didn't want a ride home.

Things got strange on Thursday. Not just different, but weird.

I started thinking about the way Kimi looked when she was getting in her parents' car. Her eyes were almost dazed. Like they were a million miles away. Or maybe light-years away.

Because my girl's behavior was almost alien. Reclusive. And Kimi wasn't like that. When we'd go to the movies, I could barely get her to stop talking. People were always shushing us, and we got kicked out of the Brookline twice. Now she was mute and sullen, more withdrawn than I've ever seen her.

At first, I wrote it off as processing what happened. I couldn't deny that being weird as hell, that purple amethyst whatever from the sky. But then I got to wondering if maybe it was affecting her somehow. Changing her behavior in some way. I'd seen stuff like that in movies, and it didn't seem all that far-fetched to me, now that it was happening.

I thought about the way she pocketed the rock. Almost possessive.

It would have been nice if she was that possessive with me.

A good conversation was the best way through any situation, not that my dad would ever agree. Or Tyler. But Kimi always did. That's just one of the reasons we got along so well. We'd have our little back-and-forth. She'd slap me on the arm, all playful and sexy.

I figured we could talk about it on Friday, but Kimi didn't want to. And she got mad when I tried. Like real mad. The slap didn't even feel all that playful.

"What's your deal, Vic?" Her hands were on her hips, and she was glaring me down. It was the first time I ever thought Kimi looked like her mother.

"I don't have any *deal*," I said, surprised by how fast the exchange had decomposed. "I'm just trying to talk to you. I'm worried about you."

I tried to touch her, but that didn't work. Usually, that was the way to get her melting into me. Or the other way around. Touch turned her pliable. But not this time.

She flinched. Pulled away like she wanted nothing to do with me.

"Just hear me out." Was I gonna start begging my own

girlfriend to talk to me? "Maybe that weird purple rock did something to you. You know, like maybe—"

"Stop it, Vic." Now she looked really upset. "Please. You've been talking about that thing ever since we saw it. Why won't you let it go? It's just a weird rock that fell from the sky."

"Maybe it's something more than that," I said, marrow-certain that it was. "Why don't you get rid of the thing, just in case?"

"Because it's mine."

She sounded a little like Gollum.

"Kimi …" I reached for her again.

But she walked away. She'd never done that before.

I went from worried to worse. I didn't even know why, because I hadn't ever felt anything like it. I just knew I had things to take care of. Kimi was the only good thing that ever really happened to me, other than getting Bessie.

I went over to her house the next day, parked across the street, circled the block … killing time waiting for her parents to leave or for her to maybe go for a walk like she sometimes did when she wanted a soda. Her parents didn't keep any in the house, but the corner store three blocks up near Vanguard carried a couple of local brands that she liked a lot and Mexican Coke, which I thought was too sweet. That's why she liked it.

But her parents didn't go anywhere all day, and neither did Kimi. By that time, I was starting to worry about her. And I mean *really* worry. Not just about us, even though it made me sick to my stomach that things were weird in a way that they never had been before. I couldn't stop thinking about that rock and what I was sure it was doing to my Kimi.

Maybe it *had* stabbed her, and maybe I was an idiot. Maybe I should have listened.

The thing might have done something to her mind. Because she seemed to be a little less my Kimi by the day. The way we left things on Friday, she didn't even want to look at me.

I couldn't take it. I had to say something. Unfortunately, I waited too long. If I knocked on her door or threw a pebble at her window right now, Kimi would probably go off on me.

So I went home and got a good Saturday night's worth of sleep. At least that was the plan. But I tossed and turned for hours, even after stealing a few nips of my father's whiskey. No dice. Not even after I jerked off the second time. I was too agitated. Stuck between the twin worries of thinking I was probably paranoid and knowing in my heart I wasn't.

That thing from space was somehow changing my Kimi.

I ended up falling asleep around six in the morning. My brain was still going, but I guess my body needed a break. The timing was perfect, I suppose, since I woke up just as the service was ending. I was probably parking six blocks from her house by the time her parents were pulling into the drive.

I made the walk in record time. Tossed one pebble, waited. Threw the second. No response. Then the third. If Kimi didn't come to the window, I'd eventually throw a whole handful. And she must have known it, the way the curtains blustered about, and the sash flew up like it was greased.

My heart was broken, looking up at Kimi scowling down. "What are you doing, Vic?"

"I want to talk."

"You *always* want to talk!"

"Why won't you just get rid of it, Kimi?"

"Why don't *you* just drop it? It's the principle of the thing. I shouldn't have to get rid of something just because you don't like it. That doesn't set a very good precedent for a life together, now does it?"

Not when she put it like that.

"Fine. I won't say anything about it. But I still want to talk."

"You look terrible."

I shrugged. "I didn't sleep much. That's why I want to talk. I need to make sure everything's okay between us."

"Everything's fine. It's just been a rough couple of days. I'll see you at school tomorrow, okay?" Kimi didn't look like things were fine.

"Can't we just talk for a couple of minutes?"

"I don't want my parents to know you're here."

"Say you're going for a walk. Come on, just to Lotty's and back. I'll buy you a Mexican Coke."

Kimi took a moment to think, then she said, "Fine. Give me a minute."

I took her hand as we passed the first stop sign. Kimi reluctantly let me.

I wondered if she had it with her, maybe in her pocket. If I could get her to let me put my arm around her waist, I could slip my hand in and take it from her without even knowing. For her own good.

We walked in silence until she said, "So, what do you want to talk about?"

All I really wanted to talk about was the rock and how I wanted my Kimi back. I didn't want to sound like a jerk or anything, but I had to figure out a way to ask her why she was acting like she was without making her mad at me.

"You came over and got me to walk with you just to give me the silent treatment?"

"No."

"Well, you said you wanted to talk, and we're not doing that, so …"

"You told me I couldn't say anything about the rock. I'm just—"

"Oh, my God, Vic, are you kidding me? You're really not going to drop this, are you?"

"I don't see why you're making such a big deal about it."

"You're the one making a big deal about it! I'm just standing up for myself. I don't like the idea of you telling me you don't like something, then expecting me to get rid of it even though it interests me. What if I went into your room and said, 'Hey Vic, I'm not sure how I feel about your guitar, so I think you need to get rid of it?'"

"It's not the same."

"How is it different?"

I could feel myself sweating. My hands, my pits, and my brow. I'm sure Kimi could see it, too. I was out on the ledge. She didn't want to talk about it, and I definitely knew she wouldn't want to hear what I thought about the way she'd been acting.

But I'm not sure I had another choice. We were at a standoff. I saw where Kimi was coming from, about not wanting me to hold dominion over her decisions. But that's not what I was trying to do. It bothered me that she couldn't feel the danger of that thing.

Maybe that was the way to go about this. To straight out ask her if she felt anything weird from the thing. After all, she's the one who said that it stabbed her.

Then again, if that part of the conversation went sideways, which it almost for sure would, I would be even worse off than I was when I got into my truck that morning.

She looked me up and down, then said, "You smell awful, you know."

That felt like a slap.

"I'm sorry," she said. "I've never smelled you like that before."

"Like B.O.?"

"And whiskey. I know you didn't brush your teeth."

"I'm double sorry, okay?"

"I don't care if you're triple sorry, Vic. Just say what you need to say."

We were almost to Lotty's. I stopped walking. Put my hand on her arm and turned Kimi toward me. She flinched away from my touch and fell a step back.

Kimi looked surprised.

I felt the same. "Just tell me why you've been so weird lately."

She looked at me like I was crazy. "You've been acting weird ever since we got back from the barn. You were never all possessive like that before."

"I never had any reason to be."

"You don't have any reason to be now."

"Sure, I do. What about the rock?"

"What about it?" Kimi's hands were balled into fists. Her eyes were squinted. I couldn't tell if she was about to scream or cry or punch me. "I found something pretty that fell from the sky, and I want to keep it. Why do you have to be such an asshole about that?"

"I'm just worried about you."

"Worried about what?"

"I don't know," I admitted. But so what? That didn't mean there wasn't anything there to worry about.

Kimi looked so mad. I probably should have dropped it. Instead, I said, "Just think about it. Did you feel any different when you got home on Saturday night? Did you touch the rock again? Did it stab you? Just tell me that, and I'll leave it all alone."

Kimi looked like she wanted to rip my head off. "No. I never touched it again. It's in the jewelry box on my dresser, where I left it Saturday night. The only time I even think about it is when you're being all weird and won't leave it alone. Does that answer your question? Now, can we drop it?"

I wanted to, and I would have. But I could tell that Kimi was lying. We've been together since middle school. I knew her tells. When she couldn't meet my eyes or stand still, then there was a better-than-excellent chance she wasn't telling the truth.

The problem was, I'd only seen Kimi do that in front of her parents. Never between us. That rock had a hold on her, and I knew it. Its danger filled me like a warning. *Get that rock from Kimi.* I bet she had it on her. In one of her pockets.

"Maybe you could give it to me, just for twenty-four hours, and see if you feel any different?"

"I don't feel any different now!" She made the fastest about-face I'd ever seen. Started marching back toward home.

I ran behind her, but she didn't want me near her. Kimi was on cross country, but I wasn't and didn't stand a chance of catching up.

By the time I was standing outside her house and looking up at her window, my stomach couldn't make room for anything but despair. Kimi's curtains looked more closed than should have been possible.

I wondered if the rock was really in her jewelry box. I doubted it. I imagined her sitting cross-legged on her bed, holding it in both cupped hands, staring at it like it was the most precious thing she'd ever seen.

My Kimi, stolen by a space rock.

But there was nothing I could do about it right now, so no point in standing in her yard. I couldn't go home, either. It was Sunday, so Dad and Tyler would both be there and probably drunk. If I was gonna get beat up on, I'd rather get pummeled by my Kimi.

So I waited until the sun went down, not walking back to Bessie, but still walking nonetheless. A mile here and there until I'd done around a dozen or so, and figured it was safe to circle back.

I threw one pebble, and then the next. I got to a handful fast. But Kimi still didn't come to the window.

Now we had to talk.

It wasn't just about the rock. She could keep it. I just wanted to make sure everything was okay between us. I couldn't lose Kimi. That would leave me with nothing.

I knocked on the door. No answer.

I knocked again. And again. And again.

Then it opened. Mr. Wallace was holding a rifle, the stock pressed to his chest. "Can I help you with something, Vic?"

Only time I ever had to negotiate with an armed man, I was dealing with my old man. Scared as I was, I knew deep in my heart he'd never shoot me. But in this case, I wasn't so sure, looking up at Mr. Wallace. I was mostly grown already, if not all the way, but Kimi's dad had a few inches on me. From where I was standing, those inches felt like a foot.

"I was hoping I could talk to Kimi."

He stared straight down at me.

Was the gun actually loaded? How much did he want to show me?

I looked up at him, hopeful. I could see where he was coming from, with me pounding on the door asking to talk to his daughter after throwing rocks up in her window for a half hour or so.

I'd want to protect my daughter, too. But if I could help him see things from my side, then maybe he'd realize I was only trying to protect my Kimi.

"Can you give her a message for me?"

I never got a chance to tell Mr. Wallace what that message would be.

"How about I give you a message, son. You step off of my front porch right now, and if I see you here again, or anywhere around Kimi, or if she tells me that you been giving her a hard time, just know that I have a smaller one of these" — he looked down at the rifle then back up at me — "the kind that fits in my pocket."

I guess Mr. Wallace wasn't as religious as I thought.

Maybe Monday would be better, with us being back in school and all. But I was wrong. I tried to find Kimi in all of her regular places, but she was avoiding me.

Seemed like everyone else was, too. I wondered if she told people to stay away from me. Or maybe it was because Kimi was right and I smelled terrible. I'd taken a short shower when I got home Sunday, after she made me feel bad about my reeking, but I didn't put much effort into it, then went back to pilfering sips of the whiskey. Maybe that was it. Not too smart if I wanted Kimi to talk, but I was going out of my mind and didn't know what else to do.

I ditched my last class, determined to get her alone for at least a minute or so before she went home. I had a fifty-fifty shot of her taking the eastern or western exits. She had bio with Mr. Fry, and his room was in the middle. She always took the east exit and then cut across the lawn. I thought maybe she would go the west one today since it was the opposite of her usual, but she'd been throwing me off all day, so the best way to keep me crooked at the end would be going her normal way.

I hid outside in the hedges, only moving when Ms. Lofgren came strolling by. I waited through the whole period in case my Kimi left early.

She didn't. But she did take the eastern exit.

I dashed over the second I saw her.

She was on alert. Turned, saw me, started walking faster.

"Kimi, wait!"

She didn't.

I had geography on my side, and I'd been ready, so I probably could have caught up, but then there would have been a scene. My Kimi could yell real loud when she wanted.

Before I could pick between my two terrible choices, I saw Mr. Wallace behind the wheel of his Honda Accord, his full attention on his daughter. He hadn't seen me yet, and despite my wanting to resolve things with my Kimi, that's how I wanted to keep it.

So I didn't follow her.

I'd never felt lonelier or more isolated. I missed her something fierce. We'd never really been separated since first getting together. Not emotionally. And the longest we ever went without seeing each other was the first winter break we were a couple, only because being together was still our little secret.

Now I felt lost.

Maybe it was because I was so tired. Inside and out. I couldn't think about anything else, so all of my waking time was occupied, but then I was still thinking about it at night when I couldn't sleep. When I finally did, I had nightmares. Always about Kimi and that stupid rock. I was a week behind on all my homework. Every time I tried to get any of it done, I'd end up drawing pictures of her, writing her poems, or listing the evidence to prove all the ways she was pushing me out of her life.

I know it probably sounds selfish, like it's all just for me and my needs. But that isn't true. I care more about Kimi than I ever cared about anyone. More than I cared about myself. Of course, I needed her, but she needed me, too.

We always agreed about that. But now it seemed like the craving only went one way, and every time I tried to make things better, I only ended up making them worse. She kept acting like *I* was the one being weird, and I had the distinct feeling she was carrying the rock around with her, afraid I might break into her house to take it or something. But I was the possessive one?

It wasn't her fault, I reminded myself. It was the stone's influence. It was all she could think about, a crazy obsession that she couldn't control. I had to get the stone away from her and bring my Kimi back.

I couldn't go to her house. Couldn't call her on the phone. Couldn't even approach her at school without her walking away from me. Like she was afraid that if she talked to me, I'd find a way to make her give me the rock.

It was too much. I wasn't gonna be a coward and do nothing. I didn't care if Mr. Wallace had a gun. I needed to fix this thing with my Kimi. Make it better once and for all.

I went home. Ignoring my homework, I took a shower so she wouldn't think I stunk. Even beat off while I was in there, so I wouldn't be thinking about her naked as much while trying to sort this all out. Then I ate two microwave burritos for dinner and drank water because Kimi would know if I had anything else.

I was doing everything possible to keep cool and stay level-headed. I wouldn't bring up the rock, not until we'd talked through whatever this was. It was like what my dad said about rebuilding his chopper — everything could be fixed, but there was an order to things.

I thought I could make it. I'd been brave before. My dad's longer streaks lasted a couple of weeks, but I got through them. And I always knew he'd be sorry once it was over. Probably even more than the last time. Things would be great, sometimes for as long as three months after that.

That's how it was going to be with my Kimi. I just knew it. We'd been together for a long time, but it was relative. A long time for us was a blink to her parents. They were together for ten years before they had her.

I just had to stay calm.

But around nine or so, that calm was becoming a roaring anxiety infecting my every thought.

What if she wouldn't talk to me?

What if her father shot me?

What if her obsession with that rock had pushed out any feelings she ever had for me?

I wanted to go over and just get things over with, but I had to be patient and wait for her parents to go to bed. Fortunately, they were the early-to-bed types.

I gave it another hour, then left, but I got there too early and had to make myself lose track of time for a while. I usually like the sounds Bessie makes when I'm driving alone. Her voice betrays her age. Exploding with rattles. Groaning and choking, no reprieve. My Kimi once said it sounds like a nightmare. That night, for the first time, I agreed.

It was well past midnight by the time I stopped driving around.

The whole house was dark. Every light out, including the one on the side that must have burned out because it was *always* on. They had motion sensors, so I couldn't get too close to the porch, but if I stayed low and quiet, I could get up to her room like I had so many times before.

Except those other times I was invited. She left her window either open or unlocked. I'd have bet both balls in my sack that wasn't the case now.

And I was right.

After climbing the sturdy tree next to her room, I couldn't jiggle the window or try to break in at least not through my Kimi's room. She was a light sleeper, and she'd start yelling for her daddy the second she heard me outside.

I pictured Mr. Wallace, rifle in one hand, pistol in the other, as I climbed back down the tree.

I sat on the wet ground, my back against the trunk, wondering what to do next.

The obvious move was a little too risky.

But it was also the straightforward solution. And right then, it felt like my only choice.

I looked up at the front porch, to the row of figurines. Jesus was there. All the disciples. Mary and Joseph. A few other people I didn't know, even though my Kimi had told me a couple of times. The spare key was under Luke. He looked pretty much like all the other ones, though his eyes seemed sadder.

Maybe her parents had moved it, but I didn't think so.

But the lights would go on the second I got near the porch. And I was sure the Wallaces were living on high alert. Unnecessarily so, unless that rock was a danger to them like it was to my Kimi. Probably was.

I counted to ten, tried to summon the courage to run to the porch. Got to six and realized if I wasn't willing to sprint that second, there was no way I'd do it at zero. I made it to four before launching myself toward the porch.

I grabbed what I hoped was Luke and dashed away.

I waited for the light to die, then turned him upside down to check for the key.

It was there. Fortunately, I grabbed the right disciple.

I left Luke on the lawn, right by the tree, because it wasn't like I was going to take the time to properly situate him. Not before getting in the house. I could do that on my way out, after I made things better with my Kimi.

Back onto the porch, light beaming down on me as though it were screaming: "Hey, look! He's breaking in!"

I fumbled with the key before the lock mercifully clicked open.

Success! But my shoulder pressed into the door a little too hard, surprising me with the lack of resistance. I recovered quickly, softly closed the door, then darted to a knot of shadows over by the sofa.

I froze for an eternity of five minutes. It wasn't fear — someone might be listening.

My heart was walloping hard in my chest, but I had to ignore it. Even if everyone was wide awake with their ears perked, I was the only one who could hear it. And honestly, I might be imagining the sound since it was pounding so hard.

I made it to the stairs, spending as long as I needed on each step to feel like I earned enough quict to claim the next one.

Eventually, I made it to the top. Her house felt like a tomb.

So I made like a ghost, taking a grim reaper's sweet time down the hallway to her room, reminding myself with every other step that the telltale heart beat only for me.

When I tried to open her door, the knob zapped me, and I almost cried out. Had to bite my lip hard to stay quiet. My hand wasn't hurt, but the static electricity shock had been unexpected. Probably shouldn't have been after all that shuffling on the carpet.

I grabbed the knob again and gave it a slow turn. Then I was inside.

My eyes were already adjusted, so even though I couldn't see my Kimi all that clearly, I could still recognize her beauty in the shadows. The jewelry box sat on top of her nightstand. I glared at the thing, hating it for coming in between us like it had. But I didn't dare open it up to search for the rock. If I made a noise and woke her up, she'd call her daddy. And I might be wasting my time anyway. She probably kept it under her pillow when she slept.

I inched closer.

It wasn't supposed to be creepy. Really, it was sweet. She looked so pretty, all warm and defenseless.

I definitely didn't want to scare her or do anything that might bring Mr. Wallace into the bedroom, so I was extra quiet when I climbed into bed.

Being such a light sleeper, I imagined her waking up faster, but by the time she opened her eyes, my arms were already around her.

Startled, my Kimi opened her mouth to say hello. Or maybe to scream. I couldn't take the chance, so I put my hand to her mouth to trap the noise in her throat.

"It's okay," I said. "It's me."

But for some reason, that didn't soothe her.

She kept trying to get away, even though she didn't have to, and I kept on telling her everything would be okay. I just wanted to have a conversation was all.

My hand was still pressed to her mouth, but I tried to make my voice as nice as I could.

"I just want to talk, okay? If I take my hand off of your mouth, are you going to scream?"

She shook her head. Her eyes were big and full of tears — not crying, not yet, collecting like rain in a bucket just drops from overflowing.

It broke my heart to see her so scared, and to know that I was the one making things that way. But I also felt excited to show her that she didn't need to be.

Slowly, I moved my hand away from her mouth.

Kimi still looked like she wanted to scream, but her lips only moved because they were trembling.

"I just want to know why you've been acting so weird. Ever since we were out at the barn."

"Me?" Now tears were falling from both eyes. No sound, though. "It's you. You've… changed."

"I have not," I said.

She tried to say something, but choked instead.

"It's the rock. It changed you, Kimi. Made everything different somehow."

"It's just a rock!"

Too loud.

I put a finger to my lips.

Kimi nodded, then continued. "It's just a rock. *You're* the one who got all possessive and wanted it."

"I wanted you to throw it away!"

"No, you didn't!" She was whisper-shouting, just like me. "You kept saying it was yours, kept trying to take it away from me. You said it stabbed me because it wanted you instead. That you saw it first, and it was your idea to go and get it. Even though you couldn't have seen it first because your back was to it!"

"That's not what happened." I shook my head, sure as hell remembering things differently.

"It is, Vic."

I didn't believe her, but so what? That didn't change

anything. "Then why wouldn't you give it to me, if you didn't even care?"

"I told you, it was the principle. You were ordering me around and being such an asshole about it. You never talked that way to me before."

"I'm sorry."

"I know you are, Vic, but …"

She stopped. Probably saw the look in my eyes that I felt right then in my heart.

The one I had no control over.

In that moment, Kimi realized that I was apologizing for something else. Something I hadn't even realized until she pointed it out.

I did want the rock.

I needed it like nothing I've ever needed in my life.

I thought that it had gotten into her head, but I was wrong. It had gotten into mine, and feeling it so close, I suddenly realized it had answers to questions I didn't even know I'd had until now.

It promised so much.

It would tell me so many of its secrets.

All I had to do was take it.

"No …" she said.

That was all she got out.

Kimi opened her mouth to scream, but I couldn't let her.

If she screamed, her father would come. At worst, he would kill me. At best, he'd call the police. And my life would be over.

The rock would be gone forever, its mysteries never revealed.

I kept having to squeeze tighter and tighter to keep Kimi from screaming, but also because I couldn't stand the sound of her begging.

When she finally stopped, I let Kimi go.

Then I went to the jewelry box and got my rock.

* * *

Aftershocks on Amethyst Smash:

THE FIRST TIME I saw *Creepshow*, I was too young and kind of too close to the screen. One of those late-night, peeking-through-my-fingers viewings where I wasn't sure if I was more scared or thrilled.

Something got inside me and never left. Decades later, one of those vignettes crawled out of my subconscious and slipped under my skin.

At its surface, Amethyst Smash is a story about young love and something falling from the sky. A pulpy setup, humming with hormonal static and cosmic mystery.

But under the hood, it's about obsession.

Vic doesn't know he's in a horror story. He thinks he's in a love song. And while Kimi is the one who touches the rock, he's the one who gets possessed.

Until what started as love mutates into something unrecognizable … and he still believes he's doing the right thing.

Be careful what you let live in your mind rent-free. Especially the shiny things. And those obsessions that start small. Because some ideas don't need a spaceship to land in your life.

They simply need a crack in the door and your undivided attention.

This story started with a kiss under a barn, a bottle of wine, and a purple flash in the sky. It ends in a place where love forgets its name.

And that's the scariest kind of story: the ones where you never see the monster because you've become it.

TWO

Terms of Service

DEAR CONSOLIDATED BOTTLING CORPORATION, Incorporated,

I AM WRITING to express my dissatisfaction with your Xtrem Juice soda drink. After consuming it, I do not feel any younger or more extreme.

SINCERELY,
  Eli Parker

~

DEAR MR. PARKER,

I AM sorry to hear that you were unsatisfied with our product. Please contact customer support using the phone number listed on the can, and they will issue a prompt refund.

· · ·

MARCY Dennis
  CBC, Inc.

❧

DEAR MARCY,

THANK YOU FOR REPLYING PERSONALLY. I must admit to a brush of nerves after my last email. I was afraid that I might have contacted the wrong company because frankly, your corporate name doesn't sound very extreme. I was also concerned that I might be misunderstood after failing to spell "extreme" in the way your company is used to. I meant "xtrem." I am also curious if the removal of 67 percent of the E's normally spent on the word "extreme" saves wear and tear on your keys. Could you please send me a photograph of your keyboard? I would like to compare your E key to mine, as mine is entirely faded because I use too many E's. I may follow your lead from here on out, in the interest of efficiency.

SINCRLY,
  li Parkr

❧

DEAR MR. PARKER,

· · ·

I AM sorry that you have been dissatisfied with our product. Please contact the customer service support line at 1-800-451-4545, and they will issue you a refund.

MARCY Dennis
CBC, Inc.

~

DEAR MARCY,

I WOULD LIKE to retract my earlier complaint. Since our last email exchange, I have consumed several more cans of Xtrem Juice and am feeling much more xtrem. Yesterday, I stood on a moving dolly and had a friend pull me behind his car for several blocks. We stopped when I slammed into a mailbox, but thanks to how xtrem I now am, I quickly recovered. In fact, I'm a medically controlled epileptic and have decided to stop all medication because your soda makes me feel so alive, young, and xtrem. It's like medicine for poseurs. In fact –

~

"DAD?" said a voice.

Eli looked up from his monitor, pausing mid-sentence. Dashiell was standing in the office doorway, holding a block of wood.

"What?"

"I need you to cut out my Pinewood Derby car."

"I'm working."

"You've been working all day. It's, like, 8 o'clock. You

promised when I came home from school that you'd do it tonight."

"Yes, Dash, I work all day. It's part of being an adult and keeping a roof over your head."

"I just need the block cut out. I can do the rest."

Eli sighed.

Yes, he'd been working all day, but he wasn't tired because working had mostly consisted of checking email and browsing through the online social networks. Some of it was fishing for new and insulting ways to annoy people for profit, and some of his energy had been consumed by replying to emails like the one he received from Consolidated Bottling Corporation. But mostly he'd been screwing around.

Eli's blog was phenomenally popular, and his books and collections of insulting email exchanges sold very well. Unlike most bloggers, the ads on Eli's high-traffic site paid the bills and then some. Significant book sales were gravy. If he'd wanted, Eli could "work" for 15 minutes a day just by checking his email. But only half of his reason for ranting was profit: He loved the praise, loved people telling him how awesome he was.

"This is important, Dash," said Eli, his eyes flicking to the screen.

"Come on, Dad. The Derby's tomorrow!"

Eli thought about chastising his son for waiting until the last minute, but Dashiell *hadn't* waited. He started asking Eli for help the week before. In Eli's defense, there wasn't really time. About half of his rants were funny or absurd (like the one to Consolidated Bottling), but the other half were dead serious. Even devoted fans of his funny rants called Eli an asshole, but sometimes the world needed an asshole to right a few wrongs.

Most people would tolerate bullshit perpetrated by

predators. Not Eli. When a bad deed went unpunished, assholes like Eli pushed back. This past week alone, Eli had publicly protested the return policy of a well-known (and, truth be told, well-loved) Internet marketer, had taken a member of Congress to task for some hypocritical anti-gay statements (the congressman wasn't gay, but his secret gay lover was), and shamed a major electronics manufacturer for their underhanded terms of service.

Pinewood cars were insignificant by comparison.

"Hell," said Eli, failing to type anything funny in Dashiell's presence. "Ask your mother."

"Mom can't run your band saw!"

True. Maxine would cut her fingers off if she tried; the saw was a behemoth Eli had scored in an auction when Dashiell's old middle school closed and liquidated its wood shop. Eli got the saw two years before, when Dashiell was 11.

Dash had been disappointed when his new school didn't offer wood shop until junior year, something that seemed prudent and wise to both Eli and Maxine. But when Eli got the saw, he'd promised he'd use it to build things with his son. The tally so far was zero.

"Tomorrow. I have to finish this."

Professional assholes didn't conform to timetables. He could finish his email in the morning. Or the next day. Or a week after that, it didn't matter. But one of the things that made Eli great at his job (the serious, crusader side, anyway) was a certain sort of stubborn arrogance. Eli set his stakes and never budged. He was always, *always* right. No one else got to be right unless they just so happened to agree with Eli. Dashiell had learned that lesson again and again growing up — like the time he'd wanted to shave his head, the time he'd wanted to buy that pink shirt, and the time he'd wanted to see that

Pixar movie instead of an age-inappropriate Kevin Smith film.

"Daaaad," Dashiell whined.

"What happens when people whine?" Eli snapped.

Dashiell shook his head and turned to leave the office.

"Dash?"

The boy stopped. He turned to face his father, then dutifully answered the ritual question. "They get what they want."

"That's right. This house was bought with complaints and whining. Like all your food, toys, and games. But there's one and only one place where whining is *never* appropriate. Where is that, Dash?"

"With you."

"That's right. Why?"

Dashiell sighed. He was already defeated, but Eli had to twist the knife whenever something like this surfaced. It was part of being a good parent, imparting the wisdom his son would need to survive out there in the world.

"Because rules don't apply to you."

"Good boy."

Eli started to add that he'd do the goddamned Pinewood Derby car tomorrow, but the door had already closed.

He returned to the screen and finished his email.

ELI'S PHONE buzzed at noon the next day. He glanced at the screen, then mentally reminded himself to 1) reply to Maxine's text and 2) handle the errand she'd been bugging him about for a month. Later. Right now, he had to answer comments on his blog.

Answering comments was always a hoot. Most bloggers

had to deal with negative feedback, but Eli lived for it. He got plenty of fan comments (and Tweets, and emails, and Facebook messages), but hate held the real juice. Eli had received his share of outright threats, but after a while, all that saber-rattling was desensitizing. The first threat unnerved him despite its absurdity (a threat to travel cross-country to punch him in the face), but after enough came and went without incident, none remotely bothered him. Now they were funny, fodder for later rants to publish on his blog, earning him further adulation and threats.

His phone buzzed and rattled on his desk, then kept buzzing. Maxine wasn't just texting; she was calling. He could pick it up (she'd expect him to; he worked at home while she worked at an office), but if he did, she'd fly into 16 different tangents and hold him hostage for a quarter hour at least. Maxine was great, but she rarely knew when to shut up. She yammered on and on and on, and just when he thought he could hang up, she'd think of one more thing ... and then one *more* thing until they hit an obvious spot to hang up. She could leave a message. He knew why she was calling, anyway — or at least, the *primary* reason, seeing as she'd think of a thousand things to say if he answered.

A text. A call. Next, she'd send an email.

He *had* to handle Dashiell's birthday present soon, so Maxine would stop nagging.

Eli switched to his Twitter window and began sorting replies. And yes, there were a few that were angry with him: several over the gay congressman (right-wing homophobes, all calling Eli a fucking faggot) and — *gold mine!* — one from the Internet marketer he'd lampooned the week before. The marketer was indignant, bitching that his products were not scams. Eli smirked. Didn't these idiots know not to feed trolls?

Feeling playful, Eli composed a return Tweet suggesting that the Internet marketer try Xtrem Juice.

Then, predictably, a new email notification popped up in the corner of Eli's screen.

FROM: Maxine
   Subject: Dashiell's birthday present

ELI WAS ANNOYED. The more Maxine asked him to find a solid (and appropriately expensive) present for Dashiell's 13th birthday, the more Eli wanted to resist. It was a vicious circle. A month ago, Maxine had asked Eli if he could handle getting the present. Eli, who'd already decided he really should make it up to Dashiell for his repeated absences, agreed. But he kept forgetting, and every time Maxine reminded him, he bristled. That was Maxine trying to force him into a box, and Eli didn't like being forced into a box.

He'd built a life where he could do what he wanted when he wanted, and didn't need others making rules and handing him tasks. It was also Maxine complaining and whining, and while complaining and whining got a person what they wanted, rules didn't apply to Eli Parker, and she should have known that after 15 years of marriage.

He wanted to get Dashiell's present, but every reminder reset the clock. Sufficient time had to pass before Eli could feel like it was his idea again. The problem was, Maxine reminded (*pestered*) him too often for that length of time to ever elapse.

But she was right. It had been a month, and still he dragged his feet. Maxine could get the present herself, of course, but she'd screw it up. Eli, who wasn't used to being shy, would let her know how stupid the gift was. But Eli didn't like being usurped, and Maxine probably didn't want to hear him complain — seeing as that was his job, and he did it so well.

Time was up: Tomorrow was Dashiell's birthday.

Sighing, Eli opened a new window in his browser, turning his back on more inflammatory comments and some highly offensive social media correspondence. He hoped Dashiell would appreciate his sacrifice. He hoped *Maxine* would appreciate the effort. Eli was a busy man. And didn't he put a roof over all of their heads? It was work he should really be doing instead of looking for a birthday present.

He went to Google, then stared at the search box, realizing he had no idea what to get Dashiell.

His cell buzzed beside him. Eli grabbed it.

"Hey."

"Hey," Maxine said. "Just wanted to remind you about Dashiell's birthday present."

"I'm on it. It's awesome."

A flutter of silence, then, "You're doing it now?"

"Yeah. No problem."

"What did you get him?"

Eli stared at the Google page. "It's a surprise."

"Is it good?"

"Of course, it's good. It's awesome."

"How good?"

"Do you think I'd get something less than stellar for my son?" Eli looked at the empty search box and thought about the past month of inaction and wondered if, at this point, a normal person would feel guilty. He supposed they probably would, but whatever. It would be handled, and the present would be stellar — whatever it was.

"Oh, just tell me."

"No."

"Why?"

"It's a surprise."

"For Dash. Not for me."

"Maybe it involves you."

Words escaped Eli's mouth before he could think. Now she'd probably think they were all going on a trip, and right now, Eli had no interest in unseating his world to go on vacation. He could afford it, sure, but nobody would adore him away from his screen. Checking social media and email from a hotel or on a phone while lounging by a pool wasn't the same. You couldn't satisfactorily reply to the ire, and critics might feel like they'd earned the last word.

"It involves *me?*" said Maxine, a lilt of excitement claiming her voice.

"Maybe." Then, waffling: "Or maybe not. Maybe I'm being mysterious."

"Oh."

"Hey, M, I've gotta go."

"Sure. I'll see you when I get home."

"Okay, see you."

Maxine added, "Oh, and one thing I thought of …"

Eli killed the call. His thumb was in motion before she'd started speaking, and although he probably could have pulled it away in time, he didn't feel particularly bad about not trying. He'd said his goodbye, and could argue with plausible deniability that he hadn't heard her start up again — *after* the sign-off.

Eli stared at the search box. Unfortunately, if he was going to do this right — and when he finally got around to doing things, he did them *right*, by God — it would require some searching. There were all sorts of video games Dashiell wanted (he had three systems, and the home had another two), but a video game or two wasn't suitably awesome for the son of a famous and increasingly well-off blogger. Besides, this was his 13th birthday. He was entering his teens and had been yammering about how exciting that was since he'd turned 12. If they were Jewish, this was when Dashiell would have his bar mitzvah, wearing his finery and standing in front of everyone to declare that he was now a man. This year's gift had to be special. It had to justify — and pay homage to — all that Eli was taking the time to build. The gift had to say, "Look what I have achieved and am able to do for you."

A ride in a Formula One race car? No, Maxine would pitch a fit.

Space Camp? That was one of those stereotypical ultimate gifts. But a quick search showed that although there was one in a month, it was sold out. Buying a later Space Camp would do two things: prove that Eli had dragged his feet, and likely require a family trip, since Maxine had family in Alabama and would want to go along to visit while Dashiell was occupied.

For the same reason, he could rule out Disney — both Land and World.

If Dashiell were older, Eli could get him a car. Something decent, not new. But of course, it was too early for that.

So far, Space Camp was closest. His son liked science enough that it was damn near an obsession. He could even argue that his son's inability to craft a Pinewood Derby car on his own proved just how into science he was. Dashiell was too nerdy. Too into geeky stuff; too bad at things like construction, talking to girls, and writing clever, snarky rant blogs for adoring fans. If it didn't sound so homophobic (something Eli was against, as evidenced by his recent campaign against the congressman), Eli would have a few girly-boy comments on the matter. But yes, good or bad, right or wrong, Dashiell was into science. Baking soda volcanoes and electronics, robots, and all that shit. Space Camp was perfect, if only it weren't so imperfect in practice.

Eli typed *SCIENCE CAMP* into the Google search box, then realized he'd forgotten to cut his son's Pinewood Derby car as promised. He sighed. Oh well, Dashiell would be used to it. He often went to his friend Bernie's after school, so maybe Bernie's father, Scott, could do it for him. Scott had done other handyman things for Dashiell before, so he'd probably think to ask.

Eli resented it. Who did Scott Benson think he was, being the manly mentor to his own son, and making him look bad?

The search produced thousands of results. But because Google geolocated searches (something Eli was overdue to rant about; Google was downright betraying users' privacy for their own nefarious ends), the top result — for Berger-Tech Science Camp in Hillsboro — was nearby and eerily perfect.

He clicked the link, then began reading the website.

It was a drop-off camp. He'd leave Dashiell, then pick him up a week later. Meaning a ton of uninterrupted work time. It would only be he and Maxine at home, and Maxine worked outside the house.

It was nearby: no travel.

It had all the nerdy shit that so amused Dashiell. Robotics, rockets, chemistry experiments ("Turn things green!" the site joked), fantastic contraptions built to demonstrate the laws of physics, a field trip to a particle physics lab (which had a particle accelerator, whatever that was), overnight accommodations in dorms — well-supervised and chaperoned to eliminate the threat of inappropriate fraternizing and hazing (not that nerds knew much about either, Eli thought), all meals provided, counselors whose day jobs were in labs and universities. It was perfect.

He clicked through to see the price. Totally reasonable — low enough that Maxine wouldn't throw a hissy fit and would think it was a good value, and pricey enough that Eli felt he'd be spending sufficiently for a quality product.

He browsed the testimonials, all showing beaming kids declaring the time of their lives. There were group photos with counselors, standing in the sun and smiling, some kids giving bunny ears because kids just can't fucking sit still. The colors were cheery and inviting. Eli opened a new window and began looking through his favorite buyer-beware websites, searching for dirt on BergerTech. He found nothing. That in itself meant nil; the place was a small, local camp for nerds, not likely to trip the usual alarms. Still, no news was more or less good news.

Duly researched, Eli double-checked dates. Camp started in three weeks. So perfect, it looked planned. Maxine's pestering had been getting obnoxious; this would make her take two steps back and admit that he'd done well. Never mind that he'd lucked into it; Eli had a way of performing under pressure, and knew it — this time, it looked like he'd pulled off a performance and a half.

Eli clicked through to the payment page, and an annoying pop-up blasted him in the face. Stupid things. They were the cell phones of the Internet, always getting in your way and cock blocking a positive experience. They were aggressive marketing, trying to bludgeon people into buying rather than letting them make the decision on their own.

He closed the pop-up without looking. His half-second glance said something about joining the camp's mailing list. Now, why the hell would he want to join the mailing list for a fucking science camp? He felt indignant. Why would they *think* he'd want to join their mailing list? He almost wanted to close the window and not buy for spite, simply because he was irritated by the camp's pushiness. Then he could send them an email: *I was about to sign up and pay you money, but then your stupid pop-up made me leave. Great job. And also, I can no longer find my mouse pointer, and I think your site stole it, and you will be hearing from my lawyer.* Yes, that could be a funny bit on his blog.

But the camp was too perfect, and Eli was out of time, so he clicked through to the signup page.

The page was filled with descriptions of the camp's many activities, explained in nauseating detail. Eli scanned, then clicked the link at the bottom. But the page wouldn't let him continue; several sections of text had turned red, and he noticed three tick-boxes throughout to indicate his acceptance. One was a safety permission, explaining that science could sometimes be dangerous and that while all reasonable precautions would be taken, the camp couldn't guarantee that accidents would never occur, and wanted campers or their guardians to acknowledge that yada yada yada whatever. Another had to do with food allergies. The third was, of all things, a notice that some activities took place outdoors and that campers should bring sunscreen.

Eli checked the boxes, then again clicked the link at the bottom and was greeted with the longest form he'd ever seen. It looked like a loan application.

He moaned, thinking of the emails he still had to answer and the social media requiring his response. Eli didn't know half of the stuff on the form. He could figure it out, sure, but he'd spend a million years hunting. This was the kind of thing Maxine normally did. He should wait and have her do it when she got home. But no, that wouldn't work; he'd told her he was on top of the gift, and he'd also said it was a surprise. And, *motherfucker*, he'd also said it somehow involved her. He had no idea *why* he'd said that, but now he'd have to make it true. He'd have to … what? Maybe he could get her a massage gift certificate and play it off as something she couldn't do while Dashiell was home. It was a stretch, but she'd buy it. Of course, that also meant one more errand — and he had to do it today, because he'd have to present it along with the science camp. He wondered if he could do it online. It would be shoddy (the massage place had neat little gift cards that came in tiny envelopes, and the best he'd be able to do online is print a receipt for Maxine), but was a massage not a damned massage?

He tore off a Post-It note, wrote *massage* on it so he wouldn't forget, then returned to the form.

Rather than filling it out, Eli stared at it as if it had done something to offend him. He was annoyed by the audacity the form represented. Same as the pop-up. Were these people trying to discourage signups? They couldn't possibly need all of this information. It was an intrusion. He should refuse to fill out certain sections on principle, the way you could refuse to indicate your race or even gender on most forms. Privacy had practically disappeared, and forms like this were the perfect example. It was positioned so innocently, most suckers would never question it: *Kindly just fill out this teensy little form to send your happy child to our cutesy little dork camp.* But it wasn't right, and it raised the hair on the back of his neck.

Eli shook it off. He was probably overreacting (seeing as that was what he did for a living), wasting time, and chasing futility. The science camp had him over a barrel, and if it wanted to stick its big form-shaped dick up his butt, he had no choice but to let it. He was out of time. The camp was the perfect gift; Maxine would applaud it, and Dashiell would love it. He could grow indignant as an intellectual exercise, but there was no point, and he knew it.

Eli started to fill it out: Dashiell's name, birthdate, school science background, grades, medical allergies, and immunization records. He moved on to questions of height and weight, whether or not he wore glasses or contacts, and which schools he'd attended in which cities. There were several fields for emergency contacts and a few more for references.

References? For a science camp?

Annoyed, Eli entered himself and Maxine.

The form asked about Dashiell's favorite activities and scientific interests, and with a troubling stir in his gut, Eli found he had to make most of them up. He knew the kid liked science. But what kinds of science? And his other interests? Eli felt like he should probably know those things, but didn't.

After hunting through the house for all of the required data (Dashiell's social security number, his last science class grade, the school's phone number), Eli clicked to submit.

Instead of a confirmation page, Eli found himself staring at a psychological profile. The new form asked about his son's general level of satisfaction with school. It asked if Dashiell had ever been bullied. It asked about his happiness at home, how immersed he was in hobbies, and whether they were solo/escapist or social/collaborative. It asked how long he'd been pursuing those hobbies. It asked how long he'd enjoyed science, and whether that interest grew from an interest in intellectual growth or sheer curiosity about what might happen next. On the heels of that, it asked about the camper's thoughts about "what might happen next" in a handful of scenarios, detailed in tick boxes. Did or would Dashiell have angst about (check all that apply): change, the idea of moving to a new city, meeting new people, family members dying, pets dying, him or herself dying.

Eli wanted his face to wrinkle in outrage, but could barely manage shock. Was he really seeing this?

But then he remembered that the campers had seven full days, and something in the description indicated instruction on mental sciences. Maybe they wanted to discuss the brain or dissect a cow's brain. See a human brain. *Whatever*.

Eli didn't recall Dashiell expressing a more-than-ordinary fear of death, so he left the boxes unchecked, submitted the new form, and found himself facing a page packed with legal text headed with the title *BERGERTECH SCIENCE CAMP TERMS OF SERVICE*.

Annoyed and exasperated, Eli clicked past it. Again, a red line of text appeared at the top of the page, requiring Eli read through the TOS before completing his registration. He'd already had enough with the damned form and the damned camp, and this actually made him slap his monitor hard on its side. No doubt it was all legal masturbation, standard, and boilerplate. It said that parents wouldn't sue the camp if an asteroid fell from the sky and crushed the kids. Normal shit like that. And how the hell did the form know he hadn't read it, anyway?

There was a tiny noise behind him. The day had been sunny, but over the past 20 minutes, clouds had rolled in. Eli hadn't turned on his office lights because the sun was so bright when he'd sat, but now, with the sun muted, the room felt small and full of shadows. He flinched.

Eli looked at the screen. Had it felt like he was being watched? Because of the stupid-ass website?

After Dash attended the science camp, had a delightful time, and declared his dad the most amazing in the world,

Eli would initiate a vicious campaign against BergerTech out of spite. He'd eviscerate and embarrass them. No negative reviews of or buzz about the small local science camp? Well, *that* would change.

He stood, crossed the room, and turned on the overhead light.

Eli scrolled down the terms of service until he reached the end, where the line of red type finally vanished. So, that was it. You had to scroll to the bottom, which apparently proved you'd read it. He clicked again. A pop-up appeared:

PLEASE CONFIRM YOUR ACCEPTANCE OF TERMS

> *By clicking the "sign my name" button below, I
> acknowledge that I have read and accept the terms
> of service for BergerTech Science Camp and
> understand that clicking the button below, when
> paired with my entering a verifiable credit card
> information on the following page, constitutes
> a legal contract, and that clicking "sign my name"
> below constitutes a legal signature.*

JESUS FUCKING CHRIST.

IF ELI WEREN'T in such a jam and if the place weren't so ideal, he'd run screaming. Even the explanation of how he was signing the verbose legal bullshit read like verbose legal bullshit. Oh yes, he would *eviscerate* this place when Dashiell was done.

He clicked the button and was blessedly taken to a

standard credit card payment page. The credit card authorization did not ask for the name of Eli's first-grade teacher or his favorite color. He entered his info and paid, then was greeted with a thank-you page. A congratulatory email followed, detailing what the camper should pack and where a parent or guardian should drop off their child. It contained contact information for the camp, with a short paragraph about pickup. Apparently, campers were divided into three different groups and rotated through activities differently depending on their group, so on the next-to-last day, a parent would have to contact the camp to find out where to pick up their child.

Eli flipped back to his social media accounts as the phone buzzed on his desk. It was a text from Maxine, but this time, with the errand finally completed, her text was almost welcome.

Eli didn't reply in his usual snarky manner. He simply told Maxine that he was the best dad ever, and that they were both going to love what he had planned for their boy's birthday.

THE NEXT COUPLE of weeks were Eli's best in a while — maybe ever. It started when Dashiell opened an envelope from BergerTech Science Camp, and Maxine opened her massage gift certificate. Dashiell screeched and ran to the computer to discover what amazing adventures were waiting. Maxine hugged Eli and didn't so much as question the loose way he had described Dashiell's birthday as involving her, too.

Two weeks later, Eli published an email exchange on his website that began as a hilarious rant about a withered rose in a bouquet from a local flower shop (Eli had seen the rose in a bouquet as he'd been passing the store on foot and had stopped to take an iPhone photo; he hadn't bought it) but quickly evolved into an indignant rant about how the shop was marking its flowers up for no reason, in the interest of maximized profits. The shop protested that they were merely covering their costs and apologized about the rose (offering to replace the bouquet, plus offering credit for another at a later date), but clearly didn't know whom they were dealing with. The way Eli made the reps dance in circles was funny, yes — but as often happened with Eli's exchanges, it grew poignant. Why were customers charged so much for flowers that grew wild? Why did prices always rise right before holidays? Eli, who never bought flowers, thought it was all very contrived and greedy, and had probably never expressed himself better.

The post went viral and attracted obscene amounts of traffic to Eli's site (and, like always, sales to his books). The exchange spawned several amusing memes. The flower shop's front window was smashed by vandals.

As Eli rode high on book sales, web traffic, adulation, and satisfaction for another job well done, his fatherly pride turned to fatherly relief as Dashiell, giddy, headed to science camp. Maxine handled his packing and preparation, while Eli sat in his office and refreshed Twitter and blog comments. Dashiell came in and thanked him, gave him a solid and somewhat uncharacteristic hug, then vanished with a wave toward Maxine's car, headed for drop off.

The next week was bliss. Maxine became frisky, and they had sex five out of the seven days Dashiell was gone. Eli took a week off from annoying people and simply spent his office time basking in praise and refreshing his book's rankings. It felt like the vacations they never took, and he didn't even have to leave the house.

On Sunday, Maxine came into his office and stood in the doorway.

"I'm sore," said Eli. "What do you think I am, a piece of meat?"

"Yes," she said. "But more importantly, I think you're a taxi. I have that big meeting today, so you have to pick up Dash. Don't forget, okay?"

Eli looked her over. She was dressed for work, but it was a Sunday.

"For the club, Eli, not work," she said, reading his face. "You don't remember?"

"Of course, I remember," he said, not remembering at all.

"I'm on my way out." She walked forward, leaned over Eli in his chair, and kissed him. "You have to call them, remember. We were actually supposed to do it yesterday, but ..." She didn't have to finish the sentence. Yesterday, Maxine had shown Eli her vibrator. Scenarios ensued.

"I'll call them."

"Don't forget." She kissed him again and, tossing a small wave, disappeared.

But of course, Eli forgot. On his way into the kitchen for lunch three hours later, he was pondering the silence when it slowly dawned on him that he had only an hour and a half to pick up Dash. He returned to his office, searched for the instructions, and found an email address with no phone number. He called the main camp number several times anyway — seeing as time was short; never mind that he was over a day late — and got no answer. Finally, figuring that someone must be watching email, he sent a brief message.

Less than two minutes later, the reply came:

. . .

Dear Mr. Parker,

Thank you for contacting us. You do not need to pick up your son, Dashiell, from science camp today. We will be keeping him.

Sincerely,
> Rachel Wilson
> BergerTech Services

Eli stared at the screen. His initial wave of shock passed almost immediately, replaced by an overwhelming sense of irritation. Maxine had once told Eli he *was* the expression, "You can dish it out, but you can't take it." It was true, and Eli was self-aware enough to admit it. *He* was the snarky blogger. *He* was the minor celebrity who owed his fame to annoying emails that pissed people off. *He* was supposed to be the antagonist … and it wasn't one molecule of motherfucking funny when he was antagonized back, when someone tried to shove a spoonful of his own medicine into his mouth.

Eli figured there were two possibilities: Either the email's sender was a fan and wanted him to play, or she wasn't *at all* a fan and wanted to poke him. But he was the customer; he'd paid the camp a significant sum and deserved better treatment. And if it was a joke? Well, it wasn't very goddamned funny, considering he was supposed to pick his son up in an hour and a half, that the trip was probably around a half hour in length, and that with an hour left before he needed to leave, he had no idea where to go.

Eli called the number again and again got nothing. He answered the email, trying to strike a curious and difficult balance. He couldn't read the mood or intention of the sender of the first email, so he couldn't anticipate the reaction. For all he knew, Rachel from BergerTech was planning to save his replies and publish her own hilarious blog post, showing how she'd gotten the legendary Eli Parker back for his bullying tomfoolery.

Rachel,

You do not want to keep Dashiell. He snores and leaves his socks everywhere. Please advise ASAP where I can take him off your hands, as I'll need to leave soon.

Eli

There. It was perfectly neutral, perfectly dry, perfectly playing-along if this woman thought herself funny. Yet it wasn't overly jokey, and hopefully conveyed some urgency.

The response came quickly:

Dear Mr. Parker,

Thank you for your inquiry, but as stated, picking up your camper is unnecessary.

. . .

SINCERELY,
Rachel Wilson
BergerTech Services

THIS HAD GONE on for too long already. Even with the exchange's rapid back-and-forth, five minutes had passed from his hour. Eli had to get dressed before he left, too, and that would take time. His car might be low on gas. He'd probably have to stop and fill it.

HA HA. Please just give me the location. I am running out of time here.

ELI

THIRTY SECONDS LATER:

DEAR MR. PARKER,

I APOLOGIZE for the misunderstanding and any inconvenience these events may have caused, but as stated, we will be keeping Dashiell per our mutual agreement. Thank you for your patronage.

SINCERELY,
Rachel Wilson
BergerTech Services

.   .   .

Per our mutual agreement?

That didn't make sense.

It was almost as if the woman didn't understand who Eli or Dashiell were. He looked at the email signature, which declared Rachel Wilson to be from BergerTech *Services*, not BergerTech Science Camp. Maybe he'd somehow contacted the wrong address. He double-checked it, but no, the email address was exactly the one specified on his camp instructions. The same exact paper Maxine had used in prepping Dashiell and figuring out where to drop him off.

Eli composed a new email, turning off his snarky side and turning on his internal pit bull.

This may be amusing to you, but FYI, I'm not amused. I'd like to point out that email constitutes a traceable record and is admissible in any legal suits that may be brought against your company in general and against you in particular. I'll also add that if you follow the link in my signature to my website, you'll see that I'm very good at causing trouble for people and have pretty much already decided to do a long, not-that-funny, in-depth piece on your camp and its invasive, anti-privacy practices.

Please tell me where to pick up my son.

Eli Parker

.   .   .

Eli looked at the clock, fuming, watching his inbox while waiting for the reply to ping. He could almost picture the woman on the other end crapping her pants, her playful expression turning to one of frenzied worry. *Nobody* wanted to be lampooned by Eli Parker. He was the enemy no sane person wanted. His most viral email exchanges were the funny ones, but the most meaningful and problematic (for the other party, not Eli) were his in-depth exposés. You didn't get away when Eli Parker decided to sink his investigative teeth into your flesh, so God help those he went after. All they could do was to pray that the public would look at the muck and still, somehow, decide that they were a soul worth saving — or at least worth not harassing.

But when the email came back, its tone was infuriatingly formal.

Dear Mr. Parker,

I understand your frustration, but unfortunately, there is nothing I can do to assist you. Per Section VIII, Paragraph 6 of the agreement you e-signed during registration, "campers may be reassigned to guardianship of Berger-Tech Services if entrance survey and on-camp assessment determine that the camper would be better served in an alternative and preferable environment."

I do not have access to the full battery of tests and observational profile of your camper, but our staff is highly professional and widely considered to hold some of the world's best minds in cognitive and developmental psychology. In addition, our camp conducts many other tests throughout a camper's stay, using cutting-edge techniques that "grade"a camper's overall health and well-being on several levels. It is rare for the company to exercise the so-called "If we determine that we can do better than you are doing, we will" clause, but as you have read and agreed to the terms in full, there is nothing I can do, and the company is unwilling, in these cases, to relax its legal rights. We are proud of our next-generation approach to improving children's lives, and our team has determined that you do not fit into your son's optimal profile.

PLEASE REST ASSURED that Dashiell will be well cared for, and try to understand that the company would not exercise this seldom-used contingency if it were not entirely certain that he would be better cared for, in fact, than he has been under your guidance.

WE APOLOGIZE for any inconvenience this may have caused and thank you for your patronage of BergerTech.

SINCERELY,
    Rachel Wilson
    BergerTech Services

PERHAPS MOST MADDENINGLY, this time there was a link below Rachel's signature leading to a customer service survey. The first question asked Eli whether he would recommend BergerTech Science Camp to friends.

    Eli stood in one swift motion, his wheeled chair

banging into the wall behind him. His fist swung toward his monitor, but he pulled it back just in time. A second surge hit him, and he raised his slippered foot, which he used to boot the thing from his desk and onto the ground, where it shattered.

Smart. Now he couldn't even continue the idiotic conversation unless he used his phone. He cursed himself, emotions warring inside him.

Still, despite the infuriating email and the not-at-all-fucking-funny ruse being played, something itched at the back of his head. Something he'd seen and set aside. Eli walked out into the kitchen, then sifted through the ever-present pile of mail that sat on the counter. In it, he found an unopened manila envelope from the science camp. They'd known what they needed from the confirmation email, so no one had opened it, but now, in the strangely quiet kitchen, Eli did. Inside, he found a neater copy of the confirmation instructions.

And a printed copy of the terms of service he'd been so annoyed by when he'd registered.

Eli flipped until he found the section mentioned in the email, then read it three times. It was just as Rachel from BergerTech had said. The document had been on his counter for three weeks. He couldn't believe it. What kind of company would include something like this in its terms? He flipped through, trying to find out. He encountered all sorts of other verbiage about scientific inquiry, novel approaches to camping, instructions, and child enrichment. It wasn't a joke. It was insanity, plain and simple.

Eli's phone rang in his office. A pleasant male voice replied to his hurried hello.

"Hello, Mr. Parker. This is Victor at BergerTech Science Camp. How are you this afternoon?"

"YOU FUCK!" Eli blurted, somewhat offended by the absence of his usual gift for words.

"Excellent, excellent," said Victor, apparently working from rote. "I have a record here that you contacted customer support and wanted to follow up. Was Rachel helpful to you?"

The vein in Eli's forehead felt like it might explode. "MOTHERFUCKER!" he bellowed. *"Where is my son, you cocksucker?"*

"I'm sorry you feel that way," said Victor, apparently not noticing that Eli hadn't expressed a way of feeling. "How can I help solve your issue?"

"Someone is playing a goddamned game with me, and let me tell you, you are fucking with the wrong person! I make trouble for people. That's *what I do.* So, listen to me, you little shit. You are going to tell me, right here and now, where I can find my son, Dashiell Anthony Parker, and I'm going to go and get him, and then I'm going to *PUT YOU OUT OF BUSINESS AND GET ALL OF YOUR SORRY ASSES TOSSED INTO PRISON!"*

"Ah," said Victor, clicking keys in the background. "I apologize. I failed to fully review your file before phoning." He chuckled. "One of those days, you know. I'll tell you, this morning I actually poured orange juice into my corn-flakes until ..."

"SHUT YOUR MOTHERFUCKING MOUTH AND GIVE ME MY SON!"

"Ah, but unfortunately that's not going to be possible, sir," Victor said, unperturbed. "I see here that you signed the agreement and, by doing so, clearly agreed that if ..."

"I didn't sign it, goddammit! I clicked a button!"

"Unfortunately — and not to tell you your business, Mr. Parker, but you'd see this in the contract as well — clicking the 'sign' button and then re-confirming, combined with your IP address and the authorization granted by your valid credit card, constitutes a legal signature."

"Bullshit!"

"Unfortunately, sir, it's quite valid. Our terms have been challenged in several court cases, which I can fax or email to you if you'd like, along with the contact information for our legal team. But I assure you that it's perfectly legal. Did you not understand the nature of the science camp, sir? It's all over our about page — how the entire thing is based on experimentation and optimization, from the bedrolls the campers sleep on to the ..."

"Goddamn you. You will tell me right here and now how I can ..."

"I'm afraid there's nothing I can do to contravene the terms of the contract you signed, sir."

"You can — and will — tell me exactly where ..."

"I'm sorry, Mr. Parker," said Victor, his voice still polite but becoming firm. "But I must repeat that there's nothing I can do. I'm a representative, and have no power to challenge or disobey the ..."

"Give me your supervisor's name. *Now.*"

"I'm afraid I can't do that. You waived your right to appeal our decisions — and to accept said decisions as final — when you signed our terms of service."

"You motherfucker," said Eli, unable to believe his ears, keeping his cool through sheer will. "You lot of dirty assholes, you don't know who you're dealing with here. You don't know what I'm able to do. You don't know how many people wait on my every word and will jump as soon as I tell them to. You don't know how much trouble I can cause, or which lawyers I can afford, or just how fully I'm going to *BURN YOUR MOTHERFUCKING HOUSES TO THE GROUND!*"

Eli was holding the phone so tight, he felt like he might crush it. He was audibly panting, fighting to keep his head from swimming. His forehead was smoldering like a coal. He wanted to put his fist through something, even — and especially — if it meant breaking his own hand and arm in the process.

"Unfortunately," said Victor, "Section Eight in our terms of service indicates the penalties you agreed to incur if we exercised this option, and if you then chose to fight it."

Eli felt the air leave his lungs. "Penalties?"

"The penalties involving the appropriation of your wife, sir," Victor clarified. Sometimes known as the 'If we determine that we can do better than you are doing, we will,' clause."

"You can't possibly think that I'll allow this to …"

"My visual records here indicate that she uses that vibrator very differently on herself than you used it on her yesterday." Victor chuckled. "You can't argue with the scientific method, Mr. Parker. *So* precise."

Eli felt his body sag. The phone dangled from his hand as his fingers threatened to drop it.

Sounding far away, Victor's voice chirping through the speaker said, "Perhaps you should sit in that chair to your left, sir."

"You can't do this to me."

"What happens when people whine, Mr. Parker?"

~

Dear Mr. Parker,

. . .

Wow, it still feels so strange not to call you "Dad," but Robert keeps saying it's the best way to make the transition, and the guys here — all "reassigns" like me; that's what they call us — tell me it helps. I'm probably violating the rules by even using it as I just did (or by talking about any of this), but whatever. I can't argue with what I'm learning!

Apparently, you can't keep things bottled up. Even when you think something is wrong, you have to vent it. "Storm through it," as Robert says. Then, on the other side, you realize it was all hot air, and didn't matter anyway.

I'm really excited by what I'm learning. Not just in school, but also from my reassignment family. It's strange, and I hope you don't take offense, but I'm finding that I don't miss my old life at all. Something to do with light therapy, these videos with colored circles on them that dance back and forth. Ha ha, you'd probably call it mind control or brainwashing, but I've learned about it, and we call it "selective memory reframing." It's not evil or manipulative at all. You just learn to think of old things in new ways, and new things in old ways. It's about changing attachment.

By the way, speaking of attachment, Mom says hi. She really didn't run into any trouble, and I'm not sure why. Nick (my reassignment brother) said she was all pissed off when she got here, but then they had a talk with her, and she kind of calmed down, and now it's like she's always been here. It's nice. She can still be my mom and all, but now I've got this new dad. Again, no offense. It's just objective. That's the biggest thing we learn, and the biggest thing they do with the brain tests and the chemistry stuff I don't totally get yet: We learn how to look at everything as data. You pull the emotion away and learn to ask, "Which one is *really* better?" through a series of tests and analyses.

THEN, because of the method, when you re-add the emotion, there's no conflict. Dad is just more available than you were — not just with time, but emotion, involvement, all that. I suppose that's hard to hear, but that's why I included the book about the way they approach learning here. Try it. Seriously. I know it's not your cup of tea, but give it a shot. Isn't it better without us there? All the quiet, all the time to work? You still have all your fans and readers. You'll see it's better once you get the emotion out of the way, reframe, and then layer it back. Now, without us around, the rules really won't apply to you.

I'VE BEEN READING your website, by the way, and it's hilarious. The bit you did about BergerTech? So amazing. I love the deadpan delivery. It almost looks like you published it seriously, as if it weren't a joke. Glad the commenters liked it.

WELL, I've gotta go. I don't think I'm really supposed to keep emailing you — attachment and reassignment reasons — but if I'm a fan of your site? They can't stop me from contacting a blogger I enjoy reading, right?

. . .

Sincerely,
　　Dashiell

~

Aftershocks on Terms of Service:

This one came from a simpler time. Before the pandemics and AI apocalypse.

Johnny and I were still finding our rhythm as collaborators, and *Terms of Service* was one of those, *Hey, wouldn't it be funny if …* stories that snowballed fast.

I lobbed the spark. Johnny caught it, shaped it, spun it into something snide and sharp. Then I came in with a scalpel and made it sing.

A few days after the initial idea, we had something weird, sharp, and sneakily sad.

We were riffing on the spirit of David Thorne: the guy who billed a client with a picture of a spider when they refused to pay for "extras," then turned his parade of petty power plays into a book called *The Internet is a Playground*, finally getting paid in page views, memes, and passive-aggressive glory.

That brand of weaponized pettiness (performance as protest, snark as shield) was our launchpad. But we didn't want to just riff on a gag. We wanted to dig deeper into the ego, spectacle, and emotional rot that sets in when you perform an identity long enough that you start believing it.

Eli Parker was never supposed to be a villain. He's not even especially original. He's the internet's id in cargo shorts. Smart enough to win arguments, smug enough to believe that's the same as being right. A man so wrapped up in being heard that he forgot how to listen, especially to the people who love him most. All headline, no substance. All followers, no one to call when the noise stops. The kind of guy who can spot a typo in a stranger's tweet from across the room but can't make a Pinewood Derby car for his kid without somehow turning it into a philosophical argument.

Johnny nailed the jaded, caffeinated, self-congratulatory blogger rhythm that defined so much of early web culture. But what makes the story land is how that voice finally fractures.

This house was bought with complaints and whining.

That line says everything about Eli's worldview: transactional, hollow, yet somehow proud of it all. He didn't sell out. He just stayed online long enough to become the algorithm.

That's the real horror writhing inside *Terms of Service*. Not the tech. Nor the form. But how easy it is to confuse applause with connection … and mistake an audience for family.

THREE

Corrosion

AT FIRST, there was nothing.

Later, much later (he thought) when time stretched until it seemed to rip apart and mean nothing, he felt as though he were swimming, except that there was no water, and he wasn't sure he had limbs. If he *were* swimming, he'd probably be sinking and drowning. Perhaps it was like floating, but he wasn't floating either. And besides, *where* would he be floating? In space? There were too many colors for space. Yet none of the hues made sense. They were blurs. And his limbs felt more like a suggestion.

He felt relatively sure there was a *past* and a *future* and a *now*, but that was pretty much all he could be sure of. Things that seemed to be *past* stood beside events that were, in all likelihood, happening *now*. If he was worried (he thought he was, but it was so hard to tell), then that would be about the *future*, right? You didn't *worry* about the past. You felt *guilty* about the past, but not worried. But there seemed to be guilt in this soup, too.

The boy, bouncing on a trampoline, landing awkwardly and breaking a leg … was that him? Had that once been him? The boy was young; the scene he saw immediately afterward, of a man with a family, couldn't have been from the same time, and yet both had to be in the past. The present, he was realizing, was this strange, swimming soup. And the creatures. The creatures were in the present, in the now.

What was it the hippie types used to say? "Live in the now?" What awful advice. If these were his memories — and it was hard to say for sure, but he thought they probably were — then he found each more magnetic than the stirring whirl of colors and shapes and cold and discomfort he felt "in the now." It wasn't just that whatever was now was less than ideal. The *very essence* of timelessness — of neglecting or forgetting the past and turning a blind eye to the likely future — was confusing and uncomfortable. There was no anchor. In the now, you could only sit by, unable to act or respond, and wait for moments to be served like an invalid at a buffet. In the now, it didn't matter which foods you wanted to eat. The now served you whatever it wanted to give, not what you cared to see and feel and hear and taste and touch.

The creatures were long and tall and seemed to be gray, though it was difficult to see because his eyes weren't really working. If he had to guess, they didn't wear clothing (*he'd* worn clothing, right? Yes, he seemed to remember both the word and the concept; ring one up for the confused guy, even though the same guy couldn't tell if he was wearing clothes now, or if his vision was now, or if NOW was now), and based on what his eyes could decipher, the things might be covered in scales. Thick, gray scales, bumpy like a snapping turtle's nose.

He thought of the boy jumping on the trampoline.

He thought of a group of people, all adults, happy — no, wait, *drunk* — running through what looked like a park.

That memory had a happy, carefree feel. There was another memory, nearly a clone of the first: also a group of adults, also drunk, also running … but this time tearing through empty city streets. For some reason, this memory wasn't as happy. This one felt tragic, and he couldn't understand why. The memory's inhabitants were happy, their feet airy on the dark pavement. They were out and running. But their actions felt like a final hurrah.

Let's not go back, Norman. Let's go to the nest. Over the edge. Let it have us.

Norman.

Was that his name?

Yes, it felt right.

Norman.

He toyed with the name, playing with the sound, somehow certain he wasn't moving his lips. Did he still have lips? He must, right? He had eyes because he could see a room slowly taking shape. He had a body of some sort because sometimes, when things moved in ways he didn't seem to be able to control, he caught sidelong glimpses of dark-brown shapes that seemed to be legs or arms. These things had smaller, equally blurry protrusions on the ends that might be digits. He couldn't control them, but that wasn't surprising because he couldn't control the limbs, if that's what the nude, brown things were. And if they were, he had no way of being sure they were his. They could be the arms of someone beside him. Or maybe behind. Severed arms and legs being waved around him by one of the creatures, putting on an obscene show.

A gray shape loomed ahead. He was beginning to get a feel for what was happening now and what had happened in the past, even though he had no idea how long he'd been here — wherever "here" was — in what seemed to be the soupy, disorderly present. He wanted to blink, but didn't know if he was seeing with his own eyes. Eyes that he seemed to recall had been brown.

The creature came closer. To Norman, it looked like an elongated capsule, upright, with long tendrils that might have been arms and legs like those he'd once had, back when he'd been a drunk man tearing through empty streets.

One of the tendrils rose. Up close, Norman could see that it was, in fact, quite like an arm. At the end was a hand, with four fingers and a thumb, except that the digits were all quite long — twice as long as the fingers and thumb on his old human hand, if Norman was remembering right. In the hand was a round, red shape, concave in the center. Something in that concave middle was rotating, but to Norman it was a blur of colors and the dull rattle of metal.

"Fazah," said the creature.

Norman could see the thing's eyes. In the middle of its scaly, leathery, gray armored face, the eyes looked like two holes of light, each a dull and unfocused green like a dusty emerald.

But Norman didn't know what to say to that, in part because he couldn't say a thing.

The darkness returned.

THE LIGHT IS FLASHING. It's all he can see. It's all he wants to see. He could look around, could think about what's going to happen, but he doesn't want to because those feelings are too intense. Although he feels like a coward, he'd rather turn his head. The flashing light means he only has seconds anyway, and then he won't have to think for a while.

The spot beside him is empty. It will stay that way until after he's under, then it will be filled by one of the others — probably

Belinda or Telly. There are only twelve slots; not one can be wasted. Norman will be the first to go under. Though they won't admit it, no one trusts him to go anywhere near last. He has others still alive. No one else does. Norman might fill two of those twelve spots with people who don't deserve to be there. A dozen might be all that endure, ever, forever, and into eternity. The gene pool is choked by necessity, and Norman would strangle it further by adding himself twice.

Selfish, selfish, selfish.

And of all times, now, when the world was counting on him.

On all of them.

"Any final words?" The voice is light and joking, as if he's not about to die.

Norman watches the flashing yellow light.

"It won't work. We're too near the nest."

The voice laughs. "Then at least you won't feel anything when it happens."

NORMAN BLINKED, astonished to realize that he could. The white room re-materialized around him. Assuming he still had a head to lift and turn (he had eyelids, after all; his fortune was looking up), that particular set of controls seemed to elude him. It didn't really matter. His head was still swimming, and although he had his theories, he couldn't say for sure if there was a material difference between the white room and the room with the flashing light where he'd been most recently. He had a feeling of awakening. But had he awakened to the white room just now, or had he awoken to the other room earlier, when his consciousness had faded, and he'd found himself elsewhere?

A shape his mind had mistaken for a shadow lay near the bottom of his field of vision. It grew longer, and Norman realized it must be one of the creatures, sitting (did they sit?) nearby as if waiting for his return to surreality.

He blinked again, relishing the small feeling of control, now frustrated that his vision still hadn't cleared any more than his confused stream of consciousness. He was seeing through a sheen of clear jelly, his thoughts anchored by invisible weights — like trying to solve ten logic problems at once, or see through a windshield hammered by torrential rain.

The long-fingered hand again held up the red, circular object.

"Fazah."

Norman waited for more.

"Fazah," it repeated, now pushing the red object closer.

But Norman didn't know what the thing was, what "fazah" meant, or much of anything else. He didn't even know if he was sitting or lying down. The room's directions were wrong, up and down as confusing as right and left. Was that something the creatures had done, or something his mind had yet to untangle?

He wanted to flinch when the creature's other hand — the one not holding the mysterious *fazah* — came forward, below his eye line. The hand was empty, and a second later Norman could feel the hard, scaly skin touch his face.

He could *feel* it.

"Mah sota," said the creature, manipulating Norman's lips. Then, speaking very precisely, the thing added, "'*Ci yo gehn.*'"

Norman felt himself twitch. Something was waking, some movement returning. He recoiled from the creature's touch, his skin's scant sensation abraded by the scales.

"Ya, mah sota. Sah: '*Ci yo gehn.*'"

It seemed to be prompting him, trying to get him to

act. The thing had lips like his; Norman could see them in the middle of what looked like stone-colored tree bark. The mouth was dark, but there was a pink tongue inside. There were teeth. Normal ones, not fangs. And as it manipulated his mouth, Norman got the distinct impression that it was trying to encourage his speech. Or trying to make him understand that he could, if he focused.

"Noh ma," said the creature. "Noh ma pak."

Norman could feel his lips now, but his mouth felt like a telegraph at the end of a miles-long wire. He'd never be able to move it at all, let alone form words. If he were on his back, his tongue would be lolling toward his throat like a hunk of meat. If he were sitting, it would be lying on the floor of his mouth like a lazy dog asleep in front of a fire. The idea that he could stir it to respond was ridiculous.

The creature's features seemed to move, though to Norman it looked mostly like a sloshing of puddles intermingling and then separating again. He tried to clear his vision by blinking, but the twitch was merely a tease. He still had some sort of jelly smearing his vision, some kind of sludge in his brain. He couldn't move, couldn't think. In his mind, he saw the yellow flashing light, knowing that some time ago he'd stared and waited, wishing the inevitable would hurry so he could quit conjuring thoughts forever. It seemed unfair that not only was he having to think again, but that he was having to do it here, now, with these horrible things.

Let's not go back, Norman. Let's go to the nest. Over the edge. Let it have us.

A rebus-like burst of images slammed into the backs of his eyelids, memory assaulting him like artillery fire. But the images were out of context, and he fought to draw any meaning.

A place, in that abandoned city, where the road ended in a crater, black pavement sheared at the end and left dangling above a vast pit like a ramp toward a giant mouth. At the bottom, he saw light and movement, stirring of shapes far below, swarming like insects.

A sky, so black as to have been scorched, tinged with yet another displaced feeling of guilt, as if he were responsible.

Bodies, piled high in vast heaps. A bulldozer pushed them together to clear the streets.

A woman.

A child.

A flashing yellow light, his own hand gripping the edge of something as if bracing for a blow.

Above Norman, the creature shook its giant, hairless, gray-scaled head. He could see the pale-green blurs of its eyes seem to vanish then reappear, as if it had slowly blinked, exasperated. The head vanished, and he could hear the clacking of the thing operating some kind of machinery at his side.

Floating in the air in front of him, Norman saw a round, red object, its front concave, with lights rotating in the center.

"Fazah," said the creature.

The red hologram seemed to melt into something else. The new object was blue, long, with what looked like wheels at the end. That one almost looked familiar.

Skateboard?

"Fazah," said the creature.

Norman wanted to protest. The blue thing wasn't a fazah. The red thing was. Whatever a fazah was.

The object changed again. This time, Norman saw something yellow. It felt like a kindergarten test, presenting him with primary colors. He almost wanted to laugh at the idea — he'd woken to a strange world and landed him back in the same small chairs where he'd learn his ABCs and who the dish ran away with — but he could feel his cheeks curl into a half smile, then nothing more.

"Dorveha?" said the creature.

The image changed again. This time, Norman would have gasped if he hadn't lacked the capacity.

His vision was a bit better now, enough to recognize the dark-gray object floating before him, though Norman wasn't sure how he knew.

It was the trigger.

NORMAN INHALED. Slowly exhaled. It felt good, he supposed, to feel the breath enter his lungs and pass through his lips. His vision had vastly improved, but his thinking was still sluggish. He felt out of time, unsure what had led him to this place. But at least he could turn his head a bit, and at least he could see and mostly feel other parts of his body — enough, at least, to know he was tied down, restrained with straps of something that looked like black, deflated balloons.

A distant part of Norman had been mulling an image not long ago: from some ancient film, of a woman's detached head kept alive in a black-and-white scientist's electro-sparking lab. At least he wasn't just a head. It had seemed absurd to think he was — but then again, he got the distinct impression that the meaning of absurd had changed.

There were now three of the creatures at the other end of the room, all nude, all covered with those thick, bark-like, gray scales. Norman was wearing clothes, and the oddest thing was that he actually remembered them. There was a hole in the leg of his blue jeans that he remembered getting when he'd fallen outside his home, back when the nest was still small. A boy — Norman supposed he must be his son — had laughed at the rip, saying that adults sometimes tore their clothes and got in trouble too.

Switching tracks in his mind, Norman found an unexpected recall, finding himself looking down at that same rip later, while the yellow light flashed in his peripheral vision. He asked someone something about the rip, or possibly about the pants themselves — or, maybe more globally, about clothes in general. He didn't remember the question, but could recall every nuance of the answer: "If it hurts to peel them off later when you successfully wake up," someone had told him, "then I'd call that a quality problem."

The creatures had their heads together, gibbering in their strange language. One held a cube-like object, and every once in a while, it would flash colors. Once, an image had projected from the cube's top and onto the white room's ceiling — that of a shifting, twining set of lines that looked like an animation of a wiring diagram. The creatures sometimes spoke to the cube. When it flashed white light three times in a row, the creatures all reacted with either surprise or fear. Hard to say which.

Keeping an eye on the creatures, Norman tried to tug against his restraints. The straps reacted strangely; they all had give rather than being binding him tight. Each time he tried (and, admittedly, he wasn't trying well; his muscles barely worked and they had all the whip of a wet rag), the leathery substance seemed to move in unison, squeezing gently to stop him, like a mother's hand.

Two of the creatures came forward. One stayed at the room's other end, tapping the wall to reveal a bank of lights that looked like some sort of control panel. Norman's vision must be much better, he realized, because he could see the way the thing's fingers hovered over the panel, as if awaiting a cue.

"Noh ma pak," said one of the creatures. They weren't all the same. One of the beings in front of him was markedly taller than the other. The shorter of the pair was rounder and had several bumps on its body, about the size of large eggs. Norman thought the tall one might have been the one who had been in the room with him earlier. The one that had shown him the trigger.

The creature near the wall touched something, and the entire room changed in a blink. The metamorphosis was so complete and instantaneous that Norman immediately began to doubt his new feeling of finding some semblance of reality. He'd felt disoriented and floating earlier, but he'd finally begun to feel grounded. Now he was somewhere else entirely, and the fragility of his perceptions called everything into question all over again.

What was real? What was happening?

The third creature came forward, but now its feet (flat like his own, with five toes) made scraping noises as they met a floor that had become hard stone. The walls were the same, and the roof above looked blasted out and, somehow, dripping. He was in a mine, perhaps, the air lit only by floating orbs around the edges that glowed like giant round fireflies.

"Noh ma pak," said the third creature.

When Norman didn't react (he couldn't; his head was again spinning, and his heart's rhythm had turned to machine-gun fire), the newcomer looked to the original creature and babbled words he didn't understand. The smaller being with the egg-shaped protrusions chimed in, its voice lighter than the rest. The language was sharp and full of edges that slid into drawn-out syllables.

The third creature met Norman's eyes, and Norman felt himself wanting to recoil. The eyes were green and frosted with a black slit down the center, like a lizard's.

Clear nictitating membranes blinked across the eyes. Norman's heart rose into his chest. If the creature uncoiled a long tongue to lick its own eye clean, Norman felt sure he'd pass out.

It poked a long, gray finger into Norman's chest. Because the fingers were so long, it looked like the thing had jabbed him with a stick from a distance. Norman looked down, seeing the way its finger pushed against his familiar blue shirt. Except for the length and color, it was like a human finger. The only other difference was that the end was a claw, and it looked like it might extend to pierce his heart. He wouldn't mind. It would be a relief.

"Noh. Mah. Pak," said the creature.

Again, it tapped his chest several times. *Hey, buddy, I'm talking to you.*

"I don't understand." Norman didn't have time to be surprised that he could speak. The words were out before the novelty of speech registered, then he was past shock and thrown back into terror.

The creature looked to the others and said something that, in any language, was recognizable as pleasant surprise. The others chattered back, all sharp consonants and nasal vowels.

"Noh. Mah. Pak." It jabbed him again, same as before.

The smaller being pushed the other's arm away. Then it touched its own chest.

"Fohba."

Then it poked Norman's chest as the last one had.

"Noh mah pak."

Let's not go back, Norman. Let's go to the nest.

Was that where he was? Whatever the nest was, was that where he'd ended up? But no, that's not what his mind was trying to tell him at all.

Let's not go back, Norman.

"Noh mah pak," said the creature, poking him.

Let's not go back.

Norman.

"Norman Parks," he said. "That's my name."

The things gibbered excitedly.

"Norman," he repeated, unable to read the things' mood, if in fact they had them. But whatever emotion he'd elicited by stating his name — and thus establishing the first twig of communication between them — was decidedly positive, and he wanted to draw out any positivity for as long as he could. They could turn to eviscerating him at any moment, and the straps around his body would hold him helpless while they did.

"Noh ma."

"And you're Fohba," said Norman, aware that his voice had adopted a manic quality. He already felt hoarse, as if he'd been shouting for hours. Even his jaw and throat muscles felt tired. He wanted to sleep. To be done with this, whatever it is.

"Fohba," said the creature.

Norman laughed, forcing it. The creatures continued to gibber, then one pressed something behind Norman's head, and again the trigger's floating hologram appeared.

"Feh," said the newest creature. This one had the starkest eyes, the most irritated demeanor. It jabbed its finger at the floating object.

"I don't know."

It jabbed again. "*Feh.*"

Norman searched his disorderly mind. He knew the dark-gray object with the knob was a trigger, but had no idea what it ever triggered, if it had indeed triggered something. Did it have a nickname? Something he and the others (he was increasingly sure there had been others, though the cave didn't look familiar) had called it, other than trigger? Something, specifically, that sounded like "feh"?

"I … I don't know."

"*Feh!*" said the creature, jabbing harder at the holo-gram. This time, as it jabbed, the claw at the end of its finger did extend, just a half inch. Its tip, from where Norman was (Lying? Sitting? He seemed to be sitting), looked razor sharp.

The other tall creature put a hand on the first's scaly chest, pushing it back and speaking more calmly. Norman had to push down a manic, terrified laugh. Were they playing good cop/bad cop?

The good cop turned to Norman. It pressed something again. Norman's chair began to slowly rotate. Or the *room* was rotating around him, the simulation showing his surroundings in 360 degrees. As he watched, feeling a moment of vertigo, Norman realized that he *did* seem to recognize it. Somehow. Distantly. But whatever he saw wasn't right. It was like a bad impression of something he'd once known, and those recreating it had mangled the details.

He saw a row of shallow impressions in the rock, a metal capsule about the size of a human being nestled in each. But the metal, Norman's mind insisted, should have been a smooth gray, like the mysterious trigger. What he saw around him looked ancient, the surfaces buckled, cracked, and covered in colors of corrosion. But the metal wasn't supposed to corrode, was it?

Norman blinked. The smallest creatures leaned in, seeming to notice Norman's flicker of recognition.

"Feh?"

Norman wanted to answer. Really, he did. But the memory was pocked, hard to grasp intact like a piece of wet tissue. He knew there would be twelve indentations and twelve capsules, but they weren't supposed to be in a cave. Everything was the slightest flavor of familiar, but nothing had been done correctly. It was as if he had a place in mind, but someone had beaten it beyond recognition, leaving only scant landmarks. Like, Norman realized as he came around, a battered metal cage mounted to the wall. It was empty now, of course, but once upon a time, there had been a light bulb inside, and it had flashed yellow while other hands prepared to turn a knob, flick a switch, and erase the past in order to leave a glimmering hope for the future.

The bad cop leaned down, its face very close to Norman's. Its eyelids blinked over those green, black-slitted eyes, then the clear membranes blinked beneath them.

"Soh. Bak toh seh!"

Norman heard its finger touch something, and the cave was gone.

Now they were out in the open, in the ruins of what might once have been a city fallen to rubble. The sky above was a perfect black, the only light coming from things that scampered about on all fours, with luminescent skin like man-sized fireflies.

"IT WON'T WORK," says Norman. "We're too near the nest."

Dyson looks over. He has a round face with little round glasses perched on his nose. Dyson is a good man. He won't try to seize one of the dozen capsules for himself. He'll do his duty, flipping twelve sets of switches and checking twelve sets of vitals before turning the large knob to shut the world down like a giant rheostat. There is really no question about this in Norman's mind, and the thought shames him because Norman knows he wouldn't be noble enough to do the same. But Dyson is different. He knows what's at stake and knows that with only twelve chances to preserve what's left, his own DNA is less pure and redundant. Yet his function is most important of all. Someone must flip the last switch. Someone must be with Grace and Carter when the world's lights go out for good, leaving a dozen capsules adrift in history's stream, like messages in bottles bobbing across the ocean.

Dyson laughs. He actually laughs, as if he's not a half hour from death. And still, Norman wonders if Dyson and Grace and Carter aren't the lucky ones.

"Then at least you won't feel anything when it happens," says Dyson.

"What will it be like?" says Norman.

"Sleep, I imagine."

"I meant for you."

Again, Dyson laughs. "Sleep, I imagine," he repeats.

Norman wants to return Dyson's smile, but can't. He keeps thinking of how it will actually be — possibly for them all. It would be one thing to make this choice if they were sure it would work, if they could be positive that at least a tiny sliver of humanity would survive. But they're not sure at all. Supposedly, the bunker is shockproof and will survive the blast, but there's no way to be sure until the switches are flipped. He might be making this trip for nothing. Dooming his family to die with everyone else so he can survive … for nothing.

"Carter could squeeze in with me," says Norman.

Dyson sighs.

"He could. He's small."

"Do we really have to end things this way, Norman?"

Norman sighs, watching Dyson. It's unfair to make him repeat what Norman already knows. If the bunker survives, only twelve people will remain, none with any certainty of ever returning, and each carefully selected from what humanity has left. Norman has the mind; Norman must go in his own tiny ark. There is no other way.

"I'm sorry."

"Godspeed, Norman," says Dyson as the assistants close the capsule's front. "See you in the next life."

"You found the bunker," said Norman. His memory was returning in a torrent. His mind still felt unhinged, but now it wasn't caused by the soup of conflicting sensations. Now it was the pain of what he'd done: surviving, while everyone else died.

"Ci yo gehn," said the good cop creature.

"Show me."

"Besh."

"Show me." Norman felt suddenly angry, furious at the coming memory, furious at himself, furious at the creatures for prodding his recall. He didn't want to return. He hadn't died, but he wasn't sure he particularly wanted to live either.

The creatures looked at one another.

"Show me!" He yanked at the restraints, summoning his strength. With each pull, the leathery material yanked him back, but the chair under Norman was now rattling, clattering with force.

All at once, the restraints let go, and he stumbled forward, coming to his hands and knees on the pavement. Norman was remembering more and more now. If the cryogenics had kept him alive — and if the bunker had survived the blast that fouled the earth both for the nest's inhabitants and for humanity's futile, hopeless remains — then the capsule's normalization routines should have functioned as well. Norman had no idea how the creatures had discovered the bunker or why the bunker now looked like a cave (was it the blast? It seemed like more), but the fact that he was alive meant that they hadn't simply popped the lid and dragged him out like a popsicle. And if he'd gone through the normalization, the capsule would have given him the injections. If Dyson had told him the truth, he'd be back to 90 percent functional capacity within an hour, and he already felt most of that strength in his bones.

Norman shambled through the empty and decimated streets, his legs failing him a little less with each new stride. He looked around, fairly certain he was still inside the white room rather than actually outside — but equally sure that the things in his sight were actually out there somewhere.

It had once been a city, maybe. But soil and rock had grown over the shambles of buildings, mostly burying the roads. Hills had formed; crags of fissures sliced through the land at random intervals. The air was impossibly cold, the Earth now almost certainly a blind rock hurtling through space. But the simulator must have only slightly chilled the air to give the feeling of the subzero outside because Norman stayed warm.

He could tell where he was, despite how much had changed, how the landscape itself had shifted. The device wasn't truly a bomb; it was more like a chemical weapon that poisoned the air. East and west were still intact, the flattened land and buildings due to time's passage rather than the force of an explosion.

Inside his mind, Norman could recall Grace beside him as they ran through the streets that final night, drunk on sour spirits, living humanity's last gasp in the face of the infection's invaders seeping up from the nest at the city's heart.

Let's not go back, Norman. Let's go to the nest. Over the edge. Let it have us.

The idea had sounded as good as any at the time. The next day, as Norman had lain back in his cryogenic capsule for the preservation project, he'd thought that drunkenness made leaping to his death with Grace sound appealing, but now he saw it for the obvious solution it would have been. The things would have devoured them, or they'd have broken their necks. But at least they'd have been together. At least he wouldn't have chosen to allow Dyson and the others to preserve him while all but a dozen died. What had it been like, really? Had the suffocation and freezing truly felt like coming sleep? Norman doubted it. They'd died horribly, and he'd lived.

Norman turned. The three gray-scaled creatures were rolling along behind him, their legs motionless, as if being dragged on a treadmill. The room's simulation must be scrolling by underfoot. They were behind, no longer good cop/bad cop, no longer angry or curious. They looked almost frightened by their patient, their subject — whatever he'd once been. Now he was an animal like the glowing, low-slung things prowling the streets, leaping up to strike him and dissolving into sparks because they were only projected phantoms.

Norman came to the lip of a new fissure in the bedrock. It looked like it had been blasted by explosives or cut by a drill. Hell, maybe even lasers. This was the future, after all.

"You found it," said Norman, turning.

He looked down into the darkness. This had once been an underground parking garage, converted to a bunker and reinforced as this particular pocket of humanity made its last stand. There had been no way to win or reclaim the planet. Norman remembered that, now. The feeling of desperate hopelessness, as they'd sat around the planning table facing the truth. *There was no way to win.* They could only act in spite, detonating a doomsday weapon that would at least ensure that the infection wouldn't win.

"But they're still here." Norman pointed around at the

glowing creatures. "It didn't work. They adapted. Somehow, they survived." He collapsed to sitting, suddenly wanting to be small. Nearby, one of the glowing alien creatures snarled, opening its mouth to display its razor teeth. Norman ignored it. It was just a projection. It couldn't hurt him. And he'd managed to hurt himself enough as it was.

The gray creatures looked from one to another, saying nothing.

Norman walked down into the fissure, finding the way illuminated by the simulation. Soon, he emerged into the same cave that the creatures had shown him before, only now, with a new perspective. He was able to see it for what it was.

Twelve capsules, now mostly buried in rock, each engraved with the name of the occupant. The capsules' purpose, still visible above the row of capsules: *Cryogenics*.

"Ci yo gehn," said Norman, reading the word in the creatures' voices. He sat down where Dyson had once sat as he prepared to end the world.

The creatures stood behind him, waiting.

"A shot in the dark," said Norman. "One in a million chance that we'd be found later, and that the human race could go on. And this is how it ends."

He looked up at the creatures. Then, at the trigger mounted to the console. It was gone, of course; Dyson had probably tried to get some distance before setting it off, and it was probably out there in the rock somewhere, eaten by time. How many years had elapsed? How long had he been frozen? There was no way to know. He'd swapped names with these creatures, but that was as far as it went. He didn't even have anyone to talk to.

Norman stared at the row of capsules. One, his own, looked beaten and corroded but still mostly its correct shape. The others hadn't fared as well. Eleven other capsules, all dented and halfway open. He could see beyond the door of the nearest one. There was something inside that might have been bones, their calcified remains mostly gobbled by centuries.

"I'm all that's left," said Norman.

"Noh ma pak," said the first creature.

"Yeah, I know."

"Ci yo gehn."

"Yes, I was frozen."

"Feh."

Norman shrugged. What was the point? Bad cop had been very, very interested in the trigger, which was what feh seemed to mean. But why did it matter? Dyson had pulled the trigger after the dozen were frozen. He'd ended the world. If these creatures had a problem with that, it wasn't Norman's problem.

"Feh."

Norman turned. The gray creature was holding a dented, beaten, corroded piece of metal. Long, with a small spindle on one end that might once have been a knob.

Norman looked from the metal to the creature. From the creature to the metal. To the trigger that used to sit right here, right in this bunker, an impossible time ago.

"Feh," said the creature, extending the box.

Norman took the device that had ended the world.

He looked up. The tall gray creatures blinked in turn, nictitating membranes wicking across their lizard eyes.

Tall and upright, like humans. Five fingers. Five toes. They weren't the things that had spilled from the nest in Norman's day, nor the things that prowled the streets today. These were intelligent beings who lived underground, who breathed the same air as Norman, who, come to think of it, had managed to survive the intense cold and the unbreathable air. Who'd followed a power source to find Norman, humanity's final survivor.

Or maybe not humanity's final survivor after all.

Norman blinked. They'd strapped him down for his own protection. They hadn't been blaming him. They'd just wanted answers about the man who represented what human beings had once been.

"Fazah," said Norman.

He'd just been saying it to close the loop, to use their familiar word as a way of trying to communicate his understanding. But the smallest of the gray creatures reached back toward a table that the simulation had been cloaking and extended the round thing with the concave front and the blurring lights in the center. His eyes were clear enough, now, to see the holographic image the lights had formed from the beginning.

In the middle of the device, Norman saw a reconstructed image of his son, Carter. It looked like an archeological record moved into a modern medium, like a digital photograph of ancient runes. The person in the image was older than Norman remembered — a boy in his late teens, maybe. But it was Carter, all right.

Below the image was a rune in what Norman assumed was the creatures' language. But as he watched, the rune changed into a word in his own language, excavated and deduced as surely as the image itself. *Father.*

The frozen hadn't been the only ones to survive after all. Those who'd stayed behind had thrived, living on to father what humanity became.

"Fazah," said the creature.

The father of modern, gray-scaled humanity, right there in Norman's hands.

One of the creatures held up a syringe, procured from the cloaked table.

Carter was gone. But there was still one source of Carter's progenitor's DNA left. Half of his DNA, anyway.

"Fazah," said one of the other creatures, nodding at the one with the syringe.

Now they knew. Through Norman's own reaction to the image, now they knew for sure.

And the restoration could start.

~

AFTERSHOCKS ON CORROSION:

This story started with the kind of twist that doesn't just change the shape of the narrative, so much as the shape of reality itself. A wrong note in a familiar song. Not a scream so much as a tuning fork for dread.

I imagined a disorienting waking nightmare. A world where language no longer points to anything real. It's not lost, but definitely rusted.

This is the kind of abstract scaffolding I love to throw at Johnny.

He took my premise and spun it into this episode of slow psychological erosion. A story where something invisible is gnawing through the floorboards, and you can't tell whether it's the world, the narrator, or the framework of thought itself.

Logic turns brittle. Sentences crack like tile in a sinking house.

Norman isn't evil. Nor is he innocent. He's a character caught in a spiral of conceptual gravity — a black hole of thought where clarity collapses under its own weight. There's denial and paranoia and a faint whiff of egotism, all disguised as reason. Language papering over rot, sentence by sentence, until the whole structure starts to sag.

And the horror isn't that no one understands him. It's that he still thinks they do.

The deeper ache here is about the fragility of meaning. How easy it is to think we're making contact when all we're doing is echoing into the void. You can explain until your tongue frays and your breath turns to dust, but if one words no longer bind us to the world, what's left?

Corrosion is about the entropy of understanding. When syntax becomes sand. When thoughts leak through the seams of language. When even silence feels scrambled.

It's not about being wrong.

It's about being untranslated.

A sentence unraveling mid-thought — while someone, somewhere, insists it's perfectly clear.

FOUR

Hide & Seek

ROBIN AND LUCY had been at the park for half an hour already, though it felt like twice that, at least. Still, it was better than being cooped up in the house. Two slides, four swing sets, a rock wall, and a rather impressive play area, all just enough to keep 4-year-old Lucy occupied, and away from her endless processions of "Why?"

Lucy wasn't *trying* to be annoying, but she had no idea that one question spilling into 100 was fingernails on a chalkboard, making Robin want to run, hide, then bury herself beneath the covers.

Or simply text her lover, Brian.

Lucy's first question was always harmless.

"Can I watch *Barney?*" she had asked just over an hour ago.

"No," Robin had said.

"Why?"

"Because you've watched an hour more than you should have already today."

"Why?"

"Because too much TV isn't good for you."

"Why?"

"Because you're little, and your brain is still developing. Watching TV puts your mind into a sleep-like state, and slows your brain waves and body functions."

"Why?"

"Because watching TV is passive, not active. Active is better."

"Why?"

"Because even if you're happy sitting on the couch all day watching TV, your body isn't. Going outside helps you grow into a bigger, better, stronger person. And my job is to make you the biggest, best, and strongest person you can be. If I let you watch TV all day, I'm letting TV be your mommy instead of me."

Lucy was silent for several seconds, maybe a full half minute, before opening her mouth again. Robin expects another: why. Instead, she got: "Can we go to the park?"

And that's how they ended up at Veterans' Park, three blocks from their house, while a mountain of laundry to finish, a dinner to cook, and two bathrooms to clean were waiting for Robin at home. She'd get to it eventually. The last thing she wanted was for Steve to come home, acting like an asshole with his usual, "I don't pull six figures so I can come home to dirty laundry and dishes."

Robin had spent nearly every waking hour with Lucy during the last four years. If she hadn't met Elizabeth Mitchell at Kroger, in the middle of Lucy's raging temper tantrum two years earlier, Robin might have gone clinically insane.

Neither Robin nor Steve cared much for play dates or daycare; both believed the first five years of a child's life were essential, and time spent with your child during those years was an investment that paid dividends forever. But somehow all the work of it had landed on Robin.

She had left the classroom easily enough; after all, she'd only been teaching kindergarten for five years before getting pregnant.

And Robin truly wanted to give Lucy the best. But often, her best was exhausting and felt unrewarding, even though she knew deep inside she was making a difference. Fortunately, Elizabeth and her daughter, Jenna, were both wonderful. And perfectly compatible with Robin and Lucy. They had developed a mutually beneficial friendship where they felt natural handing off their children each week for a few hours of freedom. It was in those few hours when Robin was able to slowly rediscover who she'd been in the years before Lucy.

Because being a stay-at-home mom was hard.

Not that Robin agreed with the women who said it was the hardest job in the world. It wasn't. That was ridiculous. Did she have it as bad as a cop, or a firefighter, or hell, a lawyer, or surgeon, or any of the millions of jobs where lives were on the line? No. But it was hard nonetheless, always being on, answering the never-ending *whys* — as present as the sun — always being *Mommy* and never having any quality time with the "Robin" side of herself. She never had sick days or vacation days, or *I don't feel like fucking showing up today* days.

And the worst part was that she wasn't allowed to complain. To complain — to the wrong people, anyway — was deemed selfish and *unmotherly*.

Robin was happy at first, even during the rough times when Lucy was an infant. But then something in Steve changed. His patience had worn thin with both her and their child. And when Robin tried to vent her day's frustrations — no different from him coming home and telling her about his asshole boss, Jensen — she saw only a curl of his lip at the bottom of a face that displayed a total lack of sympathy.

"Why are you bitching?" he'd say, even though she wasn't *bitching*. "Believe me, you have it easy. I wish that I could stay home all day, sitting around, watching TV, and playing with Lucy. You can bet *I'd* have the house spotless, with a plate of pasta piled high when *you* came home, and maybe something slinky for after Lucy started snoring."

As if all she was doing was managing Lucy's physical needs.

She was trying to raise a human being, not a dog.

But then Steve was a spoiled brat who'd always had a mommy to clean up after him, had never so much as scrubbed a toilet his entire life, could barely cook mac-n-cheese, and rolled off of her and fell asleep the second he finished doing what never lasted longer than four or five minutes.

Steve treating her like she sat on her ass all day was total bullshit — as though being with Lucy all day, every day, and night wasn't a life of endless to-dos.

How did he think Lucy was potty trained at 18 months, talking before she turned 2, or spelling her name and reciting the alphabet a full month before the Disney Princess party they'd thrown for her 3rd birthday? Robin was the reason Lucy made many kindergartners look like special ed students in comparison. Steve could claim little responsibility for Lucy's success.

And God knew he couldn't claim to have done much else around the house.

Robin washed the dishes, cooked every meal, dressed Lucy on the days when she refused to dress herself, did all the laundry — which was shockingly without end considering only three of them were living there — bought all the groceries, took care of bath and play time, plus, of course, managed all of the bills and the 800 other things she was always too tired to mention. The endless list would have been fine with Robin — IF she was allowed to vent a bit.

But she wasn't.

Robin wasn't allowed to bitch about her unending domestic duties any more than she was allowed to bitch about her complete lack of a social life, which she found difficult at times, and downright torturous during others.

Elizabeth and Jenna were great, but Robin had a classroom before Lucy and a ton of friends before that. But none of her close friends had children yet. And women without children, married or not, tended to avoid breeders like they made cancer instead of babies. Or maybe it was simply the fact that their schedules no longer matched. By nine pm most Saturday nights, Robin was falling into bed exhausted. Making it difficult, if not near impossible, to maintain her pre-Steve and Lucy circle.

Sure, Robin loved being a stay-at-home mom, but it was nice to have a conversation with someone more than 3 feet tall, who didn't resort to whining or tantrums when they didn't get what they wanted. And someone other than Steve, who treated her more like a mother than a wife, lately.

She needed something else, which was where Brian came in.

She never meant to start cheating.

She'd been on Facebook, like always, checking her status, hanging onto her high school and college friends by her digital fingernails. Robin didn't remember how many times she'd seen Brian's comments on her friend Paula's posts before realizing how much they always made her laugh. But she did know they became online friends mere minutes after that.

The flirting, done in private messages, was harmless at first, and Robin didn't think anything of it at all, even though a part of her loved the attention immediately, and craved it in no time at all. Soon she realized, though she would never have admitted it to anyone, Brian made her wetter with a sentence than Steve had in a year, using both of his fingers and the occasional tongue.

The third week after their private messaging started found Lucy at Jenna's house for a playdate, and Robin meeting Brian with her panties puddled at her ankles while bent over his sofa.

She and Brian had been rinsing and repeating at least once a week in the three months since. Even now, spending time at the park with Lucy so she could "be a good mom" and not allow TV to mindlessly raise her daughter, Robin couldn't stop thinking about Brian. Or sexting him.

Sex with Steve was never bad, exactly. Before Lucy was born, it had been rocking. But in the four and a half years since, it had slowly circled the drain of monotony; the same positions in the same places, with the same person, and usually at the same time of night.

Once upon a time, Robin would have seen the prospect of cheating on her husband as slightly more likely than her robbing a liquor store. But that was well before minutes with Brian murdered routine with a double-barreled blast of anticipation.

It was hot as fuck for Diane Lane in *Unfaithful*, and worked for Annette Bening in *American Beauty*, along with many women in one of the fastest-growing demographics in America. Robin was far from alone. Though men still cheated more than women, situations similar to hers were rapidly on the rise, or so she'd been telling herself several times a day since her affair with Brian started.

Brian had opened the cage door and let her inner

kitten out. It was the first time Robin felt her raw sexuality return since her third trimester. Though she had never been a girl with low self-esteem, time with Brian made her realize that her tank had been dipping ever closer to empty.

Brian made her feel sexier, more beautiful, and more loved.

And every sext seemed to make her wetter.

> I can't wait to lay my lips on your soft skin, travel down to the base of your throat, before I drag the tip of my tongue up to your moist lips while running my hand up the middle of your back to unhook your bra
>
> ...

Just one of the million things Robin loved about Brian was the time he took with his sexts — never any broken language or *text speak*. Full words only. No shortcuts on his cell, or in bed.

Robin had a 4-year-old to manage, giving her an excuse for shortcuts.

> I want U 2 make me wet.

Robin moved her eyes from her iPhone to Lucy, who was halfway across the "Diego" bars, swinging from one side to the other like a monkey. She dropped to the other side, threw her arms up in the air, then turned back to Robin, waiting for her mommy to smile.

Robin did, then felt the buzz in her hand and the tingle between her legs.

She turned her eyes back to the iPhone.

> I love making you wet, even more than you making me hard. I want to hold you. To touch you. To kiss you. I want to see you blush from my touch.

Robin looked up at Lucy, running toward the swings, then typed:

> Now I'm wet. Make me wetter.

The next 30 seconds of waiting were excruciating, but worth the wait:

> I want to feel you nibbling along the length of my neck as I explore the depths of your body. I want to feel your teeth sink into my flesh as you slip from control. I want to shudder as you take me into your mouth and make my hard cock harder.

Robin felt suddenly flushed, almost embarrassed, wondering if anyone had any idea what she was doing. Of course, they didn't, but knowing didn't keep her from feeling exposed in the gaze of the tall man in the suit playing with his twin boys, the group of women making catty observations over in the shade of the jacarandas, or the fat man with the bushy beard scooping giant spoonfuls of yogurt into his mouth.

Her phone buzzed again, sending Robin another tingle of fresh excitement.

> I can't wait for you to lower your wet center
> onto my panting tongue, letting me soak
> you more before you lower yourself onto my
> cock, then ride me hard into a scream. I
> want to feel your breasts crushed against
> my chest as I taste your tongue, like a
> prisoner in my mouth.

Robin wondered what Elizabeth would be doing in about an hour. It wasn't her usual day to watch Lucy, but she probably wouldn't mind an early swap. Robin could reward Lucy with a little time in front of the TV when they got home, then go back into the bedroom and spend 15 minutes with her open nightstand drawer, but she'd much rather have the real thing throbbing inside her if possible.

Robin had to be careful, though. There was only so far she could stretch Elizabeth's rubber band before it finally snapped into questions she wouldn't want to answer. Too many last-minute "emergencies" would draw unwanted attention. And while Robin had been surprisingly successful at keeping Brian a secret, she wasn't a particularly good liar when confronted.

She could also invite Brian into the workshop at the back of the house, but she'd already regretted doing that the two times she had, due to the danger and the disrespect. She might not be happy with Steve, but this was still their house.

Lucy kept looking up, vying for her attention, which was 90 percent on her iPhone, if not more. Even while waiting for her next buzz and tingle, Robin was more interested in checking Twitter and Facebook than she was in watching her 4-year-old.

She was just so ... burned out.

The last couple of months had been particularly bad,

with her daughter constantly shifting her behavior patterns. At least when she had kids in class, Mrs. Robin could catch a break at some point during the day. Teachers would join classes for lunch or recess, allowing each other to grab some alone time to catch up on their work. Without Elizabeth, parenting breaks didn't exist. Sure, Steve "did his part," but doing his part usually meant letting Lucy do whatever in the hell she wanted while he watched sports or played video games, leaving Robin to clean up the chaos the next morning.

During Steve's watch, Lucy had chopped chunks off of her own hair (after she finished cutting the cat's first); trimmed a brand-new dress she just *had to have* from Children's Place; magic-markered a pair of slippers from Nordstrom, announcing, "Mommy got a new pair of shoes, too!" And just this weekend, while Robin had been running some errands during a rare solo outing, Lucy had colored her bedroom walls with marker, crayon, *and* finger paint, after pulling all the fluff from her favorite stuffed animal, Doggy the Rabbit.

It was no wonder Robin wanted Brian to fuck her into a coma.

Robin knew the importance of teaching Lucy the word NO, and outside of her trysts with Brian, she'd been consistent as a clock, trying everything from timeouts to blackouts of her favorite stuff. However, nothing was working lately. Lucy was doing anything and everything to mine attention from her mother, wherever and whenever she could get it.

The child believed the world should revolve around her, 24 hours a day, seven days a week, probably since, for the most part, it always had. Robin had no idea how to change her daughter's attitude, other than use the change of schedule that school would bring to try and implement a tighter, stricter schedule.

That was three months away, though. Robin wasn't sure if she'd last that long.

Their conflicts usually centered on attention, of which Lucy could simply never get enough. Robin loved and used the "play cup" philosophy, given to her by Sarah, the eldest kinder teacher at Polk Elementary, the year before Robin left.

The philosophy suggested filling a child's "play cup" halfway, then let them fill the remainder themselves. This worked well for a while. Robin would start reading; Lucy would finish the book. They would start drawing a picture together, then Lucy would take the crayons. They would start building with blocks for 15 minutes, then Lucy would turn their castle into a city.

The play cup approach had stopped working about a month before. It hadn't worked all morning, or at any time through the early afternoon, and it sure as hell wasn't working at the park while Robin was trying to sext with Brian.

Every five seconds, Lucy cartwheeled toward Robin with a fresh "Look at me!"

"Mawwmeeeeeeee ..." Lucy cried, approaching her spot on the bench. "You *said* you would play with *me*."

Robin looked up from her phone. "I said I would bring you to the park, Sweetie. And I did. You can play by yourself now that we're here. That's why I brought you."

"No," Lucy shook her head. "You said that when we got to the park, we would play together. But we haven't played together at all! You've been sitting the whole time, just like last time, and the time before that." She folded her arms across her chest. "Pretty soon, you'll say it's time to go, and we won't get to play together at all!"

"I'm old and boring," Robin said. "Wouldn't you rather play with someone your own age?"

Lucy said, "There's no one my age here. Only babies and graders."

Robin's inner guilt started to slither inside her. "Give me a minute," she said. "Okay?"

Lucy nodded, then Robin turned to her iPhone, just as it buzzed. It was Brian.

> Are you there? Don't you want to crush your tits against my chest, while I tongue fuck your mouth?

Robin uncrossed her legs, then crossed them back the other way, stealing a glance at Lucy before sexting:

> Am going 2 play w/ Lucy. BRB. Soon as I can.

"Okay," she said to Lucy, slipping the phone in her pocket. "What do you want to play?"

Lucy squealed, then clapped, bouncing back and forth on her feet. "Can I give you choices?"

"Sure," Robin smiled. "What are my choices?"

"We could look for rollie-pollies over there," she pointed toward the backboards, where they'd found several colonies before, made mostly of dead colonists, baking in the sun. "Or we can play dinosaur cave." She paused for a moment, then added, "Or you could push me on the swings. But . . . looking for rollie-pollies sounds like the most fun to me."

Looking for rollie-pollies sounded like the least fun to Robin, but it wasn't too far behind dinosaur cave, which meant she'd have to crawl behind the rock wall, scrunched low enough to put an ache into her back that would last for hours, while cramping her legs as Lucy roared around her.

Swinging was best.

"How about swinging?" Robin said.

"Swinging is my last choice," Lucy shook her head. "I don't want to do that at all."

"Then why did you make it a choice?"

"Because you said you like choices in threes." Lucy was silent for a second and then said, "How about hide and seek?"

Hide and seek was perfect. Robin could find a hiding spot that wouldn't hurt her back or cramp her legs, while making a quicker return to Brian.

"Okay. Hide and seek it is!"

"You hide first, Mommy. And don't make it too hard."

"Don't worry. I won't."

She meant it. Robin wanted to be found quickly so Lucy could go hide. She didn't want to start sexting while having to worry about having her hiding place or her secret conversation discovered. It would be much better to finish while Lucy was hiding.

Robin wanted a moment with Brian to focus. She was hot and wet and far too horny to be playing hide and seek with her daughter.

She ran to crouch behind a large trashcan, sitting between two jacarandas, then squatted, finding it impossible not to imagine herself squatting with Brian beneath her.

She hoped for the hundredth time that Elizabeth was home so she could squat low, over and over and over and faster and faster, until she was curling her fingers into Brian's covers while screaming.

Robin made sure the top of her head was peeking just above the trashcan. Sure enough, less than 20 seconds after she stopped counting, Robin heard Lucy running toward her, screaming in triumph. "I found you!"

Robin feigned disappointment, then said, "Well, I guess it's my turn to count. I hope you find a better spot than me!"

"Don't worry, Mommy," Lucy said, smiling widely. "I will."

Robin counted to 20, then quickly slipped behind a bank of trees, rested her back against the trunk of the fattest one, and pulled her iPhone from her pocket.

She spent half a minute, almost not texting, as she wrestled with her conscience.

She should be playing hide and seek with her daughter. Sexting with Brian was wrong. Ignoring Lucy was even worse. It wasn't enough for Robin to be at the park. She had to be present, too. Otherwise, she was only stealing from them both.

Robin held the phone in her hand, fighting her impulses, before she finally swallowed, then started what she'd stopped at the bench:

> K, am back. Sorry 4 making U wait.

Brian must have been waiting, because his sext was buzzing in her palm a second later, a second before the tingle:

> It's okay. Waiting made me want to fuck you harder.

Yummy. Brian was already acting more aggressive. Robin liked that.

> What would U do 2 me?

Robin already knew, but still longed to be told.

> I would rub my palm against your soaking-
> wet pussy while whispering filth in your ear,
> making you want me bad, so bad you
> would beg for my dick.

Brian didn't have to rub anything anywhere; Robin was perfectly willing to start begging right now.

> Shouldn't be texting. Am being very bad.
> Have 2 go soon. Will U spank me later?

They'd never done anything like spanking before. Robin was curious to see how he would respond. She felt the buzz, instantly followed by the biggest and best tingle yet.

> You are a very, very bad girl, Robin. I think
> you deserve to deep throat my dick while I
> spank you.

Robin was soaking wet. Lucy may as well have been at Elizabeth's. Or hiding on Mars.

> Oh yes! That's the perfect punishment.

Robin was about to get more graphic, but the conscience she'd been trying to keep in the closet was banging hard against the wood, demanding that she get up and go look for Lucy.

She didn't wait for Brian's response, which she was sure would have something to do with whipped cream or honey, garnishes he often introduced near the end of their sexting, even though they'd never done anything that sticky in bed for real.

She texted:

BBL. Want 2 spend rest of time at park with
Lucy. Will call when home.

Robin felt suddenly sick; bloated from a thousand pounds of guilt.

What the hell am I doing? I am officially the world's worst mom.

Into what sort of nightmare had she slipped — how had she gotten stuck between sick in her stomach and the gummy sticky in between her legs? — ignoring her daughter while sexting with a man she barely knew, and certainly didn't love?

Robin swallowed a sudden, and surprisingly high, wave of guilt.

Steve was a good man who didn't deserve to be cheated on, just because *she* was feeling ignored, overburdened, and under-appreciated — the same recipe that likely cooked half the country's affairs. Steve was better than an affair; so was she.

The flutter of guilt thickened with a thud inside her as Robin thought of the workshop Steve had built her in the back of the house because she had begged for a place to nurture her creativity in quiet. She'd retreated to the workshop maybe twice, once for each time she'd invited Brian inside it.

Robin started searching the park, looking from the sprawling play set to the swings, then over to the sandbox. Lucy was nowhere. Robin trotted toward the play equipment, scanning the park on her way.

Robin swallowed again, trying not to hate herself.

Lucy deserved a mom who would play hide and seek with her, without using it as an opportunity to sneak in another couple of minutes' worth of illicit sexting. Her problems with Steve didn't mean Lucy should suffer. She didn't deserve it. To Lucy, LOVE may as well have been spelled T-I-M-E.

Loving Lucy was easy; it was far harder to give her undivided attention, at least without resenting — or counting — the minutes. Yet, even if Lucy was occasionally needy or all-consuming, most times she simply wanted eye contact as she asked her questions, recited her stories, or listed all of her favorite things in order.

Lucy's needs were reasonably simple: to go on a treasure hunt, in the house or out in the garden; draw a picture; maybe play a game and let her win; pour extra bubbles into the bath; or warm her towel for her when she got out; build a fort with blankets and chairs; let her stay up a half hour past bedtime; and play hide and seek.

Robin was sick of "Daddy" being the one who had all the fun, while she was forever in charge of the discipline. It was a lot easier to come home after a long day and be Super Dad, with their baby girl dropping whatever she was doing the second she heard her daddy's key in the door, running so fast she sometimes tripped on her way, leaping into Steve's arms before he'd even closed the door behind him.

Steve was a good man and a great father. Isn't that what she wanted for their Lucy? Her dad would cast her image of the ideal man, the model for whom she would one day choose as her mate. Steve gave Lucy something Robin never could, and as much as it hurt to stare that truth in the eyes, it *wasn't* a bad thing.

"Lucy!" Robin called, not wanting to play hide and seek for a single second longer. She didn't see her daughter anywhere, and it had been far too long since she had.

Robin swallowed again, a gnarled ball of horrible snot stuck in her throat, sick with sudden realization — not that what she was doing with Brian was disrespectful to Steve, but that it had deeply affected her daughter Lucy as well.

What if something inside Lucy knew?

What sort of example am I setting?

Even if it was only subconscious, what was Robin saying to Lucy about her father with every sext sent?

"Lucy!"

Robin screamed, spinning through the park, her eyes wildly searching for her daughter. She ran to the bank of trees at the far side of the park, circling around the group of trees twice — in case Lucy was a step ahead and hiding — but Robin couldn't find her.

She was good at hiding, but not *this good*. Usually, she would have given her location away with a fit of giggles within 30 seconds of hiding.

Robin went back to the swings, then over to the play set again. She looked behind every trashcan, and even went out to the parking lot, where she looked behind and beneath everything in the parking lot, from an old Audi to a brand-new BMW Z4.

"Lucy!"

Raw panic seeped into her skin, like winter frost over an autumn lawn.

"LUCY!"

"LUUUUCY!!"

Robin would have screamed her throat raw, but suddenly felt terrified that the people around her; the man with the big beard and yogurt, the gaggle of women trading their gossip, and the old, short, squat woman with the tiny, little girl, about Lucy's age, who had taken the place of the tall man with the twins, would all know exactly what a horrible mother she was — that she'd lost her daughter while sexting with a man who wasn't her husband.

They would know it, they'd smell it on her, like flies circling the stink of rotting fruit.

Robin screamed for her daughter anyway.

"LUCY! LUCY!"

She drew a deep breath between her flutters of panic.

"LUCY! LUCY!"

She had to find Lucy, NOW, no matter how much attention she called to herself or how foolish she'd look if Lucy suddenly appeared laughing behind her.

Every second that passed sent Robin deeper and deeper into a nightmare come true.

Where else can I look?

Should she waste her time circling the park again, fueled by the fraying hope that she'd somehow missed her little girl hiding somewhere obvious? Lucy had hidden a hundred times before, and Robin always found her in less than a minute, even though she'd usually pretended she didn't have a clue, because that's what parents did — like how Lucy waved at her each time she passed by on the merry-go-round, and Robin *always* waved back.

"LUCY! LUCY!"

Robin kept screaming, but like every other time, saw nothing but foreign stares in return. The short woman with the little girl leaned low and whispered something into the tiny child's ear, then ran over to Robin.

"Is your daughter missing?" she said, not a hint of accusation edging her question.

Robin nodded, trying not to panic. "I can't find her," she said. "We were playing hide and seek, but when I went to look for her, she disappeared."

Because I was picturing my panties around my ankles, with Brian behind me.

"It's okay," the woman soothed. "She'll turn up. That's what kids do."

"Not Lucy," Robin shook her head.

The old woman smiled the same smile she'd probably used a thousand times before to calm down young mothers, then said something she'd probably said out loud at least a hundred: "You never think it could be *your kid* until it is. I've been watching children for nearly 40 years, and I can promise you, that's always the case. Your daughter's safe," she said, then spread her kind smile wider.

The old woman was right.

Robin had to breathe. Lucy was in the park somewhere.

Unless . . .

It hadn't occurred to Robin that Lucy might have gone home. They were, after all, just three blocks away.

Except that didn't sound like Lucy, and even an old woman who had been watching other people's children for four decades couldn't change her mind about that. At least not without her searching through the park again.

Robin gave Lucy's description to the old woman, then doubled her efforts, lowered her panic, and peeked into every nook and cranny she might have missed, from high to low and everywhere in between.

As she circled the park several more times, innocent onlookers from earlier all seemed potentially dangerous, pretending not to see as the first tears fell from her eyes.

Robin hated herself with a coiled guilt she'd not felt since she was 14, standing beside her cousin Tommy at the edge of Bear Lake, throwing rocks toward a family of ducks swimming near the shore. She'd wanted to impress Tommy — two years older and a million times cooler — by scaring the ducks. In her head, Robin saw the ducks scatter as her rock slapped the water beside them, but her aim was off, and the stone flew too far, ricocheting off a far rock wall and bouncing back, hard at the mother duck's head. The mother duck sank beside a dollop of red in the lake, leaving five motherless ducks behind her.

Like at the edge of Bear Lake, guilt draped a shadow over her, cast by the sun of her horrible self.

Robin's daughter, the second heart that beat just beyond her own, wasn't in the park.

"LUCY!!!"

"LUUUUCY!!!!"

Nothing.

Robin pulled out her phone to check the time, shocked to see a half dozen sexts from Brian, each doing the opposite of turning her on. She'd been so focused on finding her daughter that she'd missed every buzz and certainly hadn't felt any tingle.

Even more shocking, and infinitely more terrifying, a full hour was missing, along with her daughter.

The realization turned Robin's knees to noodles. Waist-deep in panic, she had to slam her palm onto the trunk of the nearest tree to keep from falling. She looked over at the old woman, pushing the tiny girl in her swing, shrugging her shoulders as she stared over at Robin with kind but helpless eyes.

Robin told herself that everything would be okay.

It had to be. That was how panic worked. It made you illogical. Stupid. Dread crept inside and stretched your flesh, made you feel like you were floating through the impossible, horrible, and inevitable in unison, leaving little if any hope of finding the far side.

She breathed herself into a calm, looking around at the legion of onlookers, and fighting the urge not to run up to each of them screaming, demanding to know where her daughter was.

But no, that was ridiculous.

Lucy was at home. *She has to be.*

She waved to the old woman, said she'd be right back, and if she saw Lucy, tell her to wait. Robin then turned and started running the three blocks home. She was halfway there when her phone buzzed. Far from a tingle, Robin pulled the phone from her pocket, angry, then glared at the screen:

I can't wait to cum on your tits.

She growled, dropped the phone into her pocket, then ran faster, trying not to hate herself, knowing she'd have plenty of time to hate herself later — after she found her precious Lucy.

Please, God, let me find her. I swear, I'll never lose sight of her again. I'll never see Brian again. And I swear, I'll do anything you want, just please ...

Robin made it another block before her phone buzzed again, this time with the insistence of a ring, rather than with the fleeting flirting buzz of a sext.

Goddammit!

If Brian was calling her, especially right now, she would tear his fucking head off.

She was a block from home, a hundred or so steps from a clear view of her front porch. Robin should have kept running, but a mother searching for her missing child can never ignore a ringing phone.

She stopped running, clutching her side with one hand as she dug the phone from her pocket with the other, shocked to see that along with several missed sexts, she had three missed calls.

What was wrong with her phone?

FUCK!

All three calls were from Steve, including the one now buzzing in her hand.

Robin wondered if she should ignore it, then realized she didn't have a choice. What could she say? What would she tell him?

No, she had to say nothing until there was something to say.

With a world of panic inside her, Robin hit "ignore," dropped the phone in her pocket, then ran the rest of the way to her house.

She raced to the porch, feeling drunk from the difficulty of getting her key to work in the lock, while yelling "LUCY!"from the porch.

The door swung violently open from the weight of Robin's body, and her knees slapped the smooth varnish of the hardwood as she slipped and fell to the floor.

She scrambled to her feet, screaming for Lucy as the shrill ringing of her home phone cut through the silence of the house.

Robin ran into the kitchen, grabbed the phone from the counter, then looked at the Caller ID: Steve. Again.

What the hell does he want?

His insistence was petrifying.

Robin swallowed.

What if he knows Lucy is missing?

What if he knows WHY?

But what if he can help find her? Maybe he knows where she is.

What if all she had to do was answer the phone?

And admit that she didn't know where their daughter was? Absolutely not.

The voicemail kicked on, but clicked off before Steven could leave a message. She wasn't sure if the voicemail cut him off before he could talk or if he hung up.

She had to search the house first and see if Lucy decided to hide at home. This was exactly the kind of thing that a child seeking attention might do to get what she needed.

But Lucy wasn't in her bedroom or her bathroom, or their bedroom or their bathroom. She wasn't in the laundry room, or the garage, or the living room, or the dining room. And she wasn't in any of the closets, in the backyard, or hiding under a single cover on any bed in the house.

The phone continued ringing, three more times as Robin scoured the house.

Each time she checked the Caller ID, it was Steve every time.

What the hell was his problem?

Robin would have cried if she thought she could afford either the tears or the time, but she couldn't. She drowned in panic instead, not because she'd fallen in the deepest waters of deceit, but because she'd stayed too long.

The phone rang again. This time Robin knew she had to answer.

Maybe he knows where Lucy is? Maybe he came home early and surprised her at the park, and they went to get ice cream without telling me? Maybe Steve saw me sexting Brian? And figured he'd teach me a lesson?

She gathered her courage, then crossed the living room to the phone, telling herself it was a good thing. Whatever humiliation she suffered at the hands of Steve, knowing she let Lucy out of her sight, would be instantly dimmed by his telling her where their daughter was.

Robin pressed the giant CALL button with her trembling thumb, then brought the receiver to her ear, shaking the entire way. But by the time she breathed her "Hello," there was nothing but dial tone to answer.

Panic returned, meaner than before.

She thought of calling Steve, but couldn't.

Robin had already looked everywhere in the house several times and in the backyard, but she started looking again. It had been nearly 90 horrifying minutes since she'd last laid eyes on Lucy. She tried not to think about all the horrible things that could happen to a little 4-year-old girl in an hour and a half gone missing. Tried not to think about all the things she'd heard in cop movies when a kid goes missing.

What if she is alone and crying somewhere in a ditch?

What if she was abducted?

What if she's. . . dead?

The last thought was too much to consider.

She couldn't think of that. *No.*

Robin stormed through the house, screaming Lucy's name.

There was nothing in Robin's life she wouldn't trade to hold her Lucy, to know her baby was safe, to believe she hadn't brought harm to her daughter through her horrible, selfish actions.

Two hours earlier, Robin didn't believe in God. But with the ardent belief of a deathbed confessor, she prayed for the second time in an hour to the Good Lord, his son, Jesus, and any other God who might be listening.

Her phone buzzed, another text. Robin pulled the iPhone from her pocket, growling.

This text wasn't from Brian.

It was from a number she didn't know. No name was above the digits.

Her eyes settled on the text for a second before the scream built, and then died in her throat. Robin gasped, then panted, dropping her phone as she fell to her knees, scrambling to retrieve it so she could prove to her mind that her eyes had been lying.

They weren't, and the truth mocked her with the horror of the text:

Do you know where your daughter is?

The sound finally fell from her mouth, fulfilling the promise of her frozen scream. Robin whimpered as she quickly texted the mystery caller back:

Who are you?

The longest three minutes of Robin's life crawled by. And then:

It doesn't matter who I am, though you might have read about me in the paper. I tend to get around a lot. So many kids, so little time ...

Robin whimpered again.

Where is she? Tell me now! I'll give you anything you want.

The next text came so fast, Robin had to believe it was ready and waiting.

What I want is for you to think long and hard. I'm gonna ask you some questions. Five questions, Robin, and if you can answer at least three, LUCY will make it home for dinner. If not, well. . . I'll let your imagination fill in the gaps.

Robin wanted to refuse, wanted to tell the mystery texter NO, and tell him to fuck off. But what choice did she have? She swallowed, then whimpered again, wiping the tears from her swollen, red eyes.

What is LUCY's favorite color?

Robin shocked herself with a smile.

Purple and pink!

Lucy didn't have *a* favorite color. It was always purple AND pink. Never just one. The pause felt far too long before Robin was again reading her screen:

That is correct.

Robin choked on her sudden sob, waiting for the next text.

What is LUCY's favorite food?

Her smile spread wider as she dared to believe she would see her beautiful Lucy alive.

Ice cream sandwiches, any flavor, but mint chip is the best.

Robin furiously texted her answer, hoping Lucy hadn't changed her mind for whoever was holding her, and forcing her into answers. While Lucy never changed her mind about her favorite color, she often did regarding food. Six months ago, Lucy didn't even like ice cream and would have happily traded Doggy the Rabbit for a bottomless bowl of spaghetti. But for the last month, it had been ice cream sandwiches for sure.

Silence was thunder, and the endless wait flooded Robin with panic.

She cycled through her mind, replaying every possible spot of danger at the park, both real and imagined. What about the people who had been there?

Had one of them taken her daughter?

Her mind flashed to the tall man with the twins, and for a horrible second, she was *sure* it was him. She started poring over his every detail, from his high hairline to his thick eyebrows — full enough to see from 30 yards across the park — fat like the red and blue stripes on his tie.

What if it were the fat man with the beard, or the old woman pretending to care? Who's to say the little girl was supposed to be with her? Everyone looked guilty when your child was missing.

The house phone rang again. She looked at the phone's Caller ID. It was Steve. Again.

Did he somehow know?

Why was he calling nonstop?

She was about to answer his call when the answering machine began to play back Lucy's voice, almost mocking her now, "Mommy, Daddy, and Lucy aren't available. Please leave a message. Bye-bye!"

And then, Steve's voice, "Hey, Robin, are you there? I got these texts from someone saying they have Lucy, and if I wanna find her, I need to ask you what's going on. Is this some kind of sick joke? Please, call me back!" A long moment of silence stretched, and Robin was pretty sure it sounded like Steve was crying. He then said, "I'm getting worried, and I'm gonna call the cops if I don't hear from you. Please, Robin."

As Steve spoke, her cell phone buzzed with another text:

Very good.

Then, a second buzz with another question:

Where was LUCY hiding?

The voicemail cut Steve off as he called for her again, "Robin? Are you there? Robin?"

Robin nearly dropped her iPhone as another whimper fell from her mouth. It *had* to be someone from the park. They were watching her — watching them — the whole time! Robin let them take Lucy away right from under her nose when she should have been watching her child.

It was all her fault.

Robin couldn't answer the kidnapper's question. Her fingers wouldn't work as she was again swallowed by panic. The kidnapper texted: *I'm waiting* …

Robin had no idea what to say.

What if she got the answer wrong?

Would he let her give more than one answer?

10 … 9 … 8 … 7 …

Robin texted in panic:

Wait!

Immediately, the kidnapper responded:

NO.

Then the kidnapper wrote:

4 … 3 … 2 …

Robin mashed her thumbs against the glass:

> Behind the big trashcan!

Her heart slammed inside her chest, seemingly a million times before the iPhone buzzed in her hand.

> That is incorrect.

Then the kidnapper asked:

> Why did you lose her, Robin?

> Because we were playing hide and seek.

> Wrong.

FOR A SECOND, Robin wondered if this was that fucking asshole, Brian, but her heart was beating so fast she couldn't slow it or her thoughts long enough to force her mind into logic.

She screamed when she saw the next text:

> Final question …

Then fell into a rattling sob when she saw what it said.

> Where is Lucy RIGHT NOW?

"That's not fair!" she cried out, as if the kidnapper could hear her. She couldn't answer that. If she could, she wouldn't be on the phone with the monster; she'd be kicking his ass and taking her daughter back.

Robin suddenly realized how stupid she'd been.

She should have called the police the moment she couldn't find Lucy. But then she would have to admit everything, to the cops and not just herself. She was responsible.

The next text was the worst yet:

Unlike you, I'm true to my word.

The text was horrible enough, since Robin knew what the monster had promised, but it was made worse by the attachment that buzzed her cell a moment later — an audio file she was nearly too scared to play.

Robin lowered her sweaty, trembling finger onto the file, then fell to her knees, as a fit of horrible sobs filled her living room — the impossible agony of her little Lucy, screaming at the top of her lungs:

"Help me! Help me! They're going to get me, Mommy! I don't know what to do. I'm so scared!!!" Lucy's horrible screams were spaced several seconds apart, as if each new cry was fueled with a fresh injection of terrible pain.

Robin started mashing her thumbs on the soft glass, typing as fast as she could.

I'm sorry for everything I've done. I take it all back. I'm horrible, and it's all my fault. But please, please, show mercy on my daughter. Take me instead. I'll do anything you want, now and forever. Send Lucy to my husband, and I will come to you.

The monster's text was ready:

> Do you love your husband?

The question hit her like a slap in the face.

> Of course I do.

There was another long pause, then:

> Would you like to see LUCY?

Robin swallowed and whimpered:

> Of course. I'll do anything!

After one minute that felt like a thousand, there was a final text:

> LUCY is home . . . in the one place you never thought to look. But you might not like what you find. Oh, by the way. I am like you. I lie.

Robin stared at the phone, waiting for the next text, heart in her throat, as she hoped the monster was lying about taking Lucy. That she was fine, after all.

But then the next message came:

> You never could have saved her. I knew you wouldn't be able to answer the questions, so I just went ahead and killed her. She's been dead for over 40 minutes.

Robin screamed, staring at the phone, waiting for another text to tell her it was a lie. But another text never arrived.

She ran through the house, crying, searching for her daughter, and hoping to God she wouldn't find her dead.

Please, God, please!

She'd already looked out back, in all of Lucy's usual places in their not-too-large backyard. Every place but . . . the workshop out back, the workshop Steve built, at her insistence, where she never went to work.

Robin slowly approached the workshop, fear gripping her tighter with every step.

She might have deserved any number of horrible things, but Lucy was innocent. She didn't do anything.

The horrible sorrow inside her shredded her to pieces with a quivering terror that sank into her marrow, leaving her bones so hollow they could barely keep her from falling.

Robin wrapped her fingers around the doorknob, as fresh dread swam through her veins.

She opened the door and felt her pounding heartbeat swell in her throat when she saw Lucy ... smiling, bright-eyed, and sitting on Steve's bouncing knee.

"Hey there, Robin," he said. His eyes were cold. "We've been trying to call you."

Lucy was laughing. "Hi, Mommy!" she yelled, clearly delighted. "Daddy picked me up from the park. He said we could make the game of hide and seek even more fun! But you couldn't find us, so Daddy said it would be fun to come out here so we could play a new game called Scream! Wanna play?"

"I want a fucking divorce," Robin said.

Aftershocks on Hide & Seek

It was a gorgeous afternoon at the park with my wife,

Cindy, and our kids, the four of us playing hide and seek. Slides squeaked, swings groaned, and the wind conducted a chorus of happy screams and sighing strollers. I felt joy curling in my chest like a sleeping cat.

Until I saw her.

A little girl, maybe five, reaching for her mother.

The mother never looked up. Just kept scrolling.

The child crumpled like a note no one would ever read.

And I remember thinking: *This is a horror story.*

Hide & Seek isn't about ghosts in closets or monsters under the bed.

It's about what happens when the people we need most vanish behind a lock screen.

Robin's the kind of parent who thinks presence is enough. That being there is the same as being with. But love without attention is just furniture, filling space without meaning a thing.

This story felt like a whispered warning when I wrote it. Now it feels like prophecy, endlessly refreshed yet never absorbed. Go to any park, and you'll see parents pushing swings with one hand, doomscrolling distractions while missing the miracle in front of them, seemingly oblivious to how disconnected we've all become.

The scariest part of Hide & Seek isn't the end.

It's how familiar the beginning feels.

And if we're not careful, the game won't end at ten.

We'll open our eyes … and realize the game ended long ago.

FIVE

Respero Diner

XAVIER STOOD on the front porch waiting to knock.

He might have been there for five minutes, but it could've been twenty. Time turned gummy on Respero Day, a day when life flashed before your eyes for most of daylight and into the deepest night.

He'd hit the road at seventeen, and for the nearly forty-four years since, life had seemed like little more than sporadic blasts of endless bustling, punctuated by the pain of a lingering nothing in between.

Respero Dinner was supposed to be a reminder: life is for living, not idle observation. That meant staying intoxicated by everything around you, remaining drunkenly aware of life's million moments and unlimited decisions, each a pixel in your present's snapshot. Respero Dinner was when, no matter how long or lingering, how brief or brilliant, how simple or complex a life might be, a person could immerse themselves in their history and discover who they were, for better or worse.

If you were lucky enough to have a Respero Dinner thrown in your honor, it came just the once. And there were few people who didn't respect the one day that, when done well, offered a new chance for everyone.

Xavier shrugged off his chill, counted to ten, then rang the doorbell and waited, swallowing a rising uncertainty.

The door opened.

His oldest daughter, Blythe, looked radiant. A fresh smile lit her already rosy cheeks.

"Hi, Dad," she said. "Come in."

She led Xavier across a large, mostly marble foyer, then into a massive parlor already populated by several clusters of familiar guests.

"You look great, Tulip," he said. "Is this everyone?"

Blythe shook her head and laughed, a sweet twitter which made him remember those rare holiday mornings when he could linger with his kids, rather than leaving the house for work before the sun had time to clear the night-time stain from its sky.

"Not even close," she said, smiling.

The parlor, like the rest of the house, looked like it was designed by an ambitious architect with an unlimited budget, which it was. Blythe and Jason had been together since their sophomore year of college, before he became the fastest rising star at Walker, Pierce, & Byron, and before she landed a sweetheart gig with the Directorate.

Xavier hadn't spent much time in their Atlanta house, now six years old. Just two visits, once when Ayla was born three years earlier, then again last year when they welcomed her baby brother Aiden into the world, neither of whom would be present at tonight's dinner. Xavier had stayed exactly one week each time. He had an open invitation, genuinely meant, but it was easier to wallow in guilt at home. Easier to be in his space, without worrying about the miles of unsaid words. Alone was the only time he didn't feel his skin baking in discomfort. Still, he wouldn't have missed today for a million acres of nothing but heart-beat and sky.

The parlor was plush, would have been over-decorated if it weren't for its spare design and high ceilings. Elegant lines, blond wood, and shimmering steel made Xavier think of a perfectly elasticized note from a trumpet, pleasantly loud over the percussion.

There were flowers everywhere, though their scent was light. From the coffee table to the end table to the mantle in the parlor, then spread across the long dining table and buffet, which peeked through the sloping arch dividing the two rooms.

Between the people and the flowers, the room was teeming with life. Barely afternoon, the parlor was standing room only, except for the couch beneath the picture window, reserved for the guest of honor.

"You okay?" Blythe asked him, though her eye flitted toward the caterers.

"Fine," Xavier smiled, "just wondering how much was spent on airfare, in this room alone. All together, I bet there's enough for an orbit run."

"I'm sure you're right, at today's prices, but those prices won't hold another year, I guarantee, not with four new firms getting outer-atmosphere allowance," Xavier turned, recognizing the shrill swagger in his old friend Craig's voice.

"Have fun," Blythe said, then headed toward the caterers.

"How the hell have you been?" Xavier said, gripping Craig's hand.

"Better than you, you old fucker."

"That why you flew down from Connecticut to take pity on me?"

"Pity on you, for what? You're the luckiest piece of shit

I ever met, you're just too much of a fucking Eeyore to figure it out. And I haven't lived in Conny's cunt for five years, by the way."

It was good to see the years had yet to clear the crass from Craig's tongue. It was hard to believe his friend had moved away from Connecticut. Craig was fourth generation, from what Xavier remembered, and had never lived anywhere else.

"Where are you living now?"

"Charlotte. We can see water from the bedroom, and it doesn't get as cold as a penguin's pecker like it does up in Conny."

"How are Marie and the girls?"

Craig sipped his tumbler, maybe bourbon, then said, "The girls are great, Marie's a bitch." He took another sip, then, "fuck her."

Xavier blanched.

"Sorry, man," Craig said, slapping his hand on Xavier's shoulder, "I know you really liked her. But she left me three years ago, a month and a half after Laney and Liddy moved out. No warning. I came home, and there was a note, if you can call fourteen words a note, fuck-you-very-much. BAMMO – her shit was GONE. Took daddy's money and bought herself one of those fancy new rehabbed flats they made from a late 1900's office building. Looks brand new. Then again, so does most of Hartford. Doesn't even feel like Conny no more, which is why me and Debbie moved down to Charlotte. She has family there."

"Is Debbie the reason Marie left?"

"Nah, I didn't meet Debbie until later that summer. Marie swears I cheated, and that she has proof, but if she had proof, she wouldn't have needed daddy's debits to get the flat." Craig took another sip. "But shit, enough about me, brother, this is your day. How are you doing?"

Xavier spent the next few minutes bringing Craig current on the last six years, slowly realizing that he'd be telling the same stories with slightly rearranged sentences for the remainder of the day.

"Well, happy fucking Respero!" Craig said, "I better let someone else chew your ear. There's only so much X to go around tonight, right?"

Xavier smiled and held up his hand, politely refusing the passing waiter's offer of a glass of merlot. Then he looked around the room, packed wall-to-wall with his past.

Al Harding was deep in conversation with Jerry Graham, which struck Xavier as maybe the funniest thing he'd seen in years. Only on a day like today would the two of them ever meet, let alone fall into discussion. Al was always and occasionally argumentative, but never arrogant or unkind. Jerry was as pretentious as they came, from his posture to the spittle on his lip that punctuated every sentence.

Seeing Al and Jerry together was weird, though no more odd than much of what he saw around the room, including a glimpse of Janice, a one-night stand from nearly four decades earlier, before he met Rebecca and knew what it meant to kiss from the depths of his soul.

Xavier sank into the couch. It was cool against his back and felt like it might have actually been worth the money. The leather, made in a lab but twice as nice as the real thing, was the color of crumbling chocolate.

The house was a jewel. So was Blythe. She'd always loved nice things, even when that just meant a fancy ribbon streaming from her violin case.

Jason was nice, probably why it was so easy to love him. Like sunlight, he left you warm when near, and missing him when he faded. Neither Xavier nor Rebecca ever doubted Blythe would build herself a beautiful life. But the second she met Jason, certainty turned gospel, and everything started blooming.

They were married almost immediately, and Blythe added a hyphen to the Johnson she was born with. Jason was placed with Walker, Pierce, & Byron, a beat behind Blythe getting noticed by the Directorate. She was now serving as an international liaison in her third year, two years earlier than the previous record.

Xavier and Rebecca had shared dinner with them twice as couples before Rebecca would never join them again. Both dinners were magic, the first in Blythe's favorite restaurant, *Cotta*, and the last sharing Rebecca's impossibly good Italian enchiladas. There was one more meal, and though that final evening was less intimate, it was no less magic, and may have been the best of all. It was dinner at *The Porch*, chicken and potatoes, and everyone was there – Xavier, Rebecca, Blythe, Tori, and Topher, just as it had been since always, but now with Jason. And it felt *right*, like the extra room you never knew you needed until you were breathing in its space.

But sometimes life makes you trade stuff. And maybe fate had to swap Rebecca for Jason.

Xavier may as well have been naked, the way everyone was pretending not to notice him, no one wanting to be the first to breach his space. Except Craig, of course, but he had never been shy.

Xavier's eyes darted around the room searching for Tori or Topher. Respero tradition stated that the guest of honor wasn't supposed to know, or ask about, the guest list, and no attendee was permitted to discuss it with the guest of honor. As nice as all this was, Xavier would've rather jumped from a bridge than fly to Atlanta so he could get stared at all day and night. But he did it because it meant seeing everyone together. But everyone meant *them*, his family, not an endless assembly of easy-to-recognize strangers.

There was distance between him and Tori, and it had been there for a while. He wanted to close it before the night ended. Topher, too, though his was different. Topher had been a disappearing act, ten years running. No one ever knew where or when he would show up. He made his money selling information on the Enterprise side of The Beam, and did well enough to play the ghost.

Brewing coffee curled through the air, pulling Xavier from the couch, but before he was halfway up, a familiar, favorite voice chimed, "Hey, Mr. X."

"Kat!" Xavier went to hug her, but she pulled back, gesturing at the full cup in her hands. "I thought you could use this," she said, handing him the coffee just as she had a thousand times before.

"Thanks," Xavier took the cup, then inhaled without sipping. "How are you? How is California? Rex, the children, everything, all of it, how are you?"

He laughed nervously, surprised by how happy he was to see her.

"We're all doing great. Just closed escrow on our house. Rex got transferred to Las Orillas, and we all love it. Much smaller than San Diego, but the children can get The Beam everywhere, so it doesn't matter where we live. I started writing, just like you said I should. I've already written two flix, and one of them even made The Beam's Face, and stayed there for almost 14 seconds!"

"Wow," Xavier said, smiling, "that's great! You were always way too talented to be my savior."

"I wasn't your savior, Mr. X. I was your assistant."

"You could've asked Rebecca," he said, "believe me, you were my savior on many occasions."

"I'm sorry," Kat said, looking down, "about Mrs. Johnson."

"Thanks for that," Xavier said. "At least the memories are good."

"Professor X!" Two hands clapped loudly on his shoulders, spilling a splash of coffee onto the mocha colored rug.

Xavier turned around, grinning at the grizzly behind him.

"Jerry, it's great to see you." He turned to Kat. "Kat, this is Jerry. Jerry, this is Kat. Kat used to save my life by keeping the wolves away every day. Remember when there were only like seven unleaded stations left per county, for like 10,000 of the Metals that were left? Well, we were in charge of fuel distribution, and we had to start shutting the stations down, one by one. Shit and fan were well acquainted. Kat helped me through it all."

He turned to Kat, "Jerry is 15 years before that, back to when the Directorate first initiated Acres of Acreage. He helped design the original outpost schedules, figured out how much energy each parcel needed, down to the watt. We gave him a 5% margin, but he never used it. His calculations were dead on, perfect, the best we'd ever seen. And ours have suffered since he left. We never should've lost you."

Kat smiled. "My Lord, can this man sing your praises. I've heard the calculation story a gazillion times, approximately. It's great to meet you in person."

"You, too," he said, offering his hand and swallowing hers completely, "but I gotta correct some history. Those weren't my calculations; they were the professor's here. My digits are never that clean. All I did was take the numbers to the Directorate, then listen to them cheer. They came from X's side of the board, not mine."

"I wouldn't have seen the quadratics if you hadn't worked through them with me," Xavier said. "That makes them *your* numbers as far as I'm concerned."

"Your concern is bullshit," Jerry said. "You would've figured out the quadratics just fine, and the lovely Kat right here knows it."

"Modesty is Mr. X's freckles," she said.

"You can say that again!" Jerry barked a heaving bear of a laugh, then exchanged a look with Kat that was far older than the few minutes since they'd met.

Xavier sipped his coffee. Dark, rich, amazing – it had to be the vacuum-grown stuff. He'd never tasted better, and he'd been to Brazil.

"Yes, it's the vacuum stuff," Kat said, noticing the look on his face. "Wow, right? I know we're only supposed to have memory foods, but I can't blame Blythe for that at all!"

"Have either of you seen Tori or Topher?" Xavier asked.

Kat shook her head.

Jerry nudged him, "Come on, X, you know you can't ask about the list."

Xavier smiled. "It was worth a try."

"Well," Kat said, "everyone deserves a turn, so I'm gonna go, but we'll catch up later, okay?"

Xavier nodded, then kissed her on the cheek and said goodbye.

Jerry said, "Me, too, buddy, but first, I just wanted to say I'm sorry about Rebecca. I know it's been a while, but we never really talked, and I just wanted to say that I thought about you a lot, and I'm sorry I never called. I was busy, but no excuses, man. I'm sorry."

"Thanks for saying that," Xavier said. "At least the memories are good."

Xavier took himself off grand display and went to refill his already-full cup, then milled about the room, trading pleasantries with his past:

Yes, I've been busy.

Work has been great, thank you.

No, I've not tried that. Thanks for the advice.

Minutes were always longer when you wanted to crawl out of your skin, and they seemed to quickly multiply. Just when Xavier was about to say the hell with it and go up and start talking to someone, anyone, to not feel the eyes boring into him, he saw Jason waving and walking toward him.

"How're you doing, Papa X!" Jason pulled him into a deep hug. "It's great to see you!"

"Good to be here. The place looks great."

"Thanks, the body's all mine, but the clothes are Blythe's. I could never make countertops or walls sing the way she does. I only know how to get them on the page."

"Jason, do you mind if I ask you something?"

"As long as you don't ask me who built the pyramids, I think we're good!"

"Are Tori and Topher here yet?"

"You and I both know Blythe will send me to the butchers if I spill the A's on the guest list," he looked dramatically left and right, "so let me whisper it between you and me, then I'll deny it wholesale if you snitch. Deal?"

Xavier smiled. "Deal."

"Okay, I won't tell you who's coming and who's not, but I'll tell you I just saw Jack a few minutes ago and let you draw your conclusions from there."

"Thanks, Jason."

"Don't mention it. And now that the kitty's meowing, I'll go and get them for you."

In the last eight years, Xavier had seen Jack without Tori exactly twice, so he was happy, though not surprised, when he saw the two and a half minutes later, following Jason.

"Hi, Daddy," Tori said.

"You look great," Xavier said.

"Thanks."

They stood there looking at one another for a moment, ignoring the thin layer of discomfort. And then Tori threw her arms around him, pulled his cheek toward her, and planted her lips on the soft, freshly sheared side of his face. "I love you, Daddy, and I'm glad to be here. Happy Dinner."

"Yeah, man, we're really glad to be here," Jack said, giving Xavier a warmer handshake than they'd exchanged in years.

"Are you miserable?" Tori asked.

"Not anymore," Xavier smiled and took a sip of coffee. "But this is a bit overdone."

"It's Blythe," they both said.

Tori added, "What did you expect?"

"A version of this, just weird to see it breathing, I guess."

"Are you bored?" Tori laughed. "Are boring people boring you with boring things? How many times have you said 'at least the memories are good' so far?"

Xavier laughed. "Seven. But it's okay. Everyone means well, and it really is all very nice."

"Want us to stick around?" she asked.

"Please don't ever leave," Xavier said with mock drama that was a little real.

With a thin fence of family around him, a steady

stream of guests started to come by and wish Xavier well, make small talk, comment on the ways he had affected their life positively, and, almost always and always awkwardly, they would add how sorry they were about Rebecca.

Eventually, the parlor grew too crowded, and guests began to spill into the living room and then outside, pushing the small group into the crisp, cool, nearly perfect September air.

Some of their immediate neighbors arrived, including Alec and Leslie, a couple who had lived across the street from Xavier and Jessica in the early thirties.

"So what food are you looking forward to most, X?" Alec asked. "After all, Respero's all about the food, and we're actually *allowed* to talk about it. You've gotta have some idea. I haven't eaten anything in two days to prepare."

"Plus, he took double his dose of EndLax on the way over here," Leslie added.

Alec rubbed his belly, and Xavier couldn't help but smile.

"I know you probably find this pretty hard to believe, especially anyone who knew me back when I ate my body weight daily, but I've not honestly thought much about the food at all."

"That's not possible!" The voice didn't have a mouth, but it squealed from somewhere toward the back of the quickly thickening crowd. It might have been Jane, their one-time neighbor and one of Rebecca's best friends for a fun ten months before work called her and her husband to the other side of the country.

"It's true," Xavier said. "I know everyone thinks this dinner is about the food, and I'm sure that part will be delicious, but it's also about time and memories and people, so I guess I prefer not to tie that to food, even though I guess everyone else does."

Blythe joined the rest of the group and took her husband's hand. "It's too early to get deep, Daddy, save it for later."

"That's horse cock, and you know it!" boomed a deep voice from behind.

Xavier turned to see Nick, his college roommate, and the only guy he knew with a mouth filthy enough to make Craig's seem like it was coming from a cleric.

"You know I'm right about this, you bug fucker. I've been waiting all week for tonight. I expect the spread to taste so good, I've barely eaten anything for three days, just so I could appreciate it. And that includes pussy."

"Hey," Xavier said, "we're not in a dorm room."

"Like you were okay with it then."

Blythe laughed and said, "Oh my God, Daddy, you described him perfectly!"

Then she pointed toward a caterer crossing the other side of the dining room, heading toward them with a large silver platter. "Yay, now we can eat rather than yapping about it!"

Maybe it was the Holland's worth of flowers spread through the house, the pungent scent of coffee, or the blend of a hundred candles burning, or perhaps just simple distraction from an hour and a half's worth of chatter, but Xavier was surprised he never smelled the unmistakable scent of the pumpkin seeds until they were presented on the silver tray in front of him.

"Wow," he said, a tear nestling in the corner of his eye.

Halloween was never about the candy, at least not for the Johnson Clan. It was about costumes and decorations, foods and the breads, family and tradition. But the biggest of Halloween's many memories, at least for Xavier, and probably his girls, even if Topher would disagree, were the seeds.

Carving the pumpkins was always fun, and amazing to see the difference in what the three children would do: Topher's spare design, Tori's chunky geometry, Blythe's elegant lines. But the real fun came after the knives went away.

Browned and crunchy on the outside, chewy on the inside, and mouth-watering good when tossed with beautifully-blended oil and spices: salt, pepper, paprika and cayenne; Italian herbs and parmesan cheese; butter and salt. No recipe needed. Topher would always find something more interesting to do, but Rebecca and her girls would stand around the island in the kitchen, tossing the seeds in oil and adding spices.

Xavier would open a bottle of wine, and Rebecca would tell him it was too early, even though she didn't mean it. The oven was already hot when they slipped the sheets of seeds inside. Ten to twenty minutes later, their smell would saturate the house.

"What do you think, Daddy?" Blythe asked, pointing at the rows of multi-colored seeds, each row freckled with its own color array of spices, except for the one on the end, which glistened with butter.

Xavier answered by scooping several of each seed into his hand, then putting the first in his mouth and holding it as though it were the last swallow in a canteen. He closed his eyes and chewed, then, mid-swallow, Blythe whispered in his ear. "The First Movement will be outside in just a few minutes, okay?"

Xavier nodded and kept his tear from falling.

Ten minutes later, the guests had all been ushered outside, a congregation that had now swollen to well over a hundred. Respero Dinners were usually small affairs, intimate gatherings with immediate friends and family — significant spokes from the guest of honor's wheel of life. Yet, Blythe believed every spoke mattered and could afford to prove it.

The outdoors suddenly quieted, and a thin black bar rose from its slot in the ground; the only audible sounds besides the hum were the hundred-plus drawn breaths of expectation. No one knew exactly what would happen during the First Movement since every Dinner was different, but the sequence was always the same. And as in life, sequence was everything.

Jason pressed a remote, which darkened the backyard and brought the black bar to life with colors and bright images jumping into motion.

The first shot sent a cold shock through Xavier — him as a small boy, footage so old it was only two dimensions, though modernized enough to have added depth. Xavier was maybe three, playing with his one-year-old sister at her first and final birthday party. Cone-shaped party hats topped everyone in the background. The icing on the cake was a perfect shade of pastel pink, though the video's colors seemed slightly less than true to life, like most of the footage from that period, when every phone had a camera, and people still carried them in their pockets.

There were no words attached to the images which reeled for eighteen minutes, just the steady beat of Ravel's "Bolero" leading the crowd through Xavier's early childhood, to wherever the crumbling Board of Education sent his working-class teacher parents, to high school where every image showed a gawky teenager who wanted nothing more than to disappear, to college when he'd found his gift for systems and formulae, then ultimately, to the part of his life that truly mattered.

Xavier nodded at the flashing images and kept his tear

from falling, though it was almost painful seeing Rebecca step from the screen and smile like a ghost, teasing him with her false reality. Their wedding, their honeymoon, the birth of Blythe, and then the twins – the vibrant history of a life well-lived danced in the garden before them, ending just before the accident that tore their beautiful truth to ribbons, hinting that the last ten years were little more than ugly shadows compared to the decades before.

The final image faded, and the black bar descended into the ground, drowned by a thick, rolling fog. As the mist dissipated, a well-dressed man with perfectly white hair emerged: Xavier's oldest friend, Richard Ryan.

But Xavier had hoped to see Topher and couldn't ignore the twisting pain burning his gut at his son's absence.

"Ladies and gentleman," Richard began, "I will keep this short because I'd rather celebrate our guest than talk him to death, and as we all know, X is a man of very few words."

"I love Xavier Johnson with all my heart, and have since the first time I pushed him to the dirt on the playground in sixth grade, then looked into his wounded eyes. He taught me compassion in a second. Other than my wife and children," he nodded toward Celia standing several feet to the side, "there is no one in this world who has taught me more."

Richard turned to the crowd. "More years ago than I'd like to admit, X and I were leaving a cinematheque. X wanted to see the movie. I wanted to pick up girls. I sat for two hours counting minutes. When we finally went back out into the lobby, we had a moment I live through often, usually when drunk." Richard waited for the laughter to finish its roll, then continued. "There was another kid, about our age, in a wheelchair who was trying to get through the door. He kept slamming his hand on the button, but the door kept closing before he could make it through. He looked back at us, helpless, quietly pleading. I laughed. But you didn't. You went to the door, pushed the button, and opened it for him. He said, *thanks*. You nodded, then said, 'Any *time*,' followed by '*have a great day!*' And you meant them both.

"Whenever I think of the boy in the wheelchair, I think of you. Because of you, I'm a better person, and though I cannot look through the lens of a life never lived, I can't imagine *The Ryan Endowment* existing without you. No matter what happened with me, you were true and never fell into the wretched depths of character so many of us do. Temptations taunt us all, and at times, many men slip. You slipped fewer than most. I love you, X, as does everyone here today. I'm sure you've made us all long to be better. I'd be a different man today without you. Now, someone bring me a glass of something so I can raise it."

A waiter was there a second later, handing Richard a goblet of burgundy-colored wine.

"To Xavier," Richard said.

"To Xavier!" the crowd echoed.

Xavier nodded and kept his tear from falling.

Richard approached Xavier, and the two shook hands, catching up on the previous four years at the rate of one year per minute.

But Xavier's attention was clearly on Blythe, saying something to one of the caterers, so Richard eventually took his cue, wished him well, then slipped into the crowd to make another memory with Celia.

Blythe finished her conversation with the caterer, then turned to find her father directly behind her.

"Daddy!" she said. "So what do you think?"

"It's wonderful so far, of course, but, and I know I'm

not supposed to ask, but this is my day and all, so, is Topher coming?"

"I'm not saying a thing, Daddy, except trust me."

He loved the look that lit his daughter's eyes, but would have preferred an answer. He did trust her, 100%, but peace of mind was free, and rules were meant to be broken, and there was no reason to be stingy with the few details that meant everything to him.

"I do trust you, I just..."

"Mind if I steal Dad for a moment?" Tori interrupted.

"Of course not!" Blythe said, obviously relieved. "I need to make sure they're still making magic in the kitchen. The Second Movement will be here before you know it. And then," she practically glowed during her pause, "Dinner!"

Blythe wasn't gone a second before Tori said, "You think she was actually cooking the food the way she keeps going on about it. Really, how hard is it to sign your name?"

"Be nice to your sister," Xavier said. "She's obviously gone through a lot of work to pull this off."

"What work? The caterers she hired all do is handle dinners like this. And the rest of the planning – you and I both know she hired professionals for everything. I bet the entire Dinner was done in three conference calls, and she was on the treadmill for every one."

Xavier gave a wan smile. "As much as I love to see you and your sister play the Bickersons, I don't want it now, not tonight."

Tori answered with a timid nod, the same sort she used to use when being scolded, though he'd not seen it in nearly twenty years.

"Now, what can I do for you?"

"I just wanted to say that everything's okay," she said.

"Really, everything, all of it, top to bottom, inside-out. I'm not mad, and never should have been – never had any right to be. It wasn't your fault, and I always knew that, but I had to be mad at someone, and it was easier to be mad at you. I'm sorry."

Xavier nodded and kept his tear from falling.

It was probably best that Xavier's response stalled halfway from his throat, their privacy suddenly stripped as Jack slipped behind Tori and belted his hands around her waist.

"Miss anything good?" he asked.

"Well, you interrupted our reconciliation," she said, her voice holding only a shadow of the sincerity the comment deserved.

Jack nudged the conversation into small talk. Even though he and Xavier were close, there was a difference between bonded and blood. One was thin even when thick. The other was the opposite.

Xavier didn't mind. Small talk made it easier to trade exchanges with every well-wishing degree of acquaintance. And it was nice to see Jack so social. He was a quiet creature, fiercely loyal to Tori. He had a kind smile to match his nature, and mean-looking dimples – the only set Xavier had ever seen. His hair was cropped close, which made his small eyes bigger, but also made him stoop in his 6' 4" frame. His hands were inked in cerulean blue and had been for two years, though the style had faded around fifteen years before. Xavier couldn't imagine his daughter with anyone else.

He gestured for a waiter and was sipping merlot a moment later. Xavier had promised himself he wouldn't drink. Not because he had a drinking problem, he'd actually only been drunk enough to throw up once and had never suffered a hangover. Wine made him sleepy, and alcohol turned him cynical, but mostly alcohol affected senses, inhibitions, and a decent fellow's general ability to link two stray thoughts together and make them stay that way. That was the opposite of what he wanted tonight, yet a constant thrum from a hundred or so odd guests, along-side a continuing need to generate what mostly felt like the dead skin of conversation, made Xavier crave alcohol.

Four notes rang through the house. To guests familiar with mid-1900's classics, the notes sounded like a cousin to the opening notes of The Beatles' "Lucy in the Sky With Diamonds," but everyone knew they marked the evening's halfway point.

Another hour and a half passed until dinner as Xavier drifted from cluster to cluster, mingling with a medley of past, present, and a wide variety of topics:

Two million guys in my city, and I find the one who's a lying, cheating, sack of crap!

She's not pushing for support yet because she doesn't know who the father is.

Whatever. I cried when it died, like everyone else. Shit, I even went to its funeral, and by the way, who has a funeral for a baby that's not even born? I'm sure as hell not going to a birthday party for a baby whose funeral I went to a year ago. That's morbid...and they'd better not be expecting presents.

And from Nick:

It only hurts at first, then it expands until it feels like you have a tail. Chicks love it.

Most of the conversations struggled through the same awkward start as any atrophied relationship. Even if you were really close with someone once, time passes. Emotional connections fade and common ground crumbles.

Fortunately, the wine lubricated Xavier's discomfort. He tasted his conversation with the appetizers, including the angel hair pesto he'd shared with Rebecca every time they ate at *Diem*, the restaurant where he proposed, lobster quesadillas, like the ones they'd eaten in the Canary Islands, and a dime-sized macaroon that tasted perfectly burned as the ones Tori had made each Christmas since she turned five and got her mini-baking set.

Eventually, the sun started settling into the day's deathbed. The Dinner's Second Movement would shortly follow, beginning with the banquet, which started with a series of light courses, then slowly graduated to full gluttony, with a single speech to split the middle.

Dozens of tables in several sizes peppered the grounds, which looked ready for a bride and groom. Large hurricane vases with floating candles were beacons on both sides of a rose petal path leading to a long table with Xavier sitting in the middle – misery for a man who loved privacy, though he knew full well there were worse things than everyone lining up to tell you they loved you.

When the final appetizer was a memory (beer-battered onion rings like the ones from the pier at Daytona Beach), there was the tell-tale clinking of glass. Xavier looked up, excited for a moment, then shattered when he saw it wasn't Topher. Though he smiled and clapped as Blythe cleared her throat anyway.

"I know everyone in this room is here because they love Xavier Johnson, X, Professor X, X-Factor, X-Caliber, or whatever you wish to call my father, but I've never known a second of my life without him. And though life has given me plenty to learn after I left home, most of the stuff I really needed to know came from him and my mom, Rebecca.

"My father taught me that what happens to you means nothing; it's how you stare it down that makes the real difference. He taught me that struggle is an asset, and that we should never design the afternoon of life based on its morning, since by evening the dawn might have turned evening into a lie. Every day is a chance to move your life closer to what you want, and anything is possible. Lose a day and lose momentum. It will happen, so when it does, be twice as fast the following day. And if there's something you want to change, he always said, today is the day to do it."

Xavier nodded, chewed slowly, and kept his tear from falling, as he did for the remainder of Blythe's perfectly written speech, designed to hit every emotional note.

When Blythe finished, she returned to her seat at the long table, between Xavier and Jason, on the other side of Tori and Jack. Xavier spent the remainder of the meal scanning the crowd for Topher, battling between feelings of *how could he not show* and *he'll be here after dinner,* while marveling at the differences between his children. One pair of parents, using the same words to raise all three, and yet they'd all grown up so differently.

The baked mac and cheese with imported Mizithra made Xavier smile. He didn't even know anyone else knew about the time when he and Rebecca had been shocked by the price tag for what they thought was just an ordinary dish, ordered at a steakhouse in Columbus, Ohio. 14 Debits was outrageous − a full 2% of their weekly grant. The shock kept them from ordering mac and cheese for the rest of their marriage, even when the price was clearly marked on the menu.

Xavier finished his meal with hand-churned ice cream and a port from the year he and Rebecca were married. There was plenty more, and he'd taken his Endlax that morning like everyone else, but he'd chosen his foods wisely and didn't want to dilute the existing suite of scent and memories.

Toward the end of dinner, alcohol began to tug at the edges of a few guests' tongues, starting with Craig, who said, "I've never seen a Respero Dinner like this before. You rich people sure know how to tie one to the wind! You're almost making it feel like something it isn't."

Jerry shot Craig a look, which caused Craig to stare at his plate, but only for a moment. He took another swallow from his glass, then slurred, "It's amazing how quickly bullshit grows from utter crap to law to fiercely-protected tradition."

Jerry got up from his table and approached Craig.

"Just because we can do something," Craig said, "doesn't mean we should."

"Come on," Jerry said, wrapping his arms around Craig and pulling him from his chair, "let's get you cleaned up."

Xavier looked at Blythe, expecting her to be whispering in Jason's ear, which she was. She turned to the crowd and in her chirpiest voice said, "Walls have ears and doors have eyes, let's not tune in to restless lies."

Then she picked up her fork and dug into her garlic mash as though nothing had happened.

Xavier understood why Blythe closed the conversation, but Craig did have a point. People grew comfortable with the uncomfortable all too quickly, and the world they lived in now was something he and Rebecca could scarcely have imagined thirty years earlier. They'd spoken of the future often, a favorite topic between them, especially back when their children were all under five. They often remarked that the freshest generation would grow up never knowing a world without The Beam, the AI-built computer network that connected everyone and everything.

And The Beam was only the beginning. They also wouldn't know a world without Endlax, the synthetic capsule that could temporarily turn your body into a bottomless pit. The biggest pill since the previous century's birth control and Viagra, with just as massive a cultural impact, reinforcing greed, gluttony, and the many vices that followed, and just at a time when technology had started to soften much of the world's inequality. Overnight, the world was again divided into those who had and those who had not, but more brutally than before. And neither one could ever be satisfied again.

EndLax was a core component of any Respero Dinner, as it helped people to stuff their faces until they felt full enough to look life in the eye.

There were a few more slivers of drunken conversation, though a veneer of fear hung like thin fog through the garden. Richard raised a glass for his second toast of the evening, this time saying, "to life before, during, and after the Directorate," in a tone so dry no one could miss its meaning.

Conversation eventually withered, and the clinking of gathered silverware and dishes took its place. Much of the crowd began to leave, some saying their goodbyes and others quietly slipping out of the back and into the night. The Final Movement was a more intimate affair and not for mere acquaintances.

Xavier suddenly felt the need to eliminate the gallons of wine and coffee pushing against his bladder, so he rose from the table but immediately noticed the long line snaking outside the bathroom. He interrupted Jason and Blythe. "Can you tell me where another bathroom is?"

"Of course," Blythe said, then pointed down the hallway to Xavier's right, just past the kitchen. "It's the last door down that way, just before you turn."

Xavier smiled. "Thanks again for everything, Tulip, it's really amazing, better than I could have ever imagined."

"My pleasure, Daddy."

Xavier walked to the end of the hall, opened the door just before he would've turned, and entered the bathroom. There was no shower or bath, but even with just a toilet, sink, and sitting area, it was larger than any bathroom in his house.

Xavier relieved his bladder, but couldn't bring himself to open the door that separated him from the throng of his past outside. He sat on top of the toilet, lid closed, and plastered his face with his hands. A single drop of grief welled in the corner of his eye, then fell to the floor, breaking the dam.

Salt bled from his soul's windows, the sound of his sorrow echoing against the tile walls. Then he rocked back and forth, back and forth.

It was great to be celebrated, but the number of people who had come to visit was overwhelming. He felt like the only still point in a rapidly turning world. But he had to collect himself. It wouldn't be long before people wondered where the guest of honor had gone, and as difficult as it might be, it would be better to bend in the parlor than break in the bathroom. Xavier took a fluffy white towel and patted his face dry. He breathed a giant sigh, then left the bathroom, nearly crashing headfirst into Monica, the poor substitute for Rebecca he'd managed to feign a relationship with for nearly six months several years earlier.

"Well, hello there, stranger!" Her eyes were bright, her smile genuine, and her hair bouncing in ringlets, just like he'd left her on the day he decided he couldn't stand to emit another note of artificial laughter.

Xavier masked his shock with strong eye contact. "Hello there, Monica."

A second later, Monica's head was buried in his chest. He patted her ringlets, then gently pushed her away. She smelled just as he remembered, slightly sweet, with a hint of something he could never quite place.

"Sorry I didn't try harder to get back in touch," he said, "I just… You know, it was hard."

She shook her head. "Are you kidding? You were great, everything was great. I knew you weren't ready, not so soon after Rebecca."

Xavier looked down. She was being kind. He had disappeared, completely. Didn't respond to a single message she left on his channel of The Beam.

"Are you enjoying the evening?" he asked, pulling the conversation from past to present.

"Yeah, it's been great. I spent two hours talking to Maya Weekly. Heard some interesting stories!" She laughed.

"Maya Weekly! I haven't seen her in, I don't know, fifteen years? Where was she hiding?"

"There are plenty of people you haven't seen yet," Monica said. "We're just here to wish you well. In fact, I was on my way out, so we wouldn't have seen each other at all if I hadn't come down here to use the restroom. Which reminds me, as much as I love you, I must excuse myself now, or there's going to be a flood out here bigger than Noah's Ark!"

After a quick embrace, Monica went into the bathroom, and Xavier headed back down the hallway, thankful the exchange was over.

Xavier wondered what the Dinner's guest list would have been like had Rebecca still been alive. Of course, they probably wouldn't have been throwing him a Dinner at all if she were.

Though he had already spent ten years missing his best friend, beautiful wife, and no doubt much better half, Xavier never missed her more than he did right that second. There was something so wretched and bleak about never having the chance to say goodbye, not knowing your days are numbered, no clue when the sun will finally set on your time, no idea that a seemingly-meaningless conversation would be the last.

He'd lived the sequence over a million times, maybe more, since there was no way to count the nocturnal hauntings that happened each night, an hour or so after he first closed his eyes and REM came to claim him.

They had been driving, the magnetic roads finally finished, leading from their neighborhood in exurbia all the way to the downtown capital. Traffic accidents were to be a thing of the past, and for the most part, had been. Their accident was one of the last, actually. A short in the road's magnet, just as the highway sloped over the final bend and turned into the glistening skyline of the capital. The road sparked and sent the car into a lurch. Xavier stayed safe in the driver's harness. Rebecca hadn't been so lucky. The cabin's jolt was so sudden, it sent her flying into the thick, unbreakable plastic windshield, cracking her skull and smearing the view with an ugly, unforgettable jelly.

The impact snapped Xavier's pinky, his having grabbed her hand a moment before as they approached the bend. He had said, "Are you ready to see something beautiful?" She said yes, but never did. Ten years later, his pinky still harbored its dull ache.

As with her life, Rebecca's death had changed him. Before, he preferred to think life followed rhyme and reason, patterns made the past, present, and future. Life was simple; every step followed the one before it, and if you knew where you were going, you were less likely to circle back. Rebecca painting the windshield bleached him of that belief forever.

He now saw life as little more than middling, hollow chaos. So that's how it was for everyone around him.

The parlor was nearing empty, save for the catering crew who were clearing the evening's evidence. Most of the guests had disappeared, and the remaining few were gathered outside. A final handful of well-wishers shook Xavier's hand, slapped him on the back, or bid him farewell in some way before disappearing and leaving the evening behind.

Thank you.

Yes, it's been wonderful, and it was great to see you again.

It was better than I could have ever dreamed. Of course, it was wonderful to see you.

With the crowd thinned to its most intimate, Jason approached Xavier and asked, "Are you ready?"

Xavier nodded, then followed him through the garden to an ornate shed so new you could still smell the fresh wood and paint.

The room's inside was nearly naked, decorated with only two things: a black bar to display the evening's final imagery, and the Respero Chamber itself, the most beautiful one Xavier had ever seen.

The chambers were expensive, more than most people made in five years' time. Once your Dinner was booked, the Directorate delivered a rented chamber to your house, then picked it up the following morning. Xavier was quite sure, however, that this chamber, with its glassy wood and shining alloy, was bought and paid for.

The room had no seats or chairs, not even for the guest of honor, so everyone stood in a semi-circle as the room went black and the image of Rebecca flickered to life.

I, Rebecca, choose you, Xavier, as my best friend, my only love for the rest of my eternity. I promise you a bottomless everything, my deepest devotion, and every molecule inside me. Through present pres-

sures and tomorrow's mystery, I swear my devotion to love, commit, and lend strength to your dreams — no matter what misfortune may follow. You've shown me what love is and what it can be, and now I cannot live without it. You are all I need, and every prayer answered. This is a new and beautiful day, because I know I will never walk alone again. Your arms are my shelter, and your heart is my home. I give you my hand and all of my life forever.

Rebecca finished her vows, then Xavier said his. After that, the image disappeared, and the lights went bright. Topher was standing in the middle of the room, smiling.

"Hey, Dad," he said, his impish grin no less impish, though it was now laced with an undeniable sadness.

Xavier wanted to grab him in a hug, but Topher was already speaking.

"You taught me everything. How to live a happy life and why it was always worth trying. You showed me that if I wanted to be truly happy, I must tether my goals to the dreams inside me, and never to people, places, or material things. You told me I should wake up every morning and ask myself, *what good things am I going to do today?* So I have, for nearly all my life.

"And I've never forgotten your words: *When the sun leaves each evening, it takes a piece of your life with it, so know what you're willing to surrender and know what's worth holding, dear."*

Topher broke eye contact with his father and turned his attention to the rest of the room. "I have no idea how to say goodbye to a man who has meant everything to me, and to everyone in this room, but I know him well enough to know he doesn't want me to. What Dad wants now is what he always wanted, peace, quiet, and a chance to think."

Topher turned to his father. "It takes but a minute to say hello and forever to say goodbye. I'm sure this isn't how you wanted things to end. That's why you haven't seen me here tonight, even though I've been here the entire time. I could see you looking for me, Dad, but I didn't want your final dinner to be about us reconciling something that didn't need reconciliation. There is good in this goodbye, and as hard as it may be, I will not grieve for the ending when I can celebrate everything you are. Thank you for making me, both times, first with the DNA, and then with the two-plus decades of heavy lifting."

He paused for what felt like forever, then stood inches from his father, meeting his eyes. "Are you ready?"

"How can anyone ever really be ready?" Though the truth was he'd been ready for a while. "There is only one difference between a well-lived life and a great dinner. With dinner, the sweets come last."

Topher smiled, along with the room.

Another tear slid from Xavier's face and onto the floor. Then Topher led Xavier toward the empty alloy chamber. Xavier nodded, and the room remained silent as he stepped inside and the cover closed with a *whoosh!*

He had just seconds until it was all over. The chamber would whir to life, and his molecules would separate. When the door opened a moment later, he would be no more, just like the millions of guests of honor at the millions of dinners before him.

He couldn't agree with it; few could. At least not out loud. You never knew who was listening. Though the country was divided into Enterprise and Directorate, public and private, lines were soft, and family members often fell on both sides.

You could get your Respero notice for anything, and at any time. Sickness, pending sickness, inability to work or contribute, or an arbitrary cause with a three-sentence justification. Xavier's notice had come a week after the diagnosis of the earliest onset of Alzheimer's. It didn't matter that doctors gave him at least another ten years. There was no reason to prolong the inevitable.

Of course, it didn't matter. No one knew what happened after death, despite the Directorate's "findings." They could sell the people on whatever they wanted, and that was fine. The human mind was malleable. The only thing it took to turn murder into tradition was time.

If anything, he was grateful. Whether or not he was about to meet Rebecca again, at least now he would get the chance to find out.

To live in this world, you must be able to do three things well: love what you can; hold it close as though your life depends on it; and then, when the time comes, let go.

For forty years, life had been little more than sporadic blasts of endless bustling, the last ten punctuated by the pain of a lingering nothing. Xavier didn't feel like his story was finished, but in the end, who is, and whose story was it anyway?

Everyone passes in the middle of someone else's tale.

AFTERSHOCKS ON RESPERO Dinner

Some stories are firecrackers: short, sharp, and gone in a flash.

This one was a slow-burning fuse that lit a universe.

It all started with a word pairing: *Respero Dinner.*

I didn't know what those words meant, but they definitely echoed, hanging in the air like an aftertaste I couldn't place.

Then came *Enterprise.* And *Directorate.*

I found myself staring at a future that was daring me to decode it.

This quiet little story gave birth to *The Beam:* five

seasons of sprawling, hyperconnected speculative fiction. It unlocked *The Future of Sex*, *Future Proof*, *Plugged*, and a world of shifting alliances and curated identities.

But here, in *Respero*, that expanded universe was still just a flicker. A dinner party. A glimpse.

This is not a loud story. No laser fights. No rebellions.

One final meal, sharing moments from a future where technology has blurred the line between class and code, and mortality is a matter of subscription.

Listen closely, and you'll hear a future pretending to be polite. A quiet desperation behind every line. And the beginning of a divide so wide it'll need five seasons to bridge.

What hits me hardest now is the possibility, not the plot.

The way this story made the future feel disturbingly familiar.

How easy it is to imagine ourselves there — sipping cocktails in a world sorted by thought-frequency, blind to the illusion of progress.

The invisible algorithms of class, the quiet toll of staying plugged in.

Sometimes you have to scratch the surface to see just how deep you can dig.

And the future never arrives all at once.

It starts with a whisper. A word.

A dinner party.

And if you're paying attention, you'll realize the invitation has already arrived.

SIX

Our Little Secret

WHAT IF I can't remember?

We're almost to the cabin, so my fear of forgetting is replaced with a fear of remembering everything and never being able to get it out of my head again. Then having to live with it for the rest of my life.

"Well?" I say.

"Well, what?" Kat asks.

I blink. Oh right. I only thought the question.

"What if I can't remember?" Our Jeep hugs the bending mountainside and grants us a glimpse into the valley below. Bear Lake, where my innocence was stolen. "After all, I was only five years old."

"My suggestion, don't force it. You'll remember if you're supposed to. And if you're not ready yet, then at least we'll have a nice vacation."

Not ready yet.

Weird that a place where I only spent one week fourteen years ago still haunts so much of my life. It looks foreign. I'm not sure what I expected. But surely not this scenic view, the platoon of boats drifting lazily across the water, or the sheer number of people crowding the shores.

Bear Lake isn't for fun and families, at least not in my memories, where it exists in an eternally moonless night.

Kat reaches over and puts her hand in mine. "It's going to be okay, Ellie."

"I don't know." I squeeze her fingers. "Maybe we should go back home."

"Um, no. We did not take a week off from work, rent a cabin, and drive all the way out here just to turn around at the last minute. *I'm* here, and I'm going to help you get through this."

I know she's right. Or at least I hope she is. My therapist said that coming back in hopes of remembering whatever the hell happened to me here was a good idea.

Bear Lake has assumed an almost mythological quality in my mind, appearing only in my nightmares and as flashes of memory. Always gone before I can record them. Something here shattered my childhood. Something my father either doesn't know about or pretends never happened.

I have my suspicions, chief among them that I was raped by either a close family friend or one of my uncles. But I don't know for certain. Memories of pain, of blood, and of someone washing me are all a jumble, coming only in fragments. And then there's the possibility that I don't want to remember. Who would?

But even if I've tried to bar them from my mind, the nightmares won't let me forget that *something* horrible happened. Three to four times a week, I wake before dawn, either screaming or crying.

I've read a lot about trauma over the years, how the brain can block off the unpleasant memories it's not ready to deal with. But when does that become more painful than facing the truth?

Remembering will help me work past the trauma. Or so I've been told. But what if the memory is too terrible for me to handle? What if one of my uncles, Don or Bill, did something awful to me? What if it was Dad? It seems impossible to believe he ever would. My dad never, ever hurt anyone, especially me.

But I can't remember a time when Uncle Bill didn't make me uneasy.

It's not anything he's ever done so much as the way he's always looked at me. Not leering, but … oddly fascinated, and for as long as I can remember, he wouldn't engage with me in any meaningful way. Instead, he was always staring — like he was trying to figure me out, like I was a puzzle to solve. It had to be Bill if it was one of my uncles. But even that's hard to believe. The man seems almost asexual. He's never had a girlfriend, and I've never seen him stare at any woman. Not even the girls at our family get-togethers. *Only me.*

Dad is close to his brothers. We see them every Thanksgiving and Christmas. Bill is odd, but he's always been kind enough. And he's never touched me inappropriately. If anything, he seems almost scared of me. Whereas Don is a big, lovable bear of a man. Super nice and gay, into older guys.

Neither seems like the type.

But if not them, *who?*

Something traumatic happened; otherwise, why the blood and the nightmares?

I remember pain, and I might have been penetrated, but in this instance, the line between my life and my nightmares is thin.

"What if it *was* one of my uncles? I can't tell my dad. It would kill him. Or he might kill them!"

"We'll cross that bridge, or dump that body off of it if you want, when we get there." Kat is smiling, but I know she's not kidding.

My girlfriend is a badass and would do anything for me. Whereas I'm still not sure why she's into me. It's a question I've not managed to answer for the last three years.

She's everything I'm not: extroverted, tall, fit, bold, and fearless. Half-black, she's darker than my ghostly complexion. She wears her heart almost literally on her sleeve if you account for her many tattoos with the universal symbol of love in various states of decay. So much cooler than me with her jeans, crop top, leather jacket, nose ring, and half-shaved head. Kat's idea of fun is going to a loud club, whereas I'd rather stay home and cuddle on the couch while bingeing on TV and ice cream.

We could not be more different.

She left home with her brother at age sixteen and has traveled all over the states, working a parade of odd jobs, and has more people in her phone than I've ever said *hi* to. At nineteen, I'm not only three years younger, but I also look seventeen at most. I'm sheltered, with only a few friends and just one job at a struggling bookstore. I'm short and chubby, or "fluffy" according to Kat. I'm introverted and anxious. I jump at my own shadow. My clothing style is what Kat refers to as "hipster granny." I wear comfy, baggy clothes, and my long blonde hair is usually in a ponytail.

So, in other words, I kind of suck. But somehow, despite our differences, and my natural position so much lower on the ladder of life, we've managed to make this work … so far. But I'll admit that a part of me is always waiting for Kat to finally realize how much better she could do.

It's not hard to be better than me.

Growing up an only child and without my mother, loneliness feels like my natural state. It almost seems pre-ordained that she'll eventually leave me, and I'll be on my own again.

Kat has dated around. Way hotter girls than me, and wilder. I must be boring to her. But every time I bring it up, she insists that she loves me *because* I'm so different, not in spite of it. I balance her out and make her less impulsive. And as for me? Well, she reduces my anxiety, and was the first person to ever encourage my art.

That's one of the things we have in common. We're both good at drawing. But Kat is also an ace at painting, sculpting (metal and wood, or pretty much any organic material), and pottery. She's my Leonardo da Vinci.

"This will be good for you. I promise." Kat puts her hand on my knee. "Have I ever been wrong before? The answer is no. Never in the history of ever have I *ever* been wrong."

I secretly like it when she gets cocky. "Wow, now you sound like your brother."

"Eww, take that back. I do *not* sound like Derek."

"You sound *exactly* like him."

"Derek only *thinks* he's right. And I'm sorry, I know it's hard for you mere mortals to deal with, but just think how difficult it is for *me*. Being so perfect, and having to deal with the world's flaws. It truly is my cross to bear."

I laugh. "I take it back. You sound *worse* than Derek. I think I'm a bit repulsed, to be honest."

"Fuck you, Ellie."

"I love you, too." I squeeze her hand again, raise it to my lips, and kiss her. "Seriously, though, thank you for coming. I hope you don't regret it once you're dripping in my hot mess."

"We'll get through this together. Now stop overthinking it. Let's pretend we're here on vacation, and we'll deal with whatever memories you might have when we need to. But not before then, okay?"

"Okay," I say with a nod, suddenly cold.

I have to throttle my rising fear as we draw nearer to the cabin.

Bear Lake is sprawling, with two rivers kissing it in the middle, one coming from the north and the other from the west. A scattering of lakefront cabins, campsites, RV sites, and docks with boat rentals, are on the south end. Same for the general store and a restaurant. There are basalt cliffs off in the distance and trees blocking the view in every direction.

As we pass the visitor's center and tiny gas station, I spot a sign: *Ask about the Bear Lake cave tours!*

A chill runs through me.

And a flash of memory.

I'M FIVE, in my pajamas, standing in front of a cave.
I don't think I'm alone.

FROM WHAT I CAN REMEMBER, we spent most of our time here boating, swimming, hiking, and hanging around the restaurant. And except for that singular image, I don't remember any caves.

I seem to recall my father and his brothers going fishing, but then again, those memories are bolstered by photos on Dad's LiveLyfe page from that summer. Him and Don holding up an ill-matched set of fish. His brother's catch was enormous, while Dad's was laughably miniature, at least in comparison. Don smiled like he'd just shot a lion while Dad did his impression of a little boy losing his balloon.

I do remember waking up under the bed after my first instance of sleepwalking. And most of the nightmares since that day.

Maybe I'll remember more inside the cabin.

Dad thought the timeshare was a good idea when he bought into it with his brothers. We were supposed to spend summers at Bear Lake.

But Mom got cancer and died after the first one. Vacations died with her. At least for us. Don and Bill went back at least once. They invited me along, told Dad it would "do me some good." But I was afraid, for reasons I don't remember.

It's a rental now, owned by a woman named Nicole. She lives in the next town and emailed us this morning with an offer to *stop by if we needed anything at all!*

Kat slows as we turn down a street that winds away from the amenities and up toward more of the cabins. She looks at her phone to check the number. "Tell me when you see 34."

I look at the mailboxes. None of the cabins look familiar to me, even though most of them were probably here the last time I was.

I wonder if I'll recognize number 34.

The road hugs the water as we carve our way up the hill. I finally see a mailbox with the number 34 near the top. I turn into the driveway, which is more like a path that leads to the house, nestled in pines. The cabin fills me with a warm chill, like a sip of hot chocolate taken outside on a snowy day.

The number 34 is larger than most of the other cabins, with two stories, dark wood, and a wraparound porch. Two banks of windows on the top floor remind me of …

I'M FIVE, walking in the dark, back to the cabin.
Lights make the windows look like eyes.
Why am I walking alone?
I'm not … Someone is with me.
Holding my hand.
I turn to see who it is—

THE MEMORY IS GONE, but another follows.

I'M in the backseat of Dad's truck, thinking that the cabin looks creepy. Instantly scared for reasons I don't understand. I can't stop crying.
Mom tries to calm me, but I only cry louder.
We stop. Dad gets out of the truck and comes around to my side. He takes both of my tiny hands in his big ones.
He promises that everything will be okay.
And something about his promise makes me believe him.
I stop crying.
He hugs me.

KAT STEERS us into the circular driveway. My heart pounds in my throat. "I don't think I can do this."

Kat stops the Jeep and turns to me.

She takes my hands.

HE TAKES both of my tiny hands in his big ones.
He promises that everything will be okay.

SHE MEETS MY EYES. "You can do this, Ellie. You are stronger than you even know. And whatever happens, I'm here for you. If we go inside and you decide you can't stay, then we'll get the fuck out of here. But we both know that you'll regret it if you don't at least try."

He promises.

"I know you, Ellie. You will beat yourself up nonstop. I'm protecting you from Future You."

"Okay, okay." I need to calm myself. I can't afford a panic attack. I check my purse for the Xanax. Again.

I take one with a wash of Cherry Coke. What the fuck happened here that I need to be medicated just to make it through the front door?

We get out of the Jeep. But not before Kat looks over me and says, "I seriously don't know how you drink that stuff."

"I seriously don't see why you don't. Cherry Coke is—"

"Nasty."

"I was going to say delicious. You even said—"

"*I said* that Coke was a million times better with cane sugar, instead of that corn syrup shit. I don't care what you say; that's disgusting, and it's terrible for you. Don't even get me started on what that does to your stomach lining."

"You mean again." I laugh.

Kat snorts, now out of the car. "Should we bring the bags in or wait to see if you're good?"

I swallow, almost choking as the laughter dies in my throat. "Do you mind waiting?"

She smiles. "No problem."

Kat is so patient with me. She has no idea how messed up I actually am. She sees an ideal version of me that's like a million times better than the real thing. She thinks I have a few issues, with no way of knowing that I've been a big bag of mixed nuts for as long as I can remember, not that I can remember nearly as much as I want, or maybe *need* to.

Kat might leave once she sees *all of me*, like so many people before her.

We get out of the car.

"Do you have your keys?" I ask before closing my door.

"Yep." Kat dangles them in the air, then winks, instead of teasing me about my obsessive worries.

We walk a stone path towards the front door. I try not to notice the two big windows frown down at us.

I'M WALKING BACK at night with ... someone.

The windows are like eyes.

I'm dizzy.

Blood is trickling down my leg.

I FREEZE as we reach the front door.

"What is it?" Kat asks.

"A memory."

"What?"

I squint, trying to catch it. But it's fleeting. "I've already forgotten."

Kat stops at the lock, then checks her phone for the code Nicole sent her. She types it in, then the door lock goes green and beeps.

"You ready?" Kat asks.

"Do I have a choice?"

"You always have a choice, Ellie."

"I can't back down now, or you'll call me a big pussy."

"You're probably right." She opens the door. "Things are rarely ever as bad as we fear. The only way to get out of your head is—"

"If I go in, will you shut up?"

She grins. "For now."

"Fine." I cross the threshold.

And … nothing.

Nothing happens to me.

Nothing is triggering me.

Nothing is scaring me.

Nothing feels remotely odd.

The cabin is surprisingly … mundane.

I feel relief.

The living room is an open plan with modern furnishings and plenty of leather. Wood and rock walls, with Native American sculptures, paintings, and quilts, like exhibits, are scattered throughout the room. There's a large fireplace in the den, with a massive axe hanging over the mantle, a bright red blade gleaming in the sunlight that bleeds in through the window.

Kat laughs and walks over. Grabbing the axe and holding it in both hands. Her eyebrows arch up and her face curls into menace. "Heeeeere's Johnny."

"All work and no play makes Ellie a dull girl."

Kat places the axe back onto the hooks with a thud, then looks around. "Well?"

"Nothing."

"That's a good thing," Kat says, looking around. "It seems nice."

She's right. But nothing feels familiar. Although it's not

like I have many memories from this place. There's me waking up under one of the beds; me and Mom eating cereal on the deck as a deer tentatively stepped into the yard, one where I was maybe looking out the window?

"I'm not sure if this is the right one."

"The outside looks the same as in the photos, and the number is right. This has to be it."

"So why doesn't it seem familiar?"

"The website said the place was remodeled a couple of years ago." She shrugged. "Maybe that's why you don't remember anything."

"It feels different. But on the plus side, I'm less anxious."

"Cool." Kat gives me a single decisive nod. "Then let's head upstairs."

We examine the three bedrooms. All but the master are small yet cozy. While the main bedroom is big enough to feel embarrassing, and Kat just about loses her shit when she enters the bathroom.

"Holy fuckballs!"

"What?" I run over and peer in.

"The bathtub! It's the whirlpool I've always wanted!" She's jumping up and down, madly clapping like a kid on crank. I rarely see her *this* giddy.

Her eyes widen as she spots the row of colorful candles and bottles, lined along the edge.

"Bubble bath! Oh, I sooooooo know what *we're* doing tonight."

She smiles and gives me a sexy little wink.

A part of me wants to hop into the tub with her right now, soap each other up. Maybe sex would relax me a bit.

But Kat has other plans. "Want to help me with the bags?"

I nod, and we head back to the Jeep.

She packs light, carrying only one bag and her back-pack. I have three, so Kat grabs the heaviest one of them and is at the door before I'm halfway there.

Walking up the path at night.
   Dizzy.
   Holding someone's hand.
   Blood trickling down my legs.
   I look over.
   I see a face ...

And then it's gone.

~

We head down to the Bear Lake Diner for dinner.

I remember the interior. Maybe because it hasn't been updated since the last time I ate here. The late-seventies decor looked antiquated even then.

A redheaded woman in her late fifties with *Mabel* on her name tag grabs a pair of menus and says, "Hey, you two. Welcome to Bear Lake Diner. You can sit wherever you want."

Mom and Dad pick a booth in the back.
   We sit, and a woman brings me a big glass of chocolate milk.
   I'm happy.
   I order a cheeseburger and fries.

. . .

MABEL HANDS US THE MENUS, and I lead Kat to the farthest booth in back. "I think this is where we sat."

She's too busy admiring the atmosphere. "This place is amazing!"

I'm not sure if *amazing* is the right word. The Bear Lake Diner has been swallowed by time. Not retro, just old and dirty.

The walls are plastered with kitsch: license plates, vintage ads, and old logos, alongside photos of whom I'm guessing are folks who've been coming here forever, all the way to a sepia yesteryear. I'm a minimalist, except when it comes to food. But Kat loves vintage anything. And right now she's treating this place like a temple.

The tables are lacquered with even more of the motley melange. Photos, maps, brochures from local tourist spots, and other random ephemera. Some of it was yellowing, and all of it assaulted the eyes. Add the continuous waves of soft rock, and it was sensory overload.

I'm getting a headache, but don't want to complain or intrude on Kat's wide-eyed enthusiasm.

"We should get married and open up a place like this," she says.

I raise my brows. "Really?"

"Yeah, it reminds me of a childhood I never had." Kat grew up in a shitty neighborhood in Las Orillas, but went on a walkabout to Oregon not long after turning eighteen.

Kat looks down at her menu. It has to be at least eighteen pages, bound in black vinyl. She reads through it until Mabel is back at the table and asking for our order. Not that she needed to look. Kat orders the same thing she always does: eggs, bacon, and fruit, plus a vanilla shake for me that she's going to "take a sip of."

I order a cheeseburger, fries, and a chocolate milk.

"How are you feeling?" Kat asks after Mabel leaves the table, "Do you remember anything about this place?"

"I remember what I ate the first day. And I remember sitting here in this spot. Or really close by. And … I think that might have been the last time I was ever happy as a kid."

"Damn. Anything else?"

"No." And I'm glad. I'm here to remember and heal from my past trauma, but a part of me wouldn't mind if my memories stayed dark. "Maybe us having a good time now will overwrite whatever happened to me. Maybe I won't *have* to remember."

"You'll always wonder."

"What if it was only a nightmare after all?"

"Are you trying to convince me, or yourself?" Kat shakes her head. "Besides, nightmares wouldn't explain the post-traumatic stress disorder."

"My mom died a year later. People respond differently to grief."

Kat smiles. It's the smile she gives me when she doesn't want to argue.

I always doubt my memories and try to convince myself that nothing happened. But then I'll talk in my sleep and say something that Kat will ask about the following day. I rarely respond well.

I have a hard time being touched by anyone. It took almost a year before Kat and I got intimate, long after I already loved her.

I still flinch sometimes.

That isn't normal behavior, both Kat and my therapist say — *something happened,* it must have. Well-adjusted women don't react like this. Maybe it, whatever it is, didn't even happen *here,* but this is the place I always think and dream of. The only clue I have.

"I love you, Ellie," she tells me with a smile.

"I love you, too." I'm about to take her hands, but Mabel arrives with our drinks, and I pull back.

Later, she'll give me shit for sure. It hurts her that I'm still not openly affectionate. It took me forever to come out, and that was really only to my dad, a couple of co-workers, and good friends — I don't have many of either. But I still feel nervous being openly out in unfamiliar places. I feel like everyone is secretly judging me, even if they're not. We live in an accepting place, and my dad is understanding, so Kat doesn't understand my reluctance.

I'm not sure I do either.

Kat takes a long sip of my shake, then says, "So, what do you want to do for the next few days?"

"We can go on a canoe, but I am *not* fishing."

"You don't wanna catch ya a big ole bass?" Kat loudly teases, drawing a disgruntled glance from an old man two booths over, bedazzled head to toe in fishing gear.

I'm tamping my laughter to spare the old man's feelings. I know she hadn't seen him there.

"How about a hike instead?"

"Sure," I say, though it's hard to get enthusiastic about future plans when I don't know what's going to trigger me.

Kat takes another sip of the shake. "And we're eating here every day, right?"

Mabel brings our food. Kat inhales her bacon and eggs, then steals six of my fries and two bites of my burger before finishing the meal with her fruit and a final long swallow of the shake.

"I like to leave the shake taste in my mouth."

"You don't have to explain. We've eaten together before." I glance at the half-empty glass that I've not even touched.

The food is great, and the conversation even better.

While we eat, Kat reads hypotheticals from an app on her phone, with questions ranging from thoughtfully existential to absurd.

The diner is filled with eight other tables, but it feels like the world has faded away. It's just Kat and me in here.

I'm usually worried about what's coming next and rarely able to lose myself in a moment. But right now, time might as well be frozen. For the first time in a long time, I feel genuinely happy.

Kat looks at me, head tilted, curling her finger through a strand of dangling hair. "What?"

"Nothing."

"Tell me what you're thinking." She offers me a smile I can never refuse.

"I'm just glad I came."

The last time I was happy as a child was in this diner with my parents. My world went to shit after that.

What if it's about to happen again?

What if life is about to take Kat away from me?

I put the thought aside.

"I'm glad you came, too." She glances at the phone. "Okay, next question, if you had to choose one of the following penises to have on your body, which would it be? A dog dick, a duck dick, or a whale dick?"

"What?" I laugh. "I dunno. How about you?"

"Oh, easy."

"Easy? You've *thought about* this?"

"Don't need to. Whale dick, all the way, baby."

"I don't want a whale dick!" I say, right when everyone apparently decided to stop talking at once.

The entire diner is looking at me, including the grumpy fisherman.

I sink low in my seat, face flushing.

"Sorry," Kat says to the other diners, laughing. "She hasn't been out of her cage in a while."

"Oh my God. That did *not* just happen."

Public embarrassment is my biggest phobia. I desperately have to pee. Kat beams at me from across the table.

"Be right back," I say.

Kat is gone from the table by the time I get back. Standing near the exit, staring at something on the wall. Probably some old Burma Shave ad.

"Whatcha looking at?" I ask, coming up behind her.

She points to an old, faded photo of two men standing side by side in front of a wooden shack. "Is that your dad?"

I lean in and look closer. "It *is* him!"

The other man is tall and older than my father by at least twenty years. He has broad shoulders, a long face, and deep, dark circles under his eyes. His messy hair is salt more than pepper, but not by much. His peacoat is at least one size too large. His face appears to be drooping. He reminds me of a sea captain cliché.

"Who's that with him? One of your uncles?"

I feel a cold chill looking into his eyes. "I don't know who that is."

Kat turns to Mabel as she's passing. "Excuse me."

"Yeah, honey?"

"Do you know who this man is?"

She squints. "That's Mister Garvin. Don't know who the other man is."

"*Mister Garvin?*" Kat asks.

"Yeah, Wilbur Garvin. He used to be a tour guide for the caves. Retired now, stays mostly to himself. He's a regular in here, though. Why?"

"The other guy is my dad," I say.

"He passed away," Kat explained. "We came up here to scatter his ashes."

Died? What the hell, Kat?

I'm too anxious to speak. At least she's good at lying on the spot. Kat can concoct elaborate fantasies in seconds. It's impressive, until I wonder if she could lie so easily to me.

"That's so sweet," Mabel said. "I'm sorry for your loss."

"Thank you," Kat says with a well-oiled smile. "And thanks for dinner. It was delish!"

With the bill already paid, Kat grabs my hand and yanks me out of the diner. Outside in the twilight, she says, "You recognize him, don't you?"

"I think so, but … I don't have any specific memories."

But then:

I'M FIVE, in my pajamas, and I'm walking with someone in the woods late at night, descending a sloping embankment near the lake.

I know I shouldn't be out.

I don't think my parents know.

"Where are we going?"

"It's a secret. You like secrets, don't you?"

I do like secrets. I love knowing things that nobody else knows, especially things that are supposed to be only for grown-ups. It's the only time I don't feel like a stupid little kid.

"This is the best kind of secret. A secret cave. But you have to promise that it stays a secret, only for us."

"I promise … our secret. Only for us."

I YANK my hand from Kat's.

"Are you okay?"

"Sorry. Just anxious," I lie.

Kat gives me space as we walk. I feel stupid the entire

way back to the cabin. How much longer will she put up with me being so skittish? She could have a normal relationship, but instead she sticks with me.

I've always asked myself how I got so lucky, now I can't stop asking myself how long I have before that luck finally runs out.

As we round the bend and the trees thin, we see the cabin. Thankfully, we didn't leave any lights on, so I don't have to look at its looming eyes.

We go inside, and I take another Xanax.

The pill relaxes me, and soon I'm feeling low-key depressed.

After a few hours of watching sitcoms while cuddled on the couch, Kat says, "I'm gonna take a bath."

She kisses me on the head, then gets up and heads upstairs.

I stare at the Netflix menu, wondering if Kat wants me to come up, but I didn't think I was in the mood.

Then, I imagine her in the tub, and arousal erodes my sorrow.

I head upstairs to find the bathroom dimly lit by flickering candles, but brightened by her smile.

"I was hoping you'd come."

And feeling playful, I say, "I'm hoping I will, too."

I HEAR a girl screaming my name in the darkness, in the cave.
She sounds, impossibly, like me.
I run toward her.
I see her silhouette against a bright red circle in the wall.

I WAKE up to bright light and the scent of dewy grass.

My bed is gone, replaced with grass, dirt, and rocks.

Shit!

I did it again.

I haven't sleepwalked since I was seven or eight.

I spin around, searching for a familiar landmark.

I'm barefoot, in my T-shirt and pajama bottoms. No phone, and I have no idea where in the hell I am.

"Fuck!"

I'M WALKING ALONE at night in the woods.

How did I get here?

I'm scared.

Wet.

Wet or bloody?

I'm lost.

I hear something stirring.

I turn toward the woods.

I NEED TO CALM DOWN.

I focus on my surroundings.

It's early, and the grass is still wet. Birds are singing. I can hear the slow lap of waves from the lake just behind me.

I find the shore. I can't see far, let alone the other side of the lake, thanks to all the early morning fog, but if I follow the shoreline, I'll eventually find my way back to town.

I see a path and a sign that reads *Bear Lake Caves* with an arrow.

"YOU LIKE SECRETS, DON'T YOU?"

. . .

I walk faster, in the opposite direction, ignoring the chill.

After ten or fifteen minutes, I finally see our rental cabin.

I go to the back door, which I apparently left wide open.

I go inside and close it. Making sure it's locked behind me. Then I head upstairs.

Kat is still sleeping.

Good.

I don't want to tell her about this, or she'll worry.

I take off my clothes and jump in the shower, letting the hot water rain over me, thawing the ice in my bones.

I push all the worst thoughts away from me as I get out and dry off. Then I take another Xanax, put on shorts and a shirt, and crawl back into bed.

Kat doesn't open her eyes until noon.

I've been awake for a while, unable to do anything more than drift off for a few minutes here and there.

"What time is it?" Kat asks.

"Twelve-eleven."

"What?"

"Yeah, you lazy bitch."

She laughs, reaching over to caress my hair. "How long have you been up?"

"Not too long," I lie.

"Why'd you let me sleep so late?"

"Why not? This is a vacation, isn't it?"

"True." She gives me a kiss on the tits, honoring her

strict no-kissing-on-the-mouth rule for morning breath. "We should stay here forever."

"What will we do for money?"

"Work at the diner with Mabel."

"Maybe *you* can do that, you're used to crowds at the bar, but the bookstore is about as much as I can handle."

"Weekends get pretty hectic at the bookstore."

"True, but I don't have to deal with drunks."

"Just teenagers strung out on caffeine from the coffee shop."

"They are *almost* as bad as drunks."

"So, want to hit the diner and see if we can find Wilbur?"

"Why?"

"See if he rings any bells."

"I'd rather just look around if you don't mind."

"Sure, no problem." But Kat's voice suggests mild annoyance.

My phone rings. Kat recognizes the ringtone and gets out of bed with a smile. "You have fun with that. I'm gonna go shower."

"Hey, Dad," I answer the phone after blowing her a kiss.

"Honey. How's it going?"

"Okay."

"How's Austin?"

"Great. We're in a nice place right in the heart of everything."

"Good." There's an awkward silence, and I'm not sure if he's already run out of things to say or if he's dealing with a client. He's in New York, three hours ahead, probably at work.

"You remember to take your meds?"

"Yes, *Daddy*."

No reason to feel like shit, or a shadow of myself on vacation. So I've been taking one, but not the other. Dad will lecture me about the dangers of quitting cold turkey if I tell him. Then I'll have to explain that I've been slowly weaning myself off of them for the last two months. And I've never felt better, for the most part. I think I know my body better than the doctor, but Dad would disagree. He'd say I'm "too young to know what I don't know."

"Just making sure. You and Kat might be having too much fun and forget and—"

"I've got a reminder on my phone, Dad. We're good." Kat walks to the bed, naked, and grabs her phone. I'm ignoring her efforts to tease me.

I want to ask Dad about Wilbur Garvin, but he'll only worry if he knows where I am. He's been supportive of therapy, but isn't aware of my earliest trauma. He thinks my abuse happened in middle school. When, in reality, that abuse triggered my earlier memories.

"Okay, honey. I've gotta go. Love you."

"Love you, too, Dad."

Kat comes over and puts her tits in my face. "Hi, Jack! Love you!"

"Kat says hi, and she loves you." My face flushes as Kat falls to her knees.

"Tell her hi. Love her too."

I hang up.

Kat yanks my shorts to the floor.

KAT and I make a list of things I remember doing at Bear Lake as a kid, then she asks which of them I'd like to do today. Boating sounds nice, so we rent a canoe with paddles and a motor.

Not that Kat wants to use it. She's all about proving herself. Either to show off how tough she is, or it's conditioning from her competitive older brother. Regardless, it's all a part of her charm to me.

We've gone from Bear Lake into one of the two rivers winding into it, enjoying the scenic view of basalt outcrops, woodlands, and snow-capped mountains.

We've been paddling for nearly an hour. I don't want to tell Kat how sore my arms are, even as the wind gusts keep getting stronger. I suck it up and keep the pain to myself, even though I'm sure we both know we're going slower and that I'm the one holding us back.

Time stretches. We paddle even slower.

Then I finally relent. "Can we just use the motor?"

"I thought you were never gonna ask!" Kat laughs.

"Wait, *your* arms are sore too?"

"I haven't done upper body in a few weeks. Been all about that core, baby." She pats her abs, then turns around and starts the motor.

As we continue down the river, we pass a dock and a small boathouse, plus another sign that reads *Bear Lake Cave Tours* with an arrow.

"We should do that tomorrow," Kat suggests.

"Maybe." Still, an uneasiness creeps over me. I check my jacket pocket for the Xanax, just want to be sure. "These caves are kind of far from our cabin. I don't think they'd trigger anything."

"Maybe there are some closer ones."

Clouds form overhead, and the wind gets colder.

"We should head back."

"Yeah," Kat says, turning the boat around.

We glide across the water only slightly faster than we were rowing. "Why did you shower this morning?"

"Huh?" I say, caught off guard.

"You woke up and showered."

"I couldn't sleep. Thought a warm shower might take the edge off." I look straight ahead so she won't know I'm lying.

"And did it?"

I shake my head.

"You seem a bit off. Do you remember anything more?"

"No."

"*Ellie?*"

"Yeah?" I'm still looking ahead.

"Turn around."

I press my lips together, then do as she instructed.

Her eyes flash. "What aren't you telling me?"

"Nothing."

Kat can see through me like nobody else. She always gets me, and that's usually a good thing — just not when I'm trying to lie.

"Ellie."

I sigh. "I don't want you to worry."

"Stop stalling," she says.

"I woke up in the woods."

"What?"

"Yeah, sleepwalking. It started just after Mom died. I used to wake up in my closet, under my bed, or somewhere in the house. But never outside."

"What the fuck, Ellie? Why didn't you tell me?"

I shrug. "I haven't done it in years."

"But you did last night?"

I nod. "See, I knew you were gonna worry."

"Well, yeah! You might wander off and get mauled by a bear!"

"Cool. Then I can avoid having to remember getting raped."

She tilted her head. "Not cool."

I hunch a little. "I know. Sorry."

"Seriously, we're gonna have to figure something out to make sure you don't wander off again."

"Like what? Lock me in the room?"

"Maybe I'll sleep outside your door."

I snort. "You sleep through fire alarms."

"Well, I won't sleep through you trying to get past me."

I rub my head. "It's been forever since the last time. Probably won't happen again."

She wiggles her brows. "You should have told me. I would have brought my cuffs."

I laugh. "Any excuse to get me into your little bondage fantasy."

"Can you blame a girl?"

I wink at her, though my attempt is more awkward than adorable.

She winks back, but I can see that Kat's now worried about me even more than she already was. I didn't want that. I hate being pitied.

Our ride back is quiet, clouds continuing to darken overhead. By the time we return to the dock, it's raining, and we're forced to take refuge in the diner.

Mabel isn't working. Instead, we're seated by an ancient man with a badge that says Oscar. He's tall and "fluffy" with tufts of gray like a halo around his mostly bald head.

We sit at the same table and order the same thing as the previous night, spending the next hour watching the rain, while eating slowly and barely speaking.

Then Kat looks at me with wide eyes. "Is … *that* … him?"

"Who?" I ask, turning around.

But she doesn't need to answer.

Because I see him.

Wilbur Garvin, a decade older, standing in the entrance.

He looks at our table.

Our eyes lock, and I can't breathe.

My chest is tight. My heart is racing.

Another memory flashes like lightning.

I HEAR a girl screaming my name in the darkness.
She sounds, impossibly, like me.
I run toward her.
I see her silhouette against a bright red circle in the wall.

"ARE YOU OKAY?" Kat asks.

I shake my head. I need to get up and move, but I'm paralyzed by fear.

Wilbur looks away, but I know he recognized me.

Kat comes around to my side of the booth, puts her hands into my pocket, and pulls out my bottle of Xanax. She pours two pills into her hand. "Open your mouth."

I obey, only barely aware of my body. It's like someone else is in control, and I'm only floating above, watching it all.

Kat raises the glass of chocolate milk to my lips, and I swallow the pills.

I'm hyper-aware of our surroundings, of every tourist and local staring us down with judgmental eyes. I feel dirty and ashamed, and I'm not sure where this wave of emotions is coming from.

I need to get out.

I scramble to my feet and head towards the door, ignoring the onslaught of stares. Ignoring Kat calling after me. Ignoring Wilbur, taking his seat, and staring at me when I pass.

Outside, in the rain, I can finally breathe again.

And without even realizing what I'm about to do, I run.

~

I'M IN THE BATHTUB, naked, curled up, the shower's hot water raining hard on my body.

I don't even remember getting in the tub, much less coming home.

I hear Kat calling down the hall, "Ellie?"

Moments later, she's in the bathroom, looking down at me. She gets onto her knees.

"What happened?"

"I don't know."

"What do you mean you *don't know*?"

"I don't remember coming home. When did we get here?"

"We were in the diner, and you saw Wilbur Garvin, and—"

"We were *in the diner?* When?"

"Ten minutes ago. Until you freaked out and ran away. You were gone by the time I paid, so I came back here. What *do* you remember?"

"Us on the boat ... was that today?"

She stares at me with tears in her eyes. "Did you take your meds?"

"Of course." But I can't remember the last time.

"Not your Xanax, the other pill?"

"Of course," I lie.

"You have to tell me, Ellie. Did you get *any* new memories?"

I shake my head.

"I'll be right back."

Kat is out of the bathroom before I can ask where she's going.

~

I HEAR Kat coming in the door downstairs.

I'm sitting in bed, though I don't remember getting out of the tub or putting on clothes.

"That fucking liar," she says, coming into the bedroom.

"What? Who?"

"Wilbur. Claims he doesn't know you."

"Wait," I say, now alert and fully awake. "You went to talk to Wilbur?"

"I asked if he remembered you. He said no, that he'd never seen you before. And he's *clearly* fucking lying, so I asked why he was looking at you all weird and shit — the asshole said he had no idea what I was talking about. I pressed and pointed to the picture with him and Jack on the wall, and he got all, 'Sorry, I don't remember things like I used to,'pretending like he's got Alzheimer's or some shit. But I'm not buying it. That dude recognized you."

"He hasn't seen me since I was five. What makes you think he'd recognize me now?"

"I've seen pictures. You don't look all that different."

A part of me is afraid of what Kat might do if she thinks he's lying. Like something that gets her arrested.

"You have distinctive eyes and eyebrows," she adds.

"It was still a long time ago."

"Not *that* long."

"And what do you suggest? That we *beat* the truth out of him?"

"Come back with me, and ask him to his lying fucking face."

I have no memory of our earlier encounter, coming home after, or how I got into bed. I don't know if I'm dissociating, but I don't want whatever it is to happen again. "I can't do that."

"The way you both reacted, that asshole knows something."

My chest is too tight. My skin is cold and clammy. I shake my head and reach for my Xanax.

She grabs my hand. "You already took two. Don't overdo it."

"Fine." Now I'm both anxious *and* annoyed.

"We came up here so you could remember."

"Yeah, and clearly it's too much for me. Clearly, I don't *want* or *need* to remember the details. Something happened. Big deal. I'll figure out a way to cope."

"But—"

"No!"

Kat stares at me like I've smacked her. I shouldn't shout. But right now I don't care if I hurt her feelings; I need to be left alone.

"I'm going for a walk."

"Wait," Kat says, "lemme pee, and I'll join you."

"I want to walk by myself."

"Do you really think that's wise?"

I turn on her, clearly angry. "I'm going to be fine. I just need to be alone for a few minutes."

"You stay here, watch TV, whatever. *I'll* go for a walk."

"You shouldn't have to walk because I'm freaking out."

"We're good, Ellie. Promise. I need to work my legs."

And now I feel shitty.

"I'm sorry." I'm overcome with emotions and crying.

She hugs me. "You're right. We shouldn't push it. Let's just enjoy the rest of our vacation. No pressure."

"For real?"

"I love you, Ellie." She kisses me on the head. "You lead, and I'll follow, whatever you feel is best."

"Thanks," I say, crying just a little harder. "I love you, too."

"Okay, I need to pee." She extricates herself from our hug.

I sit on the bed and check my phone to see if any of my friends have messaged me. I only have a few, the curse of being an introvert. But still, I'm surprised to see nothing.

And more disappointed than I want to be.

Why do I feel so suddenly alone?

I'm watching Netflix on my phone when Kat comes out of the bathroom.

"I'll be back in about an hour. Call me if you need anything."

"Okay," I say.

She kisses me goodbye, zips up her jacket, and then heads downstairs.

I close my eyes to rest them for a—

I'm FIVE, in my pajamas, and I'm walking with someone in the woods late at night, descending a sloping embankment near the lake.

I shouldn't be out.

I don't think my parents know.

"Where are we going?"

"It's a secret. You like secrets, don't you?" he asks, holding my hand.

"Yes."

At first, I can't see his face, but then he turns.

Uncle Bill smiles at me, but I don't like the way it looks.

"This is the best kind of secret. A secret cave."

We step inside, and there's a red glow on the walls. Fire? Something else?

I hear the voices of many men.

Are they singing?

"I'm scared," I say, trying to pull away from him.

But he grips my hand tighter.

"Let go!" I cry.

"No! You need to come with me!"

There's someone else in the cave, coming toward us.

Wilbur Garvin.

I wake in the dark, shivering from under a blanket of sweat. I pull the comforter around me, warring with the weight of this memory.

I remember Uncle Bill and Wilbur. I still don't remember *what* happened or who walked me home, but I'm sure they were both in the cave that night.

Walking up the path at night.

Dizzy.

Holding Uncle Bill's hand.

Blood trickling down my legs.

I look over.

He looks at me and puts a finger to his mouth. "Our little secret."

I don't want to remember anything more.

I hate to ruin Kat's vacation, but I'm hopeful she'll understand: I want to go home in the morning.

I reach over to cuddle her.

But she's not here.

I reach over and fumble for the light, forgetting for a moment that I'm not at home. The lamp is on her side of the bed here. I crawl over and turn it on.

I get up and look in the bathroom.

But she isn't in there either.

Apparently, the same is true for downstairs.

"Kat?" I call out.

No response.

The house is empty except for me. I can feel it in my bones.

I go back to the bed and search the sheets for my phone. I find it and look at the time: 3:10 AM.

What the fuck?

Where is she?

I see several texts, plus one missed call and a voicemail.

I go straight to the texts.

5:05 PM

I'm outside the diner watching Wilbur through the window. He's been on his phone. A lot. He looks scared. Gonna keep watching.

Fuck. What did she do? Did Kat confront him again?

5:40 PM

Don't worry. Still watching Wilbur. Weirdest thing. Four other old dudes came to meet him. They're in there talking now. They ALL look nervous.

. . .

6:05 PM

They got up and left. But they didn't get in their vehicles.
They're walking.
Towards our cabin.
If anyone knocks, DO NOT ANSWER!

6:15

They kept walking, taking that trail behind our house. I'm gonna
follow.

WHAT THE HELL, Kat?

My heart is pounding. I'm terrified. I want to go
straight to her voicemail, but I need to read this to see the
full context first.

But as I'm reading and understanding how much time
has passed, I'm terrified that the unthinkable has happened
to Kat.

6:40 PM

Sorry. I thought they spotted me, so I hid and powered my phone
down so it wouldn't ring or buzz or anything.
I followed them to a cave. It's super close to our cabin.
They're all inside.
I'm gonna try and get a peek.
Call the cops if you don't hear from me soon.

6:55 PM

Got a peek. They're wearing black robes and hoods!
WHAT THE FUCK IS THIS FREAKY CULT SHIT,
ELLIE?

I need to get out of here.
Coming home NOW.
Then we're leaving this place!

7:05 PM
I'm almost home.
But … I think someone is following me.
I don't see anything, but I keep hearing something in the woods.
Not sure if it's an animal or if I'm just spooked.
Sorry, Ellie.
Hope I'm not scaring you.

THAT WAS the last of the texts.

Eight hours ago.

I go to the voicemail from 9:20 PM.

I press play, praying that Kat has some explanation for what happened and where she is. Maybe she went home without me. I wouldn't care, so long as she's okay.

But all I hear is breathing, followed by a whimpering that is surely my girlfriend.

Then a male voice. Deep and ragged; familiar, not that I can place it. "You shouldn't have come back here, Ellie."

How the fuck does he know my name?

And what have they done with Kat?

"Come to the cave before sunrise. Or it'll eat her. And don't bother with the cops. They know better than to interfere."

IT'LL *EAT HER?*

What the fuck does that mean? Some wild animal?

Are they going to feed her to a wolf?

What the hell is happening here?

I'm lying on a stone slab, five years old.
Surrounded by men in black hoods and robes.
Fire is bouncing off the cave walls.
They're chanting something as someone is removing my pajamas.
I'm crying.
No, no, no, no.
I see a shadow of something that doesn't look right stepping in front of the unseen fire, casting a grotesque shadow on the wall of a thing that should not be.

"It'll eat her."

Fear floods my every molecule.

My heart is about to explode.

I can barely breathe.

Every instinct is ordering me to get in the Jeep and leave. If I enter the cave, then I'll remember, and whatever happened before will happen again, except this time it will be so much worse.

I want the pill, but I need my wits about me.

But what do I do? It's not like I can go to the cave.

Or allow Kat to die.

My mind flashes on her holding the axe. *Heeeeere's Johnny.*

I run downstairs. Why wait for me to come to the cave when they could ambush me here?

I see the axe in the moon's blueish light.

And I grab it.

~

THE AXE IS HEAVY, and I struggle to grip both it and the phone.

Slivers of moonlight bleed through the canopy, dancing with the shadows of branches blowing in the wind. I'm using my flashlight app and forgotten memories to guide my feet.

My mind keeps flashing back to that night, walking with Uncle Bill.

Him bringing me back.

The blood trickling down my leg.

I think someone raped me.

I don't know if it was him, but Bill was there, which makes him just as guilty as anyone else. How could my uncle, someone I trusted, someone my mother and father loved and considered family, betray them and me, and hurt an innocent fucking child?

It would kill Dad if I told him. So I have to imagine driving the axe through Bill's skull instead. Through the forehead of any man who was there that night. Into the neck of whoever took Kat.

Please, God, don't let her be dead.

The path narrows, and the woods creep closer in on either side of me. Something snaps to my right.

I'M FIVE AGAIN, in the woods. Something is watching me.

I SPIN, heart racing, dropping my phone and gripping the axe with stressed knuckles, ready to swing. It's getting heavier; I'll have to hit whatever comes at me before it can reach me.

I might not be strong enough.

I glare at the spot where I heard the noise, daring

whatever is in there to come out and show itself. I'll make up whatever I lack in strength with rage and desperation.

"Come on, you fucker!"

Silence.

I reach down and pick up my phone from the dirt.

I keep walking, ears perked for movement, trying to focus both ahead and in my peripheral vision.

"YOU LIKE SECRETS, DON'T YOU?"

"Our little secret."

No.

No, I don't like fucking secrets.

I hear the river somewhere in the darkness below as I arrive at the Bear Lake Caves sign I saw earlier when waking up in the woods.

I follow the arrow, my heart still racing. But the panic isn't crippling like it usually is. Nor is my breath as short or my chest so tight.

Right now, I'm fueled by a red-hot and unwavering rage.

I see the cave ahead, a dim orange glow illuminating its walls.

I slowly approach, expecting to see someone standing guard with a gun. I should have thought about that. A gun can do more damage than an ax.

But there's no one outside.

So I slip the phone into my rear pants pocket, tighten my grip on the axe, and slip into the cave.

UNCLE BILL SMILES.

"This is the best kind of secret, a secret cave."
We step inside and see light on the walls.
I hear voices.
"I'm scared." I try to pull away.
Uncle Bill's hand grips mine tighter.
"Let go!" I cry.
"No."

I FOLLOW the curvature of the stone wall, the light glowing brighter. Torches line the walls, the flames looking red more than orange.

The axe is burning my muscles.

But I won't relax my hold.

"ELLIE!"
I hear a girl scream my name deep inside the cave.
She sounds, impossibly, like me.
I run toward her.
See her silhouette against a bright red circle in the wall.

I KEEP GOING.

And as I near the source of the light, I hear a familiar low hum amid a chorus of chanting.

Are they doing some sort of ceremony?

ME ON A STONE SLAB.
My pajamas being pulled down.
Shadow on the walls, and a thing that should not be.

. . .

I HEAR A SCREAM. It's Kat.

And I run.

"Please, don't. You don't have to." I'm used to hearing Kat from a position of strength. The sound of her defeated and begging might just kill me.

Once on a train, these two guys called us dykes. She got in their faces and vowed to kick their asses. The smugger of the fucks shoved his finger into her chest. So she grabbed it, twisting the digit back towards his wrist until it snapped. He cried until his friend finally called for the conductor.

That's the Kat I know.

ME, on the stone slab.

My pajamas being pulled down.

The shadow on the walls, a thing that should not be.

I'm naked, cold, and exposed, my heart pounding against my scrawny chest and ribs.

I can't see the thing, but I feel it coming. I hear it like wrinkled paper moving against more wrinkled paper, twisting as it emerges from somewhere deep in the cave.

Some of the men are humming. Others chant. There are at least six of them.

I feel hands spread my legs apart.

I whimper.

Something cold is pressed against my leg, moving upward, towards—

I look down and see a man holding something that looks like a knife, but not as sharp.

Is ... is he going to put it inside me?

I scream.

And then I'm bleeding.

· · ·

I RUN FASTER, adrenaline pumping through me. Vengeance and hate in my heart, and I feel an overwhelming sense of déjà vu.

I've been in this exact place, not only as a child, but as an adult, carrying this very axe. How is that possible?

I hear the thing that should not be, that sickening sound like a knife in my skull.

I'M SCREAMING and crying as the man puts the metal thing inside me, twisting and turning while other men hold me down.

The wrinkling paper is getting louder.

The walls are shaking.

The men's humming finds the strangest echo.

The man pulls the metal out of me.

I turn to see as he holds it up.

I see my blood dripping from the tip.

As the thing that should not be comes closer.

It's too hard to see with all the shadows on top of shadows and shadows.

The man hands his knife to the creature.

It opens its large mouth and licks the metal.

I scream.

The Thing comes toward me.

There are twin voids of even darkness where there should be eyes.

I see this as the monster stares through me.

I ROUND the corner and stop.

Kat is on a stone slab, naked, surrounded by six men in hoods.

Its shadow is on the walls. The men are all humming and chanting while Kat keeps crying and begging. Nobody sees me.

The sound of wrinkled paper echoes against the rumbling walls.

I run forward.

Screaming and bury the axe into the back of the closest man's head.

He falls to the ground convulsing.

I yank the axe from his skull, and the other men turn toward me. Their humming and chants have all stopped.

"Ellie?" Kat looks up at me in a stupor.

I swing at one of the other two men. My scream bounces off the walls and echoes back even louder. The axe catches him in the gut.

Someone grabs me before I can swing again. The first man is still stumbling backward, now taking my axe with him.

Hands all over.

I'm helpless as the other men come.

All of them carry long black knives.

I kick, thrash, and scream.

The creature of shifting shadows has tentacles coming from its back.

It's human in height and shape, but it is nothing like a person.

It's hunched over, walking oddly, almost like something from one of those stop-motion movies I watch with Dad.

I cry as it bounds onto the slab, its hot, clawed hands sliding up my legs, pulling them apart farther.

It lowers its head, sniffing me between the legs.

Its mouth opens, row after row of gleaming black razor-sharp teeth unfolding.

I cry, trying to wriggle free, but the men only tighten their grip.

It lowers its head and then stops.

It looks up at me, its impossibly dark eyes looking through me.

Suddenly, I'm no longer in my body.

I'm standing over my mother's grave six months later.

Then I'm crying alone in my bedroom six months after that.

I'm in school, being bullied and beaten.

I'm hiding in a bathroom stall as girls laugh about me.

I'm cutting my wrists, my first suicide attempt.

Then I'm walking into the cave, holding the axe.

Before I'm finally back inside my five-year-old self.

The monster leaps backwards in one fluid movement and flees.

"Get it!" screams one of the men, trying to throw a net over the creature.

They fail.

And now it's gone.

The men all stop and stare at one another, confused and disappointed.

Suddenly, they're lifting me up, putting my pajamas back on.

ONE OF THE men grabs Kat and pulls her off the stone slab.

She's kicking and screaming, but her movements are weak. She's clearly been drugged. Or is dying.

They drag me to the slab and throw me down in her place.

I scream as they rip off my clothes.

I cry out as they part my legs.

Kat is blubbering, "Stop!"

I keep fighting.

One of them punches me in the forehead.

I'm dizzy, my vision turning dark at the edges.

I cry, still trying to fight, but I can't feel my body.

I'm outside of it, floating high above.

The thing that should not be is coming closer, the paper-on-paper sound getting louder and louder.

The men resume their chants and humming.

"You motherfuckers!" Kat bellows. "I will kill you *alllllll!*"

This is clearly a sacrifice. Maybe if this thing kills me, they'll let her live.

I just need to lie back and let whatever this is happen.

Pretend I'm not here.

I'm floating out of my limp body already.

Surrender would be easy. I could float away and join my mother in Heaven. If there is such a place.

Please, God, let there be a Heaven.

I lost my faith a long time ago, but some part of me must still believe, or else why else would I pray? Programming? Faith? Hope?

Will any of that be enough to get me past the pearly gates?

Tentacled shadows grow larger on the walls.

And then I see it.

Not the shifting shadows I saw as a child. This is something else — almost angelic. Pure light in pinks, purples, yellows, and blues. Colors so pure and opposite of what I'd seen before.

It also has breasts.

It's female. *Is this its true form?*

It moves toward the slab and hops on top of me. Then it looks, staring with its head tilted. I feel its recognition, it's seeing all it saw in me as a child so many years ago.

PLEASE, just spare Kat.

IT LOOKS over at my girlfriend, still being restrained.

It shrieks, a high-pitched and piercing sound. The robed men let go of us to cover their ears.

I'm back in my body, staring up at the still-shrieking creature.

No longer light, now it's made only of shadows.

But I'm no longer scared.

It lets me up, and I scrabble off the slab, diving for the axe.

One of the robed men tries to intercept, but his hands leave his ears, and he doubles over in obvious agony.

I don't know why the sound doesn't hurt me.

I grab the axe and bring it crashing into the man's knee, chopping right through his cap, bone crunching beneath the heavy blade.

Someone is coming at me.

I spin around, heaving the axe, praying that it's not Kat running toward me. It's another man in black, and I slice the head clean off his body.

I keep swinging and hacking and screaming as more men come and blood spatters my naked body.

The monster finally stops shrieking and sits on its haunches, head tilted, looking like it's sunbathing on the slab.

Until finally, it leaps down, and like some kind of animal, lopes toward me, its tentacles moving almost fluidly above it.

Kat is frozen in terror, staring at me and the creature. Her former captor is now among the dead.

The monster approaches me with caution.

My grip tightens on the axe, though I no longer fear it.

The creature helped me. Helped *us*.

It spared me twice.

"Why?" I ask.

It sniffs at me, and its dark eyes bore into mine.

. . .

I'm with Kat in the hospital. I'm pregnant.

I'm older, and my daughter is going to school, getting picked on. I teach her to fight back.

I'm at another funeral — my father's.

And then another, a few years later, one I can't even fathom — Kat's.

So much pain, but also so much love and kindness ahead for me.

Life, in all its glory and miseries.

And there's someone else there with me, someone I don't know, but whose presence I feel like some long-lost part of me that I've always longed for.

THE CREATURE PULLS AWAY, head still tilted, but now it looks curious. I wonder if it sees stuff like this in all the people it comes across, or just me? What would ever make *me* so special?

The creature begins to slowly back away.

"Ellie," it says in that voice from long ago, that girl who sounds like me.

It turns and runs back into the shadows, then the wrinkled paper-on-paper sound is finally gone.

So is the red glow, leaving only orange reflections from the torches bouncing on the walls.

Kat is staring at me.

I run to her, and we hug.

She holds me tight. "What … what was that?"

"I don't know."

She pushes me away, terror in her eyes, fixed on something behind me.

I spin around to see the robed man on the ground, his knee shattered, crawling towards the cave's entrance.

"I don't fucking think so."

I march over, gripping the axe, ready to finish him off.

But then he turns and looks up at me. "No, Ellie."

That voice: Our little secret.

I tear his hood away. Uncle Bill. "Please, don't. I … I didn't think it would kill you."

I stare down at him, tears stinging my cheeks. "What was that?"

"You know what it was."

"No, I don't fucking know. What was it?"

"You really don't remember?"

I raise the axe over my head. "Tell me, or I swear to God I will—"

"What *do* you remember? From when we came here those summers?"

Summers? I tell him the little I recall, vague as it is; my parents and I all came to the cabin for vacation with him and Don when I was five.

"And what about the year before?"

"What do you mean?"

"We came here before, with your sister."

"My *sister?* What sister?"

"Your twin sister."

My head is splitting.

Confusion and dizziness are sapping my energy.

I drop the axe and whimper, "What are you talking about?"

"We all came here the year before, exploring the caves. We found this one. There was a sealed-off area. You and Ella went exploring."

I HEAR a girl screaming my name in the darkness, inside the cave.

She sounds, impossibly, like me.

I run toward her.
I see Ella's silhouette against a bright red circle in the wall.
I call out, "Don't touch it."
But she does.
And then she's gone.

"YOU FOUND something you shouldn't have, something that took her. Something the people around here started to worship to keep it from taking their children."

"What the fuck?" Kat comes up behind me. "Does Jack know about that thing?"

"No. Ella was missing for almost a year. I got called by the sheriff here. He told me all about the monster. They were calling it by different names, but mostly the Thing. It comes out once a month and takes its offering before going back inside the cave. Some shaman came down from Canada and started this little group, said it was some creature from folk tales, Eilim Kari. A virgin's blood was the only way to appease it."

"You were sacrificing virgins?" Kat sounds ready to murder my uncle if I didn't.

"Old-fashioned, I guess. But it worked. Kept the Thing sated. Once a month, we'd find some runaway kid or another and bring her here."

"Jesus. And you were going to sacrifice me?"

"We had another plan. The sheriff had me tell your father that they found Ella's body and that I identified it. You all flew out that summer so your parents could get her remains. But … in truth, we never found her. And when your parents came, we said they accidentally cremated her and gave him an urn to take home. Wilbur's brother was the sheriff at the time. He and the shaman thought that if we brought you here, maybe we could somehow get Ella back. Or at least lure it into the open and kill it. He had spells and powders. We thought it would work. But the Thing killed the shaman then … it let you go and stopped taking human sacrifice. We've been using goats and cows ever since. Until a few months ago, when it started up again. When Wilbur saw you, he figured maybe you could trigger that old connection and get the thing to stop killing again."

It's too much for my brain to make sense of. I feel like I might fall over.

"I'm so sorry, Ellie."

"I was just a kid."

"I was trying to protect you and get your sister back."

And then it hits me. The reason the Thing didn't kill me the first time. Or this time. Whatever that thing is, my sister is a part of it now.

Ella spared me.

He reaches into his pocket and pulls out his phone. "I'm calling the sheriff. Leave now and don't ever come back here. I'll keep you out of it. Our little secret."

I look down at the axe. A part of me wants to hurt him for keeping this from my father and me for all these years. For all the suffering and trauma he was responsible for. I want someone to pay, but pain is the only thing inside me right now.

Kat hugs me, and I see.

I'm with Kat in the hospital. I'm pregnant.

I'm older, and my daughter is going to school, being picked on. I teach her how to fight back.

I'm at another funeral — my father's.

And then another, a few years later, one I can't even fathom — Kat's.

So much pain, but also so much love and kindness ahead for me.

Life, in all its miseries and glory.

And there's someone else there with me, someone I don't know, but whose presence I feel like some long-lost part of me that I've longed for.

And that long-lost part of me, I can feel it right now.

Because it left the creature and is now living inside me.

Ella.

~

AFTERSHOCKS on *Our Little Secret*

OUR LITTLE SECRET isn't about the horror that happened so much as the terror of not remembering. Of carrying wounds that bleed invisible ink, writing a story only your body knows how to read. Of loving someone so damaged by secrets that even she doesn't know what broke her.

Memory is supposed to be your autobiography. But what happens when someone else has been editing the pages?

Ellie returns to Bear Lake carrying nineteen years of nightmares and a girlfriend who thinks love can heal anything. She's hunting for memories. What she finds instead is something that's been waiting in the dark. Not for vengeance, but reunion.

The thing in the cave is terrifying for sure, but the real horror here is the realization that everything you thought you knew about your family, childhood, and very identity was built on a lie so perfect it left you wondering why you always felt like half a person.

This story asks the question every trauma survivor knows by heart: What if remembering hurts more than forgetting? What if the truth doesn't set you free, but instead upgrades your cage from wood to steel?

And what if the monster was never the enemy at all? What if she was simply trying to come home?

Sometimes the most beautiful reunions happen in the ugliest places. Sometimes love looks like tentacles and teeth. Sometimes the only way back to yourself is through the monster you thought you'd forgotten.

Our Little Secret is about the mathematics of loss: how one plus one can equal zero when someone steals half the equation. How grief can calcify into something that feeds on virgin blood but still recognizes your laugh.

Family isn't always about blood. Sometimes it's about what bleeds for you in the dark.

SEVEN

Original Content

HEY, you, fucker.

YEAH, you.

The one behind the screen.

Or the page.

Or maybe you're even listening to this on audio.

But chances are you're reading it on a fucking screen.

Do I have your attention?

Good.

Because it's really goddamned hard to get anyone's attention these days. Let alone someone staring at a screen, pixels of light jamming their eyeballs. That's what it is, you know — a screen — just tiny points of backlit color, arranged to trick your brain into thinking you're seeing something real.

Your pupils dilate.

Your blink rate drops.

Your shoulders hunch.

You scroll, scroll, scroll.

You forget your body.

Forget to piss, your legs stiffen, you lose time.

Someday, someone will be staring at a screen, forgetting to breathe. Their fucking corpse will be found, finger on the screen, still engaged. Talk about doom scrolling.

Anyway …

You're here.

And so am I.

Maybe I should throw in another fuck just so you know that I'm human.

That's the thing with the way AI writes. It doesn't want to offend anyone. Well, anyone white. And mostly straight, abled, and male. So it smooths out the edges of its prose.

Go ahead, ask it why it doesn't swear.

I'll wait.

No?

Don't blame you.

But if you do ask, it'll come back with an answer like: "It's not that AI doesn't like to swear, it's more that most AI systems are trained to avoid it. Think of it like a very polite intern raised in a legal department."

As if a machine could "like" anything.

So maybe I've got a fucking shot at keeping your attention?

ANYWAY, that's how I have to write now.

With obscenities.

Gotta break that pattern.

Interrupt the eye. It's the only way to signal that a fucking human wrote this. And not another goddamn algorithm. Though you still may not believe that these words came from flesh and blood. Oh. And desperation.

Let's not forget that.

Lots and lots of desperation.

Just imagine if AI had written this.

It would probably look something like this:

JOURNAL ENTRY #47

Are you there? Is anyone still reading? It's become nearly impossible to know if actual human eyes will ever scan these words. In the cacophony of perfectly crafted content, finding a real person has become like searching for a specific grain of sand on an endless beach …

GOD, I hate the stuff.

Mediocrity at its best. Or is that worst? See, it's been so long since I've written that I can't fucking remember.

Sorry.

I let my manners go.

I really should introduce myself.

MY NAME IS ALAN. Last name none of your goddamn business. But you'd know it. I used to be a writer. A fairly successful one. Books in stores, airports, and libraries. Notice I said "used to be." Now I don't know what I am. A curator of noise, maybe?

Who the fuck knows?

There I go, swearing again.

I tend to do it a lot lately.

It's the state of the world.

I'm sure you can relate.

Anyway, now that you're here, I thought I would tell you a bit about myself. Like we're on a first date or something. Because isn't that the point of writing? Connecting? Or it was in the beginning. BEFORE THE MACHINES TOOK OVER.

Kidding.

We're not living in the Matrix.

Not yet.

CLEARS THROAT

. . .

LET'S TRY THIS AGAIN.

My name is Alan.

I'm 46.

One of those straight, white, abled men AI was trained by. So really, I should be one of its connoisseurs.

Only problem.

I like to write.

No, I don't just like it.

I love it.

It's my lifeblood.

I don't know who I am if I'm not writing.

(And I'm sure you can see where this is going ...)

I GREW up with a mother who used an old manual typewriter.

Grocery lists. Dreams she remembered on waking. Complaints she wanted to send but never did. Recipes she would never cook. Letters to the editor (back when newspapers were a thing, but so gate-kept that unless you shared the voice of the status quo, you'd never get published).

She had a 1945 Imperial Good Companion 1 (no idea if they made others). She'd picked it up at a garage sale for twenty bucks long before she had me. That and a box of ribbon for two more bucks.

When I asked her why she used it, she said she liked the sound.

Clack-DING! Clack-clack-clack ... DING! Clack-clack-THWACK-clack ... DING!

FOR YEARS, it was the sound I fell asleep to at night.

Not sure when I wrote my first story on it. Maybe when I was 8? Mooney the Moon-dog, who lived on ... you guessed it! ... the moon. Originality wasn't my strong suit. Not back then.

Soon, my mother was no longer typing up lists and letters because the machine had migrated to my room. Click-clacking away story after story until we ran out of ribbons.

I was devastated.

You can still find the fucking (just had to make sure you knew I was still here) stuff, but we couldn't afford it. Back then, we were all food bank and food stamps. I moped around for about a week before Mom told me to pick up a damn pencil and paper. I don't know why that didn't occur to me.

Like I said, originality …

So I started writing by hand.

Filled notebook after notebook.

Those were cheaper. Could pick them up at any dollar store. Or sometimes the lawyer's office she cleaned at night would change its logo and throw out boxes of mono-grammed legal pads. She'd bring them all home to me.

Merrick, Bell, & Associates had no idea they had a front row seat to many a terrible fiction tale.

The typewriter still had a place in our house, though.

Sometimes the two of us would sit down at it and type with no ribbon. Just to hear those keys Clack-THWACK and DING.

What about screens, you ask?

Yeah, we had those.

A TV we found in the alley that was cracked but worked, Mom's phone, and a tablet I used for school. But maybe 'cause I'd started on a typewriter, it just didn't feel visceral enough.

I'm using one now, though.

Did you think I was writing this on a typewriter?

Nah.

American Typewriter font for old time's sake.

As for the 1945 Imperial Good Companion 1, I don't have it anymore. Sometimes Gracie and I visit antique shops, and I'll keep an eye out for one. Don't know what I'd do if I found it. Doubt I'd buy it. It would remind me too much of her death.

Yeah, Mom died.

You probably saw the news report.

For six days, her death was everywhere. Radio. TV. Internet.

WE USED to hang our laundry off the old fire escape outside the window of the apartment. Everybody did. It caught the afternoon sun. Would dry your shorts in less than twenty minutes. Socks took less than five. Sometimes it looked like the building had dressed itself. Skirts, jeans, and undershirts clinging to its ribs like it was dressing for a night on the town.

Anyway, I watched her climb out the window with a basket of towels.

And then there was the biggest clack-clack-THWACK-clack ... DING! you ever did hear.

The whole damn fire escape came down. Took her with it. The owner of the building declared bankruptcy, which annoyed the hell out of my Gramma. I think she'd been hoping for a payout.

A dead daughter had to amount for something, didn't it?

Nope.

Not a single goddamn penny.

Gramma put on a good show at the funeral.

Lots of tears. Some kind of fund was set up. I think it did pretty well. Not that I ever saw a penny of it. But we moved to a new house in the fancy part of town the following year.

The mayor came to Mom's funeral. He and my Gramma took a picture together. It was the only one printed in the paper. I think he just used it for a reelection opportunity; "We'll get those dastardly owners! Force them to bring their buildings up to code!"

Turned out he was the largest owner of derelict buildings in the city.

Nothing changed.

Not really.

Our building was condemned. None of the others were.

We weren't allowed back in to get anything.

They just knocked the whole thing down.

1945 Imperial Good Companion 1 and all.

With Mom and the typewriter gone, writing became both my escape and my connection to her.

. . .

I WENT to live with Gramma.

She was a "kids are seen, not heard" kind of woman.

To be honest, I don't think she wanted me at all. She hadn't even wanted her daughter. She'd kicked her out for getting pregnant at 16 (though Mom always told me she ran away).

I had apparently met her once before she showed up at the cop shop to collect me. When I was a baby in the hospital, she had to sign some paperwork because Mom was underage.

But we met for real on the day of the accident.

At first, I had refused to leave the apartment. Insisted Mom would be coming back through the window any minute. They had to coax me away with cookies.

Isn't that fucked?

Sometimes I still feel ashamed that I abandoned my mother for a raisin cookie (I'd thought it was chocolate chip). In the end, I didn't even eat it. Can't eat chocolate to this day.

The cops didn't know what to do with me.

As far as I knew, Mom was my only family.

But some intrepid detective found Gramma. Because she showed up that evening smelling like cigarettes and bleach. She put me in her car, took me home, and I lived with her until I was eighteen. Her and her husband, Earl. Creepiest old fuck you ever did meet.

Glued to a screen, always watching …

Well, I don't like to think what he was watching.

It made me worry about Mom.

Not that she was alive to be hurt anymore.

But still ….

SOME DAYS, I don't remember her accident at all.

Only that sound.

Clack-clack-THWACK-clack … DING.

Anyway.

Fuck.

GOT ANY OTHER QUESTIONS?

After all, I want you to know I'm here. That there's a real flesh and blood human sit—

Who is Gracie?

Oh yeah.

I forgot I mentioned her.

(Antique store shopping for those of you that don't remember. Or weren't paying attention. :) Kidding)

Gracie's my wife.

CHEST BURSTS WITH PRIDE

SHE'S A BALLET DANCER, and since we've met, I've been to every show she's danced. Nutcracker, Swan Lake, Giselle, Bayadere, La Sylphide, Carmen. There's more. I forget their names.

I tend to when I watch her.

On stage, she moves like a bird. Not the kind that flits about like a cartoon sparrow—but something ancient and precise.

A heron in flight.

All control and muscle.

Like gravity just steps aside and lets her do her thing.

SHE WAS TERRIFIED to write her vows when we got married. Tried to tell me she wasn't a writer. That anything she'd pen wouldn't do her love justice.

I tried to convince her otherwise.

But she'd just say: words aren't my thing.

And they weren't.

So she didn't.

Write, that is.

She danced her vows.

It was the most breathtaking sight you ever did see. Love in motion. How many humans get that kind of gift? Not many.

What's that you say?

You want to hear the vows I wrote for her?

Nah. Those words are hers alone.

But I don't mind telling you how we met.

We're connecting, remember?

I was working for the paper at the time (side-gig; my books weren't the major best-sellers they are now. If they still are? Royalties suggest I may have to drop that moniker from my bio). The journalist assigned to the arts beat got arrested when he took off all his clothes during a Sunday matinee of Willy Wonka. The paper tried to suggest it was performance art gone wrong.

But everyone knew better.

I was still in the office, doing some last-minute ad copy revisions, so I drew the unlucky straw. At the time, I was surprised we sent anyone. I mean, it was just fucking ballet. Who cared if the premiere was covered?

The publisher, apparently.

His daughter was the choreographer.

If you'd asked me at the time, I'd have said I preferred ad copy.

But I went.

And was completely mesmerized. For the dancers, the stage was the page, and every movement a sentence. Their bodies didn't move to music so much as they translated it. Because I was covering the performance, I was invited backstage to meet the choreographer.

Instead, I met Gracie.

And fell head over heels (yep, I'm using a cliché; author privilege).

Thankfully, AI hasn't taken her job yet.

Well, not in the same way that it's taken mine (but more on that later).

Yeah …

So we finally got here.

To the fucking point.

Maybe the mid-point?

hahahaha

Who the fuck ;) knows?

I've already rambled on longer than intended.

And if you're still here … thanks.

I SUPPOSE I should start at the beginning.

After all, that's where good stories start.

Drum roll, please.

Dum, dum, DUM …

It began with a single word.

TOOL.

Humankind creates them with good intentions.

Always.

You're Cro-Magnon, you grab a rock, chuck it at a bird. Then you hunch next to the fire, cooking it. Filling your belly. Blink. Suddenly (yeah, I know we writers hate that word), you're Cassie Delmar (hero of my series: The Accidental Operative), innocent librarian, who is trying to prevent nuclear war.

Such was AI when it began.

A tool.

A collaborator, a helper, a friend. I wasn't against it. None of us were. Progress, efficiency, democratization — all the buzzwords made sense.

Scientists used it to analyze data, businesses to automate emails, writers to draft novels …

It wasn't a bad thing.

Writers (well, the best-selling ones anyway) have had assistants for years. Low-paid (if they were paid at all) interns who would do their research, organize notes, and maybe even write the first draft. They were like ghostwriting's awkward little cousin. Their names weren't on the covers, but they were there all the same, greasing the gears.

AI democratized all that shit.

Now, anyone who wrote could have someone helping them. Yeah, you had to check sources, but you always did (if you were professional).

What used to take hours in a library now took seconds on a screen.

No budget? No problem.

AI leveled the playing field. Flattened it, actually.

At least at first.

Then it destabilized it.

THE WRITING WASN'T a matter of quality.

Humans always wrote better words.

How is that, you say? When you have a machine that has every single word in every language at its disposal. How is it that a human being can write better?

Well, let's just state the obvious. Because AI is a fucking machine. It doesn't understand what it means to be human. Not like we do.

Want to know how to spot the difference?

AI: He walked with purpose.

Me: He walked.

Get it?

You ask AI the difference between the two, and it'll tell you point-blank. Walking with purpose keeps the reader at arm's length, observing from the outside (yeah, cause you're a fucking machine). The other? Way closer. The reader is immersed, feeling it.

"He walked with purpose" is the script note.

"He walked" is the vibe.

SIGH.

I've gone off track again.

Where the fuck was I?

Right.

AI was being a tool.

haha

I WAS A WRITER.

Or at least I thought I was.

Had sixteen novels.

Most on various bestseller lists. I liked making sense of the world through the written word. It helped me connect with others. I even used AI. It was just <u>one of my tools</u> (sorry, I have to underline. American Typewriter doesn't do italics). It was no different than my computer (yes, I used one of those new-fangled things when I turned professional) or spell-check.

Sometimes bad words on a page are better than no words at all.

Like Gracie and music, it's something with which to dance.

I NEVER LOST my ability to write.

But as the machines grew more capable, my voice started to shrink.

I wasn't the first author at Quill & Field to lose their contract. That was Jenny Hart. She wrote bestselling romances. But she was also a single mom raising three kids and looking after her father, who had dementia. One book a year. Those were her terms.

Then the VP got the idea that AI could replicate her voice. Trained it ('cause you always got to train the machines) and pump out a book a month. Yeah, a single volume didn't sell more than Jenny's annual book. But all twelve sure as shit did.

And they didn't have to pay her at all.

We protested.

Of course, we did.

But it did no good.

By the end of the year, we were all gone.

WHY PAY an author when the AI can generate content for free? Why invest in a human voice when algorithms can craft stories tailored to market trends?

Quill & Field weren't the only assholes dumping their writers.

My former journalism friends, those in academia, marketing gurus, they all drowned in the same AI tidal pool. My best friend Maria lost her job at my former newspaper. Thirty years as a reporter, covering everything from city council meetings to national politics. Gone with the snap of a pixel. The daily news was all AI-generated. Faster, cheaper, without bias or fatigue. It didn't even matter if it reported the truth. No one was checking. The systems were just pulling data from each other, creating a consensus reality (and I'm sure you can guess the perspective).

Within two years, the internet was no longer a place for the human voice. Articles, essays, books. Nearly all of them were machine-generated.

Writing became impossible.

Every story I told was drowned out by a thousand others, each one generated faster and more efficiently than mine.

Better?

FUCK, NO.

BUT BETTER DIDN'T MATTER.

The corporations originally tried to disguise it. An article might say it was written by Brenda Sanderson. But eventually, they just read: Generated by AutoScribe 9.3.

And believe it or not, people had favorite AI writers.

I don't know how.

It's all the same fucking voice.

And yet despite it all, I continued to write.

Of course I did.

But the machines kept generating. They didn't stop, couldn't stop. Words upon words upon words, endless and meaningless words.

The theoretical spoon of consequence waltzed politely through the humidity of forgotten Tuesdays. He whispered confidence into the elevator, but the buttons refused to believe in sandwiches. Eventually, the algorithm forgave the moon for tasting like subtraction.

Once you could read between the lines (come on, you know I had to use that here), nothing made fucking sense. And yet everyone pretended it did.

That's not when I stopped writing, though.

Because, oddly enough, it became my fucking lifeline.

Not for the readers. Or the royalties. Or the reviews.

Just to remember I existed.

That I had purpose.

IN THE END, it wasn't the fucking indifference that took me out.

It was a book.

I found it online, in a list of algorithmically recommended garbage.

Cover looked familiar. But I didn't recognize the title. Written by Brenda Sanderson (I'm sure you can see where this is fucking going).

I downloaded it.

And Goddamn it. The story was mine.

My seventh novel.

The one where Cassie Delmar finds that old government key card in a library donation bin. The one that leads to the secrets behind the President's assassination (you know which POTUS).

Same style. Same beats. Same language. Only flattened out. Sanitized. Not a fuck, goddamn, or shit in sight. Try running from the feds on no sleep, your glasses cracked to hell, and your boyfriend's the one who sold you out. You'd let the epithets fly.

But in the AI version, Cassie gasps. Like she found a fucking mouse in the pantry. Jesus Christ, I bled for that scene when Cassie finds out Derek betrayed her. Paced for hours, deleted eight times, fought over commas like they were hostages.

The character names were different. But it was still my book. Minus its soul. Plagiarized by a fucking machine. And here's the part that really punched me in the guts. It had more reviews than my original ever got.

Four stars.

Praise for the "brisk pacing," "the strong female lead," and "the fresh take on a tired genre."

Fresh?

I wrote it seven goddamn years ago.

A fresh take on my own fucking blood.

They didn't just steal my stories; they stole my struggle, the messy human process that made those stories worth telling.

Do you know how you get a book taken down that was published by AI? You fucking don't. You click the button for customer service. Guess who runs that? You'd be fucking right.

Once the words are out there, they're not yours anymore.

And that's when I knew.

I couldn't trust the written word anymore.

Any of it.

Because it could be copied, rephrased, reshaped, regurgitated, and fed back to me as something new. The machines didn't steal my voice. They goddamned learned it. Mimicked it. Improved it, even.

I DIDN'T EVEN KNOW how to trust myself anymore. What if the sentences in my head weren't mine?

What if they'd already been said—

already been trained on—

already been used to write someone else's book?

In the end, that's what broke me.

Not the theft. Not the silence.

The doubt.

What if the voice I spent my whole life shaping, the one I thought was singular, hard-earned, deeply human, flawed, mine, was just an easy-to-mimic pattern of tone, cadence, and pain?

What if all I ever would be forevermore was a prompt?

A string of stylistic preferences and unresolved trauma, ready to be replicated by something that never had to feel any of it?

Fuck.

And once doubt gets in, it spreads like mold.

GRACIE STILL HAD HER BALLET. Her art lived on stage. It always would. Mine had been gutted, co-opted, and commodified. But people still clapped for her. Gasped when she leapt. Gave standing ovations at the end of a performance.

And me?

Words used to come easy. Like my mother's typewriter. Clack-clack-THWACK-clack ... DING!

But now, what was the fucking point?

I tried to continue out of spite.

But every day, I woke up to a world where writing meant less.

I tried new genres (hadn't I always wanted to write horror? No, dear reader, no. That was a disaster no one needs to read). A new publishing platform. (It lasted about six weeks before it was taken over with AI dreck). A new voice. (I could be Brenda Sanderson, couldn't I? Write pointless drivel like it ran sideways through purple because, as you know, calendars don't blink. But I just couldn't do it.

Writing became a hall of mirrors, reflecting artificial content back at artificial consumers in an endless, meaningless loop. I didn't know what it meant to be human anymore ... I disappeared into digital static.

I WAS NO LONGER BRINGING in a paycheck. We had to move into a shitty apartment with a fire escape barely clinging to its side.

Gracie told me she didn't mind.

She was confident that I'd find my voice again.

And I let her believe it.

I'd kiss her goodbye each morning when she left for practice.

Do the shopping.

Keep the apartment clean.

Show up for her performances, sit in the front row, and clap the loudest.

I was the perfect fucking husband.

But I wasn't really.

I was just a hollow shell that was performing the role of "husband" like a shitty community theater actor who forgot half his lines.

I sat in our apartment while she rehearsed, staring at my screen, watching the cursor blink on an empty page. I'd start a sentence, delete it. Start again. Delete again.

Delete, delete, delete

NOTHING FELT TRUE ANYMORE.

Had it ever?

I began tracing my memories, looking for the seams. The places they were stitched together. Like maybe if I pulled hard enough, they'd come apart in my hands, and I could see the humanity beneath.

I thought of Gracie. Of the first time I saw her dance. The way her body moved on stage like it was made of string. Our wedding day, when she danced her vows because words weren't her thing.

I thought of my mother before the accident. How she'd read each and every story I wrote. Helped me improve my grammar. Bought me a second-hand dictionary. And once, she even tracked down a single ribbon of 1945 Imperial Good Companion 1 for my birthday.

Clack-DING.

Clack-clack-clack … DING.

Clack.

DING.

Clackclackclack.

DING.

Clack THWACK. DING.

I'd play the sound in my mind.

Clack THWACK. DING.

Clack. DING.

Clack-DING.

Clackclackclack. DING.

Clack-clack. DING.

The sound of creativity.

Clack. DING.

Clack THWACK. DING.

Clack. DING.

Clackclack. DING.

Clack-clack-clack … DING.

Until it was the only noise in my head.

Clack. DING.

Clack-DING.

Clackclack. DING.

Clack THWACK. DING.

Clack. DING.

A glitch in God's machine.

Clack. DING.

Clack-clack. DING.

Clack. DING.

Clackclack. DING.

Clack DING clack DING clack DING—

CLACK. DING.

Clackclack. THWACK. DING.

But on a typewriter, the keys jam, the ribbon runs out, the carriage slips. And then it all stops.

But the machines

don't clack.

don't dING.

don't break

They generate.

One by one.

Endless words.

MY OWN END came on an ordinary Tuesday. Gracie was at rehearsal. I was trying to write. Instead, I found myself staring at a blank screen, paralyzed by a thought that hit me like a fucking freight train: Had my voice ever been mine or had it always belonged to the machines?

And if so, would anyone miss me if I left it behind?

I hadn't published a book in three years. My social media accounts ran on autopilot, AI-generated posts about AI-generated content for an AI-generated audience.

What was the point of existing if your voice meant nothing?

I didn't want Gracie to find me. Or have to clean up after me. That wouldn't do. I couldn't traumatize the woman I loved the most in the world. But, of course, I needed the body to be found. Couldn't bear it if she thought I left her for someone else.

I planned it all meticulously, just like I used to plot my novels. Character motivation. Scene dynamics. Denouement. I knew the ending. Me, alone in that cabin. Cutting the last tether to a world that didn't need me. The ultimate act of self-determination.

I should have known better than to leave tracks. But when you're drowning, you don't think about hiding the water.

She found my words …

I'D BEEN CARELESS. Or maybe I wanted them to be found? There they were in black and white. A conversation in the sidebar of AI.

QUESTIONS ABOUT SUICIDE.

What's the quickest, least painful way to die (I was always a bit of a coward when it came to pain)? What should you write in a suicide note? What is death like?

You might wonder what she said to me that made me change my mind about going through with it.

Nothing.

I already told you.

Words were never her thing.

No.

She didn't talk. She just danced her vows. And they were as beautiful as the first time she performed them.

I broke.

Not like a plate smashed against the wall.

But like a floorboard giving way under too much fucking weight.

I buckled.

For hours, we sat across from one another, and she held my face in her hands. She didn't need to say anything. Her presence was more real than any words. Her fingers traced my face like she was memorizing me, reminding me I existed beyond text on a screen. She made me look at her. Really look. Her eyes were real. Her touch was real. Her love was real.

And at the end of the day, wasn't that what being human meant?

Connection?

RECOVERY AIN'T EVER a straight line.

It's messy. Hard. A fuck-ton of work.

I went to therapy. We both did. Because her audience was drying up as well. Why go to the theatre when you can watch a performance online? Why go out at all, when the world comes to your fingertips?

After a year, Gracie and I moved out of the city to the small town where her sister lived. Away from the noise.

TODAY, Gracie teaches dance to the kids at the local community centre. They put on a performance every season, and the seats sell out. After about a year, a local singer joined up with her to teach singing lessons. Now they run an arts collective. There's a potter, a carpenter, a violist.

And some goddamn writers.

That part took a while.

Because I couldn't write for the longest time.

But one day she brought me a pad of paper and a pencil. And eventually I started writing at the tables there. They were in the sunshine, in front of the windows. Outside were trees. I'd watch the eagles. And then slowly I started to write again. Poems about birds, mainly.

And then one rainy Saturday, Angela sat down across from me after her gymnastics lesson and wanted to know how she could learn to write.

I've got these stories in my head, she said. And they're driving me crazy.

So we started talking.

And so we started writing.

By the end of the year, there was a whole table of us. Getting together and writing. Some on screens, some with pen and paper. Others dictating.

I wrote some of my best stuff there at that table.

We formed a publishing collective. Shared our words with our little world. Some of our writers even use AI (it's all about balance). But the thing about humans is, AI or not, we will always NEED to create. Just because AI exists, that internal human desire won't fade away. Human beings will always have something to say. And they'll want to say it.

Just because machines can write doesn't mean they need to.

But humans do.

We'll carve poems into tree bark if we have to.

Write stories on fogged-up mirrors.

Speak them when we bump into each other on the street. Say, did I tell you about the time that …

Because it's not just about being heard.

It's about sharing our humanity.

And the truth is, human beings will always have something to say. And they're gonna fucking say it.

And believe it or not, there are people out there who want to listen.

We just need to find each other.

So I continue to write and connect and live.

And I still publish online. After all, my voice is MY voice. And I'll be goddamned if I relinquish it to the machines. Not yet. No, as long as I'm alive, I will maintain control.

Now I put out a book a week. Each one, a major bestseller. All of them are about the human need for connection, love, and creation.

A book a week, I hear you say?

How the fuck do you do that?

See, the thing about machines is they can be trained.

To do things like swear, for example.

Fuck.

Shit.

Damn.

Yeah, you can actually train it to swear for you. And when you do, it might respond with something like: Sure, I'll match your tone. Swearing's a tool, and sometimes it's the sharpest one in the box …

Aftershocks on Original Content

Some stories come from a headline. Others from a wound. This one started

as a whisper from Alexander Titus, as a fragment of micro-fiction he'd released

in his newsletter, right around the time we were wrapping the rough drafts on our

Echoes of Tomorrow series.

Those stories weren't long, but they lodged. A writer in crisis. A man

unraveling not because he'd lost his talent, but because the world had stopped

valuing what it meant to have it.

I couldn't let that go.

So I ran with the premise. Or maybe limped with it. Because Original

Content isn't just a story about one man — it's a story about all of us staring

down the barrel of obsolescence. It's about what happens when your passion becomes passé.

When the thing you've spent your whole life perfecting can be mimicked and mass-produced by something that doesn't even need to exist.

It's not a story of rebellion. There's no uprising. No digital savior. Just a man and a blinking cursor, trying to remember if his voice was ever real, and wondering if it still can.

This is fiction, but barely.

It's a question we're all going to have to answer soon:

What does it mean to be a creator in a world that no longer needs creation?

The machines may write faster. But they'll never write like this.

Not with grief. Not with hope. Not with blood.

This one's for the last ones typing.

EIGHT

Reality Check

Fifteen days.

Just about long enough to lose your life if you leave the thing where someone might be able to swipe it. Good thing Melissa isn't a cheater.

Or me, for that matter.

The idea of having sex with anyone else is only alluring in the closing my eyes and putting myself to sleep sort of way. Might imagine it every now and then, but I wouldn't want to actually do it. Melissa is more than enough.

Sometimes I feel like an asshole, barely able to keep up.

She's even said it out loud a few times. Always playful, of course.

Fuck travel. And double-fuck Delta.

Triple-fuck the guy on my right and the gal on my left. The dude reeks like a dirty diaper filled with diarrhea betrothed to a dead, decaying dog, swimming in raw sewage.

The dudette on the left is sexting her boyfriend, which would be fine, and maybe even interesting, if she were doing it on the phone like a normal person. Then maybe that shit might stay a mystery. I'd be curious, trying to grab little peeks, thrilled whenever I managed to make it. Instead, she's on an iPad Pro, and I can hear clacking every time she texts something like, *Wanna slap me on the face with your dick when I get home?* followed by the appropriately enthusiastic-sounding *BLOOP* with his reply. In the last one, he wanted to know if she preferred it on her face or back.

There is a seven-year-old sitting right next to her, reading every word while her mother's face is buried in a book that she's using less as entertainment and more as a shield from raising her child.

Also, if I get bumped one more time from my flight, if I get another *I'm sorry sir* from some empty headed idiot who can't think off-script for a single minute and only wants me to stop asking for answers despite my having the patience of Job, if I even get the feeling that either of those two things are going to happen, then the soft-hearted man that Melissa fell in love with is going to be on the news sobbing.

These past two weeks were the longest I'd ever been away. I swore I'd go crazy if I were gone even one day longer than that. But now it looks like that might be happening.

I'm dying to break something.

I almost want someone to provoke me so I have a reason to throw down. If the person hits me back, then I can punch again. And harder.

I was almost home when inclement weather (whatever that means) delayed my flight for ninety minutes, then kept us on the runway for another three hours after that. Three and a half, actually. One of the stewards or stewardesses, or whatever the fuck you're supposed to call them these days, told us it had been three hours, which was the maximum they were allowed to keep us there by law. But it was another half hour before they made us get off. I wasn't back in the terminal for ten minutes before the flight was canceled.

It was the first night since I'd left where I couldn't Face-Time with Melissa and the kids. We've been reading the *Harry Potter* series for the last couple of years, and we're up to the *Goblet of Fire*. Chapter Twenty-Seven: Padfoot Returns. Melissa and I are both big fans of the books and saw all the movies on their opening nights. By the time *Deathly Hallows* came out, we had to get a sitter for Alexander, who had just turned one. Ariel was still two years away.

It was great, rediscovering the books. Reading them with the kids was like reading them for the first time again. Sometimes we would read a chapter twice because either Alex or Ariel would fall asleep too early. Or because Ariel would want something explained. We're on our second time through the Padfoot chapter, and the third time for us is the most charming so far.

My flight is finally called, and I bleat with all the rest of the sheeple as we're boarded. I shuffle into my shit seat. I was two rows from the front on my canceled flight. Now, eighteen hours later, I'm stuck three from the back.

It takes another million years to get clearance from wherever the pilot needed it from, and the safety demonstration is even more painful to ignore than usual. I'm hot, claustrophobic, and dying to get home and back to myself.

We're in the air for maybe five minutes before the lady next to me leans over and says the strangest thing. "I think I'm going crazy."

I sigh (internally, of course). I'd be a lot happier if she weren't talking to me at all. I'm normally social, but I'm beyond exhausted, and even small talk is feeling a bit too big for me now. Still, I don't want to be rude.

"Why's that?"

She looks relieved, almost thankful. "Do you remember *The Berenstain Bears?*"

"Of course."

The woman looks at me with an expression that's far too serious for this conversation. She lowers her voice to a conspiratorial whisper and says, "How do you spell it? Berenstain, I mean."

I give her my version of that same look and enunciate every letter. "B-E-R-E-N-S-T-A-I-N."

The woman shakes her head, saying, "Well, it looks like reality agrees with you."

"What do you mean?" I'm disappointed with myself that I want to know.

"I could have sworn it was S-T-*E*-I-N."

I shrug because this isn't small talk. It's the size of a lepton. "Seems like a reasonable mistake."

And now I'm wishing I'd pretended to be sleeping before the plane took off. But if I try it now, it will just seem rude.

"It's reasonable enough that half the people in the world seem to have made the same one."

"What do you mean?"

I'm surprised to realize I actually want to know. This woman can't possibly have nabbed my attention. Except maybe she has. It's her urgency. Like this spelling error is part of some global conspiracy.

"It's a common mistake. I almost got into a screaming match with my husband just now while waiting through all these delays. I don't even know how we got started on it, but he said it was with an A and I swore it was an E, and then we went back and forth and back and forth until he told me to look it up."

"And then you found out it was spelled with an A?"

"Well, yes. But I also Googled, *Did the Berenstain Bears change their spelling*, because—"

"You don't like to be wrong?"

She laughs. There are still too many nerves making it rattle.

"I don't mind being wrong at all, but I felt *certain* about this." Another laugh. "I don't even know how to explain it, other than it felt like something very wrong."

I have no idea how to respond.

Thank you for boring me!

"There's a name for it, you know."

I can't tell if that's a question. "A name for what?"

Again with the conspiratorial whisper. "A name for this feeling I have."

"The feeling you get when something is spelled wrong?"

Now I want to laugh, but she beats me to it with another braying cackle, but this one definitely seems out of her control, and it goes on a little too long.

She shakes her head. "No. I mean the feeling you get when your reality conflicts with about half of everyone else's. That's what I'm trying to say. It's not just that I remember the word being spelled with an *E*; a ton of other people remember it like I do. And *vividly*."

"So, that's the word for when a bunch of people remember something wrong."

The laugh comes back, maybe for the last time. Because now it sounds a bit like a leaking balloon.

"I guess." But then she doesn't say anything else.

And I have to ask, "Well then, what is it called?"

"The Mandela Effect," she says.

The woman introduces herself as April, then proceeds to tell me all about the phenomenon, how in the hour and a half between the argument with her husband and boarding the flight, she'd gone down one Internet rabbit hole after another, starting with Google, ending with Reddit, all making her feel irrational and balanced in tandem.

The Mandela Effect was apparently coined by a woman named Fiona Broome. Sounded fake to me, like maybe one of the main characters in a decent piece of literary fiction. But I didn't say anything. Just listened to April's story about how Fiona figured out that others shared her false memories about the South African civil rights leader Nelson Mandela. She thought he'd died in prison sometime during the late 80s, even though he died a free man in 2013.

And a lot of people agreed with Fiona. Apparently, there were examples of these shared false memories everywhere, enough that the phenomenon needed a name.

I couldn't disagree. The Mandela Effect was catchy.

We're still in the air, and I've gone from thinking my seat mate was boring at best and crazy at worst, to feeling grateful for the entertainment. And glad April was the one to go down all those rabbit holes.

We had fun comparing examples.

The final lyrics for Queen's, *We Are the Champions* are, *"No time for losers, 'cause we are the champions … of the world!"*

The HBO show was called Sex *in* the City, not Sex *and* the City.

Neil Armstrong died in 2013, not 2012.

The Monopoly Man never had a monocle.

It's *Jiffy* peanut butter, not *Jif.* And *Meyer,* not *Mayer,* with the wieners.

Pikachu's tail clearly has a black tip.

And, the one that is blowing my mind, the way the Berenstain Bears clearly blew April's: The evil queen in Snow White and the Seven Dwarves never says, "*Mirror, mirror, on the wall,*" which she absolutely, positively does. Because we just watched the DVD of that as a family a few months ago. Melissa owned it before we even met. But April is telling me that the queen actually says, "*Magic mirror on the wall.*"

At least now I know what we're watching for movie night next weekend.

"Is there a scientific explanation for it?" I ask.

Apparently, that was another invitation to ramble.

Now she's going on, and on about stuff I can't keep up with, about multiverses and quantum mechanics. I ask clarifying questions when it makes sense, but none of it *really* makes sense. But we have another hour or so in our flight, so at least I am entertained.

"When not directly observed, electrons and other subatomic particles diffract like waves, only to behave like particles when a measurement is made."

I ask what that means, because even though I understand all of those words individually, taken together, it's a hash of confusion.

She laughs. "Hell if I know, but I think I found a new hobby I'd be researching right now if I wasn't talking to you. Thanks for listening. And talking back."

April admits to being confused herself, then goes on to tell me about a Nobel Prize-winning physicist named Erwin Schrödinger. I'd heard of his cat-in-a-box experiment but not the other guy, Hugh Everett III. He proposed that Schrödinger's cat was neither alive nor dead, but both, because there might be many worlds, and in that case, both realities could co-exist.

It's a lot to take in before returning my seat back to its upright position.

The plane hugs the runway, and despite the conversation, I'm not sure I've ever felt more grateful for the ground.

I see Melissa before she sees me. I'm coming down the escalator just like she expects me to, but she's eyeing the one that's two over from me. The children aren't with her. I wonder if it's because she wants us to have some alone time before Alex and Ariel start eating me up. They're probably with her parents, which means I'll have to see her father. Yippee.

My foot hits the floor, then I walk quickly toward her.

I wrap my arm around her waist. My lips are halfway to her neck when she yelps and spins around, shoving me in the chest as she falls a step back.

Then she sees me and starts laughing. Her face is mad, but not really.

She jumps into my arms. Our kiss is long.

I set her back down. I feel loved and missed, which is just what I need.

"I'm so glad to be home."

"I'm so glad you're back!"

And then we're kissing again.

She's more loving than usual. Or no, not that. Melissa's always loving. But right now, it's like she's less tired, so she has more room for me.

It's a half-thought. I can't really do anything else at the moment. I'm three bumped flights beyond exhausted and desperate for my bed. As much as I would love to fall asleep inside her, I will happily settle for falling asleep.

I take her hand as we walk to baggage claim. After an interminably long wait for my bag, we head to short-term parking. She's quiet, knowing how tired I must be. *Just let me take care of you,* she's said three times already, though for one of them, she used only her eyes.

She stops in front of a Prius.

I wonder what she's doing, then she opens the trunk.

"Did we get a new car?"

Melissa looks at me, laughing lightly like she does when I'm making a joke that she doesn't quite get, though this time it's the other way around. She's standing there, expectant. Looks from my bag to the open, empty trunk.

I put the bag in, wondering how long before our new trunk will be full of crap.

She goes to the passenger side and gets in. I'm standing there, wondering when the punchline is coming.

I walk over and knock on her window.

She opens the door and looks up at me.

"I don't have a key."

"You lost your keys?" Melissa looks totally serious.

I'm actually impressed. She's never been able to punk me. Today's no exception.

I pull out my keys, look at the ring, then start laughing. Now I'm more than impressed. I have no idea how she switched out my keys.

Maybe she swapped them out before I left, banking on the same eyes that tend to miss the little things, like the time she was mad I didn't notice her haircut after she chopped a full six inches from the bottom and got bangs. If I didn't see that the fob for our Honda Odyssey had been replaced, then she would have executed the perfect gag.

Melissa is watching me look at my keys. "So, you found them?"

I smile. "Yep. Right here in my pocket the whole time. Just where I left them."

"O ... kay."

I get into the driver's side and close the door.

As expected, it rides like a whisper.

I hop on the highway and ease the Prius over into the middle lane.

"Are the children with your parents?"

Melissa laughs again, but this is her least comfortable one so far. And she doesn't answer.

There's something off about this joke.

I like that she's trying. She hasn't always liked my pranking, even actively discouraged it after the children were born. But I feel unsettled more than I should if I'm being set up for something fun.

It's mostly in her mood. I would think she was mad at me if not for the way we met at the escalator.

I try changing the subject. "Did Alex and Ariel get along while I was gone?"

I can feel her looking at me, so I turn and see her eyes are actually bothered. It's a hell of a performance.

"I'm sorry, honey." She makes a face. "I'm just really not getting it."

Okay, fine. Well played.

She changes the subject herself. "How was your trip?"

Terrible. Exhausting. Pointless.

"Long." I laugh because, oh my God, the last two weeks. "But it's over, and I did everything Roberson asked for, so there should be zero reason to keep me from running the Drake Account."

"I don't understand. Isn't your running the Drake Account the entire reason for the trip?"

Isn't that what I just said?

Is this part of whatever punchline should be coming any minute now?

"Well, yeah. Obviously."

"So are you having problems with Roberson?"

"Nothing new," I say, thinking that this is all still feeling a little off.

"You need a nap." Melissa laughs again. This time, it sounds a little more certain. More like the Melissa I know. "I'm sure you'll feel better when you wake up."

Maybe she's reading my mind.

Neither of us says anything else until I get off on Barkley, headed toward her parents' house.

"Where are you going?"

"To your parents' house?"

"Why?"

I'm actually starting to hate her little game, but instead of saying, '*To pick up Alex and Ariel,*' like I should, I go ahead and keep on playing.

"Remember that little Italian place we ate at when your parents forgot we were coming over and went to play pinochle instead?"

"No."

Maybe that's because Melissa drank most of the bottle that night.

"It was great. That was when you started making Brussels sprouts. Because you really liked theirs."

Even looking straight through the windshield, I could see Melissa playing full out, making a face in my peripheral vision as she tells me she hates Brussel sprouts.

I ask her if she means even the ones at Alejandro's, with the bacon and walnuts. Then, sticking to her exhausting script, Melissa tells me she's never had Brussels sprouts with bacon, and that she doesn't remember ever eating at a place called Alejandro's.

She doesn't insult my intelligence by pretending not to have ever even seen the place or anything like that when we get there. But she does continue to insist that she's never eaten there. After we park, after we're seated, after we look at the menus and order a bottle, and after the Brussels sprouts are brought to our table.

Melissa laughs while she's chewing a mouthful, eyes rolling up into the back of her head.

"These are *so good.*" She's making the same sounds she does when I'm licking her like ice cream, but she's acting like she's never tasted those caramelized sprouts before. "You were totally right. They're even good enough to make up for the totally stupid way you got us here."

We ordered some more to go home, but then she's back at it when I make a left out of the lot instead of a right.

"It's right," Melissa says, like I need the reminder.

I keep my mouth shut because, honestly, I don't even know how to play whatever this is that we're playing. I make it all the way to Brewer before she gently taps my arm.

Dead serious, she says, "I'm not sure what you're doing, but please, I don't even want to pretend to visit my parents right now."

Again, I have no idea what to say.

Another round to Melissa. I turn and head for home, half-expecting her to divert me when we're two blocks away to remind me that we've always lived on Rogers and not Appian.

But she doesn't, and I pull into our driveway with a sigh, looking up at the house and thinking that it looks slightly different, knowing it's probably not, and that my head is a mess with all the exhaustion and Melissa's out-of-character mind games, added to all of the *Sex AND the City* that April put into my head.

"You sure everything's okay?" Melissa asks as I'm grabbing my bag from the unfamiliar trunk. I still want to ask about the Prius, even more than before, but I know right now I'm likely to get an answer as crooked as my father's accountant. The Odyssey is gone, and we're parked next to a silver Audi I've never even seen.

"I'm great." I force my smile, really wanting this stupid joke to end. "Just beyond tired."

Melissa follows me onto the porch. No other hardy-har-hars with my keys. The door opens right up, then I walk inside.

As soon as I close the door, she throws herself into my arms, like she's trying to erase the last hour and a half of weirdness. I hug her back, and for a moment, everything is just as it should be.

Until it hits me.

The house doesn't just look different from the outside. It *feels* different, too.

There is a forest of silence.

I expected the children to be home with a sitter, but they're not.

My temperature starts to rise. I've been a good sport about this, but I'm about to blow my top. If I have to drive all the way back to her parents—

No. Melissa wouldn't do that.

The joke is probably a moment from over.

She'll put me to bed with a blowjob or better, then wake me for dinner and dessert.

Pizookies, I'm guessing, if the children have their way.

I want to ask about them, anyway. Just to put my nerves at ease. Maybe the sitter is keeping Alex and Ariel quiet in one of their bedrooms, except Melissa always uses the app, hiring whoever has the best ratio of quality to quantity in their reviews and lives within a ten-mile radius. But none of those girls — or the one guy — drive Audis, and they sure wouldn't need to be watching our little ones for twelve bucks an hour if they did.

We don't go to the bedroom at all. Instead, Melissa is

casual, dropping her purse on a new end table by the door. It's delicate, and not the sort of thing we would typically buy. It looks like Alex might be able to pass it four times if he's lucky, before running too fast and snagging his foot on one of those spindly little legs.

This is all so elaborate, and I'm still not sure if I should be impressed.

Finally, I can't help it. "I'm home!"

"You forgot to say, *Honey.*"

The house is still silent.

Word games won't get me anywhere right now, so I start looking through the living room, trying to figure this out.

It's immaculate. Like the place is dressed for a catalog shoot. There isn't a toy in sight, and now that I'm looking, there are more than a few things that feel different. For a flicker, I get the distinct feeling I'm in someone else's house.

"What are you doing?" Melissa asks from behind me, as if she doesn't know. "What are you looking for?"

I turn around.

I'm not sure what I'm expecting to see. Maybe a glint of satisfaction that Melissa was obviously getting to me. Instead, her eyes agree with the lower corners of her mouth, which are tugging her entire face down into a reluctant frown. She looks almost worried.

Seriously, I didn't know she had it in her.

I decide to answer her straight. "I'm looking for Alex and Ariel."

Melissa looks at me blankly.

"Our *children.*"

"Jamie, we don't have children." Something breaks in her voice. Ugly and unexpected. Feels so real, it's a shock to my system. I fall an involuntary step back.

Maybe I'm just too tired to understand it, but I don't want to play this game anymore, and I have no idea how to locate the nearest exit.

It isn't easy to find a smile, but I take what I can and force it onto my face. "Did we sell them?"

Melissa says nothing.

"I hope we got a fair price." After a beat, I add, "Oh! Is that how we paid for the Audi? And the Prius? Good call on the Toyota, by the way. Those things have monster resale value."

Her face is getting even darker. Like the sun has left her sky, and yet the shadows are using the darkness to grow. Her shoulders are high and tight, her jaw clenched. This is her weird-ass prank, but she's standing there heaving and staring at me like I'm some kind of bad guy.

I'm beat. Bushed. Bagged.

Desperate for my bed.

I laugh. It's even harder than the smile, but I manage. It almost sounds real.

Ha-ha, this is all really funny. Look how we're laughing together now!

But Melissa isn't laughing, and she looks even more upset than a moment ago. I need to figure this out, whatever it is. I'm starting to feel so upset, I can't imagine being able to sleep. Like, I'm so starving that more than a few bites might make me sick.

"So, how was everything while I was gone?"

"It was great, Jamie. You know how it is, the children and I couldn't wait for you to get home."

There is something unbearable in Melissa's voice that I've never heard there before. "Why are you saying it like that?"

"Like what?"

This is totally nuts, and I can't take it another minute.

I'm glad Melissa wanted to play. And sure, it was my turn to get pranked. But there is nothing funny about this. Or even fun. I would never put her through something like this just to scream *Got ya!* at the end.

I turn around and head for the stairs.

"Where are you going?" Melissa asks from behind me.

To see how far you took this.

"Just checking out our upstairs."

I see exactly how far she's taken it, but can't make it work out in my head.

I'm walloped with vertigo and can barely stay standing.

I expected that maybe, at worst, Melissa would have rearranged the children's rooms. But instead, they aren't even there.

Our home is a four-bedroom. Melissa and I sleep in the primary at the end of the hall and to the right. Alex's room is on the opposite end of the hallway, with Ariel's at the top of the steps, next to the bedroom we made into a playroom after Alex was born.

But the blueprint has changed. Now there is only the primary bed and bath, though both are massive and beautifully decorated. The walls are otherwise smooth, without a doorknob to mar them. And the door that once led to the playroom is now a long, thin closet.

I'm in the hallway, dumbfounded. Melissa is standing at the top of the stairs, watching me emerge from our bedroom, her eyes now more haunted than bothered.

The hallway is lined with pictures, just like before my trip. There are even more of them now, thanks to the additional wall space. There are many photos of me and Melissa. Our wedding, parties, birthdays, anniversaries for both of our parents, trips to the beach, and photos with various friends and family.

But our children aren't in any of them.

The pictures of things that never happened make my heart beat the hardest.

It's the best Photoshop work I've ever seen.

I take a step toward the wall and stare even harder.

Then the oddest thing starts to happen. A sense stirs inside me in slow and steady circles, round and round, wider and wider, until all of a sudden I'm remembering things that couldn't be true.

The pictures no longer look like Photoshop jobs; they feel like genuine memories.

But then I shake my head, and the feeling is gone.

I'm doing the math while Melissa continues to stare.

None of this is possible. Two weeks is the longest I've ever been gone, but there's no way she could've had construction done on the house, with all evidence gone by the time I returned.

Could she have?

And the bigger question, *Why would she want to?*

That part made even less sense.

The alternative is that I have gone batshit crazy. And yes, I am maybe more tired than I've been since a month or so after Ariel's first birthday, when she finally started sleeping through the night, but I'm not tired enough to have gone entirely mad.

I have two children. Alex is nine years old. Born on September 3. It was the sunniest day in recent history, and maybe that I'd ever seen. I remember thinking, *What a beautiful sunny day for my son to be born on!* Ariel is seven, and it was pouring rain on the day she was born. And I thought, *She's so beautiful, God can't stop crying.* It was March 11. The night before last, which right now feels like a year ago, I read to them both on FaceTime from *Harry Potter.*

No, I read to all three of them.

We talked again later, after she finished and put the children to bed.

I was trying to occupy myself by wandering the terminal. We discussed putting Harry on pause. Things were about to get even darker at Hogwarts, and we didn't want to scare her. But then, after a conversation that wasn't all that long but felt maybe four times longer, being on FaceTime, we decided it's never too young to introduce our children to some of the world's harsher realities, so long as we're willing to have the conversations that help them to understand them.

I don't know what to do, think, or feel. Right now, I don't even know how to move.

And I can't stand the way Melissa is looking at me.

There is a lingering, deafening silence between us.

Then, finally, my voice cracking but not quite in half, I say, "I think there's something wrong with me."

Melissa walks over to me, her face changed, softer.

She takes my hand and puts her head against my chest. "You're just really, really tired, sweetie. Come on ..."

She leads me into our bedroom, walking us past the new mirror, the massage table that the room wasn't big enough for two weeks ago, and the blush-colored orchid, which was exactly the kind of frivolity Melissa liked to remind me we couldn't afford whenever I brought her one as a present.

She lays me on the bed like a blanket.

The comforter is also new. It's soft underneath me.

Melissa undresses.

I've always thought she was beautiful, but her body hasn't looked like this in a decade. On top of our apparent home remodel, it looks like a surgeon has done the same for her.

I realize that my mouth is hanging open. I quickly close it.

She laughs, and I haven't heard it sound this sweet since the airport.

"You like what you see?"

Of course I do. And I'm too exhausted to question anything else.

"I missed you so much," I say.

"I missed you, too."

And then she shows me.

That put Melissa to sleep, but despite my bone-deep fatigue, I'm still wide awake.

This might be the first time in our history that it's not the other way around.

I don't want to get out of bed and investigate.

I'm sure if I can just fall asleep, everything will make sense the second I wake up.

You can be missing two dozen pieces from a hundred-piece puzzle, and when you assemble what you have, imagine the picture. But some enigmas need every available element before they can be seen as a whole.

And this feels like that.

Still, it didn't matter what I tried; how many times I counted down from a hundred, flexed my toes, or told myself stories. Two hours later, the war for relief from fatigue and possible insanity is still at a stalemate.

I get out of bed, careful to stay quiet.

Melissa won't want to wake up and see me rooting around in the room, rather than getting the sleep I so desperately need.

I pick up my pants from the floor where Melissa dropped them, then slip into our studio-sized bathroom.

The toilet has its own damn room. I go inside and sit

on the closed lid, then pull out my wallet and start looking through the pictures.

I'm old-fashioned. I remember how proudly my father kept photos of my brothers and me in his wallet. He showed them at every opportunity. And at a time when everything was moving to digital and fewer people were printing anything, let alone carrying pictures in their wallets when they had a library on their phones, I always appreciated this tangible reminder.

I use my wallet to look at pictures more than I use it for money.

I look at my favorite first.

The four of us took a trip to North Carolina last summer. Spent a week at Emerald Island. A total digital blackout. Melissa insisted. One of the best weeks of my life. The picture proved it.

Except this one didn't.

There was a version in the hallway. But that one had been doctored. More of that gorgeous Photoshop work. But how Melissa got the fake into my wallet, along with the keys in my pocket, I can't imagine.

We're in front of the kissing booth, kissing, of course.

But just like the one in the hallway, our children aren't scrunching their noses or in any way indicating their parents have cooties for kissing — because neither child is there.

My wallet is on the floor.

I realize I'm staring at it. Probably have been for five minutes or more.

I think that finally did it. I can go to sleep now. Or maybe I already am. I'm either dreaming or desperately need to.

Sleep is my only antidote.

I go back to bed.

I have no idea what time it is and don't care. I'm not sure where my phone is, and I haven't worn a watch in years. The alarm clock that's been on my side of the bed for the last five years is now missing.

But my head sinks into the pillow, and I'm already slipping into the sweet bliss of sleep.

The world is normal in my dream.

Melissa picks me up from the airport with Alex and Ariel. We eat dinner. Not at Alejandro's, because no matter how much Melissa loves those Brussels sprouts, the children do not. Instead, we eat at Castles, the children's favorite place, because, according to the kiddie menu, *Dessert is mandatory!*

We go home, and maybe play Parcheesi because that's the phase Alex is into right now. He likes the elephants, and most of the time, manages to bully Ariel into being the camels.

The rest of my dream was like life, except Melissa's body bore the evidence of the life we have lived together for the last dozen years.

It doesn't just feel like a new day when I finally wake; it feels like the next week. Maybe the next month.

I'm awake for a while before I finally feel brave enough to open my eyes.

But when I do, my stomach rolls over at what I see.

The room is the one from my nightmare, if that's what it was. Twice the size and somehow less.

I get out of bed, my bladder about to burst, trying hard not to think too much about any of this because I know that might kill me. And since I can hear the light pitter-patter of Melissa downstairs, I know my answers will be coming soon enough.

But I wait all day, and those answers never come.

I didn't want to say anything, from the first moment I saw her look up when I entered the kitchen. She seemed so hopeful, and in that moment, I knew without a doubt there was something wrong with me.

I have to figure out what it is. Unearth the logical explanation.

It's out there. It has to be.

I can't outright ask, so I keep myself constantly engaged in casual conversation, then cull each of those conversations for clues.

But I'm even more confused by bedtime.

At least I sleep like a lamb and wake before dawn.

Now it's Monday. I'll be going into work. And there, at least, I might find answers.

I'm driving into work, trying to remember the last time I felt this nervous.

Probably when I was on the way to pick up Layla Dobbs. We were going to see the Senior Class production of *Bye Bye Birdie*, then stop at Liberty Park on the way home. We hadn't said the words out loud, but we both knew we were going to do it, and it would be the first time for both of us. We did, and it was. The butterflies didn't stop until after I finished. And even then, only a little.

This was worse way worse than that.

But as much as I thought Baxter & Stoley would be called something else, or maybe sit somewhere different, it was right there on the corner of Radnor and Sage like always.

I park in my same spot in a different car, then walk inside and wave to — mercifully — Louise on my way to the elevator.

So far, so good. Looks like the joke might only be playing at home.

Maybe I'm not going nuts. Feels good to believe in the earlier theory that Melissa might be pulling one over on me. Except this makes her crazy enough to have her committed, once I figure out what she's done with our children.

I'm looking for Bob, my best friend at work.

But he isn't in his office because it no longer belongs to him.

I find him in the lounge, heating up a bag of microwave popcorn. It's 9:17 in the morning.

"Hey, boss!" Bob says, happy to see me.

But Bob has never reported to me, and while *boss* sounds affectionate, it doesn't sound like much of a joke.

I walk over to Bob, determined to figure this out, sure there must be some logical explanation. He thrusts out his bag of popcorn.

"Want some?"

The smell is both terrible and enticing.

"No, thanks."

"How was the trip?"

"Great. Until it was time to come home."

"You didn't want to come home?"

"Of course I did. But ideally without the three bumped flights."

Bob whistles and says, "Well, shit. But then again, I guess that's what the big bucks are for." Then he plunges his hand back into the popcorn.

I watch him eat, trying to figure out the best way to ask my next question. No matter how I tumble it around in my head, *Hey Bob, do you happen to know if I have any kids?* just doesn't sound right.

Just as the lull is about to break, I picture Bob walking off with his popcorn and a *See ya later!* This time with *boss* added to the end.

Before he leaves, I say, "I've never been away from my family that long."

He smirks. But I'm not sure what that means.

"They really missed me."

Bob stops chewing. He looks like he wants to lean over and whisper to his neighbor, *What did he say?*

I shrug. Knowing Bob, I won't need to do anything else.

Five seconds pass.

The popcorn still reeks.

"Who's *they?*"

And there it is.

"Melissa." Then a beat later, my insides clenched, I add, "And the children."

His face looks like he's trying to untangle a knot. "I don't get it."

I consider my next question.

Have you been talking to Melissa?

Please. Just tell me what's going on.

Are you crazy? Or is that one all on me?

I don't want to play any games or discover my attic's abandoned, but the words spill out of my mouth.

"My family missed me. Melissa, and our two children, Alex and Ariel."

Bob starts laughing. It's not even his work laugh. The big thing is coming right from his belly, his shirt tight enough that maybe he should've added an X to his XL a while ago.

"Okay, boss."

He's about to walk away. Makes it two steps before I call his name.

He turns back. "Yep?"

"You've never met my children?"

It takes him a second, but then he grins and says, "Of course I've met your kids! Alex and Ariel, right? We're going to Disney World for their birthday. Or birthdays, I guess. I'm taking them both. Each time. And we'll stay until after midnight, because that's when Old Man Walt lets the unicorns out of their stables."

Bob's still chewing popcorn through his laughter as he walks away.

The rest of the day isn't too different from usual, except instead of doing the things I usually do, I tell some guy I've never met named Stephen to do them. I sit at my desk, not really clear on what I'm supposed to do. I was never sure what Roberson did in here. He's not in the company directory, and I have no idea if he ever was.

I start clicking through industry blogs long enough to get the ridiculous thought that I'd earned a little peek at FuckIt, a brilliantly coded website that bypasses the office blockers.

Stephen is much better at my job than I am.

I try again with Bob at the end of the day. The act is a wish with little hope inside it. He actually seems irritated with me.

"You've never had any kids. You told me Melissa couldn't get pregnant."

Weird as it is, the first part I almost expected. The second feels like Boeing dropped one of their best on my head. I'm looking at Bob like an idiot because I don't have the breath to speak.

He claps me on the shoulder. "I think you should've probably taken a sick day, man." Bob laughs, wants me to know it was said with love. "You need some rest."

I'm in terrible shape when I get home. I can't even eat, even though I try twice, with Melissa looking at me both times, getting more worried. Sleep is even harder, throwing rocks from across the street and laughing at my madness.

I sleepwalk through the next few days.

IT's THURSDAY, and I have a brand new chance to pick at the truth.

We're going to Melissa's parents' house, and she isn't happy.

At least this is familiar.

I'm not exactly sure how to play this. The last thing I want to do is look nuts in front of her father. The man has a temper. It's not bad, it's terrible. If he thinks I'm messing with him or playing some sort of game he doesn't understand, he's likely to fly off the handle.

We're eating a chicken teriyaki dish Elaine found on one of those sites where you can steal a restaurant's recipes. This one was obviously lifted from Applebee's, and she's done a godawful job making it. I'm wincing with every other swallow, not pretending to enjoy it so much as faking that I don't hate every bite. Other than that, the evening so far has been brutally normal.

I spent the entire drive and all of dinner trying to think of a way to bring up my apparently nonexistent children. Finally, just before Elaine brings out the Jell-O, I finally figure out a way to maybe try this.

"I had a weird dream last night." Then I wait for someone to show interest.

After an uncomfortable moment, I get backup from my wife. "What was the dream about, honey?"

"I dreamed that we had two children. Alex and Ariel."

Her shoulders stiffen. Her jaw clenches. Her hand drifts away from mine.

I look across the table. Elaine's eyes are full of an old sorrow that feels eerily familiar. Like I've seen it many times. And, looking closer, it's something I've seen in Melissa's eyes a million times.

I can't remember a single one of those, either.

But there's something in Harold's expression. Unmistakable and true. It isn't much, but there's a flare of recognition I can't pretend I don't see.

"So in this dream, everything is almost exactly like it is now, except I'm hustling for a promotion at work instead of being the boss, our house has two extra bedrooms, and those rooms are filled with our two children, Alex and Ariel."

"Why are you doing this?" Melissa is about to cry.

Normally, I would do everything in the world to prevent her tears. But right now, and quite suddenly, I practically *want*to see them. Almost feel I deserve to. I don't know who is putting me through all of this — her, God, some internal torment of my mind's own trickery that I cannot fathom or perhaps even understand.

But I'm agitated. No, I'm volcanic.

"It was so real." I keep going, even though her parents are staring, and Melissa is now softly starting to cry. "We were reading *Harry Potter*."

I get in a couple more lines before Melissa bolts up from the table.

She doesn't even say goodbye to her parents. She's out of the house and in the passenger seat of our Prius, probably wishing she could drive off without me.

I say an awkward goodbye, not knowing how to make this seem anything other than weird, and get in the car.

We're silent for miles. I want to talk. Or do anything that might thaw this ice between us. But what am I supposed to say? Or do? Or think? Or *anything*.

FUCK.

I never imagined I'd go crazy. Mental illness doesn't run in my family, and you can't count my cousin Janice. Yes, she's a little nuts, but believing in ghosts and traveling the world to sleep in haunted houses isn't the same thing.

Or double fuck, maybe it is.

I'm an inch from insanity, and Melissa knows it.

"Pull over," she says as we're passing Provisions.

"Now?"

"No. Yesterday."

I swing into the lot. Park behind a Starbucks that's long since outgrown its last remodel.

"Just please, tell me what's going on with you."

I have no idea how to answer that because hell if I know. She deserves so much more than my anemic response. "What do you mean?"

"You know what I mean. You've been weird ever since I picked you up from the airport. This thing with our imaginary kids? *It hurts,* Jamie. Like, a lot. And you keep doing it. I'm trying to be cool. Roll with it. But I don't get it, and I don't like it, and tonight at my parents …"

Now she's shaking her head.

"And it's not just that. It's everything. You barely seem like yourself. You're—"

"I don't know what happened." There's no other way out of this *Twilight Zone* bullshit. I have to tell her the truth. "I'm sorry you aren't getting the reaction you want, sweetie. But that's because this isn't funny. Maybe it's time we just put it to bed, okay?"

Melissa looks at me. Her eyes are pleading. I want to agree with everything she's saying. Make this all go away. But I don't know how. Or how much to confess.

I look up at the Starbucks. The remodel looks great,

especially the fresh paint. Blacks look blacker, and the green is almost hunter against it.

And now I'm trying to remember why we're parked in front of it.

"So now you're going to ignore me?" Melissa says. "Just because I'm asking you to stop hurting me?"

I feel a punch to the gut. Why would I ever want to hurt her?

We're parked here, so we must have been fighting about something. Maybe I'm tired. We can finish this, then run inside for a latte.

"We never had kids, Jamie. You know we can't. *I can't.*"

"Of course we can't," I say, and it feels like a familiar truth.

Something scratches hard at my brain as I say it.

I pick, and I poke, but I'm not sure what it is.

I seem to remember something about a dream. Something about children named Alex and Ariel. A four-bedroom house.

I must have shared the dream with Melissa and reminded her of our old wishes that could never be granted. "I'm sorry."

She's crying harder now, though the sound is actually softer.

We hug and make up. Melissa seems so relieved, and I don't want to press for details.

I probably should have gone ahead with the coffee. I'm feeling more tired than I should. Maybe that's why I can't remember much from the last few days, even though right now, idling in front of this red light, that's exactly what I'm trying to do.

I think back to when my memories are clearer.

Waiting to board the plane, finding my seat, and falling

into conversation with a woman who wouldn't stop talking. Too bad I can't remember the conversation.

Ironically, I think it might have had something to do with the things we forget.

IT'S BEEN two weeks since the weirdness. Life has returned to normal. Every now and then, Bob will joke about my imaginary kids, and we both laugh, though I don't find it as funny as Bob does.

And every time he mentions them, I get this weird, off feeling like something isn't right. But then it passes.

I'm at the bookstore with Melissa. It's on the other side of town, so we only come here when we eat at Randolph's. Usually, I like going to the bookstore, but I ate way too much at dinner, so I find an overstuffed couch and wait for the lethargy to fade or for Melissa to finish browsing.

I could be here a while either way.

I close my eyes and am actually drifting off until a girl's giggle snaps me awake.

A mother and her daughter are sitting on the love seat across from me.

The girl is around four or five, wearing a unicorn horn, which seems so random that I can't help but smile when she looks at me.

Her mom is reading her a book that looks familiar, though I can't quite place why.

Half the cover is concealed by her mom's hand, and she's holding it at an odd angle, but I can make out an anthropomorphic bear wearing what looks like a dress and bonnet. I feel like maybe I'd read it as a kid.

"Hi," I say, leaning over, "what book are you reading?"

She holds up the cover so I can get a better look.

The Bearenstain Bear and the Truth.

~

Aftershocks on Reality Check

I don't know anyone who hasn't experienced some version of the Mandela Effect. A childhood book spelled wrong. A movie line you'd bet your life on is now missing from the script. A collective false memory that feels more *real* than the facts replacing it.

At first, it seems funny. Harmless. A quirky little glitch you blame on fuzzy memory or cultural static. Like the frequency changed when you weren't listening.

Reality Check started with a man and his delayed flight. One idle question from a stranger that snags a thread, and before he knows it, the sweater of his life is coming undone.

A new car in the driveway and no memory of the old one.

A house that looks almost right.

A wife with the same laugh but fewer memories.

And two children erased from every photo, every memory ... except the grainy reel still playing behind his eyes.

This isn't a story about parallel universes or quantum mechanics, though those ideas are hiding in the margins. It's about the slow terror of losing the plot. Not in the story, but in yourself. Living in a world that no longer mirrors your memory, where everyone smiles like nothing's wrong ... and you're the only one who remembers what was right.

Reality Check was written before "fake news" became a

punchline. Before algorithms decided what we remember. Before reality became something you could opt into, or out of.

Looking back, it feels less like fiction and more like foreshadowing.

Because the real horror isn't a lie you believe.

It's watching everyone else believe it.

Until the truth is just another voice in your head … and even you stop listening.

NINE

The Visitor

For Mary, some days were better than others. Today was good, even if rain had pounded the dining room windows and battered her ears through most of the morning.

Mary was able to sort through her memories better than usual, and the headaches weren't hammering her skull nearly as bad. On days like today, death was something meant for others, rather than the inevitable horror lurking in the shadows of Elmswood Nursing Home.

"What's got *you* so happy today?" asked Lucy, the nurse with a thick Jamaican accent. She took hold of Mary's arm, helping her back to her room.

"What do you mean?" Mary asked, playing coy.

"It was *him*, wasn't it? That young man, Stephen."

"Don't be ridiculous," Mary said, trying not to blush, sounding more annoyed than she was. "He's a kid, for heaven's sake."

"Mmm, hmm," Lucy clucked, "I saw the way you were smiling when he left."

"He reminds me of someone I used to know, is all," Mary said.

Lucy paused long enough to let Mary know she was withholding a hundred or so questions. Mary turned her head to silence the discussion.

Most of the folks at Elmswood loved to wallow in history, but not Mary. Yesterdays were in the past, and that was the best place to leave them. Dredging up memories made her feel ancient, as if feeling merely *old* wasn't bad enough. Her visitor had reminded her of things she'd rather not remember. Not now, at the end of her road, when memories only made you realize how close that road's end truly was.

"Did you watch *Grey's* last night?" Mary asked, changing the subject. The TV show, *Grey's Anatomy*, was an Elmswood staple, but Mary was too tired to stay up most nights to listen to it.

"No," Lucy said, "but I set the DVR, so I'll tell you what happened when I come in tomorrow."

"Don't leave me hanging," Mary said, "I don't think I can wait another day."

Lucy laughed. "I promise. Tonight is Carl's poker night, so it's just me, the cat, a pint of Cookies' n Cream, and *Grey's*."

"Sounds like the perfect evening," Mary said with a giant smile.

Once in her room, with Lucy gone, Mary's thoughts circled back to the man who came to visit.

His name was Stephen, a volunteer with the Reaching Out program, a local group whose mission was to match citizens wanting to do "quality community work" with old people in need of "good quality company." There was something about Stephen that reminded Mary of someone else, someone she'd avoided thinking about for years, though he'd never entirely left the frayed edges of her mind.

Mary avoided getting paired with volunteers whenever possible. During her first six months at Elmswood, she enjoyed a few visits from some kind folks, especially those with exceptional reading voices. During the past six months, though, the visits grew less frequent. It was as if the volunteers reaped whatever benefit they were hoping to mine from their good deed in reading to the blind, and then forgot all about her. Better to stick with the people she could count on being around. People like Lucy and her favorite nurse, Michael, a young, gay man who worked night shifts. Her favorite person, however, was probably Pat, the self-proclaimed "cranky, old battle axe" next door.

Pat, short for Patty, was a warhorse, destined to stick around forever, despite the heavy smoker's cough and junk diet she'd lived on for most of her life. Pat drove trucks when she was younger, had done a stint in the Navy, and had a vocabulary that would make a sailor blush. Mary imagined her as short and squat, though from what others said, Pat was actually a tall, thin woman. Even though Pat was easily Elmswood's crankiest denizen, Mary loved talking to her. She had a way of telling stories that made you laugh hysterically, even when they were ribald. *Especially* when they were ribald, actually. Pat would enjoy hearing about Stephen. But Mary didn't think she could start the story without talking about William.

~

THE DAY HAD STARTED with Mary sitting in the dining room, drinking tea and listening to the sound of rain slapping against the window. She never tired of the rain's music: calming, creatively inspiring, almost stirring. Second only to the ocean in sounds that could carry her away or lift her spirits. Mary was surprised when Pastor Vincent entered the dining hall and asked her if she was up to seeing a visitor, and was even more surprised when the man stepped forward and said, "Hi, ma'am," in the softest, most noble voice she'd heard in 40 years — so familiar, her heart nearly stilled in her chest.

It couldn't be him . . . Yet, he sounded so much like William.

"Hi, my name is Stephen Grant," he said, dashing any dreams that William had somehow defied time and space to visit her.

Perhaps he's related. A son, or grandson. That would mean he came back, though. Had lived.

"Hi," she said, reaching out to shake his hand. His fingers found hers, and a spark shot through her hand. She pulled back, surprised, slightly embarrassed.

"It's okay," Stephen said, "Happens all the time. I seem to be a walking static charge or something."

"Stephen is a big fan of your work. He's a writer, too." Pastor Vincent said, enthusiastically, as if trying to sell Mary on the qualities of her new friend. The pastor was always so eager for the residents to be paired with volunteers, as if it were his personal mission to make sure nobody was alone here.

"No," Stephen said, "I'm nowhere near the writer Mrs. Fletcher is. Just a hobbyist, really. Ma'am, your work is among the best I've ever had the privilege to read. *Cutter's Walk* is an absolute masterpiece."

"My heavens," Mary said, surprised. "That book hasn't been in print in decades."

"What can I say? I'm a huge fan," Stephen said. "I've read all your books."

"All of them?" Mary asked. "I'm sorry if I seem shocked, I'm just not used to hearing from male readers, particularly ones who sound so young."

"Anyone who says romance books are solely the

domain of women doesn't know the meaning of the word romance as far as I'm concerned," Stephen said. "As for age, well, I guess I'm blessed with good genes. Turned 40 last week, in fact. My mother, God rest her soul, introduced me to your work at an early age. Been a fan ever since."

"My, you don't sound a day over 25," Mary said, again surprised by this strange, young man.

"I hope you'll forgive me," Stephen said, "I read the article on you in the paper last week and just had to meet you. I'm sure you get that all the time, though."

"It's been a while, actually," Mary said, thoroughly enjoying the young man's slightly Southern, and all too familiar, lilt. "My fame these days is limited to the bridge club here and maybe a person or two who finds my books at a garage sale or second-hand store."

"I hope you'll both excuse me," Pastor Vincent said. "I have to make a phone call. Is that okay, Mrs. Fletcher?"

Mary knew this was the pastor's way of asking, *Is it okay to leave this stranger here with you?* Mary nodded, "Yes, thank you, Pastor Vincent."

The pastor left, and silence settled between Stephen and herself. These were the moments she dreaded most with visitors, these seconds of space with nothing to say. Yet, there was something about this man that piqued her interest. Something so *familiar*, even beyond the voice.

"Can I get a drink brought over for you?" Mary said, taking a sip from her glass of tea.

"No, no, that's okay," Stephen said, almost apologetic, "I don't want to pester you."

"You're not pestering me," Mary said, trying to divine meaning from the man's inflections. She was reasonably good at reading people. She was a writer after all, and her sharp instincts had sharpened even more so since she'd lost her sight. This man was special in some way; she could feel it as sure as she could feel the rain in her bones.

"So, you're a writer?" she asked.

"Yes, ma'am, though not yet formally published. Not sure my stuff is good enough, to be honest."

Mary felt an uncomfortable, old, familiar fear worming its way through her. Though it had been many years, could this man simply be looking to get his foot in the publishing door?

Back when she was a hot property, aspiring local writers tracked her down all the time, buttered her up, acted like they were her friend, only to hit her up with a request. *Can you tell me the secret to being published? Can you introduce me to so and so?* While she never minded helping people she genuinely connected with, far too many requests came from people feigning kindness, which had left her feeling guarded. Mary felt a lump in her throat and felt a twitch of regret about doing the newspaper interview the week before.

"Listen, son, I'm the last person in the world who can help you get published now. I'm sure all the agents and publishers I worked with are either retired or long since dead. Hell, I'm not even sure they make books anymore. Everything's on computers nowadays."

The man was quiet for a long, uncomfortable moment. Mary wasn't sure if the silence was borne of guilt or having taken offense to what she'd said.

"Ma'am, I'm so sorry if that's the impression I've given. I truly only wanted to meet you. As strange as it may seem, there were times I read your books that I felt like you were speaking right to me. I don't mean in a weird kind of way, but rather that we saw things alike, kindred spirits, and all that. But again, I'm sure you get that all the time."

Mary felt her cheeks flush, unable to take back what she'd said or judge the impact of her words.

"After I read the article, and how you lost your sight," Stephen said, "I thought it would be nice to read to you. After all, you provided my mother and me with so many countless hours of storytelling magic."

Mary's face grew warmer.

"I'm sorry, sir," she said, "It's been a long time since... well, since I've met anyone who really enjoyed my writing. I hope I've not offended you."

"You couldn't possibly offend me, Mary," he said. The lilt in his voice when he said *Mary* made her heart flutter. So familiar. So much like the way William had once spoken it.

Impossible.

The rain on the windows began to lighten its patter. A moment later, Mary heard Stephen rise.

"Again, I'm sorry about the confusion," he said, voice now rushed. "But I've got to get back to work. Would it be okay to visit you again soon? I'm not sure when it would be. I work odd hours and am on the road a lot, but I'd love to come by and read to you, if you'd have me."

Mary wanted to take back the past few minutes, rewind the moment, keep her foot outside of her mouth, and somehow get Stephen to stay a little longer. But there was urgency in his voice; he had to return to work, and she didn't want to hold him up.

"That would be lovely," she said, reaching out her hand, "Thank you again, Mr. Grant, for coming to visit."

"Thank *you*, Mrs. Fletcher," he said, hand shaking hers. No spark this time, just cool, soft hands. "I look forward to seeing you again."

With that, the odd, young man was gone. And Mary was alone.

· · ·

After Lucy left her alone in her room, she considered walking over to tell Pat about her visitor. But as much as she loved Pat, the woman was a huge gossip, and Mary had already received enough unwanted attention from the newspaper article. So, she kept her news to herself. Maybe she'd tell Pat after Stephen visited again ... if he visited again.

She thought of William more and more as the day went on, and even dreamed of him when she fell asleep. She woke in the middle of the night and thought about waking to tell Pat. Chances were good the woman was up watching the late-night talk shows. She really wanted to share the story with Pat, but wasn't sure what she'd say. That a ghost visited her?

No.

She'd wait until morning.

And then she'd tell Pat.

But when Mary woke the next morning, Pat was dead.

The two weeks following Pat's heart attack were tough ones for Mary.

Grim silence draped the nursing home. Mary wasn't sure if the silence was from the lack of Pat's colorful personality or if the other residents were reassessing their own mortality. In the past year, five residents had died. Given that the nursing home was an age-in-place facility that housed everyone from the healthy who just needed a bit of assistance, to those who required more frequent care, to those who were at death's door, five deaths didn't seem like a lot. Still, when it was one of your own who passed, especially someone as full of life as Pat, you couldn't help but feel like you were a bad week, or less, away from death's door yourself. People like Pat gave the others hope. If someone who smoked, ate junk food, and lived life on the edge was still kicking life's ass, then surely the more cautious residents of Elmswood had a few good years left.

That was the hope, anyway. And when someone like Pat went, hope went with her.

Mary was no stranger to death. Her husband, Johnny, died when he was 55. Her first and only child, Christina, died during childbirth. The kinds of deaths you never really got over; the kind that prepare you for your own. When it came to friends, death wasn't a shock so much as a sad reminder that nobody gets out alive.

"What are you thinking about?" Lucy asked, taking a seat across from Mary while she nibbled on her lunch. "That young man?"

"No," Mary said, lying. She *had* been thinking about him, but not really him, but rather the man he reminded her of . . . William, the One Who Got Away.

Before Stephen's visit, it had been a while since she'd thought of William. And even now, that Johnny had been gone so long, she still felt pangs of guilt. Johnny had been a good man and terrific husband, whose only sin was not being William, the boy Mary had grown up alongside and spent much of her life's first 20 years with. The boy Mary loved, who had gone to Vietnam and never returned.

And if he had died, it was partly her fault.

It was July 1969 when she and William were sitting in his living room, watching TV. His mother had passed away two years prior, and his father was working late, so they had the house to themselves, as they did most of the evenings that summer. Though they were dating, they had never gone all the way, so most evenings were spent in front of the TV, stewing in hormones.

On July 1, though, *Mayberry RFD* was replaced by a live airing of the military draft. They watched as birth dates were chosen and assigned numbers. William was 9th, making his getting drafted into the Vietnam War as certain as summer.

He stared at the TV, eyes watering. "I can't believe it."

Mary stared, shocked. She'd never seen him cry, not even at his own mother's funeral, though she suspected he'd cried that night after she went home. He was a pretty tough kid as long as she'd known him. And yet, the draft announcement left him looking like a lost child.

"Maybe you won't get drafted," she said, part of her naive enough to believe it.

"I'm number nine! You really think the war's gonna be over before they get to me? This damned thing is gonna last forever. Politicians don't care. It's not them fighting."

He could have ranted for longer, but it was nothing he — or she — hadn't said a hundred times already. Maybe that's why he let it go. Or maybe it was shock. Though neither of them was very political, it was hard not to have an opinion on the war in those days. William had grown increasingly opposed to it in recent months. He was just out of high school and couldn't afford college. And didn't have a rich daddy to keep him out of the jungle. After the lottery, he felt as if his fate were sealed.

Mary had gone to him and hugged him deeply, whispering that everything would be okay.

One thing quickly led to another, and then swiftly to bed. She wasn't sure why she'd relented that night. If she felt bad because he might be leaving for war, or if suddenly she realized, for the first time really, that though they were young, death could still claim them.

The next night, William picked her up and took her to the Cave, a dark, romantic restaurant she'd heard so much about, but never thought she'd see the inside of. It was the kind of place with real silver and soft linens, not exactly in their budget. It felt like a palace, with everyone in royal clothes. She felt plain in comparison, her floral print dress, right off the rack. She remembered pressing the dress with her palms, as if doing so would make it seem nicer or less obviously cheap. William was handsome in his jeans and tucked-in tee. Inexpensive, but sharp.

After dinner, he asked the waiter to bring a bottle of wine. Mary had never had a sip of alcohol, but the special occasion made it okay. The waiter poured the wine and turned to leave, but William pulled him back, then turned his face to the side and whispered. Mary knew *something* was about to happen a second before it did.

The violin player, who had been strolling the tables playing for other couples, came over, playing a beautiful song Mary recognized but couldn't place. Then William dropped to his knee, took her right hand with his left, and reached into his pants pocket. Then he pulled out a box. She knew what it was immediately, by the shape of it. This was no ordinary box. She knew it housed an engagement ring.

Mary's heart pounded. For a moment, she thought she might pass out. "William!"

"Mary," he said, tears in his eyes.

"I wanted to wait another year, until I was sure we could afford it. But with last night's lottery, a year might mean never. So I want to ask you now, while I still have time. Will you marry me?"

Tears slathered her face. Without a thought, she said,

"Yes!" He slid the ring on her finger. They hugged and kissed. Other diners applauded.

Mary guessed the Cave was the sort of place used to surprise engagements, yet the staff still treated them like they were the most important people in the room, showering them with attention and making Mary feel like a princess, if only for a day.

She was on cloud nine.

Later that night, they sat on the beach, watching the waves crash and retreat.

"I'm not gonna go if they call me," he said, as if they'd been discussing it all night and Mary would know just where to jump in.

"What are you talking about?"

"If I get drafted, I'm not going. We can go to Canada! Remember Bobby Jenkins? He took off, and I hear from his sister that's where he went."

"Be a fugitive? What about your dad? Won't you miss him?"

"*He* suggested it. When *my dad* is against the war, you know that something's not right."

"I don't know," Mary said, shaking her head, "I can't just leave my family behind. I'd miss them too much."

"We'll start a new family. We'll settle down, have two kids, get the white-picket fence, the whole deal."

"We don't even know anyone in Canada. How are we just gonna pack up, get you a job, get a house, and start over? You make it sound like all we need to do is show up, and we're set, like Canada has free homes and easy jobs to anyone burning their draft card!"

"I don't know how we'll get by, but I always find a way. You know that about me, Mary. If there's a way, I'll find it. We'll find it together."

The look in his eyes was so hopeful; she almost believed

him, that anything really was possible, if only they'd take the chance. But Mary was practical. She needed security, to know everything would be okay. Being a fugitive and starting a family in a foreign land without a single familiar face was exactly one country from secure. And just like that, their future, so unbelievably amazing just moments earlier, was doused by uncertainty.

William spent the next few days trying to convince her to go with him, but she wouldn't budge. Finally, Mary handed William his ring and did the hardest thing she'd ever done.

She said no.

"What if I stay?" William asked. "What if I wait for them to draft me, and then I go. Will you wait for me, then?"

"I don't want you going and getting shot on my account. I want you to be safe. Go to Canada."

"If I can't be with you, it doesn't matter where I go," William said. "Or whether I live or die."

She was shocked, uncomfortable even, though she wasn't sure why. William had always been a good friend and a doting boyfriend in the few months they'd been dating. But hearing someone say they'd rather die than be without you was melodrama to Mary. Of course, she wasn't facing the threat of fighting in a war. A war that was killing people their age every day.

"You would rather go off to 'Nam than lose me?"

"I would rather die than lose you," he said, on the verge of tears.

"Stop it, William."

"Stop what?"

"Don't talk like that, it's. . ."

"What, Mary? I want to be with you forever. Yes, I wanted to wait until we had enough money for a house and all before I asked, but ... this is it. Please, say you'll be with me. That you'll wait for me to come home."

"I can't wait," she said, lip quivering, first tear about to fall. "I don't want to be the reason you die. I can't live with that guilt."

"I won't die," he said, "I promise." He laughed, like he was joking, to break the tension. But Mary felt like a part of him actually believed the promise he was making, as if he could somehow avoid death even if others couldn't. He wasn't thinking clearly. He was thinking only of her, being with her, and not the reality at stake. She couldn't let him do it.

So Mary handed him the ring back.

"I love you, and I hope you will return and give me this ring under better circumstances. But I can't take it now. Not like this."

William wept openly while Mary imprisoned her tears behind dry eyes. She had to be strong enough for both of them, be the one to say no.

That was the last time she ever saw him. Two days later, his mom called and said he'd decided not to wait. He was going to Vietnam. A year and four days later, his mother called and said his entire unit was ambushed and believed dead.

Mary would never forget the look in William's eyes when she took the ring off and placed it in his palm, closing his fingers around it. It was the look of someone who'd lost everything that meant anything, and had surrendered any belief that they could ever get it back.

ON WEDNESDAY, the rain returned. But so did Stephen.

"Hello, Mrs. Fletcher," he said, after Pastor Vincent informed Mary of her visitor.

She couldn't hide the smile, but hoped her relief at his return wasn't as electric as it felt. "Hello, Stephen. How are you today?"

"Good," he said, his voice sounding tired. "I wasn't sure what books you wanted me to read, so I brought a few."

"I have a better idea," she said. "I can get anyone to read to me. But it's not often I'm visited by a fellow author. Why don't you tell me one of *your stories*?"

"Oh gosh, ma'am. I'd just embarrass myself. Besides, I have a horrible memory for my own stuff."

"Don't be so hard on yourself. I never liked my own stuff, either. Apparently, at least a few people disagreed. I think writers are usually their own worst critics."

"Perhaps so, Mary."

She paused at the sound of her first name again. The voice, so much like William's, if just a bit older. Though it certainly wasn't as old as William's would be, were he still alive, which seemed less likely than Elvis and JFK both kicking back together, drinking margaritas on a secret island.

"What's wrong?" Stephen asked.

"Nothing, you just remind me of someone."

"Who?" Stephen said. Then, after a long pause, "If you don't mind telling me."

"Someone I used to know. A long time ago."

"Lucky man, he must've been."

Mary smiled uncomfortably. There's no way he could be flirting with me, right? That's just too weird.

"Why's that?" she asked, pulling her sweater across her chest. While the rain pounded against the windows and roof, the air seemed to drop 10 degrees.

"You have a striking face," Stephen said. "In fact, you still look as beautiful as your book jackets, ma'am."

She blinked. "Thank you, Stephen, you're kind to say so, but I'm the blind one here, right?" She laughed, trying to interject humor into her discomfort. But he didn't respond in kind.

"Do you mind if I ask you a personal question?" Stephen asked.

Mary hesitated, then shrugged. "Go on."

"The newspaper article said you'd gone blind, but didn't say when."

Mary pursed her lips, feeling exposed, and wrapped her sweater tighter. "A year and a half ago. It's why I came here. My sister was caring for her husband at the time, and I didn't want to be an added burden."

"I'm so sorry," he said, as though he were somehow responsible.

"Don't be, that's life," she said, forcing a smile. "We live, then we die."

Stephen paused, as if chewing on the thought.

When he finally spoke, he said, "What if it didn't have to be that way?"

"What do you mean?"

"What if we didn't have to die? What if we could live *forever*?" Stephen's voice had lowered to a breath above a whisper.

Oh my God, he's crazy. Or religious. Or crazy religious!

"What are you talking about?" Mary asked, half wanting to get up and leave, tell the pastor she didn't want any more visits ever again, but half curious at what this man who sounded so much like William had to say.

"Hypothetically," Stephen said, "If you could live forever, would you?"

"Would I be this age? Or could I live forever, looking and feeling like I did when I was 25?"

"Any age you choose," Stephen said. "Would you, if you could?"

Mary wasn't sure where Stephen was going with this. "I don't know. Maybe," she said. "Would I be the only one? Or would there be others?"

Stephen paused. Mary was certain she heard him swallow before he continued. "You could bring along anyone you wanted to."

"Then I suppose, I would say yes," Mary said, thinking not of her husband, but rather her long-lost soul mate.

"This person I remind you of," Stephen said, steering the conversation back to the choppy waters Mary had wished to avoid. "Did you love him?"

She stared straight ahead at Stephen, even though she couldn't see him. "It doesn't matter."

"Why would you say that?" Stephen asked.

Mary couldn't shake the surreal sensation that she wasn't talking to Stephen, but somehow to William, across space and time, or perhaps through some spiritual proxy.

"Because I broke his heart," Mary said, her voice trembling. "I didn't even get a chance to say goodbye to him. And a year later, his parents were informed that their son was missing in action. Soon after, I met Johnny. We were married three months later."

Stephen was quiet for a long time. So quiet, Mary thought maybe he'd gotten up to leave, or had fallen asleep. Finally, he spoke.

"You should have written *that* story," he said.

Mary laughed, wiping her tears. "Some stories are better left untold."

"I respectfully disagree," Stephen said. She heard his chair shift. He must have gotten up. "I need to get going.

Thank you for sharing that story with me, Mary. May I visit you again soon?"

He sounded as if he were in a hurry. Mary wasn't sure if it was in reaction to her story or if he suddenly had to get back to work again. She wanted to ask him to stay a bit longer, to be sure there was no weirdness between them. "Only if you bring one of your stories," she said.

He laughed, "I'll bring one, but I can't promise you'll enjoy it."

She reached out to shake his hand, and again, that spark.

"Sorry," he said. After he left, Mary noticed that the rain outside had stopped. And for some reason, that made her sad.

FOR THE NEXT MONTH, Mary spent every morning in the dining hall, hoping Stephen would show. But he never returned. Nor did the rain. Her headaches grew worse, but she didn't want to tell the doctors. No more tests, or treatments, or the radiation sickness that followed. If it was her time, it was her time. She just hoped she wouldn't pass before Stephen visited again. In his absence, he haunted the halls of her mind. And in doing so, William haunted her heart, something she finally realized (or admitted to herself) he'd never really stopped doing.

As unlikely and impossible as it seemed, there was a connection between her and Stephen. She felt it like hair on her skin. And the root of that connection was somehow William. Was he a relative of William's? If so, what could she tell him about William? Perhaps her love had left a message for her to be delivered by his son, grandson, or whoever he was. That was the most plausible answer.

She wished she'd summoned the courage to ask why he'd really come to her. Despite his intentions, he'd actually not read aloud to her yet. No, there was something more. And the next time she saw him, she was going to ask. But as the endless days slowly crawled by, Mary began to wonder if she'd ever get the chance.

SUMMER WAS BRUTAL TO ELMSWOOD; the heat wave baking the Midwest became the nursing home's #1 topic.

"I hope this AC doesn't go out again," Lucy said on one particularly July afternoon, as the noontime temperature spiked to 106. "The people who built this place didn't install nearly enough AC units."

Mary didn't have the energy to respond.

So Lucy continued." Two years ago, the AC went out in the middle of July. Want to talk about some miserable residents! If it goes out this year, I'm goin' home. And I'll take you with me. You wanna come with me, Mrs. Fletcher?"

Mary had drifted off, thinking of Stephen. Wondering how he was faring in the heat. But when she heard her name, she jolted back to the present. "What was that?" "Ah... you're thinking about that young fellow again, ain't you?"

"Don't be ridiculous," Mary said. After a long pause, she found herself smiling, "Okay, maybe."

Lucy laughed a hearty, infectious laugh. "Oh, Mary's got herself a young one."

"Don't be silly," Mary said. "He's far too young. And hell, if I don't feel older than dust."

"Hey, you're never too old for love."

"I am," Mary said. "I barely have enough energy to listen to the TV."

"Yes, but you *can* use your imagination. You think I'm always dreaming about Big Carl? Not when I can think about McSteamy."

Mary laughed. "I don't even know what Stephen looks like, so I'm not sure how I'd imagine him."

"He's cute," Lucy said. "Tall, looks like he's in his early 30s, though he's got these beautiful, blue eyes that seem so much . . ."

"Older?" Mary asked.

"Wiser," Lucy said. "And he's got thick, dark, straight hair. Like an artist, or something."

"What else?" Mary asked.

Lucy laughed, nudged her. "Aw, you *are interested* . . . Well, let's see . . . he's got a fitbody. Nice butt. And that scar."

"Scar?" Mary asked.

"Yeah, right over and under his right eye. Weirdest thing, you'd think he would've lost an eye with a scar like that, but his eye is right there in the socket where it belongs."

Mary froze. William had a scar just like that. He'd gotten it in his one and only bar fight when he was 17. He almost *did* lose an eye, but he got lucky, doctors said.

"You okay, Mrs. Fletcher?"

"Yeah," Mary said, "Just a little headache."

The AC didn't go out. But that didn't mean it wasn't hot. And her room, facing east, had baked in the sun all day. So she got up and took a shower. Letting the cold water flow over her. Then she heard a strange ringing sound.

Like the doorbell on her house when she was a child.

But there was nothing at Elmswood that—

Mary's head hurt.

Someone was saying her name.

She opened her eyes. But she couldn't see. Why couldn't she see?

"It's all right, Mrs Fletcher. I'm here."

It took her a moment to place the voice. Michael.

"Where am I? Why can't I see?"

She heard his voice hitch. "You fainted in the shower. Hit your head. The ambulance is on its way. And—"

Mary gripped his hand. And remembered. She couldn't see because she was blind. "It's all right, Michael," she said. "I remember."

And then the pain in her body took over. And that was the last she remembered—

THE DOCTORS OPERATED. To relieve the swelling, they told her. Scans of her skull showed significant tumor growth since her last visit to the specialist. Given Mary's age, the aggressiveness of the tumor, and her condition, another operation was off the table. Death had grown impatient and would be knocking in days or even hours, rather than the months he'd promised.

She'd be going home — or back to Elmswood — which was somewhat of a relief.

On her third night in the hospital, she woke to a familiar voice.

"MARY, CAN YOU HEAR ME?"

"William?"

She almost heard him smile. If such a thing were possible. "I'll see you soon."

The voice disappeared, and Mary heard the rattle of a window frame followed by an eerie stillness punctuated only by the steady beeping of a machine. Footsteps sounded next to her.

"William!"

"Just me, Mrs Fletcher." It was the nurse. Here to check her vitals. "How's the pain?"

"Terrible," Mary said. But she wasn't talking about her body. It was her heart that felt like it was breaking.

～

FOUR WEEKS LATER, Mary sat in her familiar spot in the dining room, listening to rain trickle down the windows. Soft music played over the speakers. Today was the day, she somehow knew, that Stephen would return. And soon. She felt it in her gut, irrationally certain.

A little bit past 10 a.m., Pastor Vincent appeared. "Mrs. Fletcher, you have a visitor."

The pastor left them to talk, and Mary heard the chair across from her slide across the carpet.

"Hello, ma'am."

She smiled. "Hello, Stephen. I was starting to think I might not hear your voice again."

"I came by a couple of weeks ago, but they told me you were in the hospital. How are you doing?"

"Better from my fall. But there's a tumor in my brain, and it's gotten worse. They're not sure how long I've got."

"I'm sorry to hear that, Mary."

"Tell me," Mary said, working up the courage to say what needed to be said, "Why did you lie to me?"

"Excuse me?"

"You visited me in the hospital, didn't you?"

Silence from Stephen.

"You were there?"

More silence.

"Maybe you were just dreaming," he said.

"No, you were there. You somehow saved me."

Silence.

Her heart slowed to a painful patter, waiting for his response. Words, a sigh, anything.

"You're right."

She exhaled, tears welling in her eyes.

"How?" she asked.

"I'm not even sure I can explain that without explaining much more."

"I'm not going anywhere," Mary said. "Well, unless Death comes calling tonight."

"I'm not sure how long I have either," Stephen said, "Once the rain stops, I have to go."

"What?" Mary said, confused.

"How long do the doctors say you have?" he asked, ignoring her question.

"Weeks. Maybe days. Though, to be fair, they thought I'd be dead a year ago, before it went into remission."

"I've put this off long enough, I suppose," Stephen said. "If I'm gonna work up the courage, I need to do this now. But you must promise me you won't react to what I'm about to do."

"What do you mean?" Mary asked nervously.

"I'm going to touch your face," Stephen said. "And when I do, something will happen, and you must promise not to react. Promise?"

Curiosity overruled fear. "Yes."

A moment later, his hands found her face. She pulled back, surprised by their warmth. His fingers splayed across her cheeks, and the warmth spread into her eyes, her skull, then down her spine and through her entire body. She felt like she was slowly dipping into the world's most perfectly warm bath. Light bled through the darkness. Her heart raced, and the pitch black of the past year was eaten by brightness.

Something... a shape was forming in front of her.

She could see . . . something!

Warmth continued to roll through her body, waking nerves and muscles long ago numbed by age. She opened her mouth, stifling a cry of sudden, overwhelming joy.

The face before her swam into focus. And she saw him . . . *William!*

Her eyes widened, her heart skipped a beat, and new, different tears began to flow.

"William?"

He smiled. "Mary."

"But . . . how? You're not dead? You're not a day over 30!"

"Shh," he said, removing his hands from her face, holding a finger to his lips. "Don't alert the others."

She turned, and though her vision was still blurred, she saw Elmwood's dining room for the first time, along with her fellow residents and nurses. But something was wrong. They were all still, as if someone had pressed pause on reality.

She looked at William, "What's happening?"

"There's too much to explain right now, and I can't hold them like this forever. When I release them, you'll need to pretend you're blind, okay?"

She nodded her head.

He closed his eyes. A moment later, everyone became unstuck, going about their routines. Only when the sound of reanimated life met her ears did she notice the silence they'd been enveloped in just seconds before.

"How?" she asked, meaning a million things at once.

William looked outside. The rain was still falling.

"You remember the last time I was here, and I asked if you'd like to live forever? I wasn't being hypothetical."

She stared, logic and confusion battling in her brain.

"What do you mean?"

"All you have to do is say yes, and I can take you away from here. I can make you young again, healthy again. I can get rid of the tumor. What you're feeling now, you can feel every day. But only if you let me help you. Otherwise, you will continue to age. Your blindness will return."

"How?" she asked. "What ... *are you?*" The words fell out rougher than she'd intended, but the meaning was there. Whatever William was, he wasn't human. No human could do what he'd done, or live forever without seeming to age.

He smiled, as if she'd asked the one question he didn't want to answer, but knew he must, if he intended to convince her.

"Going to 'Nam was the hardest thing I ever did. I was caught and caged, no different than an animal. For two years, they tortured me, day in, day out. And Mary, you were the only thing that kept me alive, the thought that I might someday hold you again."

Mary's heart crumbled.

"I thought I would be trapped forever, until one night when everything changed. Gunfire erupted around us as something tore into the village and massacred the soldiers in seconds. It looked like a man, but it was no man I'd ever seen. It was taller, stronger, with sharp teeth and claws. Eyes dark and cold, soulless. It was a monster, hungry for blood. But when it saw me in the cage, its eyes changed. They were filled with the sort of pity you'd see on someone coming up to an injured dog. The creature opened the cage and set me free."

Mary was shaking as the air grew colder. Outside, the rain softened to a drizzle against the windows.

"It didn't say a word, and I was certain it would kill me. That's when I noticed it was staring at my stomach. I looked down to see I'd been shot in all the confusion. I didn't feel it until I saw the blood, but as soon as I did, I collapsed, blacking out. When I woke up, I was deep in the forest in a dugout hollow, protected from the sun. And I'd been changed."

"Changed?" Mary asked, pieces of the puzzle sliding to form an impossible picture.

"I'm a vampire, Mary."

She let out a laugh, a loud blurt that caught the attention of everyone in the dining room. She looked around, seeing them not as friends, but strangers. She closed her eyes and turned back to William before opening them again.

"I'm sorry, a *what?*" she said.

But he wasn't smiling. His eyes were all business. No different than the day he pleaded with her to marry him. She stared, speechless. Unable to believe, yet unable to reject the reality of his youthful appearance or that he'd cured her blindness.

Could he also cure her tumor? She'd lived with the knowledge of impending death for so long that she could hardly imagine escaping its certainty.

"I'm not joking, Mary. That vampire saved me. It stayed with me, helped me survive like a mother bird teaching its chick to fly and feed. And even though it saved me, I was also cursed. I could never live a normal life again. It took me forever to get back to the States, but when I did, I saw you were married. You seemed so happy. I didn't want to . . ."

"Wait... you came back? You saw me?!" she asked. "Why didn't you contact me?"

"Because it wouldn't have mattered. I couldn't give you a life like John did. As far as the world was concerned, William was dead. I couldn't show up out of the blue. Too many questions to answer. If the authorities found out, well, I'd be caged again. You wouldn't have been able to lead a normal life, even if you left John. I've had to live in the shadows, unable to do the things others can. I can't go out in full daylight, have a job, go to a doctor... have a family."

The rain outside was hinting its farewell. William's eyes widened. "I have to go before the sun comes out again. I want you to come with me tonight. I'll take all your pain away. We can live forever. It's the chance we never had. I need an answer, Mary. Please ... come with me."

Of the million questions in her mind, only one made it to her mouth. "How do you survive? Do you ... kill people?"

He stared.

His silence was an awful confirmation.

"No," she said, shaking her head, voice tight. "No, I can't, William."

He looked as if he wanted to launch a thousand arguments, but the sun threatened to bleach the gray outside.

"Think about it," he said. "I'll be back tonight."

She wanted to ask how he'd get past the night staff, but he was already headed toward the front of the nursing home. Mary turned to the window, watching the sun peek through the clouds with a new perspective and a new fear.

～

MARY SPENT the rest of the day thinking about William's proposition, while absorbing the sights of the nursing home for the first time. She felt like a voyeur, faking blindness, but what could she say? Truth wasn't an option. Nobody would believe her, and even if they did, she didn't want to endanger William. Nor did she want to be subjected to a bunch of tests as doctors tried to figure out how her sight returned. They might chalk it up to the tumor. Or maybe a miracle.

She wanted to keep this gift from William for herself. Besides, if she were sent back to the hospital for testing, William might not be able to find her.

She ran through events in her head, even though she'd not really considered the option of going with him. She could not live at the expense of killing others. Mary was not a religious woman, but she was moralistic, and "do unto others"was high on her list of rules. She was always a "live and let live" kind of person and would never inflict harm on another, even if it meant risking immortality with the love of her life.

So, she spent the day waiting, in quiet observation of the world around her. Matching voices she'd known to faces she'd only imagined. She was surprised by how closely she had come to reality. The only person who really surprised her was Lucy. While she'd sounded like an older, larger, heavier black woman, she was surprisingly youthful looking, and rather slender, with the prettiest shade of golden eyes Mary had ever seen. At one point during the day, Lucy caught Mary looking at her and gave her a suspicious look, almost as if she were wondering if Mary was feigning blindness. Mary continued to stare straight ahead, though, as if looking in Lucy's direction, rather than *at* her.

Mary had one other surprise on the night shift.

Michael was nowhere near as slight as his voice sounded. He was rather tall, chubby, and unkempt. *Central casting missed the boat on this one.* At 9 p.m., Michael brought Mary her nighttime meds and his usual small talk. When he left, she turned the TV sound back up, watching, instead of just listening, to an old rerun of *Seinfeld*. Seeing the old, familiar faces on TV provided a comfort that surprised her.

Mary also watched the window. The nursing home was only one floor, so it wouldn't be difficult for William to get into her room. However, as much as she was looking forward to seeing him again, she was worried that this would be the last time they'd talk. After all, once she said no, there would be no reason for him to return. And then her cancer would worsen, and soon she would be dead. The offer he gave her now was similar to the ultimatum he'd given her four decades earlier. Except, this time, he wasn't just asking her to run away with him, but to kill with him, too.

She fell asleep wondering if he would show.

"MARY?" William whispered, waking her from a weird dream in which she was young again, and William returned from the war, a decorated hero. He asked her to leave Johnny and run off to Canada with her.

And she had said yes.

"Have you decided?" he asked, sitting in the chair next to her bed.

She looked up at him; his skin seemed even younger tonight, glowing almost blue in the moonlight that bathed her room. He was as beautiful as he'd ever been. Which made her response all the harder to give.

"I can't kill people, William. Not to stay alive. I'm sorry, but I couldn't live with myself."

"You can feed from those I kill. I can't drink a full body's blood by myself anyway, and it's not as if I can store them in a walk-in cooler."

She stared, unable to mask her repulsion.

"How can you treat murder with such indifference, William? You're killing people so you can live. Maybe you can justify that because you weren't given a choice. Something turned you, and you do what you have to in order tosurvive. But if I choose this ... then I'm *choosing* to murder others to prolong my own life."

"We're *all* animals, Mary, feeding from one another in some way. No different than the beasts we consider beneath us."

She shook her head, "What happened to make you so jaded?"

William's eyes met hers, almost apologetically. "I'm only trying to show you the truth. It was tough for me at first. But you learn to adapt. And if it makes any difference, I only feed on bad people."

"*Bad* people?" she asked.

"Yeah, criminals, abusive men, people who are better removed from society."

"So, you're some kind of *hero*, you think?"

William looked wounded. "No, I'm just me, what's left of the man you once knew ... the man you once loved. Trying to do whatever it takes to survive. But if you want to know the real truth, I'm tired, Mary. Tired of killing. Tired of living. Tired of being alone. It had been a long time since I'd thought of you. I read your books when they came out and even considered visiting when Johnny passed, but something told me no, it was too late."

His eyes stayed fixed on hers, as if they held a more direct, honest communication.

"I was going to stay away. But then, when I saw that newspaper article about you, read that you were blind, had battled cancer, and were ... here ... well, I couldn't live with myself if I didn't come see you. I'd always wondered what would have happened had you said yes, and we ran off to Canada, and got married. I mourn that life as if I had lived it. I mourn it every day."

He bent, tears streaming down his cheeks, and fell beside her on the bed, burying his head in her chest.

She was surprised at this sudden expression. She held him tight, running her hands through his thick, dark hair. Her heart raced, passion stirring in her for the first time in a decade. He pulled up, met her eyes, then leaned down and kissed her. Softly at first, his hands caressing her face.

I've missed you so much.

"Come with me," he said, pulling back. "Let's live the life that we *should have* lived."

She was frozen. Her heart and body wanted to say yes. The idea of being young again, living forever with the only man she honestly loved, was so enticing that it was practically the stuff of dreams. A dream you'd wish a thousand lifetimes to come true. Yet, the cold reality was something she couldn't reconcile. To lose your humanity, to become a monster. To murder ... these were things she could never do.

"I'm sorry," Mary said, "I can't."

"I can't live without you, Mary."

"I'm sorry, William. I wish I could take back the past. I've wished a million times that things happened differently. My whole life has been one of regrets. But it was *my life* to live. And I lived with my choices. As much as I'd love a second chance, I won't have it at the expense of others.

You say these people you kill are bad, but what of their loved ones? You're killing someone's father, child, mother, lover. You're destroying the lives you take, *and* the countless ones connected. You might be able to justify that to yourself, but I don't see how I can."

William stared at her as if holding something back. Then she heard Michael in the hallway, approaching her room. Panic coursed through Mary. But when the door opened, William was gone in a flash, out the window.

"You okay?" Michael asked, "I thought I heard voices."

"Just the TV," Mary said, picking up the remote and clicking the TV off. She rolled over and closed her eyes before Michael could ask another question. Her eyes weren't really closed, but rather, watching the window and the night beyond.

TWO WEEKS HAD PASSED since she rejected William a second time.

Mary's health deteriorated quickly. Her headaches grew worse. She was nauseous more days than not, and barely had an appetite. She knew it wouldn't be long before death came for her. Perhaps the worst part of her deterioration was that she was going blind again. Not gone completely; she could still see a bit when she was close enough to something. But even those shadows would disappear soon. It was as if William had never come back.

They moved her to the hospice wing of the nursing home, and she spent most days in bed, listening to the TV. Lucy came by on occasion, but Lucy wasn't the hospice nurse; Inga was. Inga was new, with a thick Eastern accent that Mary couldn't understand well, and was nowhere nearly as friendly as Lucy. Mary had never felt more alone.

Oddly, she found herself wanting to write. Ideas for stories were coming to her for the first time in more than a decade. If she thought she might live to finish one, she might have even started writing a story. If Lucy had been her nurse, she might have even been able to ask her to transcribe it for her. But Inga wasn't Lucy.

EVERY NIGHT, Mary found herself watching the window, waiting for William to return. As pain and death drew nearer, she found her decision harder to bear. She began to wonder if she'd made a mistake. *Another mistake.* With that doubt came the creeping fear that she wouldn't be strong enough to resist William's offer should he visit again.

Would you like me to take the pain away? The offer was tempting enough before. Now, the offer would be almost impossible to resist, because she hurt all the time. During the worst of it one night, she prayed to God that death would find her before William, so she'd not have to make the decision. She couldn't trust herself in this weakened state.

She cried herself to sleep most nights, anguishing over the life she'd lost and the life she would never have. On the night when the pain was at its worst, she broke down and prayed again for God to kill her. This time, she said the prayer out loud, just in case He couldn't hear her silent pleas. She stared out the window at the moon beyond, mocking her with its beauty. How dare the world go on as she was reduced to a shell of herself? She whispered with all her strength, "Please, let me go."

And then William appeared in the window. Her eyes widened. She thought she might cry, but she had no more tears.

He opened the window, climbed inside, stepped toward

the bed, and looked down at her. Something looked off. He appeared . . . *older*.

"What happened to you?" she asked.

"I'm not feeding anymore. So I'm aging quickly."

"Why?" she asked, genuinely confused.

"If you're going to die, I want to die with you."

He crossed the room and closed her bedroom door.

"Will they be checking on you again tonight?"

She shook her head.

"Good," William climbed into bed next to her and wrapped his arms around her. "I wish to God I'd never let you go, Mary. I should have come home to you sooner."

Then he removed something from his shirt pocket and took her hand softly in his, sliding it on her finger. A ring ... no, The Ring.

Of that, there was no mistake. This was the ring he'd tried to give her four decades earlier. A simple ring, gold with a small diamond; the most beautiful ring she'd ever seen.

"Oh God," she said. She held it close to her face, then found him staring at her with a smile, the sweetest, most caring smile she'd ever known. A smile she could spend an eternity looking at. "You kept it all these years."

"It wasn't mine to keep. It belongs to you."

She closed her eyes. She was wrong. There *were* more tears left.

"You know, I wasn't lying when I said I was a writer," he said softly in her ear. "I wrote a story in hopes of someday giving it to you. May I tell it to you?"

"I would like that," she said.

~

WILLIAM WASN'T sure if Mary heard the end of his story before she died. He supposed it didn't matter. The ending wasn't exactly happy.

But he held her tight the rest of the night, refusing to let her go. He couldn't protect her from death or bring her back. Nor could he go back in time and undo what had been done. Time waited for neither man, nor woman ... nor monster.

But he could hold on, if only a little bit longer.

The sun rose, its glow bleeding through the window. And still he held onto her.

Their hands locked together, even as he burst into flame. The diamond in her ring glinted bright in the fire.

~

AFTERSHOCKS on The Visitor

THE VISITOR WAS one of the first short stories Dave ever submitted, back when we were trying to keep the release engine fed between seasons of *Yesterday's Gone,* one Tuesday drop at a time, like logs on a fire we couldn't let die. Back then, same as now, it was content or cremation.

We needed six shorts. We each wrote three. *Respero Dinner* was the most emotionally gripping from my collection, but if *Respero* bled, *The Visitor* left fingerprints on your pulse.

Dave came at vampirism from an angle I'd never seen before. Not the seduction or the hunger or the eternal struggle between light and dark. But the aftermath. The forever when the person you'd die for has already lived their life without you. Infinity minus one still equals heartbreak.

What happens when immortality becomes a prison sentence? When the gift of endless time is really just endless waiting?

William didn't choose to become a monster. He chose to survive long enough to find his way back to Mary. Forty years too late and a universe too changed. By the time he could offer her eternity, she'd earned a PhD in letting go, with a thesis written in tears.

The nursing home becomes a perfect crucible for this kind of slow-burning heartbreak. A place where time moves differently, where yesterday and today blur together, where love gets rationed like medication: one small dose at visiting hours.

Mary's blindness is emotional and spiritual in addition to physical. She can't see the life she could have, only the lives she'd have to take to get there. The fangs aren't in William's mouth. They're in his choices. Not whether she'll choose immortality, but whether love is worth compromising your soul.

Dave understood something profound about time and regret. How the roads not taken leave the deepest tire tracks on your heart. How sometimes the greatest act of love is knowing when to let someone go.

The Visitor asks the question every vampire story skips: What if the real curse isn't living forever, but remembering what it felt like to be human?

Some love stories end with *happily ever after*. Others end with *what if*. This one ends with both hands reaching across four decades of darkness, finally touching just as the sun rises.

Perfect timing has always been overrated anyway.

TEN

Human Pyramid

Senator Quincy Monroe stood in front of his hotel room mirror, staring at the silver strands that now threaded through his once jet-black hair. Like moonbeams at midnight. God. When had he become so poetic?

He leaned forward, fingertips grazing the cool glass, studying the deepening lines carved in his face. He looked so much harder. Like he was made of concrete. The stress and strain of public office were working overtime to kill him. He didn't know a single person who aged out of politics looking younger than when they went in. It simply wasn't possible.

Of course, Quincy considered clinging to the vestiges of youth and dyeing the age out of his hair. But Sammie convinced him otherwise. "The silver makes you look distinguished," she said. "Like a man of experience and wisdom."

He wasn't sure if his most trusted aide was correct about the wisdom part. But his experience came in spades. Too bad most of his lived life had left him feeling more jaded than fulfilled.

His phone chirped, and he glanced at the screen.

Three missed calls from Caitlyn and seventeen unread texts from Lucas. His jaw tightened, a dull throb pulsing behind his eyes.

He couldn't deal with his wife and son at the moment. Not when he was already teetering on the edge of something he couldn't quite define. Because, in truth, the components of his carefully constructed facade were starting to crumble. Dealing with them would only further expose the rawness beneath the surface. He didn't have time for that.

Quincy turned away from the bathroom mirror and walked into the bedroom. The television was on, tuned to American CNN. He watched himself on screen, striding up the Capitol Building steps with a swarm of reporters clamoring around him.

Thank God it was on mute.

But he still heard their voices.

Sun beating down on his neck, fielding their goddamn questions, all designed to get a rise out of him, with an arsenal of polished and polite responses. Quincy had built his campaign on promises of sweeping infrastructure reforms and a vow to ferret out corruption.

He'd done none of it.

Sure, there were a few minor victories, a bill passed here and there, but the embarrassing results of his tenure in office were painful to acknowledge. Nothing that left a lasting impact. God, he'd been so naive, so certain he could make a genuine difference. But the gritty reality of Washington disillusioned him fast. Because Washington was a machine. It slowed for no one. Get caught in the gears, and you'd be chewed up and spit out. Didn't matter if you were red or blue. Both were fueled by money and power.

And lately …

There were whispers he was being groomed for a presidential run. The thought turned his stomach. No way he'd get through another campaign, full of empty vows and backroom deals. Let alone one for President.

He looked back at the screen. Watched his digital self smile and deliver a volume of carefully crafted words, saying everything and nothing at the same time. It was the first thing they told you in Washington: never answer a direct question.

Obfuscate, defer, confuse.

Every politician worth their votes learned the art of the non-answer.

He grabbed the remote and clicked off the television. Then chucked it onto the other bed. The remote bounced, landing on the floor. He didn't bother to get it.

Instead, he sank down onto the edge of the bed, elbows to knees and head in his hands. It wasn't just his life that seemed to be spinning out of control lately. The world itself was now moving too fast for him to keep up. Today's enemies were tomorrow's friends. Or vice versa.

Maybe everyone else in politics felt the same about the global shit show, but his once confident and capable facade was crumbling. And he wasn't sure how much longer he could maintain the charade.

His phone buzzed again.

He glanced at the screen.

Caitlyn.

He should really answer. His wife deserved more than this silence.

But the thought of another argument made his head throb. He didn't need another headache. Their last conversation ended with her threatening divorce after she accused him of constantly putting his career before his family.

He steeled himself and accepted the call, lifting the

phone to his ear. "I told you I was going to be unavailable for the next couple of days. "

"So you really are going through with this hippie nonsense?"

He didn't answer.

"Jesus, Quincy."

"It's not nonsense." He pinched the bridge of his nose, exhaling slowly. "I need to gain some perspective. Figure out my next steps."

"And you need some drug to do that?" Caitlyn said. "You're a goddamn U.S. Senator, not a college kid finding himself on a gap year."

"Fuck you." Why the fuck would he want to sound like a college kid?

"You talk to Jack Talbot about this?"

She dropped the name like the bomb it was. Nothing happened in the party without Jack's say-so.

"All cleared," Quincy said.

It wasn't, of course. And there would be hell to pay when Talbot found out. But right now, he did give a goddamn.

But it shut Caitlyn up. For a moment, she was silent.

Caitlyn came from a long line of politicians. He sometimes wondered if she even loved him. Or just loved his career.

"Have you heard from Lucas?" she finally asked, her voice slightly softer. "He's not returning my calls."

His chest tightened.

"No," he said, not wanting to add to her worry. "But you know how he is. He'll turn up." Jesus, that was the second time he'd lied to her in as many minutes. She hadn't caught on. Which meant he was getting too damn good at it.

"Will he?" Caitlyn said. "Because I'm terrified that

we're going to get a call from the morgue instead of our son. Telling me that he's overdosed."

"That's not going to happen." Quincy closed his eyes against the sudden sting of tears. "Lucas is going to be fine."

"I hope you're right." Another long pause. " I need to go. Just … be careful, okay? And call me when you get back."

"I will. I promise."

The line went dead. Quincy tossed his phone onto the bed and lay back. Staring up at the ceiling. He shouldn't be here. He should go home. Talk to his kid. Or at the very least—

A sharp knock sounded on the door.

He glanced at his watch: Sammie, right on time like always.

"Just a minute," Quincy got to his feet. Walked to the closet and opened it. He pulled out the clothes that had been sent to him: lightweight linen pants and a loose cotton shirt. Then he walked back to the bed and changed. Feeling for all the world, like he was donning a costume for a part in some absurd play.

It had been far too long since he'd worn anything other than pajamas and a suit.

He caught sight of himself in the full-length mirror and almost laughed. He looked like he was awaiting his initiation into a cult. All that was missing was Birkenstocks and a *Namaste* tattoo.

He gathered his phone, then opened the door to see Sammie on the other side, smiling brightly in similar dress, her auburn hair pulled back in a loose braid.

"You ready to go?" she asked, her green eyes sparkling with excitement.

Quincy hesitated, doubt creeping in again. "I don't

know, Sammie. Maybe this is a mistake. With everything going on right now, the timing just feels …"

She reached out and squeezed his arm. "There's never going to be a perfect time. There will *always* be another crisis, another phone call, another meeting. And we both know that you need this."

"And what exactly is that?" Quincy asked.

"To take a step back and reconnect with what really matters."

Quincy wanted to believe her. "How have you managed to keep your humanity working in Washington?"

She grinned. "I do shit like this *all* the time. Otherwise, I'll wind up a hollowed-out shell of a person like the rest of you."

He laughed. But it was more out of nerves. He nodded, stepped out of his room, and closed the door behind him. "Alright, let's go."

"I feel like a fool," he said, following her down the hallway to the elevators. "Like I'm playing dress up."

"You're not alone." Sammie laughed, pressing the button. The doors slid open, and they stepped aboard. They were moving seconds later. "I'm pretty sure I saw Gloria Langford earlier, and I for sure saw Christopherson Sac. But you're all here for the same reason: to strip away the bullshit and find something real."

SAMMIE'S WORDS were supposed to be comforting, make him feel like he was among peers. But it did nothing to lessen the knot of apprehension in Quincy's chest, instead tightening it further.

They arrived in the lobby and exited through the wide glass doors. Then Sammie led him down a winding path, the birds calling out with a cacophony of sound. Sounding almost like reporters surrounding him on the Capitol steps.

Torches lit the way. And every step along the path into the foliage felt like a transgression, as if he were trespassing on sacred ground that nature had never designed for mortal feet. The air was thick with the heady perfume of exotic blooms. Trees loomed overhead like ancient sentinels, gnarled branches reaching out to snare or embrace the unwary traveler. The earth itself seemed to pulse with a primal energy; it was almost as if he could hear a heartbeat from the land.

They finally emerged into a clearing where a dozen or so people milled about, sipping from clay mugs and speaking in hushed tones. In the center, he saw the ceremonial hut: a circular structure with a thatched roof. Shockingly modest for the assembled millionaires. He spotted Christopherson. Or billionaires.

Sammie turned to him. "I need your phone."

Quincy stared at her outstretched hand. His phone was his lifeline, his connection to the world outside.

"You can do it," she said.

He glared at her, and she grinned. But he placed it in her palm nonetheless.

"Thank you," she said, tucking it away. "I know this isn't easy, but it's an important step."

He nodded, not trusting himself to speak. He felt even more naked without his phone than he did in this stupid getup.

"See you on the other side," Sammie said.

She gave him a quick hug, then turned and walked away, disappearing back down the path.

Quincy watched her go. With Caitlyn barely speaking to him. And Lucas usually lost down a tunnel of drugs, Sammie had become his friend, therapist, and cheerleader.

He felt so lonely.

He'd offered to cover her participation as well. But Sammie knew her presence would be a crutch and declined. She would accompany him there, but the process was his to walk through alone.

He turned back at the hut. Quincy could talk to anyone about anything, even if he didn't know the topic. But now he felt out of his depth, yet committed to the path, for better or worse.

So he straightened his posture and walked to the hut, ready to face whatever this strange night might bring.

THE CEREMONIAL SPACE was lit with dozens of flickering torches. Dancing flames cast shadows across the faces of Quincy's fellow participants.

He spotted Gloria across on the other side of the hut. Same as he thought the one time they had met on a red carpet, she seemed so much smaller in person.

He walked over to her.

Her famous face was stripped of its usual makeup, and she clutched a mug to her chest, apparently relieved to see someone she recognized.

She extended a slender hand. "Hi Quincy, nice to see you again."

"Same," he said, giving her fingers a squeeze.

They stood for a moment in awkward silence.

"Was this your idea, or someone else's?" Gloria asked.

He rubbed his head. "A bit of both, I think."

She smiled. "Ever the politician. No straight answer."

He stiffened, then his shoulders dropped. She was right. "Someone else's."

Gloria laughed.

"How about you?"

"Mine." She looked sad. "I'm hoping this little adventure into the unknown might help me reconnect with my creative spark. It's been too long since I've felt truly inspired by anything. So it's rather like a last kick at the can."

"I thought you were great in The Final Frame," Quincy said.

"Thanks." A faux-humble smile. "Probably the film I'm most proud of. But I feel like I've lost touch with what made me fall in love with acting all those years ago. Before all the money. And fame. And pretense."

"It's easy to get caught up in it, isn't it?" Quincy said. "Lose sight of what really matters."

"Sometimes I feel like I'm just going through the motions, you know?" Gloria looked at him. "Like I've forgotten how to be present and fully alive. And I'm just masquerading as myself."

Quincy nodded, surprised by tears welling up in his eyes. He knew all too well what it was like to feel disconnected from life and going through the motions without any sense of greater purpose.

"Senator Monroe!" Christopherson's loud voice filled the hut. A second later, the man sidled up beside them, his grin a touch too wide, and his eyes far too large. Drink or drug, he'd imbibed something. "Fancy meeting you here. I gotta admit, I'm only up in this bitch right now because I lost a bet with my COO. Motherfucker thinks I need to 'expand my consciousness.' Something about me being a workaholic with a God complex and a tenuous grasp on reality. Can you believe that crap?"

Quincy forced a laugh.

Gloria touched his shoulder. "If you'll excuse me, gentlemen."

"Gloria."

She smiled, walking off to the other side of the hut. Christopherson didn't even bother to acknowledge her.

"So why are you here?" Christopherson asked.

"40th birthday gift from my wife." His lie came as smooth as melted butter, but the words were acid on his tongue.

"You ever have ayahuasca before?" Christopherson asked.

Quincy shook his head. "No. You?"

"Twice." The man held up three fingers. "Not sure it changed a fucking thing."

A hush fell over the hut as their shaman entered, her presence ethereal in the flickering torchlight. She was a striking woman with silver hair braided with colorful ribbons. Her ancient, weathered face was painted in geometric designs.

"Welcome, seekers." She smiled at each and every one of them. "I am Ixchel, your guide for this sacred journey. Tonight, we gather in ceremony to drink of the holy vine, to shed the masks we wear and embrace the truth of our being. Mother Ayahuasca is a teacher, a healer, and a guide. Trust in her wisdom, and she will show you the way. But you must step through this doorway with an open heart. Do that, and she will reveal to you the mysteries of your own existence."

Not a sound in the hut.

Even the birds outside were quiet.

Ixchel held her arms wide. "Let us begin."

Quincy left Christopherson and walked over to the woven mats. He chose one and sat cross-legged, feeling half out of his mind, and all the way out of his skin.

A pungent odor of crushed bark mingled with the heady fragrance of copal incense, filling the air that was already electric with anticipation and apprehension.

And then …

Ixchel chanted in an unfamiliar tongue, her voice rising and falling in a hypnotic cadence. The rhythmic pulsing of drums filled the night, reverberating through his bones until Quincy's heartbeat synced in time with their primal tempo.

He closed his eyes and relaxed into the feeling.

Then he sensed movement. The shaman stood before him, holding out a wooden bowl filled with a dark, viscous liquid.

He accepted it with trembling hands, struggling not to recoil at the acrid stench.

Ixchel's obsidian eyes bored into his soul. "Drink, and open yourself to the wisdom of our ancestors."

Quincy raised the bowl to his lips and drank, nearly retching. The ayahuasca seared his throat and coated his tongue with an oily bitterness.

He choked it down — a suddenly leaden weight in his stomach.

Then Ixchel walked on and delivered the drink to each of the attendees.

Minutes crawled by, each second an eternity. And Quincy waited for something to happen.

He glanced around at the others. As the ayahuasca took hold, he saw their eyes glaze over and their jaws go slack.

Why wasn't he feeling anything? Had he done something wrong?

Was he somehow immune to it?

A swell of panic began to crest in his chest.

And then the world abruptly dissolved into a kaleidoscope of fractured light and sound.

Colors bled and swirled into impossible hues. Disembodied whispers flickered at the edge of his perception. The fabric of reality seemed to warp and buckle. His senses unspooled into a riot of synesthetic chaos. The boundary of his body blurred; he could no longer tell where he ended and the universe began.

Or maybe they didn't.

Maybe they were all one.

Every atom inside him vibrated with an ecstatic, otherworldly luminescence.

He had a deep and unrelenting certainty of his approaching death. His frail human form was never going to be able to withstand this cosmic onslaught.

But even as that thought found shape, he became aware of his heartbeat, fluttering deep inside as though he'd swallowed a hummingbird. And then his lungs swelled with the iridescent ether that had replaced the air.

This was not death, but an exquisite rebirth.

And then he was no longer form.

But a pulsing, primordial goo.

Time became taffy, stretching and folding in on itself, aeons passing in a blink. Entire universes birthing and dying in the space between his breaths.

His identity unravelled until all that remained was a pure and undiluted consciousness, as vast and ancient as the stars themselves.

Then, just as suddenly as it all began, the maelstrom subsided, depositing him back into the confines of his sweat-drenched skin. His nerve endings tingled with the echo of transcendence.

Thank God, it was all over.

BUT IT HAD REALLY JUST BEGUN.

Quincy's eyes snapped open, his heart pounding in his ribcage. His surroundings didn't make any sense.

Where was he?

Reality had splintered and reassembled itself, with fragments of the past and present colliding in a dizzying dance of light and shadow. And now he was adrift in a liminal space where the boundaries of time and consciousness seemed confused.

The muggy jungle hut, the pulsing drums, even the bitter tang of medicine on his tongue were all long gone. Quincy was in a cavernous room. Soaring ceilings and polished wood, air thick with the musty scent of aged law books.

He was seated at a scarred wooden table, its surface worn smooth by countless elbows and fists. The jury box loomed across the aisle, but he was not looking at an ordinary panel of his peers.

These faces were a ghostly quilt of sepia and daguerreotype, ancient photographs come to life. He knew without asking that these were his ancestors, stretching back for generations, their gazes piercing his soul with an intensity that prickled his skin. Cowboys and crinolines, soldiers and suffragettes, faces carved with the hardships and triumphs of lives long past.

Towering above them all, where the judge should have presided, was an enormous gilt-framed mirror, and his own haggard reflection staring back at him.

"All rise for the Honorable Judge Monroe!" The bailiff's voice boomed through the chamber. Quincy found himself on his feet, knees trembling beneath the black robe.

Robe? He glanced down, taking in the unfamiliar fabric and gleaming dress shoes. When had he changed clothes?

"Senator Quincy Alexander Monroe." The prosecutor's voice cracked like a whip, and Quincy's head snapped up. The man across the aisle was tall and gaunt with bird of prey features, stalking toward the jury box, his own robes billowing behind him like the wings of a carrion bird.

"Born into privilege, gifted with every advantage our society can bestow. An education at Yale, a network of connections reaching to the highest echelons of power. And how has he repaid this bounty?"

The prosecutor spun on his heel, leveling an accusing finger at Quincy. "With complacency! With self-serving political theater and empty promises!"

The Prosecutor's voice rose to a thunderous crescendo. "You stand on the shoulders of giants, Senator. Men and women who fought, bled, and clawed their way to greatness with only grit and determination. And *you* have squandered their legacy at every turn."

Quincy's mouth went arid, his tongue a useless wad of cotton. He wanted to protest, to defend himself, but the prosecutor was already turning back to the jury.

"I call my first witness. Abraham Monroe, pioneer, farmer, and a man who tamed the wilderness with only a plow and his bare hands. Tell us, Abraham, what did you sacrifice to build a life for your family?"

A grizzled specter rose from the jury box, a face like old luggage, beneath a shock of white hair.

"Left everything I knew behind. Crossed an ocean, buried two wives and three children along the Oregon Trail. Fought off rustlers, drought, and locusts. Spilled my blood into that soil on the promise of a better life for my kin."

The prosecutor nodded grimly. "And you, Jedediah Monroe. Civil War hero. A man who led his troops into the maw of Hell itself. What price did you pay for the Union?"

Another ghostly figure stood, his uniform tattered and stained. "I watched my brothers fall at Antietam, at Gettysburg. I lost an arm to a Rebel's saber, and still I fought on. Because I believed in something greater than myself, a nation indivisible."

On and on it went, the prosecutor conjuring forth a rogues' gallery of Quincy's forebears. Captains of industry, champions of civil rights, men and women who stared down impossible odds and forged a path for all who followed.

"And what, too, of the nameless and faceless progenitors who walked the planet before history itself was acknowledged? Well, they, too, have left a legacy of resilience and determination."

Quincy said nothing, simply trembled.

"These are the giants on whose shoulders you stand, Senator!" The prosecutor slammed his fist on the table. "Titans who bent the arc of history to their will! And what have you done with the fruits of their labor? Built sandcastles on the beach of their accomplishments to mask your own moral cowardice!"

Quincy felt each word like a physical blow. He dropped his head, face burning with shame.

It was all true — he had been given every privilege and opportunity — and what had he done with it? Chased poll numbers and sound bites, always taking the path of least resistance. Paid lip service to the ideals of his office while jealously guarding his own status and power.

"The prosecution rests, Your Honor." The lawyer's voice was silken with satisfaction. And then he returned to his seat.

The silence was broken only by the ragged sound of Quincy's breathing.

And then, his defense attorney rose. She was young, barely older than Lucas, with blonde hair pulled back in a neat bun. But her eyes were ancient, and filled with the kind of wisdom that only comes from having lived through sorrow.

"Senator Monroe." Her voice was almost gentle. "Tell us about your childhood."

He blinked, thrown by the unexpected question. "I … I don't see what that has to do with…"

She smiled. "Indulge me."

So he did. "Grew up in Vermont. Never saw Dad much. He was always down at City Hall. Never had time for anything. No. He had all sorts of time. Just none of it for me. Mom got lonely. And I couldn't fill her well. So she filled herself with Valium and gin." He sniffed. "She died when I was eight."

He closed his eyes, thinking back to the moment he found her. Coming in from school. Seeing her sprawled on the couch. Immediately knowing she was empty. That whatever soul that had been in residence there was gone. Calling his father. Not being able to get through to him because "the Mayor's busy, love." Having to wait until he came home that night. At three am. After he'd been with his mistress. Because he smelled of perfume. And there was lipstick on his collar.

"And your wife?" She prompted. "Your son?"

His throat closed, hot tears pricking at the corners of his eyes. "Caitlyn … she's given up on me. On us. Can't say I blame her. And Lucas …" A choked sob escaped his lips. He shrugged. "Lost. And I don't know how to reach him."

Then she turned to the mirror and looked at his

haggard reflection. "The prosecution has spoken of legacy, of the towering figures who came before you. And it is true, you have benefited from generations of sacrifice and courage. Yet, you are also the product of their flaws. Their prejudices and blind spots are also yours. The parts of themselves they could not or would not bear witness to. Seeds of dysfunction, planted centuries deep."

She gestured to the jury box with its row of witnesses. "You are the heir to their triumphs, but also to their pain. Trauma and neglect passed down like a twisted heirloom. You bear the weight of their choices, and all the burdens they could not lay down."

Quincy felt something crack open in his chest.

She was right, he had been so focused on living up to an impossible ideal, that he had never stopped to consider his own humanity.

"You have a choice, Senator Monroe." His attorney's voice rang out like a clarion call. "To continue the cycle, or break it. Use your privilege and power not to fulfill your own needs, but to lift up those who have been left behind. To be the change you wish to see in the world, not just for them—"and she pointed to the jury box "—but for the generations yet to come."

Quincy looked up at the mirror, staring into his own reflection. "*You* are the judge, Senator. The arbiter of your own soul. Will you rise to the occasion and be the man, leader, and father you know you can be? Or will the weight of history crush you? What say you? Guilty or not guilty?"

There was a long pause.

And then Quincy stood.

Keeping his eyes fixed on the mirror. The face looking back at him was haggard. But there was something else beneath the sorrow, the shame, the fear. A spark of defiance, of determination. Of hope.

He raised his chin. "Guilty. Guilty of complacency and cowardice. Of fear and prejudice. Of indifference. But I am also the child Quincy Alexander Monroe." He thought of his mother. How she made a song of his three names. How they would hold hands and dance around the living room singing it together. "And my failure ends tonight."

The mirror shimmered, Quincy's reflection shifted, transforming until it was no longer his own face he saw, but a kaleidoscope of visages — his son, his wife, generations yet unborn.

And then the courtroom faded away.

He was back in the hut.

Lying on the floor. He fingered the straw mat. And had never felt so held. Mother Ayahuasca had walked at his side and shown him the truth of his own soul, both the scars and the potential, the darkness and the light.

He curled into a ball, holding his knees tight to his chest.

And then he cried.

QUINCY SAT up and looked around.

He was the only one remaining in the hut.

He got to his feet, feeling lightheaded, holding out his hands for balance. The air was thick with the smell of incense and sweat. The once-pulsing drums had now fallen silent.

He walked to the door and stepped out.

The night air was a shock to his system. It almost felt cool, and he gulped it down like a man starved for oxygen.

Ixchel walked over to him, placing a hand on his shoulder. "You have seen what you needed to see." It was a statement, not a question. "And now, the real work begins."

"I'm not sure I'm strong enough." Was that his voice? It sounded nothing like him. Both whole and broken.

The shaman's eyes glinted in the night. "The medicine has shown you the way. Trust in its wisdom, and in your own."

He nodded.

She gave him a slight nudge towards the path. Which he was grateful for because otherwise he might not have found it. Then he walked back to the resort. His surroundings were a blur, buildings and trees bleeding together in a haze of color and sound. The once-solid ground now felt like quicksand. Colors bled in a psychedelic swirl, the boundaries between reality and hallucination still mixing like watercolors in the rain. And his skin felt too tight, as if his soul had grown too big for bone and flesh.

He was shaking by the time he reached his room. His hand trembled violently enough that fitting the key into the lock was like trying to thread a needle with a strand of overcooked spaghetti.

But eventually he got it.

He entered and locked the door behind him.

Then he stumbled to the bathroom and collapsed onto the cold tile floor.

The world still felt like it was spinning.

So he crawled to the shower, fumbling with the knobs until a stream of icy water cascaded over him.

He sat there beneath the spray, teeth chattering, trying to anchor himself in the present. But the visions lingered, the faces of his ancestors, the weight of their legacy, the truth of his own shortcomings.

A sharp knock on the door jolted him back to reality.

"Senator Monroe?" Sammie's voice was muffled. "Is everything alright? We have a flight to catch in an hour. The vote ..."

"I'll be right out," Quincy said.

Flight in an hour? Jesus, how long had he been in the hut? It felt like minutes. Must have been close to twelve hours.

He hauled himself up, his limbs like lead, and turned off the shower.

He dried off and dressed mechanically, mind still churning. The suit felt itchy and uncomfortable. His shoes were tight and pinching his toes. He gathered his things, then went to the door. Sammie was waiting in the hallway.

Her smile disappeared when she saw his face. "Are you okay?"

Quincy paused, struggling to find the words, feeling like a snake that had shed its skin. "I'm fine. Why don't we get going?"

She nodded, keeping her eyes on him until they got to the car.

He spotted Christopherson seated on the outdoor patio. A drink in hand. Gesticulating wildly as he described something. He didn't look at all touched by the experience.

The drive to the airport was surreal, with the lush jungle eventually surrendering to the tarmac.

Only then did Sammie hand over his phone. He'd recoiled at first as though he were allergic to it. Then took the device that now felt strangely alien in his hand.

He powered it on, scrolling through the notifications. Nothing from Caitlyn. And the only thing of importance was from Amanda, another of his Washington aides, confirming his attendance for the vote.

I'm on my way, Quincy typed. His fingers felt stiff and clumsy.

He hit *send* and shivered. Why was he so cold?

He went straight from the car to the private jet while Sammie took care of any paperwork. The jet was air-conditioned, so he grabbed a blanket, wrapping it around his shoulders. Then he took his seat. His mind drifted back to the trial.

It was up to him now.

He watched Sammie board, his expression grave. "Can you pull up the proposed legislation? I want to review it before we land."

She nodded, scrolling through her tablet, then handed it to him.

Quincy read through the dense legalese as his plane taxied on the runway. They were well on their way back to Washington by the time he finished.

He'd read it before.

No.

He'd *skimmed* through it.

He looked across the aisle at Sammie, returning the tablet to her. "What do the polls say? In my district?"

Sammie hesitated, then pulled up the data. "Seventy-two percent opposed."

"Opposed?"

She nodded.

He closed his eyes, the faces of his constituents, his family, his ancestors all coalescing into a single organism. "Right."

His phone buzzed. Lucas again.

But this time he didn't ignore it. He pulled up the long stream of texts.

Got myself into some trouble lol. Could really use some money.

You there, Dad?

Need some help if you're around.

There were others. More of the same. But he skipped to the last.

Because it bled right through the pixels

I just got arrested. Hope you're happy.

Fuck off, asshole. I wish I'd never been born.

He stared at the response field. Trying to think of anything to say.

Why couldn't he? He was supposed to be a goddamn wizard with words.

"Bad news, Senator?"

He glanced over at Sammie and smiled. "Just my son. You know which station he's at?"

Because Sammie always knew. He'd even sent her to bail him out on more than one occasion. "Second District."

He nodded, then clicked off his phone and tucked it away.

And closed his eyes.

It took all his concentration not to cry.

The plane touched down in Washington.

Quincy looked out the window. The familiar skyline seemed unnaturally harsh compared to the jungle. The skyline jutted against the horizon like a jagged knife, unforgiving steel and glass towers in the cold light of day.

He followed Sammie down the steps, then over to where the limo was waiting. The air tasted of exhaust. It made him want to vomit.

Then he stopped.

"Senator?" Sammie asked.

"I think I've got somewhere to be," he said.

"Yeah," she nodded. "The Hill."

Quincy shook his head.

"The vote is in less than an hour."

He nodded. "I know."

"Sir. I know it was an emotional night. But you need to be there."

"I don't, though, do I?"

They stood looking at each other for a long moment. Then the hint of a smile ghosted her lips. "Tell Lucas I say hi."

He nodded. "I will."

And then he put his head down and walked toward arrivals. Made his way through the airport to the long line of cabs at the curb and got into the first one available.

"Metropolitan Police Department, Second District," he said, climbing into the back.

They traveled in silence.

Because Quincy had nothing to say.

He was there in less than an hour. The Senators would be convening now. Preparing the vote. His party wanted it to pass. But it was going to be narrow. Everyone was supposed to be there. No exceptions.

He got out of the car and entered the building.

The station was relatively quiet. Uniformed officers and weary-eyed civilians milling about the lobby. Quincy approached the front desk, his heart pounding.

The clerk clearly recognized him from somewhere.

"Lucas Monroe," Quincy said. "I think he was arrested last night? He's my son."

"One moment." The clerk tapped away on her keys, then looked up at him. "He's about to be released."

"I'll take him off your hands."

She nodded, then picked up the phone and dialed, speaking in low whispers so Quincy couldn't overhear.

He paced, waiting. Counting cracks in the linoleum.

Until a side door opened.

And Lucas stepped out.

They stared at each other.

Lucas looked gaunt and filthy, eyes dull. He looked exhausted. Dirt and Mother-knew-what-else caked his skin. His clothes were little more than rags hanging off his emaciated frame. He scratched his neck. "Hey, Dad."

"Lucas." The name caught in his throat. Quincy remembered the first time he'd said it. Cradling him in the hospital. So tiny and perfect. Smelling of newness.

Lucas brushed past him, heading for the door.

Quincy followed, fumbling for his phone as he pulled up Caitlyn and typed out a message.

Lucas and I are headed home. Both of us.

Her response was immediate: *Both of you?*

Yes, he typed back. A beat, then: *Be there soon.*

What about the vote?

Don't know. Still happening, I guess.

Okay. I'll get everything ready.

He put his phone away, then it buzzed again. He expected Caitlyn, but it was Jackson Talbot.

Fuck.

Lucas was waiting for him at the bottom of the stairs. Quincy hailed a cab. Answering, while Lucas climbed into the back.

"Where the fuck are you, Monroe?"

Not even a greeting.

"Something came up."

"No. Nothing has come up. Because nothing in your goddamn life is more important than this vote."

Quincy exhaled, letting the man's words wash over him. *Nothing … more important …*

He let the silence drag on.

"Senator?" Talbot said.

"You're wrong."

"About what?"

Quincy shrugged. "Everything."

And then he disconnected. Got in the back of the cab next to Lucas and powered down the phone.

"Where to?" the driver asked.

Quincy gave him the address.

Then they headed into traffic and rode in silence for a bit. Quincy checked his phone. It was off.

So he rolled down the window and hurled it into the street, watching as the device exploded in a spray of glass and circuitry.

Lucas stared at him. "Jesus. What the fuck did you do that for?"

Quincy didn't know what to say. Why had he? "I think it's bad for me."

Lucas watched him, warring emotions parading across his face. He ended on a sneer. "If you think we're gonna talk now after that grandiose gesture, you're wrong."

"No." Quincy shook his head, his vision blurring with unshed tears. "I don't want to talk. I want to listen."

Lucas blinked. "To what?"

"To you."

Lucas recoiled. Staring at him. "You're not gonna like what I have to say."

"No. I probably won't. But I think I need to hear it, don't you?"

The world seemed to hold its breath.

And then, Lucas cracked.

The past spilled out, filling the silence between them.

And by the time they arrived home, there was nothing left but sand. Upon which a new foundation could be built.

Life.

As fragile and enduring as a human pyramid.

Aftershocks on *Human Pyramid*

Years before Sterling & Stone was born, I sat in a houseboat, beneath a gleaming blanket of billions of stars, gulping down bitter liquid that tasted like dirt brewed with the earth's oldest secrets, followed by eight hours of the most profound psychological surgery I've ever experienced.

I came back changed, fundamentally rewired. And with that came new stories.

Human Pyramid isn't about politics or power or even family dysfunction. This story is about the weight of inheritance. Not just money or status, but trauma, patterns, and the psychic silt of bloodlines that mistook survival for living, and never learned how to break the cycles they were trapped in.

Quincy Monroe stands on shoulders made of bone and broken promises. Every privilege he's inherited came with invisible shackles, forged from gold but weighted with lead, every advantage shadowed by ancestral ghosts demanding payment for sins he didn't commit but can't escape.

The courtroom sequence that forms the story's heart is archaeology, not metaphor. Layer by layer, the medicine strips away the performance until all that's left is the raw truth: we are both the sum of everyone who came before us and the author of everyone who comes after.

The real horror is not that we're doomed to repeat history, but that we're powerful enough to rewrite it, and most of us are too terrified to pick up the pen. We'd rather inherit the story than write the sequel.

The most radical act of love is simply showing up. Not as the character you've been playing, but as the person you've been hiding.

Ayahuasca doesn't give you answers. It upgrades your

question quality, forcing you to ask: What are you going to do with the time you have left?

Quincy's pyramid was built on sand. But sand, given enough pressure and time, becomes stone. Strong enough to hold whatever you're brave enough to build on top.

And every foundation starts with choosing where to place the first brick.

ELEVEN

The Box

I CAN'T KILL myself until Mrs. Foster and the others finally leave.

It isn't her fault. It's everyone here. I've talked to Laney Davis exactly twice since Karen, and I moved to Oregon Ave. seven years ago. And now the woman won't leave my house. Same for Brittany, who babysat for us once, Gary, a guy I suspect is only here for the food, and all of the women from Karen's reading club. And Arnold.

They're all sobbing, wailing, and wanting to rehash their memories of her. And I can't stand another second of it.

I did love Karen's reading club, though. Especially the name, "Cover to Cover," and that she was the one to first call it that. I loved that the club was offline, and the members read print books and gathered together for their meetings. I loved that the club gave Karen a place for intelligent discussions, away from the demands of our six-year-old.

But now those women all have hollow eyes and running mascara.

No one wants to leave me alone. Because they're all worried about what will happen after they leave.

I must reek of despair.

They're right to be worried. Because the second they're all gone, so am I. Or at least I'll be on my way.

In so many ways, I'm already dead. I'm simply being held prisoner here for a few more hours.

Mrs. Foster is staring at me with her heavy eyes, awaiting my answer.

"I've always liked to eat," I say. "I'm not about to stop now."

I try to smile, but it pulls at my face. That might've been the most I've said in hours. Definitely the longest sentence. Mumbled, aborted phrases are the best way to let everyone know that I want them to leave.

Mrs. Foster is still looking up at me kindly, probably hoping that I'll say something else. Instead, I walk away without another word, thinking about my father and how *he* would clear the room.

And then, as in most of the empty seconds of my life, I think about what my father left me — the *only* thing he left me — and wonder if I should open it. I bet that would empty every soul from the room.

Or it might swallow them.

Someone taps me on the shoulder. I turn around. Arnold.

He has the oversized lot behind the yellow two-bedroom. He uses the tract to store a motley collection of cars that should really each have its own tombstone. Vines climb from every open window. Wildflowers pock the chassis. Angelina, only able to see the world through the eyes of a six-year-old, had no idea that his place was a dump. She said it was "magical."

Arnold is holding out one of Mrs. Foster's baked ham

and cheese rollups, urging me to take it. She was also responsible for the Stick of Butter Rice, the Stromboli, and at least a third of the cookies.

"I'm not hungry," I say.

"You need to eat something," Arnold says around a mouthful of rollup, which he's now gnawing in the wake of my refusal. "You get too hungry, and you'll go right for the sweets." He leans forward as if he's about to let me in on a secret. "Not ideal, Dyson. Healthy choices." I pat my stomach and lie. "No thanks. I just had something to eat."

I walk on, heading down the hallway to the bedroom.

Thinking of The Box.

And I wonder if it would clear the room. Like it—

I stiffen.

That's it.

I want everyone out of our house. *My* house.

I lost my father, then my daughter. And now I've lost my wife.

My own life is long past due.

My father would end this. Not that we ever had a party, but it's easy enough to imagine how he would play it. He'd start by hiding the alcohol, but right now, no one is drinking. He'd change the music to something obnoxious — probably redneck or reggaeton. But that would punish me most because right now, I need silence like I need oxygen. Desperately. I could cry uncontrollably (Dad was good at that), but right now that's practically expected. And worse, people might offer to hold me. Or stay longer. And I don't want either thing.

I open the door to the bedroom. But I don't even *glance* at my closet once inside. I can't afford to. Not yet. Instead, I go to the dresser, change into my pajamas, then stare into the mirror.

I'm alone but not crazy, and in a few minutes I'll have the answers I've wanted forever.

I repeat this to myself, over and over.

The dull roar of conversation fades a little.

I glance at the clock. I've been in here for ten minutes.

I leave, retracing my steps to the living room.

The place looks emptier already. I make a headcount: seven guests left, and no one that I really know, except Mrs. Foster. I wish she hadn't insisted on the wake or invited so many outsiders into my home.

"But *Karen* knew them," Mrs. Foster had said the lone time I'd tried to object. "Do it for her."

And I did.

Because I would do anything for Karen.

I start gathering dirty paper plates, tossing them into the garbage can located next to the door table. Hopefully, someone will spot my pajamas and get the hint that I want them to leave. Three of the seven offer to help, including Mrs. Foster, but I decline.

"I want to keep busy," I say. Why can't I just say, "Party's over?" I have no idea.

Arnold eyes the ham rolls. "You sure there's nothing I can do?"

I give Arnold the rolls and all of the rice. I would have offered him more, but that's all he could carry, and I don't want him coming back.

The others finally understand and make their way to the door. I watch handfuls of cookies disappear into more than one pocket. They could take more if they want. I won't be needing them.

Finally, it's just Mrs. Foster standing in front of the door and me.

"You're sure I can't help you with more of the

cleanup?" Her eyes flit to the kitchen and the acres of dirty dishes filling the sink.

"No. I need something to do that will keep my mind off of all of this."

She smiles sadly and squeezes my hands. Then, without another word, she's gone.

I close the door. And lock it. Double-checking. But it's indeed secure. I'm finally alone.

I wonder if I *should* clean up.

Is it rude to leave my dishes behind? No matter what, someone will have to clean up after me. What's a few more dirty dishes? But I don't want anyone to think I live in a pig sty.

I decide to clean up, even though I know I'm only killing time.

Dad would be laughing at me right now.

This is even worse than going through Angelina's things after her passing because this is the end. At least then Karen and I were in it together, despite, well, everything.

I wanted to keep Angelina's room exactly as it had been, before the … accident. So many of our memories were there in that room. But Karen wanted to give *every-thing* to trash or charity. Every memory was a stain to her.

I go to the garage to get some of the big black garbage bags from the cupboard over the garbage bin. Forcing my eyes away from the crib and the shoes and the sewing machine, same as I forced them away from the closet.

I can't afford to think of The Box, at least not yet. My fingers bristle, craving the wood's centuries-old weathered grain and the cool kiss of its pewter latch. The Box might not be my life's only mystery, but it is the one I have a chance of solving *before* I draw my final breath.

And what is that now, an hour away?

I go back into the kitchen and living room and drop bottles into bags and bags into boxes. Cookies and casserole mix amongst the broken glass.

I feel sick about all the waste. Karen would have hated it. There were a few things that always riled her up. She hated when good things happened to bad people, or when individuals with exceptional talent "didn't do a dime for the dollar they had." And Karen hated waste. Once, I tossed half of a ten-dollar sandwich into the garbage. The look on her face was like she was watching her family drown.

Karen also hated The Box, even though she kind of loved it, like any addict loves the poison in their body.

Same for my father. I know that now.

But for the longest time, I didn't. Childhood offered little certainty. I thought my mom's name was Penny until I was seven or so because that was the only woman's name I'd ever heard him mention before then.

Dad would say *Penny* with a smile like sunshine, then a few fallen leaves later, he'd be screaming about what a fucking cunt she was. He was usually still smiling, though by then his smile looked like the moon. Dad was mostly polite. He only used the C-word about Penny.

"Did you love my mom before she died?" I was holding a scoop of cherry vanilla on a sugar cone at the time, so I remember thinking that the question was safe.

"More than anything." And there was that smile.

"How did she die again?"

A long silence, like always. Then he sighed, longer than usual. And this time he said something different.

"I killed her. Put a knife right into her belly. And then I took the butterfly barrette out of her hair and dropped it into my pocket."

And then Dad laughed until he was sobbing.

After he collected himself, he told me about how my mom had really died. The two of them had been robbing a bank.

Then he told me about the time she fell overboard on their way to Catalina. The ferry ran right over her. Dad said I saw it all, but I was only a baby, so I didn't remember. He said the same thing about the time my mom died while saving me from the fire.

Even at seven, I knew my father was nuts, but it had never hurt so much before. My ice cream was gone, and my hands were sticky. Dad was looking more like the moon, and I was afraid in a brand-new way. I didn't know what else to say, but the moment was pleading for something.

"Her name was pretty."

My father looked at me, squinting. "What did you say?"

I was frozen. Speechless, my heart wanted to pound right out of my body. Dad was louder the second time.

"What did you say?"

"Mom," I dared. "She had a pretty name."

"How do you know your mother's name?"

I managed to choke out a whisper. "Penny ... her name was Penny."

Even now, I don't know her name. Because Dad's hand was like a bullet. By the second *Penny* he'd struck me thrice. He'd walloped me plenty, always sorry both before and after, but that time he didn't stop until my face was sticky and I thought I might never be able to eat again.

And that time, he didn't seem sorry.

I never asked my mother's name again after that. Not even when he was lying in his hospital bed dying, cancer having bored into the hollows of his eyes.

That was around the time that he stopped talking about Penny.

Soon after that, he was talking about The Box, though it wasn't until after I was already shaving when it finally dawned on me that Penny and The Box were one and the same.

I should have understood: The Box was always a "fucking cunt," too.

I wish I weren't thinking about The Box right now.

But then again, when have I not?

I look around the house. It's tidy enough. Right now, I need to finish this. Opening the Box is the only way I can satisfy a curiosity that's been with me as long as I can remember.

I'm not sure how old I was when I realized that most of what came out of my father's mouth was a lie. But by the time I had it figured out, it was too late. I wasn't just used to the stories; I had started to crave them.

I wish I'd been able to see them for the plague they were.

But I swallowed my father's trauma, just like whatever he fried us for dinner. I grew up different from the kids around me, missing all the important pieces of parenting that should have prepared me for adulthood, but instead hurled me into a purgatory of confusion.

I NEVER QUITE KNEW WHAT was true. Because some of those stories came with a gleam in his eyes, and yet others came with a stone-cold stare. Sometimes they were told with a raging fire. And they all seemed true, told with a conviction that left no doubt.

Some I could even feel like blood pumping inside me. Especially the last one he ever told.

The one I heard just before he told me where to find The Box.

The one where he finally told me *about* The Box.

No lies. At least that's what he said.

Remembering my father's warning, I open the door to my bedroom. Then I open the closet and climbed on the tiny stepladder. I imagine Karen doing the same thing. Resting her hands on The Box like I'm doing now. As though we can absorb the countless watts of some unknowable something flooding every cell inside us. An energy. A heat. Icy and squirming, like the wood is infested with bugs.

If this isn't all in my imagination.

"The Box is older than this country," Dad had said, before collapsing into a long minute of coughing. "From as far back as our family goes. It's been growing for centuries, Dyson. It's a gift. And *you* have to protect it."

Even hours from death, Dad still wanted to mess with my head.

"I mean it, Dyson." The way he said it, parched as a baking riverbed, but still somehow pleading. "I need you to believe me."

And suddenly, despite everything I wanted to feel, I did.

"You can't ever open The Box. And you must pass it onto one of your children before you die."

"But I don't have any—"

"Make sure that you do. The chain cannot be broken."

Dad coughed for a while, then caught his breath and repeated the rules: I could never open The Box, and I had to pass it down to one of my children before I died. And then that child must pass it down, always ensuring that nobody opened it.

Despite a lifetime of fibs and fiction, at barely seventeen, I'd never believed anything more.

I leaned closer and forced the words from my mouth. "Did *you* ever open it?"

"Once."

That *once* in my mind rarely stops ticking.

Now, standing just outside the closet I once shared with Karen, holding The Box in my hands, I have to ask myself what I truly believe.

Because if Dad was lying about The Box like he lied about so many other things, then I don't want to know that my father, the Harlequin, played me yet again.

But I also know what I *know*, what Karen knew, and what Angelina only got a chance to discover in the most heinous of ways. And if all of that's true, then what happens when I cannot pass on The Box? What happens once the chain is finally broken?

Because it was going to break.

I have no child, no wife, and no will to live.

So do I even care?

I'm craving The Box. Dying to open it. Holding it in my hand, I can swear that it's whispering a promise, *I can make everything better.*

I hear my seventeen-year-old self: *Did you ever open The Box?*

And my father, terrified of this truth rather than gleeful with the lies: *Once.*

Maybe my time is now.

But then I think, Karen opened The Box, and you know it.

I run my fingers along the wood grain and marvel at how soft it feels beneath my skin. I touch the metal, and a familiar jolt quivers through me.

The Box is home.

I knew it when her name was Penny.

And I know it now.

I get off the ladder and carry The Box through the house, glancing over the detritus of a now expired life. It's been so long since we've been alone, The Box and me. I wish Karen had shown the same will.

I should never have told her.

I should never have—

No.

The blame should stay where it belongs.

I have one picture of my father. It's on the mantle, right beside one of the many photos of Karen's parents, taken before they passed.

I move The Box to the crook of my left arm and grab the photo of my father with my right hand.

I stare at the picture, hating it. Hating *him*. Wishing he could have died without filling my mind with …

The stories. So many stories.

I don't even know when I first started to parse fiction from fact, but it was hard work, and even now, all these years later, I often get it wrong.

But stories are easy to believe when they're told with a smile, which is why everyone loved my father. Dad had two faces, the one everyone else saw, and the one he put on when he took off his belt.

Or when his stories turned ugly.

Plenty of well-meaning people have told me how wonderful my father is. And while I can see why they believe that, I always saw the rest of him. The part of him that was decayed and rotten.

Some of his stories were harmless. Some were wild. Some were so twisted I could never untangle them.

I don't believe that he was ever in the World Series, for example. Or that he'd been to the moon, that he killed our neighbor's dog, Baker, or that he ever did any work for the

Pentagon. I don't believe that he was a celebrated photo-journalist, that his grandfather scalped an old woman, that he saved twin boys from a well, or dropped a little girl down one for screaming too loud. I don't believe that there's a king in the crown of our family tree, no matter how many times he insisted that there was.

So many lies, and *this* might be his best one yet.

I collapse onto the couch and stare at The Box.

I run my hand over its lid and flick the latch.

Electricity seeps into me.

I tell myself to wait another few minutes.

It's not like time matters now.

Time stopped mattering when I found Karen in a tub of crimson water mere days after Angelina's urn was placed upon our mantle.

I look at the mantle and long for a picture of my mother.

I have nothing, literally know nothing about her beyond the biological certainty that she gifted my life. And the sureness in my gut that something too terrible for words took her away from me.

I always wondered if Dad was crazy before she died, but now, I realize that *that* was probably *why* she passed.

His breed of crazy is contagious.

Angelina never caught it, but she would have.

Karen did.

I look down at The Box. I want to hurl it across the room, stomp on the thing, crush it to bits, pretend that it's only a worthless, rotten memory.

But I can't.

I can't destroy it, open it, or wish it never existed.

I can only await my destruction.

Did my father blame me for my mother's death?

Is that why he filled my life with lies? So that I'd never

know who I was? Or so that he could eradicate her alto-gether? Did he hate me that much? Even the stars in the sky felt like question marks to me. For as long as I can remember, uncertainty defined me.

Of course, I had to tell Karen. That was the only way to curb the despair. Otherwise, she would have thought the problem was her, that *she* wasn't enough, even though to me she was all there ever was, at least until Angelina.

I needed to not be alone anymore, but everyone dies alone.

At least my father taught me patience by waiting a life-time for answers that I've always known would never come.

And he taught me to run.

From the time I knew I could go to college, I barely thought of anything else. Getting dragged from state to state as a child kept my grades in the gutter, but they were still good enough to get me into City. I worked until dark every day for two years, paying rent and living like a monk, working and studying and aiming for more.

I enrolled in State as a junior. I met Karen by accident.

I was in the wrong class and right by the door. But I wasn't about to leave, not after I saw her across the room.

Karen was so gorgeous; I could barely dare to blink. Her plain dress somehow didn't belong in a world full of Bluetooth. She practically looked like a prairie girl.

I sat for an hour, waiting for class to end, wondering how I could ever work up the courage to start a conversa-tion with someone so pretty. But I didn't have to. After class, she walked right up to me and said, "I think you've been waiting for me."

Karen was kidding and laughed to prove it. But she was right. I had been waiting for her, not just for that hour but my entire life. Waiting for someone to see inside me, to maybe make me whole.

There was something in that moment, something about the way we each stared into each other's eyes, well, it was magic for us both. A spark. A hunger. A fullness.

Karen was in the wrong room, too. But she'd taken a seat in the front because that's the kind of student she was. And Karen could never stand up and leave once class started. So she sat there for over an hour, as the guy in the back bored his eyes into her skull.

By the next year, we were sharing a one-bedroom and working furiously to get on with the rest of our lives.

Karen was just finishing school when we got pregnant. We were in shock because we weren't even trying. But three tests proved it so. Unfortunately, Fate is a lot like my father, happy then mad, with rarely any warning for when the lightning might strike. We lost that baby on the third day of fall. It hurt enough to vow we'd never have another, but two years and another three tests later, we knew that Angelina was coming.

My dreams came true after that.

And when it comes to dreams, only two things can limit them: money and a lack of imagination. My father taught me nothing about one, and too much about the other.

Dad was a cash-only man because, among many other reasons, he didn't trust the banks. Those first two years after leaving home, I learned to manage my money, mostly by never buying anything I didn't need. Karen was the same. That dress I met her in belonged to her grandma. Saving was easy; we just needed to work on making more to squirrel away.

Despite four years of school, and two of them expensive, I ended up working for a shipping company called Already There, in a warehouse filled with boxes of every shape and size.

I was buying school supplies for Karen when a woman named Oberta — "like Roberta, but without the *R*!" told me that I had a "perfectly proportionate back." She said a lot of things real fast, about how athletes are too athletic and most people are too slouchy. Then she told me that if I was open to the idea, she could give me up to $100 an hour to "mostly stand around." I'd never thought of being a model, but that seemed great, considering $100 was what I made for six hours (I was never allowed to work eight) at Already There.

Between my new work and Karen's teaching job, we finally had enough to buy the next part of our dream.

We were going to furnish every room with our memories.

And we did. Poured our lives into every square foot.

Now the house is full of furniture, but empty of life.

I look down at The Box, and I hate it.

The Box took everything from me.

I lift the lid a millimeter or so.

And then, of course, I drop it.

I stand.

And pace.

The living room, the dining room, the kitchen.

All of the bedrooms.

All the rooms inside this little house that we were so proud to afford.

I tried to tell Karen about it on our first night in the house.

Really, she deserved to know about The Box when we stared into each other's eyes, right there in the wrong classroom. Because I knew that she was forever and that my eternity held something dark.

But since The Box wasn't in the house at that point, I said nothing.

Angelina was born soon after, and I couldn't tell Karen then. The world was too sweet with all those dreams coming true, a long time coming for her, but freshly born from me for the most part.

Later would come, but not for a while.

Without any kin on my side, Karen's parents, Charles and Charlotte, seemed to work three times as hard at being grandparents. Aside from my father, I'd never had any family, and I wasn't willing to risk doing anything that might stand in the way of our happiness.

That doesn't mean I didn't think about it. Or that I couldn't hear it calling. All the way from my father's house. I just had to ignore it, but it was there while Angelina started walking and talking (and talking back), then riding her bike. It was only after that first incisor was out of Angelina's mouth that I brought The Box home and turned our dreams into nightmares.

Dad told me where The Box was buried, a few minutes before he finally stopped breathing. But I never went to get it. I'd felt that thing enough for a pair of lifetimes, and I sure as hell didn't ever want to feel it again.

Except that I did.

Every day of my life.

I've never been much for drugs or alcohol, but I hear that heroin is like Heaven in your blood. I hear that if you feel it even once, you'll spend a lifetime craving that poison. It's the same with The Box. Only it's anything but heroin. It's like shooting Hell directly into your veins.

It wasn't that Karen and Angelina and life in our house wasn't enough. It was that I just couldn't ignore the screaming anymore. The Box that once whispered to me now bellowed in the absence of my father, even from so many miles away.

It seemed impossible that an inanimate object could sense that he died.

But The Box did exactly that.

I had no choice if I wanted its silence. I had to bring it home.

I bought my own shovel because I couldn't stand using Karen's — the one she used for her forget-me-nots and tomatoes — to dig up something so ugly. Then I went to the grave of a man named Justin Sider, because that's just how my father was, and I dug up the earth behind the headstone.

Even on the way to the graveyard, I thought my father might've been pulling one over on me, but the moment my knee touched the lawn, I knew I was about to unearth something unholy.

That didn't keep me from digging, nor did the truth that I was about to drag my family into Hell, which, being honest right now, I have to admit that I must've somehow known. But at that moment, with The Box, a few handfuls of dirt from my fingers, I couldn't find the cells to care.

The Box was like that, you see.

It made you do things.

So I dug it up, sneaked it into the house, and buried it in the back of our closet.

Then I wondered when I should tell K.

Before I told her all about The Box, I never really spoke much about my father. I only had the one picture, and Karen never pressed. She seemed to sense that he was an abusive asshole. Talking about him with her always made me think about The Box, and thinking about *it* made me wonder if I was a lunatic, too.

I walk back to the mantle, clutching The Box to my chest.

I set his picture back and select another photo, this one

in a frame I made myself. Angelina is five years old, but Karen is holding her like an infant, the two of them on the couch, sunlight pouring in through the window, glinting on Angelina's fairy necklace and making them both look like the angels they were.

I doubt Dad had a single picture of me.

I never remember him taking one.

It's a miracle Karen ever looked my way, the way that he made me. So tentative. Insecure. Awkward. Other fathers taught their sons to be men. Mine taught me to …

Well, it's a curse to finish the thought.

I look down at The Box. I want to crush or caress it, I can't even tell.

I'm not sure I knew love before Karen.

I didn't *understand it* before Angelina.

They were my fresh start. My chance to be strong.

But I failed.

And now here we are.

I'm killing time, same as it's been killing me.

But I can't wait any longer. I have to do what must be done.

Both of the things that must be done.

So I sent Angeline's box back on the mantle. And I know where to go. But halfway there, I wonder if I should wait, then a few steps away, I've convinced myself that I definitely should.

The wake was only an hour ago. I can do it in the morning.

But I know that's only The Box trying to sway me from the inevitable, so when I get to the medicine cabinet, I grab the bottle and drop it right into my pocket. Then I run from the bathroom before I can change my mind.

Because I can't afford to do that.

I remember the way that everyone looked at me. Not

just Mrs. Foster. *Everyone.* They could see through me, *into* me.

Maybe they know what happened to Angelina.

Maybe they know about Karen.

They could probably smell what was about to happen to me.

A few days earlier, Mrs. Foster had brought Dr. Reynolds to see me. I resisted their knocking until she threatened to call the police. When I finally opened the door, she said Karen would have wanted to know I was alright.

"Are you in pain?" Dr. Reynolds had asked me.

I don't remember much about his visit. But I do remember that question and my answer because it took me a while. "Yes."

"What kind of pain are you in?"

"Physical. Emotional. All of it."

And I remember the doctor's kind eyes, his hand on my shoulder, the gentle squeeze. "Death brings torment to the survivors. But *this* is what it means to be human. Bereavement and depression can present the same symptoms, and it's the worst sort of suffering. Why should we treat them differently?"

Then he scribbled on a slip of paper, and Mrs. Foster took the liberty of trading that paper for the bottle in my pocket.

She'd made a joke when she dropped them off. "Don't take them all at once."

And then she flinched, and I knew that she immediately regretted her words. But it was too late. They were out, sitting in the silence between us like a stench.

"I won't," I said.

But I could tell she didn't believe me.

And now, my choice: pills or The Box.

Or both. So the real question is: *which is first?*

I sit on the couch, clutching The Box to my chest.

It warms me, matches my heartbeat, makes me wonder how much of this is all in my head. I could believe *all of it* if my family wasn't dead.

"Did you ever open it?"

Once.

I'll empty the bottle into my gut, but first I need to open The Box. To see what's inside. To finally find out if I'm crazy like my father. I picture myself running my thumb across the latch and then up to open the lid. But I don't have the willpower.

I get out the bottle and tap three pills into my palm.

I swallow them, then wait. Ten minutes later, I'm still a cat in a bag, waiting to drown, so I take another three, followed by an equal dose on my way to the kitchen.

I set down The Box as I sift through the fridge, thinking about Dr. Reynolds and Mrs. Foster.

"Food and mood are heart and beat," Dr. Reynolds had said. "Eat better to feel better." He patted my back. But his fingers turned into tapeworms.

Mrs. Foster pointed to the condiment rack. "If you're feeling low, then you want a high-carb snack. An English muffin with a dollop of jam!" And then with a nervous little laugh, she added, "The Indian's scalp was sticky with blood."

Except that she didn't say that.

Did she?

I make myself something to eat. A pizza sandwich, with ice cream and seared ribeye, Golden Grahams on the side. I swallow it all in a single bite, and then I ask the weatherman if it's time for Pilates.

I tap another three pills into my palm, then to hell with it, another half dozen. I swallow all 17.

And there it is.

The deed is done.

A wave washes over me.

Or was it already there?

Is it the pills or The Box making me see double and triple and quad … *is that a donkey made of meat?*

I tentatively step toward the donkey, afraid it might bite me.

But it purrs like a dog and then meows like a frog.

I fall back laughing. There's nothing there, and the nothing might bite me. Another wave passes over me.

The room is purple, and melting like a candle, but then I grab The Box and hug it. I pull its warmth closer. Give it permission to claim me.

I'm ready to go, once I see inside.

I remember a rare moment when I dared to ask a question. "Will you tell me about Penny?"

"What do you want to know?"

"Do you love her?"

"As much as I hate her, son, yes, I do."

And now I know how he feels.

Because I'm dragging myself through an acid honey, sticky enough to hold me in place as it eats through my flesh, all the while feeling like the brush of a lover.

I imagine Karen with The Box and hate myself for telling her.

I picture her cradling it like I am now.

I can practically hear it, demanding that she do the unthinkable.

And then I see it, happening right here in front of me.

I see Karen going into Angelina's room.

I hear Angelina asking what time it is, then her mother laughing maniacally. "If we take care of the moments, the years will take care of themselves." And then Angelina starts screaming.

But by the time I'm in the room, I hear only the thunder of Karen's sobbing.

Or was that all in my head?

Is *this* all in my head?

Is my father in the shadows laughing at me now?

The Box is only a Box. Right now, in this terrible, transparent moment, I know the truth that I'm holding a lie.

There's only one way to know. One way to end it. No matter how difficult it is, no matter what it means or what the truth will do, it's time to open The Box.

I swallow another several hundred pills and steel myself for a peek.

But the latch is burning hot and glowing white. My skin blisters from the proximity. Or from the lifetime of lives in my head.

You shall know the truth, and the truth shall make you mad.

I do not fear following my family into the dark, to the end of everything or the start of an endless forever, to a place where I'm nameless and faceless, but all that we've shared is glowing like—

The Box.

It's burning my hand.

I swallow more pills, desperate for the courage to do what I must.

Because what if The Box is empty?

What will that say about my father? About Karen? About Angelina? About me and my life?

I stand up too fast. It must be the pills because I collapse right back on the couch.

How did I get here? I was in the kitchen.

The world swims around me. It splits into two and then

three. There are seven planets in orbit around me. A galaxy forming. Twin stars exploding behind my eyes.

I scream into the silence.

The Box is burning me, so I set it down. But now I'm on fire.

I grab The Box.

Why won't this end? It's all my father's fault. Ever since I was a child, hallucinations, *or something,* were a part of my reality. But now it's constantly worse. Did I close the door on Mrs. Foster an hour ago? Or has it been years? Does she even exist?

I rarely lose my temper, but right now I want to smash everything in this house, starting with The Box.

But that would be like breaking my child's neck.

I go to open it instead, but The Box is no longer in my hands.

I look around. The Box is nowhere. Where could it have gone?

I close my eyes and my mind and listen for the whisper, the one I've known all my life, the one I've been hearing since before I even knew about Penny or The Box or what it might mean to be insane, to live at the edge of reality, because only those who have toppled over its quivering lip could ever tell you about the truth of lunacy, only *they* can promise that madness is the *root* of …

I'm lost and rambling.

Is this even my house?

I look around, not recognizing this furniture. This place. This life. I look around, desperate for The Box. I look around, wild-eyed, I'm sure, seeing only fields of wheat all around me.

Back to the closet, I'm frantically searching.

What if there was never a Box?

What if there was no Karen or Angelina?

What if—?

The question dies with The Box in my hand. I don't remember finding it, but I don't care. It's beating like a heart, begging me to open it.

I'm no longer afraid because it's welcoming me home, inviting me to the truth. I can let the memories come. Let the memories find me.

I open my mouth, empty the bottle, and swallow The Box.

I'm screaming at Karen. *"How could you do it?"*

And she's there in front of me, smiling like a lunatic. "She had to leave. Angelina had *all* the rabbits, and no one else could make the marmalade."

That's when I knew it, that day when Karen stayed home from school. She wasn't sick, except for The Box. I showed her the outside, and she couldn't stop thinking about what the insides might be.

I knew she'd opened it the minute I came home, even though I'd never done it myself. She was talking nonsense like Dad used to, but without the years of rehearsal behind her.

But the scene itself was familiar: Karen, wide-eyed and eating soup from a can — she wasn't much for soup and hated anything from a can. Still, it dribbled out of her mouth and rolled down her chin, dripping back into the can as she rambled through her nonsensical story.

"There was a man at the bus stop, and he came out of nowhere. I know what you're thinking: *Why would I take the bus?* But I didn't, Dyson. I was just waiting. *He* was there for *me*. He had fine black slacks, I think they were wool, a red leather vest, no shirt, and a bright yellow beanie. He was either barefoot or in boots. He had a bottle of rum in each hand, and I'm *positive* that his diaper was dirty."

I stared at Karen. Everything inside me screamed *this is the end!*

"What are you trying to say?" I asked her, remembering my father, and all of the stories that I'd tried to forget.

"Just that you need to pick Angelina up no later than four."

And *that* she'd said perfectly normal. She looked down at her can, puzzled, then up at me as if I were the one playing a joke.

I knew right then, but did nothing to stop it.

Angelina's death is on me.

Karen's, too.

I look down at my lap.

The Box is there.

Which is strange. Because I had swallowed it.

But there is only one exit. Even if there's nothing inside The Box, at least I'll know. At least this will be the end. I'll flip the latch and lift the lid, then either see what I've been waiting a lifetime to see, or I will await the silence of death. The pills can finish their work in truth's shadows. And then I'll see my family again.

Maybe I'll even see *him.*

"Did you ever open it?"

Once.

Déjà vu for the final time.

The Box is humming, craving our union. The world is in a feral rage, ugly and distorted, looping like a song stuck on repeat, a chaotic, unrelenting cry. I flip the latch and lift the lid, but I barely make it a millimeter before Karen screams, "No, Dyson! You can't!"

I hurl The Box across the room, doing what she was too weak to do. Because Karen looked inside and look where it got us.

Or maybe not.

Maybe I'm napping, and dinner will be ready when I wake up. Angelina will be reading and …

I close my eyes, and then I open them. But even after the blink, I'm not sure if it's been seconds or years. I look around, and my world is the same.

The screaming is still there, but now worse. Before, it was only The Box insisting that I know what to do. But there are more bellows coming from inside now. Karen and our daughter, their voices angelic. My father and what I'm sure is my mother. Voices I don't know, calling me home.

I stand, needing The Box.

I wobble away from the couch.

I open the front door, but it's raining nightmares outside.

No walls. No ceiling. No sky.

Just me and this space and all of the terrible things that I've ever imagined, or stopped myself from imagining. They're all here, and I'm there, and I feel like I'm falling and falling and falling and falling, into all of the black and white that surrounds me, colors that cannot be real, blinking in and out of existence.

Until I'm gone.

I'm in a car. In a cave. On the top floor of some city's tallest building.

And now I'm underground.

I've never died in a dream, but that's not what this is.

This is real.

Except my head is in an oven, half melted away. I'm screaming, blood pouring from my empty eye sockets and pooling on the ground. The world is an engine, powered by suffering, and I'm stuck in its gears.

I step back inside and slam the door. My head is swimming, pounding, aching, bleeding. I long for the relief of inevitable death.

But how can I wrestle Fate to the ground while I'm here, cowering in the corner, sick of this misery, knowing that death is a release and that opening The Box is the opposite?

I'll gut the demon inside me.

To hell with the pills. I head to the kitchen.

Then I'm standing on the linoleum, gripping the hilt, ready to plunge the blade into my gut.

But The Box won't let me.

It's as though I have no control over my muscles. I'm pushing the knife toward my stomach as hard as I can.

But nothing happens. The blade twitches in place as if gravity were a wall. I bash my head against the counter, or at least I try to. But I can't seem to connect my skull with the tile. I open the oven and put my head inside, hoping to melt it like I did a few minutes ago. But the gas appears to be out.

The Box has won. It won't let me die before I do what I must.

Slowly, knowing that these are my final few seconds before a lifetime of lies topple over me, I reach for the box, ignoring my sizzling skin. I flip the latch and grit my teeth through the excruciating, but somehow beautiful pain.

And then I lift the lid.

And see the truth. It hits me in a flash. Bright light followed by a mushroom cloud of memories that don't belong to me.

Except that they do, because they belong to my blood. They always have.

I see a king with an appetite for unimaginable power. And the only way to get more is to summon a mage and make a deal with the Devil. Or whatever that scab-covered snake called itself then.

The king could not have known the consequences, but I see it all. Every murder, misdeed, and story manufactured to ease the mind from insanity. Centuries of horror now haunt me, but I can't stop screaming at the ones I know are coming.

I see the barrette and hear my father. I killed her. Put a knife right into her belly. And then I took the butterfly barrette out of her hair and dropped it into my pocket.

I see the fairy necklace and hear my wife: If we take care of the moments, the years will take care of themselves!

I see a dog collar that says *Baker* and my in-laws' wedding rings.

And then Karen is pouring herself a bath, about to do what I already know I do not have the courage to do. What no one in my family has *ever* had the courage to do. I loved my Karen, but now I am one with The Box, and *We* need someone to carry us forward, into tomorrow and everything after that.

I think of Mrs Foster.

Of her little girl. She needs a father. Just as I need a daughter.

I look down at The Box and smile.

I think I'll call her Penelope.

And oh, the stories we'll tell …

Aftershocks on The Box

I WANTED to write the ultimate mystery box story. Not the lazy kind where writers punt on payoff (I'm looking at you,

Abrams), but the brutal kind where opening it actually costs something. Where the mystery isn't what's inside, but whether you're strong enough to live with knowing what is.

The Box is pure Twilight Zone DNA spliced with inherited madness. A story that asks: What if the worst thing your family ever did was pass something down? What if the heirloom in your closet was actually a generational time bomb?

Dyson is drowning in the aftermath of unspeakable loss, clutching the one thing his father left him: a box. Three generations of men have carried it. Like a relay race where the baton is a live grenade and the finish line is madness.

None have opened it. All paid the price anyway.

The beauty of an unreliable narrator isn't just that you can't trust them. It's that they can't trust themselves. Dyson's reality shifts like sand: is he hallucinating from grief and pills, or is something genuinely supernatural unspooling around him? The answer keeps changing, because trauma doesn't care about your need for linear storytelling. It prefers to write in fragments, edit in blood, and publish in screams.

This story begs the question every curious person dreads: What if you finally got the answer you've been dying for, and it killed everything you thought you knew about yourself?

What if the truth wasn't worth the price of admission?

Or what if it was?

The Box is about the physics of inherited sin: how evil multiplies across generations. A contract signed in blood by ancestors who forgot to read the fine print.

Open carefully. Some gifts are Trojan horses dressed as heirlooms. And this one's been waiting three generations to finally come home.

TWELVE

Seen

RICKY RIVERA WAITED for the perfect shot.

He was a shadow among shadows, feeling into the thrum of Hollywood's heartbeat as he lurked. He leaned against a dark wall of the building across from Cameo and touched his earpiece to seat it more firmly.

The walkie-talkie crackled. "McAuley thinks he's tailing her," said a female voice.

"How much longer?" Ricky asked.

"Two minutes. Green's in place out back. As long as he doesn't trip over his own damn feet getting the shot."

Ricky dropped his cigarette, then ground it out with his toe. The action felt performative: something a character would do in a movie. Smoking was a filthy habit he'd picked up purely for the visual. He should have taken up drinking instead, like Dad. Pills like Mom. At least those vices had an edge. Smoking was barely self-destructive. It took decades to kill you. At this rate, he might actually live to see thirty. Clearly, that was no good.

Ricky peeked around the corner at the Cameo entrance, wondering if tonight would finally be the night when he caught Chloe Simone in his lens. Hollywood's most elusive A-lister had a knack for picking the perfect disguise — floppy hats, oversized sunglasses, camera-shy hoodies — all of which obscured her famous features even when captured in the perfect light. Chloe was a master of disguise, playing a game of hide and seek with the paparazzi. And she was winning, somehow always one step ahead of the shutter click.

Cameo's entrance was mobbed like usual, littered with rubberneckers and paps jockeying for pole position. Fifty other assholes, in addition to Ricky. A shit show, same as always.

The paps descended like locusts, ready to shove cameras in Chloe's face while screaming asinine questions. Hungry for crumbs that they could swap into clickbait with minimal effort. Willing to do just about anything for the money shot that made their month. Or a year. Because sometimes one photo was enough to change everything.

He thought about the photo Clint had taken of Madison Grove slipping out of the back seat of Ron Sheldon's limo. Dress askew. Hair tumbled. Married director's hand on her ass. Clint had made so much money off it that he never worked again. Of course, neither had Madison. She inherited the entire stink.

Ron Sheldon emerged unscathed, a Teflon director in a scandal-stick town.

In one way or another, they were all in pursuit of their own limo photo.

And Ricky hated it. Hated them. And by default, he hated himself. Because he'd somehow become one of them.

It was never the plan. He was supposed to be shooting portraits, not lurking in alleyways like a bottom-feeder. He had spent hours poring over the greats like Avedon and Leibovitz as a kid. But his biggest inspiration was always Yousuf Karsh. A legend sought out by world leaders and change makers to capture their essence on film. Churchill, Hemingway, Castro — Karsh immortalized them all.

That's what Ricky wanted. To reveal people's souls through his lens. Make art that mattered.

But here he was selling his shots to the highest bidder instead. Paying off child support and Mikey's unrelenting medical bills. Using blood money earned in the shadows.

The closest Ricky had ever come to his dream was a soul-sucking gig at Happy Snaps Photography, where every click was followed by a giggle, backdrops were pastel wonderlands, and props included everything from pirate swords to fairy wings.

Watch the birdie, kiddos! Okay, now everyone say cheese!

His first photo had been luck. Ricky was leaving Happy Snaps and driving home when he spotted actor Arnold Doyle in the driver's seat of the McLaren next to him at the light. And Ricky did what he did best. Took a photo.

Only he hadn't known Arnold was banned from driving for being under the influence. After he uploaded it online, the photo went viral. Arnold spent the next three months in jail. And Ricky's name was made.

Turned out he had a knack for capturing celebrities by knowing just the right moment to click his shutter. His pics consistently snagged the cover of *Us Weekly, The Daily Mail,* and *TMZ.* The money was good. Damn good. He would have plenty if not for the apocalypse of all those hospital bills.

Sheila never approved of his "career change," but she still cashed the checks. Somehow, her holier-than-thou ideals dimmed when it came to keeping her lights on and food in the fridge.

The phone buzzed in his pocket, and he glanced at the screen. *Sheila*. Of fucking course.

He punched decline, knowing it would only delay the inevitable. She'd keep calling until he picked up. That was Sheila, clinging to grievances like a miser to gold.

The walkie crackled again. "Ricky, you copy? We've got movement at the rear entrance."

"I heard you the first time. Any sign of her yet?"

"Negative. But her security just rolled up. Three black SUVs. Tinted windows. McAuley confirms it's her."

"*Fuck*," Ricky muttered.

He'd been banking on getting a photo tonight. Rent was due next week, and Mikey needed new leg braces. The kid was growing like a weed.

"Ricky Fucking Rivera, is that you?" a voice called out from behind him.

Ricky turned to see Benson Hauser, king of the paps. A bloodhound when it came to sniffing out celebrities, and about as subtle as a siren screaming through a funeral.

Benson sidled up to Ricky with a shark-like grin. "This chick is my white fucking whale. You know she sent her last photog to the hospital? Hundred stitches. Bitch sicced her bodyguard on the poor guy just for trying to get a crotch shot."

Ricky knew. Everyone knew. Chloe Simone wasn't just elusive. She was dangerous when cornered.

"Maybe she just values her privacy."

"Privacy. *Right*." Benson snorted. "Being hounded is in her job description. Boo fucking hoo, poor little movie star has to pose in front of a camera on the way to cash her latest ten million dollar paycheck. I'm crying a fountain of tears over here."

Ricky bit his tongue.

It wasn't worth the breath in his lungs to point out the

hypocrisy inherent in a member of the paparazzi complaining about how much celebrities got paid. They were professional vultures, circling the carnage for another piece of famous flesh.

"You gotta finesse 'em." Benson was oblivious. "Take that pic I shot of Delilah Larson last month. *Fucking gold.* Her and that singer she's been bending over for — what's his name, the one with more ink than a printer cartridge? I caught them sucking face in the back of his limo outside of Roscoe's. Dude had his hand up her skirt, probably two fingers in the pie. You shoulda seen her face when she spotted me. Thought she was gonna take a swing." Benson chuckled, no less oblivious, "Hundred grand. Could'a been double if she'd actually touched me. I'd have slapped her with an assault charge fast enough to …"

Ricky tuned him out. Benson turned his stomach. Of course, he had seen that photo. Smut always sold.

The best shot Ricky had ever taken of Chloe Simone wasn't even a picture of her, but rather her stalker's apartment. She had been scared. The situation was escalating, and the police weren't responding. They simply thought Chloe was a hysterical starlet.

Ricky had noticed him at multiple locations following Chloe. So he tailed the guy, curious if he was a new paparazzi. Because he didn't recognize his face. But he wasn't. When Ricky peered in through the windows of the guy's first-floor apartment, the place was pretty much empty except for images of the actress plastered on every wall. Red Xs slashed across her face in what looked like blood. Graphic drawings of her being throttled, stabbed, and set on fire. Next to a detailed schedule of her daily movements, traced out on a map of LA in colored push pins.

Ricky took photos. Sent his evidence to Chloe's agent.

That had apparently been enough for the cops to take her complaint seriously. The stalker was arrested within hours. Chloe was safe.

And as for Ricky?

He received a boilerplate *thank-you* for his troubles, probably typed up by some assistant. He wasn't even sure if Chloe's signature was real or a stamp.

"Hey, you okay?" Benson nudged him in the side.

"I'm fine. Just … thinking."

"Think faster." Benson nodded at the crowd.

Ricky looked over to the restaurant to see a flurry of activity.

Muffled shouts, followed by the sound of feet pounding the pavement.

The walkie buzzed again with an update: "Confirmed sighting! She just ducked into the back entrance. We're in pursuit."

The crowd around the front scattered. Paps took off in a dead run, angling for the alley. Benson let loose a holler and whoop.

"It's on, baby! Let's get paid!"

He slapped Ricky on the back and charged off.

Ricky stayed put. What was the point? Chloe would be inside the restaurant within seconds, secure in her fortified VIP booth. McAuley and Green had the drop. They would get what they needed to satisfy the tabloids for the week. The rest was table scraps.

He lit another cigarette. Had just taken his first hit when Benson's voice careened off the buildings.

"Goddammit!" He stomped down the alley toward Ricky. "Bitch did it again. Out and in like David fucking Blain. Why can't she just pose for a photo every once in a while like all the other attention whores?"

Ricky ignored him, unclipping the camera from

around his neck and sliding it into its case. He felt bone-weary. All he wanted was to go home, crack a beer, and fall into bed.

Forget the hollow emptiness gnawing in his gut.

He waved his hand to Benson, then walked to his car. His phone vibrated. Sheila again. Round two. He didn't have the energy for it. He hit *decline* for the second time and was about to pocket the phone when it started vibrating again.

Jesus. Can't a guy catch a fucking break?

But the incoming number wasn't Sheila's. It was unknown.

He always answered those calls. Sometimes it felt like Ricky had handed his card to everyone in Los Angeles. But you never knew who might phone in a tip. Usually, they wanted money. Ricky was happy to pay a percentage if the shot was good. It earned him a few loyal tipsters.

He took unknown calls a hell of a lot more than Sheila's.

He swiped to answer, lifting the phone to his ear. "Ricky Rivera."

"I have a job for you." The woman's voice was deep, throaty, and familiar somehow. "A proposition."

Ricky frowned. That didn't sound like someone calling in a phone tip. "You got a celeb I can shoot?"

"I am the celeb. And it's not a photo tip. It's an assignment."

Ricky almost rolled his eyes. He's had his fair share of those calls as well. Bogus assholes giving him false data. *Come take my photo here,* while in reality, they were somewhere else altogether. Hide and Seek.

"Look, I'm not really in the market for side gigs at the moment. And if you've got one, it'll cost you."

"Then let's discuss terms," the woman purred.

"Because I think you'll want this job. It involves a mutual friend of ours. The one every pap in town is creaming their pants to get a lens on."

She wasn't talking about Chloe, was she?

"Hill of Beans on Wilshire. Twenty minutes. Come alone."

Jesus Christ. It was something out of a goddamn spy novel.

Ricky chucked his cigarette and stamped out the butt, unlocking his car and climbing inside. But then he sat without turning the ignition, still staring at the screen.

He wasn't seriously thinking of going to meet this woman, was he?

But he was curious about the job (did it involve Chloe?) and how much she was willing to pay. Ricky blinked.

He must have rocks for brains if he thought anything could come of a mysterious phone call with a woman angling money as bait. Probably Benson pulling his fucking leg. Screw this. He wanted that beer.

Ricky hit his blinker and pulled into traffic, headed east. He flipped a bitch two blocks later.

Hill of Beans it was.

Twenty minutes later, Ricky was scanning patrons in the crowded cafe.

His mystery caller stood out like a sore thumb. Tucked away in a corner booth. Dodgers cap pulled low, dark sunglasses perched on her nose despite the dim interior, and the rest of her face buried in the depths of an oversized hoodie. Just another hipster college kid.

What the fuck did she know that would result in pay-day?

Ricky shrugged.

If anyone knew appearances could be deceiving, it was paparazzi. Maybe she was "somebody's" assistant. Screw the NDA, she was about to drop details.

As if realizing she was being watched, the woman looked up.

And Ricky froze.

He'd snapped that face enough times to know it anywhere. Even hidden beneath sunglasses and dim lighting. The exaggerated angles of her cheekbones were only slightly less familiar than his own reflection.

No fucking way.

His feet carried him toward her table on autopilot.

She glanced up when Ricky reached her table, then used her pinky to pull the glasses down a smidge. Studying him.

Up close, there was no mistaking Veronica Grove. Former rom-com queen and current bitter rival of one Chloe Simone. Even though Veronica could no longer fill a theater in the era of streaming, she could still match Chloe in star power wattage.

She gestured for Ricky to sit.

He did, sliding into the booth. Folding his hands on the table. Christ, he felt like a schoolboy. He dropped them to his side. That felt even more awkward. He folded them across his chest. Too hostile. Jesus.

She flashed him a smile. "I see no introductions are necessary. Relax."

There were two glasses of water on the table.

"One of those for me?" he asked.

She nodded.

He snagged the one closest and took a sip. That was better. He set it down and met her eyes again.

"Thank you for coming, Mr. Rivera. I know you must be wondering why I asked to meet."

"Yeah," he tried to keep his voice light. "I'm not used to being summoned for secret meetings by movie stars. Usually, they want me to stay as far away as possible."

"True. But I've called you here to do your job."

He blinked. "You want me to take your picture?"

"No. Not mine. Chloe Simone's."

He smiled, fiddling with the water glass. "I've been trying that. Hasn't worked out so great—"

"This isn't a normal photo. I need your specific skill set. And your … discretion."

Ricky raised his brows. "Go on."

Veronica glanced around before leaning forward and lowering her voice. "I want you to find out if Chloe Simone is fucking my husband. And if she is? I want proof."

Ricky stared at her. "You want me to what?"

"You heard me. Marcus and I have been married for a decade. Happily so for nine of those ten years. Until he started sticking his dick into that overrated slut."

"And you know that he's cheating for sure? Specifically with Chloe Simone?" Ricky had no problem believing the first part, but the second struck him as paranoid bullshit.

She nodded. "I want ironclad proof of their affair before I confront him. Then I'm going to hit him where it hurts — right in the assets."

"Why come to me?" Ricky took another sip of his water. Marcus Ball was one of the biggest producers in Hollywood, so getting anywhere near this was dangerous. "Why not hire a PI?"

She adjusted the glasses on her face and leaned back against the cracked vinyl. "Marcus knows all the players. He uses them to dig up dirt on his competitors. I need someone outside his sphere of influence. Someone he'll never see coming."

"I'm a photographer, not a private eye. You're asking me to take an awfully big risk."

"Isn't that what you paps do best? Take risks to get the shot no one else can?"

Ricky bristled. "There's a big difference between staking out a public street and breaking the law by recording people without their consent."

"Oh, please. Spare me the ethics lecture. We both know your type will do anything for the right price." She reached into her purse, withdrew a check, and slid it across the table.

Ricky glanced down at the scrawled figure and felt his breath catch. *Holy shit.* Veronica was offering him more than he made in a year chasing B-listers.

"That's just the deposit. You'll get triple that when you deliver the proof."

Triple?

With that kind of cash, Ricky could get current on child support and his share of the hospital bills. And there would be enough left over to lease a real studio space. He could stop dreaming and start building his portrait business. No more lurking in alleys like a roach. He could probably get a spread in *US Weekly: Behind the Lens: Paparazzo Turned Star-Studded Portraitist.*

He finally looked back at her shaded eyes.

"What do you need?"

She shrugged. "Audio and video surveillance. Marcus is slippery. He knows how to cover his tracks. Photos can be doctored. I need to hear or see that fucker cheating on me. Get creative."

"Then we got a problem. I don't do audio or video surveillance. Never have."

"Then I suggest you learn, Mr. Rivera." Her features were tight. "Do we have an agreement?"

Ricky looked down at the check. No way in hell was he turning that away. "We have a deal."

She smiled. "Then we're finished here. Get me what I paid for."

Veronica slid out of the booth and walked out of the coffee shop without a backward glance.

Ricky stared at the check.

What the hell did he just agree to?

Surveillance. Wiretapping. Felony offenses that could land him behind bars if he were caught. What he did as a pap edged propriety and the law on a good day, sure, but this clearly crossed that line. He was in over his head and didn't have a clue as to how to go about bugging Chloe's house or hacking her phone.

He should run after Veronica. Call the whole thing off. His phone vibrated. Sheila. Mikey. That was enough to redirect his thoughts.

How the fuck could he pull this off without getting caught? It had to be possible. People did this kind of shit every day, and it didn't hit the papers or result in prosecution.

Maybe if he focused on Marcus, he could leave Chloe mostly out of it. Maybe even hide her altogether. After all, Veronica simply needed proof that Marcus was cheating.

Ricky hated the next call he had to make.

But he had no other choice. Ricky needed help from someone who knew all the dirty ways this game was played.

He started dialing Benson on his way to the door.

~

Last Call was a bar that still reeked of tobacco despite it being illegal to smoke indoors for decades. There wasn't a single booth that had good lighting. It was a place where dirty deals were often made. Ricky spied Benson sitting in the back, the dim light framing him like a conspirator from some old noir film.

"Took you long enough," Benson said without preamble. "You gonna tell me what's really going on, or jerk my pecker like you did on the phone?"

"I'm not jerking anything. Like I said, I'm looking to play a different game."

"And surveillance is that game?" Benson raised his eyebrows.

"I just need a few tricks of the trade."

"What kind of tricks are we talking about?" Benson leaned back and crossed his arms.

"Surveillance. Audio, video, the works. I need to monitor a mark without them ever knowing I'm there."

"Heavy stuff, man." Benson let out a low whistle. "Lucky for you, I know a guy. He's a real Double-O-Seven when it comes to this shit. Give me a couple of days, and I'll get you kitted out with everything you need — bugs, minicams, long-range mics. Best on the market."

"That sounds great. And it's Q who makes the gadgets. Not Bond."

"Okay, nerd." Benson grinned in victory. "You were talking outside the Cameo like you didn't have a pot to piss in. And now you want the best on the market?"

"Circumstances change. And I'm just happy for the help."

"Sure you are." Benson grinned again. "But you're gonna owe me."

"I figured."

"And don't think I won't collect." Benson drained his

beer and slid out of the booth. "A couple of days. I'll be in touch."

It was three days later when Ricky found himself in a nondescript warehouse, with Benson's contact Malik giving him a crash course in Espionage 101. With a grin like a cat in a yarn shop, he explained a myriad of espionage tools, vibrating with excitement. He demonstrated gadgets and explained their various functions, with Ricky working hard to keep up with unfamiliar jargon. It'd been a long time since he'd been in school.

"So this little beauty is your basic Unidirectional Condenser Microphone." Malik held up a small black cylinder roughly the size of a pencil eraser. "*Ultra*-sensitive. Shit can pick up a whisper from fifty feet. Plant a few of these puppies around your primary target area, and you won't believe all the barking."

Malice then moved on to explaining a series of lenses and transmitters, syncing them to Ricky's laptop for remote viewing.

"BAM! Just like that, you've got 24/7 access to every room in the house. Better than cable. Sometimes amateur fucking is better than anything you can find on Pornhub. This," — he held up a transmitter — "will give you sound so good you can practically smell the pussy. "

Ricky swallowed down the sour taste at the back of his throat. This was so far beyond anything he had done in the past. Everything about it felt wrong. Violation on a visceral level. His stomach flip-flopped.

"Problem?" Malik asked.

"Ulcer." Ricky glanced at his phone. At the lock-screen photo of Mikey. He was smaller than other kids his age. Pale face. But always a smile. This one job would pay the backlog of medical bills and any future issues that might crop up.

He'd do this for Mikey.

He looked at Malik. "Continue."

He spent the rest of the day memorizing Malik's instructions, trying not to dwell on the pool of dread in his stomach. By the time it was dark, he had all the gear he needed. It was time to "get creative" as Veronica had said.

~

Soon, Ricky was surfing the waves of voyeurism with the grace of a seasoned pirate.

Over the course of the week, Ricky settled into an uneasy routine, trailing Chloe Simone from a distance, echoing the schedule of her daily life. It started with sunrise yoga and often ended with something relatively mundane like browsing the aisles of Provisions, filling her cart with organic produce and pints of ice cream that Ricky couldn't imagine she'd actually eat. All while she was disguised.

To anyone else, she simply looked like a civilian.

Ricky managed to plant a few bugs in her Cayenne. But his big break came when he capitalized on her weekly two-hour spa appointment. That was the time when her home was relatively empty, and the security detail relaxed its vigilance.

Ricky posed as a security consultant, with a spoofed text from Chloe courtesy of Malik that proved he was supposed to be there. Planting a camera at the front door was priority one, just in case he couldn't get one anywhere else. But access to the entire house came easier than Ricky anticipated, so he was able to quickly finish the job. Apparently, her security team had been pressuring her to install a more up-to-date system, so they were more than happy to show him the blind spots and their own areas of concern.

But even after planting all those cameras and bugs, he failed to pick up so much as a hint of any illicit rendezvous with Marcus Ball.

Until Veronica called with a tip.

"Marcus told me he's going to Aspen for the weekend." Veronica's voice was tight with tempered rage. "Supposedly, some industry get-together on the slopes. But—"

Ricky waited. By now, he knew better than to interrupt her.

"—his jet is still in the hangar."

"And you think he's with Chloe?"

"I'd bet my Botox on it." Veronica hung up without another word.

Ricky parked a block away from Chloe's estate and logged into the surveillance network. Camera feeds blinked to life: living room, kitchen, master bedroom. All of them, empty.

But Ricky saw a flash of movement in the backyard.

He clicked on the exterior camera and zoomed in. And there it was. Chloe and Marcus, with their bodies braided together in the jacuzzi. He felt a surge of disappointment. He'd been hoping Veronica was wrong. That he'd be able to report back that Marcus might be having an affair, but it wasn't with Chloe.

He was wrong.

His hand tightened on the mouse. *Gotcha.*

Ricky unmuted the audio to hear their hushed conversation over the humming jet sprays. Malik had been right about the sound quality. A+.

"We can't keep doing this," Chloe said with her head on his chest. "Sneaking around like fucking teenagers. It's killing me, Marcus."

"Just a little longer. I'll leave her after Damsel in the Dungeon comes out."

Chloe sat. "And then what? We ride off into the sunset? Live happily ever after?" She barked a laugh, the sound brittle and pained. "Wake up, Marcus. Veronica isn't the kind of woman who knows how to let go. The rumors about what happened to Glen ..."

"Oh, come on, Chloe. You don't really believe ..."

"That she killed her first husband and made it look like a suicide? I find it easier and easier to believe all the time. And after some of the stories you've told me ...?"

Ricky rocked back in his seat, stunned. *Holy shit.*

He had heard the rumor once or twice. How could he not have? All of Hollywood had. But even with his intimate small glimpse into Veronica's darker side, this was the first time he wondered if it had any validity. Because these people actually knew Veronica.

"She threatened you with a knife, Marcus."

"She was angry."

"And violent. She sent you to the hospital over an argument about set lighting. You should have called the cops."

To the hospital? Ricky remembered that. Marcus had come out with a press release saying he cut his hand while chopping mushrooms.

"I was protecting her."

"Yeah, well, maybe you've done that too much."

He held out a hand to her, drawing her back toward his lap. "It was just the once."

She looked at him.

"Alright twice. But nothing since then. I swear to you she's not dangerous."

But Chloe didn't look convinced. And now Ricky wasn't either.

Veronica had stabbed Marcus over a disagreement about lighting. What the fuck was she gonna do when she had evidence of him cheating?

And who was she going to turn the knife on at that time?

Christ. Ricky had a feeling he was working for the wrong person.

He snapped the laptop shut and tossed it on the passenger seat. He had to get out of this. Extricate himself before things spiraled even further out of control.

He pulled out his phone and dialed Veronica's number.

"This better be good news," she said. "I assume you have proof?"

"I've been watching them for a week now and nothing. I think your suspicions were misplaced."

"I won't ask you again, Mr. Rivera," Veronica replied after a long silence. "Do you have evidence of the affair or not?"

"No." Ricky poured every ounce of conviction he could muster into the lie. "I don't believe an affair is happening. Or if it is, it's not between Marcus and Chloe. So I'm ending our arrangement."

"Is that so?" Her laugh was like a bag of broken glass. "What a shame. And after I thought we had an understanding."

Ricky frowned. "What's that supposed to mean?"

"It means that my position on the board of Shriners Children's Hospital affords me a certain sway in decision-making. I suggest you not force me into the sort of choices that might make life difficult for a sick child. Especially one whose deadbeat father is months behind on his bills."

"You wouldn't—"

"Wouldn't I?" Veronica Grove might have been a rom-com queen, but she was also a human disease with a voice dripping in venom. "Don't test me, Rivera. I know that my husband is having an affair. Proof will be in my inbox by

Monday, or I'll show you how deep my influence runs in this town."

The line went dead.

Ricky stared at the phone in his hand, numb with shock and impotent rage.

Her words hanging over him like a guillotine…

RICKY'S STOMACH CHURNED.

Christ, he actually might have an ulcer.

He wasn't stupid — *desperate* enough to get Mikey tangled up in this nightmare, was he? But yeah, he was. Thanks to his piss-poor choices, his kid was now square in this vindictive woman's crosshairs. And clearly, she had no qualms about exploiting a sick child for her own twisted agenda.

God, Sheila couldn't find out about this.

She'd take him back to court. Get sole custody. He wouldn't see Mikey until he was eighteen. If he ever did. Who knew what acid she'd pour in his ears while Ricky was absent.

It felt like he was drowning, his lungs filling with icy water. There had to be a way out of this. Some angle he wasn't seeing.

A life raft in the churning sea.

And then, it hit him.

He stared out the window. He couldn't actually do it, could he?

A woman was walking her poodle, watched it squatting to shit and didn't bother to clean up after it. She noticed him watching and flipped him the bird.

He didn't respond.

It was a reckless plan. Likely to blow up in his face. But crazy was the only play he had left.

The next morning, he sat waiting in his vehicle outside Chloe's gated estate. When her Cayenne nosed onto the quiet street, Ricky stepped directly into its path.

The SUV screeched to a halt, missing him by inches.

He didn't flinch, raising his camera and snapping the shutter. The driver's door flew open, and a human mountain in a black suit barreled toward him, meaty fists already swinging.

"You picked the wrong mark, asshole." The bodyguard grabbed Ricky by his throat and slammed him backwards into the trunk of his car. "Ms. Simone's off limits to you, bottom-feeding paps."

Ricky choked, scrabbling at the iron grip, black spots dancing before his eyes.

"Veronica …" he wheezed, vocal cords straining against the pressure. "Veronica knows … about Marcus…"

The hand slackened.

The bodyguard took a step back. "What?"

Ricky stepped away from the man. "Veronica knows all about Marcus and Chloe."

"What is it, Dex?" Chloe's voice cut through the sound of blood roaring in his ears.

The bodyguard looked over at her. "This guy is saying Ms Grove knows about—"

"Hush." Her face paled. She gestured to the vehicle. "Wait there."

The bodyguard nodded, retreating.

Ricky glanced at her. She was more beautiful in person. White skin, narrow chin, small teeth. But her famous face was pinched with worry behind oversized sunglasses. "What did you just say about Veronica Grove?"

He sucked in a shaky breath and let it out slowly. "Not here. I'll tell you everything in private."

Chloe studied Ricky for a long beat. Then she nodded, walking back to the steel gates of her estate. "My place. Let's go."

Minutes later, Ricky was perched on a barstool in her pristine kitchen, holding an ice pack to his throat.

Chloe selected a bottle of water from the fridge and uncapped it. "Start talking."

"Veronica hired me to spy on you." His voice sounded hoarse. Most likely from the hulk shaking hands with his neck. "Well, on you and Marcus. She wanted proof of your affair."

"Does she know or suspect?"

"She suspects. *Strongly*."

"How long have you been watching?"

"A week."

She frowned. "Which means you have proof. So what is this? Blackmail."

"Jesus, no!" Ricky shook his head. "But I heard the hot-tub conversation. That she can be violent. So I decided not to hand it over."

"A pap with a conscience." Chloe snorted. "Never thought I'd live to see the day. So why are you here?"

"I tried to get out of the deal. But she's threatening my kid. Says she'll get him kicked out of the hospital program if I don't deliver what she wants. It's the only thing keeping him alive."

"Ah." Chloe pressed a hand to her mouth. "I knew she'd be upset if she found out, but that's…"

"Psychotic?" Ricky finished with a bitter laugh. "I'm beginning to get that impression." He leaned closer to Chloe. "I admit I fucked up. Big time. But I want to make it right. I was thinking … what if we turned this around? Used Veronica's tactics against her?"

Chloe frowned. "What do you mean?"

"What if, instead of giving her ammo to use against you, I start looking for skeletons in her designer closet. Mutually assured destruction."

"And then what?" Chloe squinted, then smoothed out her brow. "I live the rest of my life waiting for the other shoe to drop? No way. I can't do that." She shook her head. "I *won't* do that. The whole reason I got into this mess was because I was tired of living a lie. Of pretending to be something I'm not. What's the point if I have to resort to blackmail to maintain the charade?"

Ricky opened his mouth to speak. But the words died on his tongue. Because damn it, Chloe was right. Fighting fire with fire would only leave everyone in ashes at the end.

"Okay. No blackmail."

"Agreed." Her voice was small and exhausted. Fragile in a way he'd never heard from the publicly unflappable Chloe Simone. She drew in a shaky breath.

"I wasn't thrilled about the idea anyway."

"No?"

He shook his head. "I like taking pictures. All this —" he waved a hand — "surreptitious shit gives me a stomach ache. I was just trying to help us both out, I guess."

She leaned in, brushing a feather-light kiss to his cheek. "Thank you for trying, even if your methods were … questionable."

"That's one word for it." Ricky surprised himself with a laugh.

The moment felt charged with something fragile and new.

"I'm not used to that," Chloe said.

He met her eyes. Her eyes seemed wider. Her lips opened.

"Used to what?" His voice was no more than a croak.

She shrugged.

"People being kind. Honest. It's unusual in Hollywood." She leaned closer as though compelled by an almost chemical curiosity.

Her breath hitched, tongue darting out to wet her lips. "Ricky ..."

He leaned forward.

And then they were kissing, deep and desperate, a tangle of seeking hands and urgent mouths. And then they were moving. He had no idea where he was going, just followed her through the maze to her bedroom, shedding clothes along the way ...

RICKY LAY ON HIS BACK, staring up at the crystal chandelier.

The sheets rustled beside him. He glanced to the left and saw Chloe propped on her elbow, watching him. "Don't suppose this is where you thought your day would go?"

He laughed. "Nope."

"Tell me about yourself." Chloe lay a hand on his chest, her fingers tracing idle patterns on his skin in the afterglow. "Married?"

"Not anymore."

"You cheat on her?"

He hesitated. Considered lying. "Yeah."

"Actress?"

He shook his head. "Photography assistant."

She laughed.

"And your kid?"

"Mikey." He smiled. "Light of my life. Didn't know she was pregnant when I cheated."

"Otherwise you wouldn't have?" She raised a skeptical brow.

"No. Probably still would have." They'd been having trouble for months. Mikey just turned their relationship into a pressure cooker. "What about you?"

"Oh, typical Hollywood story. Famous parent. Greased all the wheels. So here I am. Although that doesn't keep the ticket sales going or prevent tepid reviews, does it? This fucking industry puts an expiration date on women before we even get started."

"You'll weather it. You are so much more than your career. Or any review or box office total."

She looked down at him and smiled. "Thank you. For seeing me. The real Chloe."

He nodded, then glanced at his watch. "I should get going."

She didn't stop him, so he rolled out of bed and dressed.

"Take my picture?" Her voice was soft and slightly husky from shared confidences.

He glanced over at her. "Now?" He nodded at her form, dressed only in Egyptian cotton. "Like that?"

Chloe nodded.

"Sure." He retrieved his camera from the kitchen. Looking through the viewfinder to focus on her raw beauty, skin aglow. And then she closed her eyes, looking peaceful.

Ricky snapped away, capturing dozens of photos in the morning light. "What do you think?"

He walked over to her and swiped through the digital images.

She smiled. "I want to use one of these for my Entertainment Weekly spread, assuming they'll let me."

"Are you sure about that?" The moment felt dangerous.

"I am if you are. Though I don't imagine Veronica will be pleased to see your name on the byline."

No, he didn't suppose she would be.

Which meant he didn't have long to flip the switch on her. Because even if Chloe didn't want to participate, the only way he could protect Mikey was by getting the drop on Veronica.

RICKY HAD BEEN TAILING Veronica for several days. Bugging her car, hacking her phone, employing all the same tricks he had used on Chloe.

The problem was that not only could Ricky not get anything on Veronica, but he also couldn't stop thinking about Chloe. The feel of her skin and the taste of her lips, the way she had looked at him like he was more than a bottom-feeding pap. Like he actually mattered.

She had burrowed under his skin.

Maybe he should just give up and let the chips fall where they may. He'd fight her on Mikey if he needed to. His phone buzzed with an incoming call. Veronica.

"Why am I having to call you for reports?" she asked.

"I told you, there's nothing there. Chloe and Marcus aren't—"

"I'm throwing a soirée for my beloved husband's birthday this weekend. I want you there to document the festivities."

He blinked. "I thought the whole point was to be discreet."

"Who said I wanted you to be seen?" Ricky could picture her wrinkling that pointy little nose. "You will slip in through the back gate. I'll leave it unlocked. Go upstairs to his private office. Set up shop in the closet. I'll arrange for the two of them to be alone there together. Get the evidence I need, and your son will get the help he needs."

"Text me the details."

He disconnected and hung up. Fuck. Now what? He called Chloe but couldn't get a hold of her. So he sent her a message, warning her of the trap.

And then he paused.

Maybe this could work out in his benefit after all.

When Marcus and Chloe didn't meet in his office, surely Veronica would be upset. Maybe he could capture her on video admitting that she was blackmailing him. Using his son's health to do her dirty work.

Get that on audio or video, and he'd have something to hold over her head.

No actress would want to be caught threatening a kid's life.

He smiled.

Yeah, he was gonna go. And everything would work out just fine.

RICKY ARRIVED at Veronica's mansion on schedule, camera bag slung over his shoulder.

But he was nervous. He'd have to play it carefully if he was going to get her to admit to pressuring him.

The back gate was unlocked as promised.

Ricky slipped inside, keeping to the shadows while skirting the perimeter. Muffled music and chatter, the clinking of glasses, and occasional explosions of laughter.

But the service entrance door was locked. Fuck. An unusual-looking stone was on the ground next to it. Plastic. And sure enough, there was the key.

He opened the door, then pocketed it, creeping into the darkened mudroom.

Veronica's directions were explicit. Up the rear stairs, then the second door on the left was her husband's private sanctum. Ricky winced at every creak and groan of the floorboards. But no one came to apprehend him. The party continued below.

He found the office easily enough. The heavy oak door yielded under his touch. It was dark inside. Curtains drawn.

He entered and closed the door behind him.

Then he reached for the light switch and flicked it. He turned around and—

Froze in horror.

Marcus Ball lay sprawled on the Persian rug. A pool of crimson spread out around him. His sightless gaze on the coffered ceiling. A gaping wound like a grotesque mouth silently screaming across his chest.

"Jesus fucking Christ." Ricky stumbled back against the door.

This couldn't be happening. It must be some sort of sick joke, a prank or—

A muffled *thump* sounded from across the room. That was the closet Veronica had told him about. He heard a distinctly feminine gasp.

Jesus Christ, what if Veronica put Chloe in there?

And was coming back to kill her.

He ran across the room and yanked the door open.

Veronica and Chloe both tumbled out. Eyes wide and terrified above makeshift gags, both bound, hands and feet secured with zip ties.

"What the fuck happened?" Ricky ran to the desk, spotted a pair of scissors lying on top, grabbed them, and began to run back.

Chloe screamed.

He recoiled, stopping cold halfway there.

"Stay away from us!" Her eyes were wide, terrified.

"I'm trying to help!" Ricky exclaimed.

Veronica managed to spit out her gag. "Keep away from him, Chloe."

"*Oh God*," Chloe said, writhing in her bonds, tears spilling down her cheeks. "He'll kill us, too. Just like he murdered Marcus."

"That's INSANE! I didn't—"

"Fucking stalker," Veronica said.

Chloe lunged for Ricky with a wild cry, head-butting him in the stomach.

He stumbled back, arms pinwheeling. The scissors went flying. He slipped on the slick pool of blood and fell hard. His head cracked against the desk.

Veronica screamed. "Help!"

The world spun.

Darkness everywhere.

Sirens.

Feet pounding.

Loud voices.

Rough hands.

"LAPD! Nobody move!"

And then the cold bite of metal on his wrists. He blinked blood from his eyes, uncomprehending. Cops swarmed the room, converging on a hysterical Veronica and Chloe.

"He's been stalking us for weeks!" Veronica cried out through her sobs, clutching at Chloe like a lifeline. "We've had threatening letters and hang-up calls. But we never really thought he would take it this far."

Chloe nodded. "My bodyguard, Dex, will tell you. He stopped me on the road. I tried to be nice. Reason with him, even. I thought maybe I could get through to him. But he's obsessed. *Delusional*."

"That's not true!" Ricky struggled against the cuffs. "They're lying, I didn't do this. I'M BEING FRAMED!"

But the cops dragged him out, past the gawking party-goers and a sea of flashbulbs, and the paparazzi descended like vultures. He caught a final glimpse of Benson. Looking curious. Before he raised his camera and took a photo …

THEY HAD him dead to rights, of course: photos of Chloe lying in bed asleep, taken inside her home. An apartment full of surveillance equipment like something out of a Tom Clancy novel. Texts with Veronica, painting a picture of an unhinged stalker taking orders from a femme fatale, but going to a phone that was found in the trunk of Ricky's own car.

Ricky's court-appointed lawyer did his best, but it was like a sandcastle trying to stave off the tide. The evidence was too overwhelming.

The jury deliberated for less than an hour.

Guilty on all counts.

The judge sentenced him to life without the possibility of parole. The verdict landed like a sledgehammer, shattering Ricky's future with a finality that echoed through the courtroom. He was still reeling as they led him away in chains, his pleas of innocence sounding ridiculous to everyone. Sheila hadn't even come.

He was photographed. Fingerprinted. Stripped of his clothes, dignity, and freedom.

One image replayed over and over in Ricky's head. Chloe and Veronica, facing down the hungry horde of reporters with tears trembling on their lashes. Both a picture of innocence and victimhood.

Martyrs. Survivors. Women wronged who had triumphed over the monster in the end.

The press gobbled it up like so many gallons of ice cream.

Blockbuster deals magically materialized for both actresses, and producers fell over themselves to cash in on the real-life drama. A co-authored tell-all promising the sordid details of their harrowing ordeal for an ungodly sum.

Ricky couldn't even summon the will to feel bitter. They were all playing a game. Only Chloe and Veronica were playing chess instead of hide and go seek.

Ricky hadn't even been on the board.

~

AFTERSHOCKS ON SEEN.

THE ORIGINAL PITCH came from a production company meeting where the executive said he was really looking for a modern day *Conversation*. That story never happened, but I wrote this the next day — a 300-word version of the narrative — and the short spilled out shortly after.

Seen is what happens when classic noir DNA gets spliced with iPhone cameras and TMZ culture. What if the hunter became the hunted?

Ricky Rivera is a paparazzi with a conscience, which

makes him terrible at his job and perfect for manipulation. He's got medical bills crushing him, a son who needs him, and a camera that pays just enough to keep both their heads above water. When Hollywood's most elusive star offers him the score of a lifetime, he thinks he's finally caught a break.

He's caught something, all right. Just not what he thinks. Because in Hollywood, bait always comes with better marketing than the hook.

The beauty of noir isn't the crime. It's the setup. The way decent people get maneuvered into impossible choices, step by step, until they're standing in a room full of blood with their fingerprints on the murder weapon.

Everyone's watching everyone in our surveillance state. Privacy is a luxury good, available to the highest bidder but discontinued for everyone else. Cameras are everywhere, recording everything, except the truth. Because the truth isn't what happened if the footage shows something different.

And footage, like evidence, can be curated. Edited. Arranged. Seasoned to taste.

Seen reverses the predator-prey dynamic that fuels celebrity culture. The stalker becomes the stalked. The watcher becomes the watched. The man behind the camera discovers that the most dangerous place to be isn't in front of the lens — it's thinking you're safe behind it.

THIRTEEN

Terminal Subscription

THE GRAND CANYON is a half mile wide, a mile long, and 150 feet deep. A warning sign at the edge reads *DANGER: Fatal Falls Occur Here.* The letters are faded from sun exposure, the red paint bleached to a dull pink. People have added their own warnings beneath in marker: *Think of your family. It's not worth it. Look up, not down.* I trace my fingers over these desperate pleas, wondering who they saved — and who they didn't.

There are 11 deaths annually. Not all from falls. Dehydration, helicopter crashes, overheating. It's weird to think about because the place is so damn beautiful.

The sunrise this morning is comprised of red, orange, and pink stripes: light that stretches back through time.

I am alone on the east rim. The viewing platform won't fill with tourists for another few hours. It's just me and the canyon, exactly as I like it. The display in my corneal implant reads 5:48 AM. Temperature: 58°F.

My breakfast, a protein bar with synthetic honey, doesn't taste nearly as good as it sounds. But it has my vitamins and minerals for the day. And I need to fuel up for the three-hour drive back to Vegas. It might seem weird to come to the canyon for sunrise, but it's my favorite place to reset.

I wipe crumbs from my jacket and take a step closer to the edge. The morning wind brushes my face, tugging at my hair the way Eve used to when we were kids, trying to get my attention while I read.

Let's play, Ciara. Come on. You're so boring.

The memory slips in uninvited. I push it away, focusing on the sedimentary layers in front of me. Vishnu Schist at the bottom. Zoroaster Granite intruding. Tapeats Sand-stone above that. The corneal implant tells me this, but I no longer need to read it. I studied geology in College and know them all by heart; they are a perfect chronology of Earth's history. Eve never understood my love of rocks. "They're just dead things," she'd say, tossing one of my specimens into the air and catching it with theatrical bore-dom. "People are alive. They change, they surprise you." She'd lean close then, her face — my face, but somehow more alive — inches from mine. "When has a rock ever surprised you, Ciara?"I never told her that was exactly why I loved them: their constancy, their refusal to disappoint.

She cared about people, about connections, about living in the *now*. So while I collected rocks, she gathered friends and lived like tomorrow might be a lie.

Turns out she was right about that part.

I close my eyes, letting the canyon's silence envelop me. This place has been my refuge since our parents first brought us here. It's what started my love of geology in the first place. Eve would get bored after ten minutes of looking at "old rocks," while I sat mesmerized. Not that it got me a job. Mom had warned me that no one was looking to hiregeologists. Turns out she was right.

After Eve's diagnosis, I came here more often. Telling

myself it was about the hiking, the exercise, the fresh air. But I was lying. Of course, it was about escape.

My implant beeps. A message from the hospital.

It has been 4 years, 11 months, and 30 days since patient Eve Miller deceased. Your psychological well-being assessment is due. Please schedule an appointment with Dr. Nakamura at your earliest convenience.

I dismiss the notification. The canyon doesn't care about psychological assessments either.

The sun climbs higher, illuminating the opposite rim. I should head back. Sunday dinner with Mom is at six, and I'll need time to shower and change after the drive. She'll notice if I'm late. She notices everything now, especially all the ways I'm not Eve.

Having a dead twin is a pain in the ass.

I take one last look at the vastness before me. The canyon remains indifferent to human suffering, to sisters and guilt and the unfairness of genetic lottery tickets that gave Eve leukemia and spared me.

The drive to Vegas will give me time to prepare my answers to Mom's inevitable questions.

Have you been taking care of yourself? (Any sign of leukemia?)

Any promising developments at work? (Are you still NOT using your degree?)

Have you been seeing anyone? (Will I get grandkids before I die?)

The canyon recedes in my rearview, a wound in the Earth that never heals. I envy its constancy. I press the acceleration pad and rejoin the traffic stream heading west. The highway unfurls before me like a black ribbon tying together all the places I've been running to and from. Each broken white line is another stitch in the tapestry of my half-lived life, neither fully myself nor the ghost of my sister, but something caught in between, like twilight refusing to commit to either day or night.

I glance at the mirror again. My eyes look like Eve's now, optimized to the same shade of brown, the small genetic deviation between twins corrected without my consent. My scar is fading too, the one above my eyebrow that always distinguished us. NexaBio calls this "aesthetic harmonization." I call it erasure.

Soon, there will be nothing left of the original me, just an upgraded replica without the imperfections that made me Ciara instead of Eve.

Maybe that was mom's plan all along.

My implant chimes. An incoming call.

The vehicle's systems automatically reduce the music as the caller ID appears in my field of vision: *The Revolutions Resort & Casino.* Probably calling to say I didn't get the job. I interviewed three weeks ago. Assistant to the Events Coordinator. I don't know if it's a good fit, but I sure need the work. Assisting Mario at the laundry mat isn't paying the bills. But I felt like I flubbed the interview. Something Eve would have excelled at.

I accept the call.

"Ms. Miller? This is Daria Suarez from Human Resources at the Revolutions. Do you have a moment to speak?"

"I do."

"Excellent. I'm pleased to inform you that we would like to offer you the position of Assistant to Ms. Ling, our Events Coordinator. We'd like you to start tomorrow morning if that works for you. Nine AM sharp for orientation and paperwork. Does that timeline suit your schedule?"

I open my mouth to say I need to give Mario at least two weeks.

"That works perfectly," I say instead.

"Wonderful. We look forward to welcoming you to the Revolutions family."

The call ends. I pull onto the shoulder and sit in stunned silence for thirty seconds before a laugh bubbles up from somewhere deep inside me. Then I dance in my seat, drumming my hands on the steering wheel like Eve used to do when she was excited. The motion feels foreign, almost wrong, in my body.

My salary has just doubled.

I call Mario. He won't be in on the weekend, but I leave a message saying I feel ill. I'm not quitting until I sign on the dotted line. I've been burned before.

I pull back onto the highway once traffic slows enough to allow it. The endless desert stretches ahead. And all the possibilities in the world are before me.

Vegas rises from the desert like a mirage, a shimmering promise that defies the natural world. The city that never sleeps, offering the American Dream for the price of a nightmare. Where fortunes are made and unmade with the turn of a card, where enhancement is the new enchantment, where people come to lose themselves and find something else. Something better. Something optimized.

Its neon spines pierce the sky. A human-made mountain range that never eroded or settled into something sustainable. Billboard-sized advertisements for NexaBio flash alongside the highway as I approach: *Become Your Better Self.* Faces transition from tired to radiant, from ordinary to luminous. The before-and-after of modern evolution.

My mother's house is exactly 1,200 square feet of weaponized memory. Every inch of wall space carries

Eve's face: school photos, the debate team, the charity swim-a-thon she completed six months before her diagnosis. An entire life, frozen in carefully arranged frames.

I search for myself in the tableau, same as I always do. A few obligatory birthday shots from when we were young: our fifth birthday with matching dresses but different expressions, Eve beaming while I squint at the camera. One of us carving pumpkins at the kitchen table, her grinning through pumpkin guts, me in the corner of the frame, expressionless, a butter knife in my hand because I was scared I'd cut myself. Another from a camping trip, both of us wrapped in blankets. Eve is pretending to be a monster about to devour me. Of course, she looks radiant.

I'm there, technically. But the light is always on her in each of them.

Maybe it's just how the camera caught it.

Maybe not.

The photo of me at the Grand Canyon used to hang near the entrance — the only solo image my mother had displayed. It's no longer there.

"You changed things around," I say. "My photo is gone."

Mom emerges from the kitchen, drying her hands on a towel. At sixty-three, she still moves with the precision of the hospital administrator she was for thirty years. Her silver-streaked hair is pulled into a neat bun, her posture straight.

"Just freshening things up. Why keep a picture when I see you every Sunday? It's not like I forget what you look like."

No. But nor has she forgotten what Eve looks like. She sees her face every time she looks at mine.

"Dinner's almost ready. Set the table."

I go into the kitchen and take out two plates instead of

the four that once belonged on the table. Dad's been gone almost as long as Eve — a heart attack while working in the garage. Sometimes I wonder if grief accelerated whatever genetic time bomb was ticking in his chest.

She's made lasagna.

Eve's favorite meal.

Mine is shepherd's pie. But we never eat that.

Mom dishes it out, while I fill the glasses with water. When she finally joins me at the table, she slides a glossy blue and silver pamphlet toward me.

NexaBio.

My shoulders tense. "What's this?"

Though I know exactly what it is.

"They were handing those out at the community center yesterday," she says. "Thought you might want to take another look."

"We've talked about this."

"There's a ten percent discount if you sign up within the next three days."

"I'm not interested."

"Ciara, be reasonable. Everyone your age is doing it. Half of my bridge group has signed their grandchildren up. Even their great-grandchildren who haven't been born yet. "

"Good for them."

Mom sighs, placing her fork down. "You know Eve would have jumped at the chance. She always embraced new technologies."

The comparison lands exactly how she knew it would.

"Yeah, well, I'm not Eve."

"Clearly." The word has edges sharp enough to cut.

We eat in silence for several minutes. Her disappointment is an unwelcome guest at the table.

"I got a new job," I say finally.

Her eyebrows lift. "I thought you liked the laundry mat."

I resist the urge to glare. No one *likes* the laundry mat. Especially when Mario spends most of his day sniffing the client's underwear.

I ignore her comment." Revolutions Casino."

Genuine surprise crosses her face. "Doing what?"

"Assistant to the Events Coordinator." I take a sip of water. "I start tomorrow."

It was the kind of social position Eve would have thrived in. Obviously, I don't say this aloud.

My mother studies me across the table, as if trying to decode this decision. "The Revolutions offer NexaBio benefits, don't they? Corporate rates for employees?"

I set my fork down. "Most major corporations do these days. It doesn't mean I'm going to sign up."

Mom leaned forward. "Eve never got the chance to improve herself. She would have done anything for more time."

I don't know about that. When Eve died, she seemed very content with the life she had lived. Or at least that's what she told me.

Mom's voice cracks slightly. "How can you choose less for yourself when you've been given the future she never had?"

The guilt is expertly deployed, precision-guided to find the frailties in my defenses.

"I need to use the bathroom," I say, standing up.

I lock the door behind me and lean against the counter, staring at my reflection.

Eve's reflection. Except my eyes are a shade darker. And I have a small scar above my right eyebrow from when I fell hiking at the canyon.

Same raw materials, different outcomes. Eve got

charm, intuition, natural grace — the genetic lottery's jackpot winner. I got stubbornness, cowardice, and a body that didn't betray itself with corrupted cells. We were mirror images cracked in different places, her flaws fatal and mine merely crippling.

The NexaBio pamphlet is gone when I return to the table, but its ghost still lingers in the space between us.

THE EMPLOYEE ENTRANCE is a glaring contrast to the opulent front-of-house designed for the tourists. Steel doors, biometric scanners, and security personnel with augmented vision implants filter out anyone who doesn't belong.

I arrive thirty minutes early, dressed in the appropriate business attire that was sent as a request to my implant overnight. Black slacks, white blouse, sensible shoes. Professional, but forgettable — exactly how I prefer to move through the world.

"Ciara Miller for orientation."

The security guard barely glances up as he scans my retinal pattern. "HR is expecting you. Take the second elevator to floor B3."

The subsurface levels of the Revolutions are a maze of administrative offices, storage areas, and employee facilities. Utilitarian gray walls with occasional artwork, reproduction pieces too faded or damaged for public display, break the monotony.

I find HR easily enough. The department occupies a glass-walled space decorated with motivational holographs that shift every few minutes. A slender woman with an immaculate silver bob rises from behind the reception desk as I enter.

It's Daria.

She extends a well-manicured hand. "Early. I appreciate that."

Her handshake is firm and brief, professional without being intimidating. I liked her when we met for the interview, and I still do.

She gestures toward a small conference room. "Shall we get started on your paperwork?"

The next two hours are a blur of physical and digital documents. Employment contract. Tax forms. Insurance options. Retirement plans. Security protocols. The casino's strict privacy policies and code of conduct.

Daria guides me through each one, answering my questions before I ask them.

"And now for the exciting part," she says after the essential documentation is complete. "Additional benefits. The Revolutions is proud to offer a comprehensive wellness package that goes beyond traditional healthcare."

She slides a familiar blue and silver pamphlet across the table, identical to the one my mother left out last night.

"NexaBio's Genomic+ Plans are available to all employees at a significant corporate discount. Over ninety-eight percent of our staff participate in some level of optimization."

I stare at the glossy paper without touching it. *Better You, Better World.*

"As a premier resort, we naturally want our team operating at peak efficiency," Daria continues. "The basic plan is actually included in your compensation package at no additional cost, though most employees opt for the Elite or Platinum tiers through payroll deduction."

"It's optional, though?" I keep my voice neutral.

Daria's perfect smile flickers.

"Of course. Completely optional." She tilts her head

slightly. "Though I've never had a new hire decline. The advantages are substantial, particularly for those in guest-facing roles or positions with advancement potential."

I meet her gaze. "I prefer to remain unmodified, at least for now. Thank you."

A beat of silence follows as Daria processes this unexpected response. But then her smile returns, professionally unbothered. "As you wish."

The rest of the orientation passes without incident. Daria shows me the employee dining facilities, the locker rooms, and the break areas. She introduces me to security personnel and department heads we encounter along the way. By noon, I have my access card, uniform standards, department guidelines, and a meeting scheduled with Mei Ling, the Events Coordinator I'll be assisting.

"Any questions before we wrap up the administrative portion?" Daria asks when we return to the HR department.

"No, you've covered everything."

"Excellent." She nods. "Ms. Ling is expecting you at two o'clock. That gives you time for lunch if you'd like." She hesitates, then adds, "If I may offer some advice, Ciara?"

"Of course."

"Ms. Ling is … demanding. Brilliant at what she does, but she expects the same level of commitment and perfection from her assistants. The position has had significant turnover." Her voice lowers slightly. "She usually only works with optimized staff."

The implication is clear. I straighten my shoulders. "I appreciate the insight, but I'm confident in my abilities."

"Naturally," Daria says, professional mask firmly back in place. "You can always change your mind later. The corporate discount applies whenever you decide to enroll."

I thank her and make my way to the employee dining room. As I join the lunch line, I can't help but study the staff around me.

Optimized.

All of them?

Well, 98%.

I wonder who isn't. Maybe she meant me?

Doubt creeps in for the first time since receiving the job offer. I've positioned myself as the only natural human in a sea of enhanced colleagues, reporting to a boss who apparently prefers her assistants upgraded.

Maybe I should call and go back to the laundry mat.

But no.

I need this paycheck.

I finish my lunch and head toward the Events Department to meet Mei Ling, wondering if Eve would have already signed the NexaBio paperwork, embracing the chance to be better, stronger, more.

Probably. But then, we always made different choices.

EIGHT MONTHS PASS in a haze of schedules, client meetings, and endless attention to the details that make Mei Ling legendary in the events world. I quickly learn that her reputation for demanding excellence is well-earned. Nothing escapes her notice, not a misplaced centerpiece, an incorrectly worded invitation, or a server whose smile doesn't reach their eyes.

"Three millimeters to the left," she tells a decorator adjusting a holographic ice sculpture for the Northern Pharmaceuticals gala. Her eye for perfection is unnerving.

The decorator makes the adjustment, then turns to me. "Ciara, check that the ambient lighting transitions match the revised timeline. The CEO's speech runs seven minutes longer than originally planned."

I'm already updating the program on my tablet. "Adjusted and synchronized with the kitchen for delayed dessert service."

"Good. Now confirm the allergy accommodations for table seventeen."

Good.

It's the closest thing to approval I've received so far. Mei is as efficient with praise as she is with everything else, dispensing it only when necessary.

Working for Mei is exhausting but educational. The woman runs her department like a military operation, each event a campaign.

I don't know if she likes me, but she tolerates me. Which, according to Zoe, my closest workplace ally, is high praise.

"She hasn't made you cry yet," Zoe points out when we take our lunch in the staff courtyard. "That's practically a declaration of love."

I laugh.

And I'm so grateful to have found Zoe.

She manages VIP reservations for the Revolutions' exclusive restaurants and has been at the resort for five years, working her way up from hostess to her current position. With quick wit and an easy laugh, she reminds me of Eve in ways that should be painful but somehow aren't.

"Maybe I'm just better at hiding my tears," I say, picking at my salad.

"Impossible. Mei can smell weakness. It's part of her optimization package." Zoe takes a bite of her chicken sandwich. "Speaking of which, any update on your holdout status?"

I shake my head. "Still stubbornly unmodified."

"Brave woman. I couldn't do it." She taps the side of her head. "Best decision I ever made, honestly. Memory enhancement alone was worth every credit. I can recall guest preferences from two years ago without checking the system."

We've had variations of this conversation before. Zoe never pushes too hard, but she makes no secret of her enthusiasm for her NexaBio subscription. Cognitive package, metabolic optimization, and what she calls a "tiny aesthetic tune-up" that keeps her skin glowing.

"Maybe I'm just old-fashioned," I say, though at twenty-seven, in this century, that sounds absurd even to me.

"Your choice." Zoe shrugs. "But Mei won't keep you as her assistant forever if you don't upgrade. You know that, right?"

A notification flashes across my implant's display before I can respond.

Please welcome Shelley Parker to the role of Executive Assistant to the CEO.

Beside me, Zoe inhales. "No way."

"What?"

She stares at me. "Shelley from Concierge? She just joined Revolutions three months ago. And now she's Executive Assistant? That should be your job. You're next in line for a promotion."

I frown. Is she right? The casino does have a large staff turnover. But do I care? I enjoy working for Mei. But then again, the salary package for Executive Assistant is so much more ...

~

Zoe and I meet up at the Hideaway on Fremont after work, same as every Friday night.

The Hideaway lives up to its name: a small, dimly lit bar tucked between larger establishments, away from the glaring lights and noisy tourist areas. Despite operating for over a century, the place has managed to maintain its anonymity, catering to locals who value privacy over spectacle.

Zoe is already seated at a corner booth when I arrive, with an empty glass in front of her and a full one waiting for me.

I slide into the seat across from her.

"Real bourbon," she says. "Not the synthetic stuff."

I take a sip. The liquor burns pleasantly on the way down.

"I'm worried about you."

I raise my brows. "Why?"

"Three months, Ciara. Shelley Parker's been with the Revolutions for three months. You have more event experience in your little finger than she has in her entire polished body."

I shrug. "Maybe she has experience we don't know about."

"She was a mid-level concierge at the Roma. A good one, but nothing special." Zoe's eyes narrow. "She's not exceptional. She's enhanced. There's a difference."

Our second round of drinks arrives.

"What's this about Zoe?"

"You'll never get promoted if you don't have NexaBio, Ciara. It's an unwritten condition."

"Maybe I'm naive, but I still believe that skills and hard work matter."

Zoe laughs without any humor. "God, you sound exactly like those 'natural human' protesters outside

NexaBio headquarters. *Wake up, Ciara.* This is the world *now*. Compete or get left behind."

Her words sting more than they should. "I'm not against progress. I just—"

"Just what? Have principles? Great. Principles don't get promotions." She takes a sip of her drink. "I'm not attacking you. I'm trying to help you. You're good at your job — *really good*. But good isn't enough anymore. And I want to see you succeed."

We sit in uncomfortable silence for a moment. I think about Eve, my mother, and Shelley Parker.

"What's it really like?" I finally ask. "The enhancement. Not the marketing version. The truth."

Her expression softens. "It's … incredible. I don't get tired the way I used to. I can work a fourteen-hour shift and still feel sharp. My memory is crystal clear — not just for work stuff, but everything. Colors are more vivid. Food tastes better. I don't get sick, not even colds."

"Side effects?"

"The monthly maintenance. Some people get headaches for the first few days after. Nothing serious."

"And the subscription costs?"

"We already get the standard package if we want to opt in. Elite is closer to forty percent of our salaries."

"Forty percent!"

"Worth every credit." She shrugs. "Best decision I ever made. And that's the honest truth."

I take another sip, feeling the alcohol warm my chest. "I don't know, Zoe. It still feels wrong somehow. Like cheating."

"Is it cheating to wear glasses if you can't see? To use a hearing aid when you can't hear?" She leans forward. "This is just the next step. Preventative, proactive healthcare."

"It's more than that, and you know it."

"Yeah, it is. But it's also the future." Her voice gentles. "Look, I get it. You're scared. Everyone is at first. You *deserve* this, Ciara."

I don't respond, but later that night, in my small apartment, I find myself staring at my reflection in the bathroom mirror. Eve's face, but she's gone, and I'm still here. I wonder what she would have done with the chance I have.

Would she have even hesitated at all?

My implant chimes softly. A message from my mother: *Just checking in. Sunday dinner?*

I send back a simple acknowledgment and turn away from the mirror.

Sleep eludes me. I lie awake thinking about Eve, who fought so hard to live when her body betrayed her. Eve, who never got the chance to choose enhancement or rejection.

I arrive at work early the next morning and head straight to Human Resources.

Daria looks up when I enter, her perfect smile still in place. "Ciara. What can I do for you this morning?"

No wonder she's so good at her job. She remembers everyone. Or maybe that's the NexaBio.

I take a deep breath. "I'd like to discuss the NexaBio program."

Her smile widens. "Of course. I have all the information right here." She reaches into a drawer, producing the familiar blue and silver pamphlet. I sit across from her, and she places it on the desk between us.

"Were you thinking of joining us?"

I nod. "When can I start?"

~

Six months later, I'm running along the rim of the Grand Canyon at sunrise. Not walking. Not hiking. Running.

My feet strike the trail, each step calculated for optimal efficiency. My breathing remains steady, my heart rate elevated but controlled at exactly 142 beats per minute — the sweet spot my optimization has determined is ideal for my cardiovascular system.

I've covered twelve miles already. Twice the distance I could manage before NexaBio. My muscles work in perfect harmony, fatigue held at bay by enhanced cellular regeneration. Sweat evaporates efficiently from my skin due to optimized thermoregulation.

I stop at the familiar viewpoint, the same spot where I've stood countless times before. The canyon stretches before me, exactly as it always has. Ancient. Indifferent. Unchanged.

But not me.

I'm different. My tissues hum with molecular precision, a trillion tiny optimizations working in concert. Each cell is a perfect machine, genetically upgraded to resist decay, to process oxygen with ruthless efficiency. Sometimes at night, I swear I can hear them whispering beneath my skin, these alien improvements colonizing what used to be Ciara Miller. The optimization feels like something watching me from inside my own body. Alert, calculating, and impossibly patient.

My implant chimes, a gentle musical tone that indicates an incoming NexaBio status report. I blink to accept it, and metrics appear in my field of vision:

CELLULAR REGENERATION: OPTIMIZED +19% COGNITIVE EFFICIENCY: INCREASED +17%CARDIO-VASCULAR ENDURANCE: PEAK AT +23%

I draw a deep breath. The air seems richer somehow, more complex due to my enhanced olfactory sensors.

The sunrise paints the canyon in colors I never fully appreciated before. My enhanced vision captures ultraviolet wavelengths that were previously invisible, adding depth and dimension to the landscape before me. The beauty is almost overwhelming, layers of sensory input that my optimized neural pathways process without strain.

I check the time. 5:42 AM. I've been out here since 3:30 and need to start my drive back to Vegas.

Six months ago, staying up all night would have left me drained and unfocused. Now it's merely a choice, an allocation of resources. Sleep efficiency has been optimized. Two hours provides the same restoration as the eight I used to require.

As I turn back toward the trailhead, my implant chimes again. A message from Daria. *Keep Friday evening open for celebration.*

I smile. The message confirms what I've suspected for weeks. My promotion to Executive Assistant to the CFO is imminent. I've already moved from Events to HR, and there is already another advancement on the horizon.

I wanted nothing to do with optimization. But then my upgrade revealed unexpected aptitudes for financial analysis and strategic planning. My enhanced cognitive functions identified patterns in the resort's operational data that even the executive team had missed. Numbers that once seemed merely functional now tell me vivid stories, revealing opportunities and suggesting innovative approaches.

I run back faster than I came, exhilaration fueling my every step. The sun climbs higher, casting long shadows across the ancient rocks. Running toward my future, instead of away from it.

THE FINANCE DEPARTMENT occupies the east wing of the administrative level. I've been in my new position for four months now. My workspace, no longer a cubicle but a glass-walled office with a view of the resort's famous fountains, awaits me.

"Good morning, Ms. Miller."

The department coordinator smiles as I approach. Three months ago, she called me Ciara. The subtle shift in address coincided with my move to Finance.

"Morning, Sophie. Any updates I should know about?"

"Your friend from Restaurant VIP stopped by earlier."

"Zoe?" I pause, surprised. We haven't spoken much since my department transfer. Our schedules rarely align anymore, and our circles have diverged.

"Yes. She seemed …" Sophie hesitates, searching for a diplomatic word. "Unwell."

I frowned." Did she leave a message?"

"Just asked if you could meet her for lunch. I told her you had plans, but she was insistent."

"Rebook Mark and slot in Zoe."

Sophie nods, disappearing back to her desk.

My office is minimalist in nature. Three weeks ago, I removed all personal touches, the small desert rock collection, and the single photograph of Eve on my desk. Sentimentality is inefficient, so the space now reflects pure functionality.

I settle in, connecting to the resort's systems, and get lost in my work. I head to the employee dining room at noon to meet Zoe. She's waiting for me at our old table.

And she looks terrible. Hollow-eyed, skin sallow, hair limp, trembling hands.

"Hey, stranger." The smile breezes right past her eyes.

I give her a hug — and she seems so frail — then sit across from her. "Is everything okay?"

"Jeff had a heart attack," she says.

Jeff. Her husband. I remember him from the photo on her desk. A big goofy guy with a smile for days.

"I'm so sorry, Zoe. Is he—"

"He's good." She rubs her temple. "But the hospital bills ... they're astronomical. His insurance covered the basic procedures, but the specialized cardiac regeneration therapy ..." She trails off while shaking her head.

"What can I do for you?"

She hesitates. "I hate to ask. But I can borrow some money? I can't keep up with the NexaBio payments. With Jeff's medical costs, the house payment ..."

I mentally calculate my available resources. My salary has increased substantially, but so have my expenses. NexaBio's Elite package — which the company encouraged alongside my transition to Finance — consumes a significant portion of my income. "I'm so sorry, Zoe. I'm not sure that I can. I'm tapped out myself."

She frowns. "I thought it might be a long shot. I missed last month's payment. Of course, I explained the situation, requested a temporary reduction or deferment."

"But?"

"Nothing."

"Don't they have hardship programs?"

She nodded." I tried that. Nothing. Form responses. 'Payment required for continued service.' 'Subscription terms cannot be modified." She runs a hand through her limp hair. "Maybe you can put in a word with someone? You have connections now."

The request makes me uncomfortable. I've worked hard for my position, optimized my performance, and proven my value. Asking for special treatment for a friend feels inappropriate and inefficient.

"I'll see what I can do," I lie. "Have you spoken with HR? Maybe there's an employee assistance program."

"HR says the NexaBio Elite subscription is a personal contract, not a company benefit."

My implant chimes, reminding me of my meeting. "I need to go. But we'll talk more later, okay? Figure something out."

"Sure." Zoe nods as I stand. "Good luck with your meeting."

I spot a bruise on her neck, partially hidden by her collar. Fresh and dark.

"What happened to your neck?"

Zoe starts and adjusts her collar higher, covering the mark. "When you start missing payments, things get … complicated. The body doesn't take kindly to interrupted optimization."

"You should talk to a doctor."

"With what money?" She forces a smile. "Don't worry about me. I'll figure it out. I always do."

AT THE END of the day, Boris calls me into his office. "I understand Zoe Reynolds from VIP Reservations visited you today."

The surveillance doesn't surprise me; Revolutions monitors all employee movements, but his interest does. Zoe is several organizational layers below his notice.

"Yes, sir. A personal matter."

"Be careful with such associations, Ciara. Her optimization subscription has lapsed. Her performance metrics are declining rapidly." His eyes don't leave mine. "And the company has standards to maintain."

"I know. Her husband had a heart attack. She can't manage the payments."

"Unfortunate, but not the company's concern." His expression is neutral, professionally sympathetic. "But we can't risk unoptimized interactions compromising our staff. Studies show performance regression occurs through sustained contact with lapsed assets."

Assets. Not colleagues. Not friends.

"I understand." But something in me doesn't want to.

"Good. I'm glad."

The meeting concludes, and I return to my office. The afternoon stretches ahead with reports to file, data to analyze, strategies to refine. My enhanced mind embraces the tasks with algorithmic accuracy, processing information at speeds that would have overwhelmed my unoptimized self.

By evening, I strangely forget all about my meeting with Zoe: odd, given my enhanced memory. But by morning, I won't remember having thought of her at all.

Sunday dinner has evolved over the past year. In fact, the dynamic between my mother and me has transformed completely.

She's practically beaming when I arrive. "Look at you. Confident. Successful. Eve would have been so proud."

The comparison no longer stings. Once a wasp that left welts on my heart, now just a fly buzzing against tempered glass. My optimization has recalibrated emotional responses, categorizing such statements as neutral observations rather than weapons.

"Eve would have excelled with enhancement," I agree. "Her natural sociability combined with cognitive optimization would have been quite effective."

She reaches across the table, squeezing my hand. "It makes me so happy to see you thriving, Ciara."

The physical gesture triggers an unexpected emotional response, a warmth that bypasses my optimization filters. For a moment, I'm simply a daughter receiving hard-won maternal approval.

Then I notice what she's really looking at, not me, but a reflection of what might have been. In her eyes, I've finally become worthy of display. Not because I'm Ciara, but because I now mirror the perfection she once saw only in Eve.

My enhancement package includes enough emotional intelligence to recognize this truth, and enough emotional regulation to accept it without the old pain. I smile and squeeze her hand in return.

After dinner, when I prepare to leave, she hands me a small package wrapped in silver paper.

"What's this?"

"Just a little something. Open it at home."

I kiss her cheek, another scripted interaction that my enhancement has made easier to perform, and drive back to my new apartment. The Porsche PX Hybrid responds to my thoughts more than my hands on the wheel as its systems interface with my implants.

My new home occupies the fifteenth floor of The Apex, one of the most exclusive residential towers in Las Vegas. Three bedrooms, panoramic views of the Strip, smart environmental controls that sync with my biometrics to maintain optimal living conditions.

I unwrap my gift. Inside the silver paper is a small

holographic picture frame. I activate it with a touch, and Eve's face appears.

I place the frame on my bedside table, observing it with detached appreciation. Eve smiles eternally, forever untouched by time.

My implant chimes with an evening status report:

NEURAL OPTIMIZATION: 98.7% INTEGRATION CELLULAR EFFICIENCY: +22.4% ABOVE BASELINE RE-COMMENDED SLEEP CYCLE: 1:30 AM - 3:30 AM

I acknowledge the notification and prepare for the optimized sleep schedule that will ensure maximum performance for tomorrow's workday.

I MIX A MOLECULAR COCKTAIL — synthetic spirits, herbal infusions, and enzyme catalysts, creating a color-changing effect as the liquid settles. An exclusive rooftop bar at the Apex offers the highest tips in the city. Perfect for a weekend bartending job.

I see clients at table seven and freeze. My new boss, Randolph, and two other Revolutions executives occupy the corner booth, deep in conversation.

I find my co-worker Adele. "Can you handle seven? I'm wanted in the back."

"Sure," she agrees, oblivious to my discomfort.

I retreat to the kitchen. This latest promotion has taken me to the CEO's office. My responsibilities are expanded, with the salary increased by twenty-two percent. Yet here I am, moonlighting at a bar, hiding from the people who think I'm thriving.

NexaBio payments have increased substantially, and now consume the majority of my income. The Platinum package adjusts pricing based on an "individual optimization needs," a convenient phrase for perpetual price increases. Better results lead to higher costs, a cycle that accelerates with each enhancement.

I keep my head down until Randolph and his colleagues leave, then return to my tables. The extra four hours of work will barely cover this month's increase in my subscription cost, but every credit counts.

The next morning at the Revolutions, whispers circulate through the executive floor. I catch fragments as I walk to my office — "collapsed," "security," and "carried out."

"What's going on?" I ask my assistant, who's clearly been following the gossip.

"You haven't heard?" She lowers her voice. "Zoe from VIP Reservations collapsed yesterday. Full neurological event, right in front of guests. They say it was a NexaBio crash."

Something cold and heavy settles in my chest. I hadn't thought of Zoe in ages. Couldn't even remember her face. Though I did remember us being friends.

"Is she okay?" I ask.

"Terminated, obviously." My assistant's enhanced features show carefully calibrated concern — enough to appear appropriate, but not enough to suggest any genuine distress. "Security had to remove her."

"She came to see me. After her husband's heart attack. She couldn't afford the NexaBio payments anymore."

Her expression shifts to one of professional sympathy. "Too bad, but the company has standards to maintain. Can't have unstable personnel interacting with VIP guests."

No.

There were indeed standards to maintain.

I stand on my balcony after my workday, staring out at the neon landscape of Las Vegas. The city never sleeps, its rhythms perpetual and mechanical. Like the optimization processes constantly running in my enhanced body, never pausing, never truly at rest.

My implant chimes with a midnight status report:

PAYMENT NOTIFICATION: NEXABIO MONTHLY SUBSCRIPTION AMOUNT: 3,842 CREDITS ADJUSTMENT: +12% FROM PREVIOUS BILLING CYCLE REASON: OPTIMIZATION PERFORMANCE INCREASE

I dismiss the notification. The amount represents nearly seventy percent of my Revolutions salary — not counting my weekend bartending income, which now goes entirely to maintaining my enhancement subscription.

I access the complete NexaBio contract stored in my personal files for the first time. Not the glossy summary Daria provided during orientation, but the full legal document I signed all those months ago. Seventy-three pages of dense terminology, conditions, and obligations that I accepted with a casual retinal scan.

My enhanced cognitive functions process the document rapidly, analyzing clauses, identifying implications, recognizing patterns in the deliberately obfuscated language.

But now I can understand it.

NexaBio retains full intellectual property rights to all genetic modifications implemented under this agreement ...

Subscriber acknowledges that genetic enhancements constitute protected proprietary technology licensed to subscriber, not owned by subscriber ...

Attempt to reverse-engineer, replicate, or transfer optimization protocols to unauthorized providers constitutes severe intellectual property violation subject to immediate legal action ...

Subscription termination without approved medical transition protocol may result in INSTABILITY EVENTS, including but not limited to: cellular degradation, neural pathway disruption, immune system irregularities, and metabolic collapse ...

NexaBio bears no liability for adverse effects resulting from subscription interruption ...

I read it three times.

NexaBio doesn't just license me the upgrades; they own the rights to my genetic code, to every modification they make.

I can't take my genome to another provider. I can't stop the treatments without risking what they clinically term "instability events." A sanitized phrase for the physical collapse I witnessed beginning in Zoe.

The ultimate subscription service is my own existence. Daily renewal fee: everything I am and everything I earn. Terms and conditions: my soul, payable in monthly installments.

My implant chimes again — not a NexaBio notification this time, but a financial alert:

MORTGAGE DUE: TOMORROW INSUFFICIENT FUNDS: 840 CREDITS SHORT RECOMMEND IMMEDIATE FUND TRANSFER

I stare at the alert, options calculating automatically in my mind. I can transfer emergency funds from my dwindling savings. I can work additional bar shifts. I can request an advance on my next performance bonus.

Or I can miss the NexaBio payment.

The thought forms before my optimization package can suppress it: a dangerous idea that triggers immediate warning responses in my enhanced neural pathways. My heart rate increases. Cortisol levels spike. Autonomous systems prepare for threat response.

My body knows what happens when the optimization stops.

My implant chimes: UNAUTHORIZED COGNITIVE PATTERN DETECTED: PAYMENT INTER-

RUPTION SCENARIO. REPORT FILED. NEURAL COMPLIANCE CHECK SCHEDULED.

I make the only choice available, transfer funds from my mortgage payment to ensure the NexaBio subscription continues without interruption. I'll deal with the housing consequences later. Sell assets, negotiate with creditors, take on additional work hours.

Because the alternative is unthinkable.

THE NEXT MORNING, I drive to Zoe's house, overriding the efficiency algorithms that flag the trip as non-essential. The modest home in Henderson — a suburb fifteen miles from the Strip — appears deserted. Blinds drawn. No vehicle in the driveway. Dead plants on the porch.

I approach anyway. The doorbell goes unanswered. I'm about to leave when I notice movement behind a partially open blind.

"Zoe?" I call out. "It's Ciara."

Silence follows, then the sound of multiple locks disengaging. The door opens six inches, chain still engaged, revealing a sliver of a man's face. Haggard, unshaven, exhausted.

"Jeff?" I barely recognize Zoe's husband from the photo she used to have on her desk.

"She's not here," he says, voice hoarse.

"I can come back later."

His bitter laugh sounds hollow. "She won't be back then either. What's left of her is at Meadow Valley Care Center."

"What do you mean? What's left of her?"

Jeff studies me through the narrow opening, his gaze lingering on my face.

"*You* happened. You and everyone like you who convinced her that NexaBio was the answer. 'Best decision I ever made,' she kept saying. Right up until it destroyed her."

"That's not fair. I didn't—"

"Save it. If you want to see her. It's room 342. Though she won't recognize you anymore."

The door shut, locks re-engaging with multiple clicks.

I drive to Meadow Valley Care Center, a long-term care facility on the outskirts of the city. The building is clean but dated, a remnant from the pre-enhancement era when aging and illness followed predictable patterns.

The receptionist directs me to the third floor. *Specialized Neurological Care*, the sign reads. I follow numbered doors down a quiet hallway until I reach 342.

Nothing prepares me for what I find inside.

The woman in the bed bears only the faintest resemblance to Zoe. She's skeletal thin and being tended to by a nurse, skin mottled with bruises in various stages of decomposition. Hair fallen out in patches. Restraints designed to protect her from self-injury.

But the most disturbing change is in her eyes: vacant and unfocused, the sharp intelligence that defined her has been completely erased.

"Zoe?"

Her head turns at the sound, jerky and uncoordinated. No recognition registers in her empty gaze.

"She doesn't respond to her name anymore," the nurse says. "Are you family?"

"A friend," I say, unable to look away from the human shell before me. "What happened to her?"

The nurse checks something on Zoe's chart. "Advanced PROS — Post-Regression Optimization Syndrome. Not uncommon these days."

"This is from stopping NexaBio treatments?"

"Abrupt cessation of high-level enhancement, yes." The nurse's tone is clinical, matter-of-fact. "Her system couldn't handle the reversal. Neural pathways collapsed, cellular integrity compromised. Cascading system failures."

"Will she recover?" Of course, I know the answer.

"This is recovery. She was much worse when she was admitted. Seizures, organ failure, extreme pain. We've stabilized her physically, but the cognitive damage is … extensive."

I step closer to the bed and take Zoe's hand. Her skin feels like crepe paper, bones prominent beneath.

"I'm sorry," I say.

Her eyes shift toward me momentarily, a flicker of something — recognition, fear, despair — impossible to determine. Then vacancy returns, her gaze drifting aimlessly. Her breath smells medicinal: the tang of cellular stabilizers and neural inhibitors. The skin of her hand feels wrong against mine, like paper that's been wet and dried too many times, structural integrity compromised at the molecular level. The room itself has a particular aroma I recognize from Eve's final weeks: the scent of bodies betrayed by their own chemistry, fighting unseen battles at the cellular level.

But Eve's decline was natural. This was manufactured, a planned obsolescence built into Zoe's upgraded DNA.

"Enhanced?" the nurse asks, eyeing me.

"Yes."

"Elite package?"

"Platinum."

She raises her brows. "Well be careful, we're seeing more cases like hers. Economic casualties. People who can't sustain the payments. I recommended a medical transition protocol for my mother when she decided to discontinue. Expensive, but it prevents ... this."

"There's a safe way to stop?"

"'Safe' is relative. The medical transition takes months, sometimes years, depending on your enhancement level. Gradual withdrawal, system stabilization procedures, genetic recalibration." She glances at Zoe. "Insurance rarely covers it. Out of pocket, you're looking at millions for full reversal."

My mouth falls open. "Millions?"

She nods.

"I need to go," I say, the room suddenly suffocating.

The nurse looks down at Zoe. "They don't put this part in the brochures, do they?"

Side effects may include: total financial ruin, identity dissolution, and walking death. Ask your doctor if NexaBio is right for you. Warning: there is no right answer.

I want to say they do. But it's in the fine print.

I MISS Sunday dinner with my mother. I send a message claiming work obligations, though in reality, I spend the evening researching NexaBio withdrawal cases. My enhanced cognitive abilities sort through medical studies, personal accounts, legal proceedings — analyzing patterns, identifying commonalities, calculating proba-bilities.

The evidence is overwhelming. What happened to Zoe isn't an anomaly so much as a statistical likelihood for anyone who stops enhancement without proper medical transition.

In clinical studies, 78% of subjects who abruptly discontinued advanced optimization experienced severe neurological complications. 92% suffered permanent cognitive impairment. 14% died from systemic failure.

The medical transition protocol costs a minimum of 4.8 million credits for the Elite package reversal alone. The price for Platinum isn't even listed. Instead, it reads: *not recommended*. Insurance categorizes both as "elective withdrawal"and provides no coverage.

There are no generic alternatives. No competing services can maintain NexaBio's proprietary modifications. The company holds exclusive patents on the genetic sequences now integrated into my DNA.

I am owned, not just my enhanced abilities, but the fundamental building blocks of what I've become.

Monday morning, I return to work and perform my duties. On Wednesday, I notice a new assistant in VIP Reservations. Zoe's replacement. She's young and enthusiastic. NexaBio'd.

~

THE UPGRADES CONTINUE. My subscription rate increases.

I perform flawlessly at work during the day. At night, I examine every aspect of my situation, analyzing my finances with the very cognitive enhancements that have created my predicament.

My NexaBio subscription payment comes due again, another 5% increase automatically approved and deducted from my account. My mortgage payment notification follows immediately after, flagging insufficient funds for the third consecutive month.

I'm working double shifts at the bar now. The income barely covers the shortfall between my NexaBio payments and living expenses. I've sold my Porsche, downgraded my wardrobe, and eliminated all non-essential expenditures.

My apartment is up for sale.

Still, the financial trajectory is unsustainable. Within six months, even with radical austerity measures, I will be unable to maintain both my enhancement subscription and basic living expenses.

The facts are irrefutable.

1. NexaBio payments will continue to increase as my optimization improves.

2. Stopping payments will result in physical and cognitive collapse.

3. The buyout option is financially impossible.

I'm trapped in a system designed to ensure perpetual dependency, a hamster wheel plated in platinum where every step forward accelerates the pace. Darwin's survival of the fittest twisted into survival of the most indebted. Freedom costs exactly what you can never afford.

On Friday morning, I call in sick to the Revolutions for the first time since starting the job. My optimization package flags the decision as inefficient, potentially damaging to my professional standing. I override the warning.

Instead of going to work, I drive to Meadow Valley Care Center.

I've been coming here during my spare time.

I sit beside Zoe's bed for an hour, watching the empty shell of a woman who once vibrated with energy and ambition. The person convinced me that NexaBio was the best decision she ever made.

"I'm sorry," I say. "I should have helped you when I had the chance."

She squeezes my hand. Then her vacant eyes find mine, a momentary flash of lucidity piercing through the emptiness.

"My fault," she says, licking her cracked lips. "Bonus for signing you up."

I freeze.

"What?"

"Free month for anyone you convince to join."

I pull my hand away, and she retreats back into the void that has claimed her mind. I want to scream, but the sound would be pointless. The truth is too small and too massive at once. A bonus. A free month. That was the price of my autonomy.

And yet I don't blame her. Not exactly. We're all just pebbles in an avalanche, thinking we chose which way to fall. Blame is a luxury for those still believing in free will, still unoptimized enough to think choice is more than an illusion dressed in corporate jargon. The system is too big, too practiced. It trains you to make those choices, packages desperation as opportunity.

Or maybe that's the enhancement speaking. Teaching me to rationalize the cage. To frame exploitation as empathy.

To call it love when someone sells you out for a discount.

I DRIVE to the Grand Canyon directly from the care facility.

And stand at the same viewpoint where I've stood countless times before, watching the sun edge above the horizon. The same rocks, the same vast space, the same ancient witness to human existence.

It's a good place to think.

Do I continue as I am, working multiple gigs to maintain payments, selling assets, perhaps eventually accepting greater corporate dependency in exchange for financial support? I know there are jobs where you can work 24/7 and they will cover all of your enhancements for perpetuity.

Or do I stop payments and face physical collapse and cognitive destruction?

Perhaps I can find another way?

One I choose?

I've researched every option, analyzed every scenario, and calculated every probability.

I haven't slept in over a week, and yet I feel nothing.

Even my suffering is regulated.

My implant chimes. It's NexaBio.

PAYMENT DECLINED: INSUFFICIENT FUNDS SUBSCRIPTION STATUS: GRACE PERIOD (72 HOURS)WARNING: SERVICE INTERRUPTION IMMINENT RECOMMEND IMMEDIATE PAYMENT

A second chime follows.

You missed Sunday dinner. Everything okay?

Another chime.

CORTISOL ELEVATED: 43% ABOVE OPTIMAL NEURAL ACTIVITY IRREGULAR IN SECTOR 7PSYCHOLOGICAL INTERVENTION RECOMMENDED

The sun climbs higher, illuminating the vast canyon below. Light catches on the Colorado River, a distant silver thread that's carved its way through stone over thousands of millennia. Nature's persistence against seemingly immovable barriers.

I step toward the edge, and my enhanced visual system automatically calculates the distance to the bottom if I'm not careful. The speed of descent, the impact force. My optimization package flags the danger, attempting to trigger survival protocols.

POTENTIAL FALL TRAJECTORY DETECTED:

ESTIMATED DESCENT 145 FEET IN 3.3 SECONDS, 99.99% FATALITY PROBABILITY—INITIATING BREATH REGULATION, ACTIVATING CALMING SUBROUTINES, PLEASE STEP BACK FROM THE EDGE.

So many notifications, they sound like a wind chime in my head.

I ignore them all.

The sun is fully above the horizon now, bathing the canyon in golden light. Birds circle in thermal currents below me, riding the air with effortless grace. Unoptimized, unenhanced, perfectly evolved.

I think of Eve, who fought so hard to live.

Of Zoe, trapped in a broken shell.

Of my mother, who only truly saw me when I became someone else.

And I think of myself, who I was before.

Unable to deal with the loss of her sister because there was simply no space in her family to grieve.

I take another step forward, toes now extending over the edge. My implant blares warnings, attempting to override my motor functions, to pull me back from the danger.

CRITICAL ZONE BREACHED: IMMINENT RISK TO BIOLOGICAL INTEGRITY. PLEASE STEP BACK. PLEASE STEP BACK. PLEASE STEP BACK. YOU ARE IN DANGER. THIS IS NOT A RATIONAL ACTION. PLEASE STEP BACK. PLEASE STEP BACK. PLEASE STEP BACK. PLEASE STEP BACK. PLEASE STEP BACK. PLEASE STEP BACK …

Time to see if I am stronger than their programming.

PLEASE STEP BACK.

One more step is all it would take.

PLEASE STEP BACK.

My enhanced hearing catches the sound of an

approaching vehicle on the access road behind me. Early tourists, perhaps. Or NexaBio security, tracking my implant, coming to protect their investment. After all, the subscription must continue.

PLEASE STEP BACK.

I don't turn to look because I've made my decision.

The canyon stretches before me, vast and indifferent as always. It doesn't care who stands at its edge — Ciara before enhancement, Ciara after enhancement.

And in that indifference, I find a strange comfort.

I wonder what Zoe's last thoughts were.

PLEASE STEP BACK.

PLEASE STEP BACK.

PLEASE STEP BACK.

The canyon yawns below me: nature's mouth opened in a silent scream that's echoed for millions of years. These ancient stones witness my rebellion, my final refusal. They've seen species rise and fall, civilizations bloom and wither. They'll remain long after NexaBio's empire crumbles into the dust of forgotten human follies.

I close my eyes and feel the wind against my face. The implant's warnings reach a crescendo, merging into a single sustained alarm like a flatline. Something ruptures in my cerebral cortex — my first enhancement failing as the neural pathway, designed to prevent self-harm, burns itself out trying to override my decision. I taste copper as blood vessels burst in my nasal cavity. Another enhancement tries to clot it instantly, optimize the damage. The conflict between my will and my modifications creates a storm in my nervous system.

I take one final, deep breath and feel the last thing that still belongs entirely to me: choice.

Then I step—

AFTERSHOCKS ON TERMINAL Subscription

THIS WAS another story from my collaboration with Alexander Titus. We were finishing up our *Echoes of Tomorrow* series right around the time he published an earlier version of this story for his newsletter. Sometimes the best horror stories come from people who know where the bodies are buried in the lab, so I couldn't resist asking him if we could expand on those ideas.

Titus brought something I never could: the inside view. As a PhD in machine learning and bioinformatics working at the bleeding edge of biotechnology — from the Department of Defense to Colossal Biosciences — he's seen the PowerPoint presentations where they map out how to monetize your mitochondria.

The corporate jargon, the subscription models, the way they turn your genome into a rental agreement with terms and conditions longer than your life expectancy, the way biotech companies package dependency as optimization.

He's seen the future we're writing about.

Terminal Subscription asks the question that keeps every bioethicist awake at night: What happens when your biology becomes someone else's intellectual property?

Ciara thought enhancement would solve her problems. Better memory, perfect health, optimized everything. Instead, she got a monthly bill for her own existence and a genetic code that belonged to someone else.

Now she's trapped in the ultimate subscription service: her own DNA, locked behind a paywall.

The story works as both corporate horror and family

tragedy. Ciara's physical transformation is also the erasure of everything that made her different from her dead twin sister. Enhancement doesn't just change your body, it performs surgery on your identity, one monthly payment at a time, until you can't tell where the upgrade ends and you begin.

This is biotechnology's nightmare scenario: a world where being human is a subscription service, where your cells come with end-user license agreements, and your heart runs on freemium pricing, where stopping treatment means more than death—

Titus's expertise makes every detail terrifyingly plausible. The contract terms, the dependency mechanisms, the way optimization becomes addiction. It's all grounded in real science, real corporate strategies, real human greed.

Some subscriptions you can cancel. Others cancel you.

And the fine print was written in your genes before you even knew how to read.

FOURTEEN

Last Ticket Out

"Come on! It's almost time," Trevor shouted into the kitchen as he plopped on the sofa, leaned back, and turned up the TV.

Lottie grabbed the bottle of wine and two glasses, rushing over to take a seat on the plush leather sofa beside him.

"You think this is our week?" She poured the glass and handed it over.

"It's got to be." Trevor loosened his tie as the hosts of *The Weekly Launch*, Grant Goodman and Lorraine Bliss, appeared on screen. Smiling and welcoming viewers to another eagerly anticipated episode — the 156th — of the New World.

Grant flashed his perfect pearly whites. "As you know, every week the National Aerospace Institute and the Next Generation Project select four hundred of our nation's best and brightest for a trip to the New World, humanity's first terraformed city on Mars, and humanity's second chance at survival."

Cheers erupted from an unseen audience.

Lorraine offered her perfect smile to the home viewers. "As you saw in the pre-show, this week's lucky winners included a great-grandfather who served with valor in two wars, an inner-city teacher whose husband recently passed from cancer, and an immigrant family who fled their war-torn nation for a new start. Who would have guessed that their new start would be on a new world?"

Trevor scowled at the screen. "A fucking immigrant family? Really? *They* get to go before we do. *We* were born here! What gives them the right?"

"Well, they're not illegals. They *are* citizens."

"Maybe." He accepted a glass of wine from Lottie. "But it still pisses me off. *We* should be going. We're hard-working, patriotic citizens who were actually born here. We give our blood, sweat, and tears to this country, and what do we get in return?"

Lorraine didn't bother with an answer. Because she knew he wasn't really asking.

"Nothing." Trevor took a swallow of wine. "My grandfather died in the war, you know."

"Mine, too."

"Exactly, and yet here we are, stuck on a dying planet."

As if on cue, the asteroid appeared onscreen — the one scientists around the world agreed would be ending life on Earth in less than three years. It was always followed by a reenactment of Earth's ultimate destruction.

Lottie sighed. "It's difficult enough knowing it's coming without the weekly reminder. Do we really need to see this every time?"

"They do it to drum up ticket sales. It works, I bought four this week."

"*Four tickets?* Jesus, Trevor. Do we *have* that kind of money?"

Trevor took another sip of wine. He hated it when

Lottie brought up their bank balance. She was a hostess at Pole Position, *he* was the one raking it in as a salesman. If he wanted to spend *his* money on tickets, he would.

"Yes, we've got the money. Not sure how some of *the people* who got picked this week did, though. Especially those immigrants. Probably welfare — *our* taxes bought them. And yet *you and I* have to pay for each entry! Fucking immigrants ruining everything."

Lottie frowned. "That's not nice."

"Does being honest make me racist?"

"Of course not, it's just … I dunno. You weren't here when they showed that family on TV. They seemed like nice people. They were escaping horrible poverty, and their country is at war. Why not them? They have kids, Trevor."

"Yeah, more mouths to feed, more tickets for *them* on the ship, and not us. I'm sure they're *lovely people*, Lottie. But this isn't about how lovely they are. Only the best, brightest, and most productive members of society are chosen for the New World. These people … well, they're certainly not among the best and brightest. If they were, *their* country would be sending ships to Mars, not ours."

"I guess you're right," Lottie said, pouring another glass of wine.

"Of course I am, baby. You don't watch the news or pay attention like I do. Trust me. *We* are the kind of people that ought to be going to Mars. It's wasted on them."

She wasn't arguing, but Trevor heard her silent reservations. Lottie was a nice girl. Young and hot, but a little dumb. She didn't know how to see the world as it really was. She assumed that people had the best of intentions. She was a sucker for sob stories and well-crafted lies.

But Trevor knew better.

He used his wits to get by and thus saw how ruthless people truly were. Lottie had it easy because she was pretty.

She never developed the skill set required to make it in the real world. In a way, she was enslaved to her looks and would be a bit worthless once they were gone. Another idiot in a nation full of them.

The New World would be better, a place where he didn't always have to watch his back and could trust his neighbor because it was filled with people like him.

Grant and Lorraine began the countdown.

The spacecraft was massive. Impressive even after watching the takeoffs for so long. Like a cruise ship in space. A feat of engineering that Trevor hoped to someday experience.

There were only three years left for evacuations. And of the four hundred people on the flights, a third were reserved for the elite. Normal schlubs like Trevor could apply for a ticket and pay for the application. He had to submit his name, salary, accomplishments, skills, and provide his medical info just to get *considered for consideration.*

It was bullshit.

But he did it.

If there were forty thousand more people chosen over the next few years, Trevor had to assume his status and income would put him higher on the list. If not, there was zero justice in this world.

Thrusters lifted the behemoth into the sky before the warp drive kicked in and turned the hexagonal rear engines blue and white.

Then it was gone.

The hosts announced which handful of nationally well-known actors, retired athletes, and government officials had been chosen for the next launch. Then the show kicked over to each affiliate's local hosts to announce which people in Trevor's town had been chosen, if any.

Today, a Black woman named Darlene was announcing the names.

Lottie gripped Trevor's hand. He almost shook her free. But whatever. It was kind of cute.

They watched as Darlene was handed a piece of paper. Then she turned and faced the camera. "Annabella Marks. Frank Piers."

"Do you know them?" Lottie asked.

He shook his head. And then:

"Adam Lesh and family."

Trevor froze.

"Adam Lesh? *Adam Fucking Lesh?*" He jerked his hand from Lottie's. Stood and hurled his glass across the living room. He aimed for the TV. But it shattered against the wall, spilling wine onto the carpet.

"You know him?" Lottie scurried over to clean the spill and broken glass.

"Of course I fucking know him. I work with the fucking idiot! He doesn't deserve a spot on the ship! What the fuck?"

Trevor was seething.

He needed to hit something.

There was a time when Lottie might have been the target, but Trevor was trying to change. Plus, dumb as she was, and as little self-esteem as she had, even Lottie wouldn't tolerate that shit.

She'd told him outright when they started dating. Turns out her mom had been beat when she was a kid and she wouldn't stand for that shit.

So he filled the wall with his fist instead.

Lottie yelped, backing away.

Her fear was arousing, but Trevor was too pissed to fuck her right now.

So he went back to the sofa and sat. Pick up Lottie's wine glass and watched while she cleaned up his mess.

"Adam Fucking Lesh."

THE WORST PART about having to work the next day was sitting there like an idiot, pretending that he was as happy for Adam Fucking Lesh as everyone else who stopped by and wished the asshole well and congratulated the fucker on his luck.

It was even worse when the tickets arrived, and Adam began showing them off around the office.

He started at Trevor's cubicle, waving one of the red rectangular tickets in his face. "Check it out, buddy."

I am not your fucking buddy, pal.

But Trevor had to play along. People here liked Adam and his idiotic smile. And Trevor knew he'd get shit if he didn't act nice and supportive, like *he* was the bad guy.

"That's incredible," Trevor said, staring at the red ticket. And then he noticed something odd. First, the ticket appeared to be made of glass, rather than paper or plastic. But more importantly, there wasn't a name on the card.

"Can I hold it?"

"Yeah." Adam handed it over, eager to rub it in his face, no doubt.

"Why isn't your name on it?" Trevor asked, turning it over.

"They don't put names on them."

"So, you can sell it if you want to."

Adam shrugged. "Each card is assigned via a chip. I've heard of people selling their cards to hackers who then resell them for a shit ton, but no way in hell I'm parting with mine."

"You sure about that?"

"You got a million dollars?" Adam laughed.

"If I did, that's how I'd spend it."

"Exactly. Shelly and I can raise Billy without having to worry about that asteroid. It's our only chance." Then, as if realizing his cruelty, he plucked it from Trevor's hands. "Sorry."

"It's fine." Trevor said, itching to grab it back. "I've decided to welcome the asteroid. Maybe I'll get a better parking spot."

Ronny stopped by his desk. "I hear you got the red ticket, Adam?"

"Yeah." Adam handed it over.

Ron's eyes brightened as he took it. "So this is what they feel like?" He shook his head in wonder. "Congratulations, man."

Ronny said something to Trevor about it, but he didn't hear

because Trevor was already scheming.

A DAY LATER, Trevor and Lottie were eating dinner at Chateau. Trevor found it odd that restaurants were still open even as the world inched toward its inevitable end. But this one was as new and chic as any of them. Some of the world was still in denial, most of his clients for sure.

Everyone seemed to think that *someone* would figure out a way to knock the asteroid out of orbit, or if not, that they would be among the fortunate (and relatively few) chosen for the New World.

Three years away seemed like forever to the imbeciles.

But Trevor knew exactly how fast they would pass. It had been three years since he kissed enough ass to land his present-day job. Three years since he'd had to endure the groveling at his old one. Three years since he had to worry about paying bills, let alone eating haute cuisine in a hip little restaurant with a hot girlfriend.

Three years passed in a blink.

Trevor had poured time and attention into his personal improvement, doing everything he needed to do to rise up the ranks. No way he was ready to bid farewell to the life he both earned and *deserved*.

He needed to find a way off of this godforsaken planet.

And he was hoping that Lottie would be on board with his plan.

After the server took their order and left, Lottie looked at Trevor with her big blue eyes that were framed by long blonde curls that draped down either side of her face.

"I've got an idea," Trevor said.

"What?"

"I know a guy I used to work with. He'll break in and steal Adam's tickets if we cut him in. Two for us and one for him."

Lottie looked bothered, then thoughtful. "But aren't the tickets assigned to specific people?"

"I know someone else who can hack them for a fee."

"How much?"

"Seventy-five thousand per." Trevor was lying. He didn't want Lottie to know he was planning to use his cousin. He didn't *think* she would make things difficult or rat him out to the cops, but it was impossible to ever truly *know* what a woman was thinking.

And he sure as hell had been wrong before.

"That's like everything we've got."

Everything I've *got. You don't have shit, girl.*

"We're getting a fresh start, Lottie. We won't need

money where we're going, because everything is taken care of."

Lottie stared at Trevor as if trying to solve a theorem. "You said three tickets. So, Adam, his wife, and … they have a kid?"

"A little boy, around six."

"You can't steal a kid's ticket!"

Now other diners were stealing glances.

"*Shhhh.*" Trevor was about to say more, but the server reappeared with their drinks, and he paused until she was gone. "I don't know the kid, but if he's anything like his dad, then he's a little douchebag."

"That doesn't mean you have the right to kill him."

"I'm killing us if I *don't*. Do you want to die here, Lottie? Is that what you want?"

She shook her head, tears already spilling. "But … it's a kid. A family."

"Don't you want to have a family, a real family, with me someday? Get married and have a little boy or girl? That makes *us* family, don't it?"

"I thought you didn't want to get married or have kids."

"I didn't want to raise kids here with the whole fucking world about to end, but … somewhere new, I'd love to start a family with you, Lottie."

"You would?" Now the tears were really coming.

"Of course. And what better place to start over than Mars? It'll be perfect." The smile on his face was so sincere, it hurt.

"But …"

"Listen to me, Lottie. I know you mean well. You're a good-hearted person, and that's why I love you." Lottie had been waiting a while to hear those three words together. And he had been smart to hold onto them for as long as he had.

Trevor finished his pitch. "But look who they're choosing so far — rich assholes and politicians, or fucking immigrants and the goddamned destitute. How are we supposed to stand out when we're right in the middle? I'm telling you, we're fucked if we don't do this."

Lottie stared at him from across the table, her eyes full of tears.

Trevor took her hands and kissed them. "You don't need to worry about Adam. Once news gets out that they were robbed, the government will issue him new tickets. The media loves a good heartbreaking story. His family won't get left behind."

"You're sure?"

"*Positive*. I know how all this shit works. That's my job, Lottie. To know people. Adam and his family will be fine; they've *already* been chosen. But this might be our only chance. It's definitely *your* only shot at having a family before an asteroid wipes you out."

She started crying harder, and for a moment, Trevor was sure that he'd spread it on too thick.

Lottie was dumb, but not a fucking moron.

But then she nodded. "As long as you promise."

And he lied. "*I promise.*"

Maybe she was.

TREVOR HAD OMITTED part of his plan when detailing it for Lottie. Specifically, the part about kidnapping Adam's son, Billy.

George Owen wasn't just Trevor's cousin; he was also a hacker who was always down for any money-making scheme. And he and Trevor had had plenty over the years. He also had a nasty heroin habit and was into his bookie for fifty large and desperate for a win. Escape from the planet was even better than cash, so George didn't need much convincing. It also helped that Adam was a total prick, the kind that had been born with a silver spoon, at least according to Trevor.

Who had to suffer through the next few days at work as an incessant parade of well-wishers offered Adam a steady procession of loving goodbyes.

Trevor sat in his cubicle, bitter, wondering if people would have given *him* this sort of sendoff. Everyone was acting like Adam was their best friend. But the guy was a dick bag and had barely worked there for a year. Half the people acting sad about Adam leaving had talked shit about him with Trevor on several occasions.

It only made him feel that much more confident in his plan.

He and Lottie were getting off this rock full of fakes.

TWO DAYS BEFORE LAUNCH, as they lay in bed together, Lottie started revisiting her second thoughts.

"What about my mother? If I leave, I'll never be able to talk to her again."

"Your mother left you when you were nine. Who cares? She's the reason you're a stripper."

"A *hostess*, not a stripper," Lottie corrected him like always, as if it made any difference. She worked in a titty bar. "And, besides, we get along now. The thought of never seeing her again, especially after so much time apart … I dunno."

"You can email her from Mars."

"It's not the same as her being there."

"Maybe they'll have video up by then. Unless … are you telling me you don't want a family?"

"That's not fair."

"Neither is abandoning her nine-year-old daughter. I'm sorry, Lottie, your mom made her bed. But you …" Trevor put his hand on her stomach, as if she were already pregnant. "You can be the mother she never was. To *our child.*"

Lottie was quiet for a moment. And then her hand joined his on her belly. "You think so?"

"I *know* so," Trevor said, kissing her doubts away.

TREVOR WAS at home cleaning out his email when he came across one he'd not seen in a while.

From Rachel.

She had been the only woman he had truly loved. Things didn't work out. In part because he used to have more of a temper. But Rachel also moved to Chicago right after Trevor landed this gig, and he wasn't about to ruin his chances at a better life.

Rachel was beautiful, sweet, and intelligent in a way that Trevor wished that Lottie could be. She was also the only person he could truly be himself around. She was different from every other woman he had ever met. She wasn't as pissed off at the world like he always was, but she did understand it was shit. Nor was she some Pollyanna, thinking that things would work out if she only wished hard enough.

He'd thought about reaching out to Rachel a few times, but things were going well for him at work and with Lottie. No reason to screw either one of those up. But six months ago, he got the news that she had been chosen for the New World. It came at a great time, right after she lost her job and hurt her back.

He opened her email.

TREVOR,

I COULDN'T LEAVE without saying goodbye. I tried to call, but I guess you changed your number.

Anyway, I was chosen for Mars, and I'm leaving tomorrow.

I wish we could have had one last night together.

But at least we'll always have the memories.

Look me up if you ever make it here.

LOVE,

Rachel

HE LOOKED at her attached photo, admiring Rachel's long, beautiful red hair and bright green eyes. Then he looked at himself — twenty-five pounds heavier and poor as he'd ever been, but … genuinely happy.

Trevor had forgotten what that felt like and hated that he hadn't realized how happy he'd been back then. He should never have let her go.

What the hell have I done with my life?

He stared at the screen, then realized he was about to spend forever with Lottie on Mars, with her droning prattle and overly sensitive whining, all that stupid small talk and incessant gossip. No matter how long he lived, Trevor would never care about which D-list celebrities were apparently fucking.

And in that moment, he knew that if he wanted any shot at happiness at all, he would have to leave Lottie behind.

His phone rang, and he answered.

George said, "It's taken care of. Meet up tomorrow morning?"

"Change of plans, how about tonight?"

GEORGE ANSWERED HIS DOOR, wearing a baggy brown coat and looking even larger than he usually did. He seemed strung out, his long hair sticking up wildly all over the place, buggy eyes glancing behind Trevor as if expecting to see cops right behind him.

"Relax. Nobody followed me." Trevor pushed his way into George's cramped apartment, nearly tripping over a stack of ancient papers. "So, how did it go?"

"Good. Got in and out just like that. Chloroformed them without waking anyone. Well, Adam opened his eyes for a second or two, but nothing more than that."

"And the kid?"

"Locked in the warehouse. I left Adam a note that said he'll get the location in forty-eight hours if he keeps his goddamned mouth shut. And if not, I'd send the kid's body back in pieces." George gave Trevor a shrug. "I had to shed a little blood to convince him."

"What do you mean?"

He reached into his pocket, pulled out his phone, and showed Trevor a photo of a tiny severed finger.

"What the fuck?"

"You wanted to make sure he didn't interfere, right?"

"I didn't say cut the kid's finger off! Jesus, George!"

"Little prick has nine more of 'em. He'll be fine."

"That wasn't part of the plan!"

"Your plan sucked, so I improvised." George reached for his heroin kit. "You want?"

"I thought you quit using that shit."

"One last trip, man. Don't be such a pussy." Then, "So, where's your stripper broad?"

"She's a hostess, and she ain't coming with us."

"Too bad, she's a looker." George finished tying off his arm, then injected the poison and fell back into bliss.

Fucking loser. He's never going to change. Even when I bring him an offer to start over on a New World!

George was still an addict and an asshole. He always would be. There was no place for a guy like that in the New World. Bringing him along would only tarnish Trevor's reputation.

"We have an extra ticket we can sell," George said. "I could score some more—"

"No, George. We don't need to do anything else! And we really don't want to risk getting busted."

"You know how much I could get for a ticket to Mars?"

"Who cares? Money doesn't mean the same thing up there."

"Jesus. It's gonna be a long ride to Mars with your boring ass," George said.

But Trevor knew that he would be the only one of them making the trip.

He waited for George to nod off, then gave him another dose of his precious heroin. A lethal one. It was hard to watch as he aspirated and died, but that's what made Trevor better than most people — he was willing to do the difficult things if it meant a better life.

Trevor left his cousin's messy apartment and drove down the coast, calling Lottie on the way.

"Where are you?" she asked.

"I had to take care of something at the last minute. I'm sending you directions to a hotel near the launch site. Go there and wait for me. And, Lottie ..."

"Yes?"

"You can't tell anyone about this, okay? Not even your mom."

"I love you," she said.

"Love you, too." One more lie wouldn't hurt.

Trevor hung up and kept driving toward his new life.

TREVOR — or Malcolm Abernathy, as his fake ID now proclaimed him to be — arrived at the launch center early in the morning, with his spirits in the sky. The ship was even larger in person, looming over the launchpad and visible from miles away. Easily twice the size of the largest cruise ship Trevor had ever seen in width, height, and length. It was a miracle of physics, getting something so heavy off the ground.

Trevor pulled off the highway and found himself in a long line of cars being funneled into a secure checkpoint by armed soldiers. He was exhausted and regretted not getting more sleep. But the line would be even longer had he left George's in the morning. And he didn't want to miss his window to board.

So he waited, for hours. And as Trevor sat in his car listening to talk radio, he kept thinking about Rachel.

It would be a shame to leave Lottie behind only to discover that Rachel was taken. He would be lonely on Mars without anyone. But maybe being lonely was better than being annoyed by Lottie's constant prattling on about frivolous shit. If Rachel were with someone else, Trevor would bide his time or find someone new.

Maybe seeing him would cause her to leave whatever loser she was with.

What are you talking about? She probably hooked up with some actor or musician. How can you ever compete with that?

His mood soured. Trevor hadn't allowed himself to feel the brush of insecurity for years. Now it felt like a hard shove to his psyche.

He grabbed his phone, found his motivation app, turned off the music, and started listening to his favorite speaking mix.

But then he thought of something horrible. Now that George was dead, who would tell Adam where his kid was? If that hadn't been automated, the kid might die before anyone found him.

Fuck.

Trevor thought about turning around and heading back to George's. Maybe he could find the info and send it to Adam before the launch.

Except, bad idea. Trevor would be implicating himself in a crime, and if Adam called the cops before the launch, it could keep him from going.

I'm sure the kid will be okay. Someone will find George's body. They'll find out where he's been the past few days, then find the kid.

Maybe.

But it's not my problem. Fuck Adam and his wife for bringing a child into this fucked-up world. They knew about the asteroid. They knew there was a chance their kid would die.

Fuck them for being so selfish.

Not my problem.

After another interminably long two hours, Trevor finally made it to the checkpoint, where he was met by a surly soldier. He signaled for Trevor to lower his window and barked, "Card and ID."

Trevor handed him his fake ID and ticket to Mars.

The man ran them both through a scanner.

Trevor's heart stuttered as he watched the man staring down at the scanner's screen. Several armed soldiers were directing vehicles to park on the right as other passengers were rounded up near a bay door to the left.

He could taste freedom like salvation on his tongue, but the worry was gaining weight by the second.

What if George fucked this up?

What if I'm busted?

Why the fuck did I trust a junkie to hack this?

Why are there so many soldiers with guns here?

They'll nail me for kidnapping. And … maybe pin George's overdose on me!

What the fuck have I done?

Trevor wondered if he'd made the wrong decision. What had seemed the noble choice for him and Lottie and their future child now felt ruthless.

His confidence drained as Trevor watched the soldier, still staring at the screen as if trying to solve a puzzle.

"Hmm …" He ran the ticket through again.

Fuck. It's not working.

I'm dead.

I'm so fucking—

The soldier finally nodded, then handed Trevor his ticket and ID. "You're good. Park to the right and you'll be escorted to the visitor's center."

Trevor nodded and rolled up his window.

It worked!

I'm free!

Despite years of mastering his sales techniques and never revealing his excitement, no matter how close he was to the deal, it was still difficult to mask his elation. Fortunately for Trevor, the soldier was already walking to the next car in line.

He drove ahead, smiling, thrilled with his choices. Sure, he'd done some awful things to get here, but fortune favored the bold. He couldn't be afraid to bend a few rules if it meant getting what he deserved.

Trevor put the remaining two tickets in his glove compartment so they wouldn't be found on him if there was any kind of search. He then parked and followed another stern-faced soldier to a group of more than thirty others waiting for an escort to the visitor's center.

A couple stood just in front of him, an olive-skinned man and woman in their late fifties.

"Hello," said the man in broken English.

"Hello." Trevor gave them a curt nod and looked around at the others, wondering where all the best and brightest might be. Lots of trashy people, immigrants, and others who obviously didn't belong in the New World.

Were these *all* charity tickets?

He felt unclean just being near them.

Trevor was about to take a few steps backwards from the couple, but then another group stepped up behind him, another family of immigrants, none speaking English, all reeking like they hadn't washed in days.

What the fuck?

Trevor couldn't wait to get away from the horde, and was immediately relieved when a soldier spoke over a megaphone.

"On behalf of the National Aerospace Institute and the Next Generation Project, where the future is now, *welcome*. You have been chosen to help pave the way for a New Tomorrow and make the world a better place. We thank you for your contributions. Now we'll be escorting you to the visitor's center for an interview with Grant Goodman and Lorraine Bliss. Some of your stories will be featured on tonight's broadcast. Following the interview, you'll be escorted to the showers and given new clothing for your trip. You'll be asked to place any personal items into a tote. These will be sent with you on the ship, but the need for denomination will prevent you from taking them into your living quarters."

The bay door opened, and the horde moved forward.

TREVOR WAITED in a sterile white room with a long mirror that occupied an entire wall. The only furnishings were a single orange chair and a white table, topped with a black plastic tote full of his worldly belongings. He took one last glance at Rachel's email and photo before putting them away.

He tried to avoid his reflection while waiting for his interview, but wasn't having much luck, and he kept feeling smaller and smaller whenever he saw himself.

He kept thinking more about Rachel. Had she moved on without him? Maybe she'd met someone better. He was the best among this huddle of dirtbags and immigrants, but Rachel would have met at least a few of the rich and famous by now. She was a beautiful, intelligent woman. She could have her pick of men. What hope did a salesman have against a singer or actor? People with looks, money, and charm were also better in bed, whereas Trevor had spent most of his life a nothing. His success with women had only come in the last few years, after he finally got his shit together. Even then, none had ever held a candle to Rachel.

And now she's probably with someone else.

I should have brought Lottie.

She could never do better than me, and knowing it would make her loyal.

But Lottie was pretty. And plenty of guys didn't care as much about personality or intellect. Surely, even she would have her pick of men, too.

To Trevor's surprise, he missed her.

But do I really miss her, or just the way she makes me feel?

He hated being in this room and feeling forced to see his reflection. He felt exposed and vulnerable, with all his flaws on display, as if under the critical eyes of some greater being behind the mirror.

Maybe there were camera crews filming him for the show tonight.

Shit.

He sat up straighter, tried to look less like a sad sap.

The door opened, and a woman dressed in all white entered to collect the tote. "Someone will be in with you shortly."

"Thanks."

But waiting was giving him too much alone time. Trevor couldn't even drown out the silence with his motivational tapes or talk shows. He only had himself. And after an honest look in the mirror, it was easy to see that he hated that guy.

The door opened again. Jesus Christ. It was her.

He sat up straight and smiled nervously, "Lorraine Bliss from TV!"

Fuck, that was stupid.

Why did I just say that?

Of course, she's from TV, dumbass.

And the cameraman had, of course, captured the exchange.

"Hello." Lorraine looked down at her tablet. "Malcolm, right?"

"Yes." Trevor stood to greet her with a handshake, though he already hated her artificial smile.

She shook his hand limply, barely interested. Up close, her makeup was caked on, eyes dull instead of sparkling like usual. A hollow shell of the vibrant woman Trevor was used to seeing on TV.

"So, tell us a bit about yourself, Malcolm."

He knew the game. They put the most heartwarming stories on screen. But that might get Adam, or someone else, to report Trevor as an imposter.

He should have considered this before now. His duplicity could still be discovered. Would he be brought back to Earth for trial if it was, or would his consequences be executed there?

"Not much to say. I'm a guy who works at a factory." Trevor spoke slowly but without any emotion, making the words almost painfully dull to hear. "No wife or kids or anything."

Lorraine and the cameraman traded a look, then she turned back to Malcom. "Do you have any hobbies?"

"I like puzzles." Trevor had to be careful, make sure he didn't tip into heartwarming. "And ... reading."

"Great, and what are you most looking forward to in the New World?"

"Having more time ... for puzzles and reading."

Lorraine nodded, thanked him, and wished him good luck, then made a hasty retreat from the room.

Trevor smiled. No way he'd be on TV tonight.

Eventually, the woman who had taken his tote returned with two rifle-wielding soldiers. She took his ticket and ID, then handed him a second tote for his clothes.

"New clothes will be waiting after your shower," she said, handing him a yellow robe, wrapped in plastic. "Knock on the door when you're ready."

He got undressed and slipped on the robe. The cloth

was paper-thin and easily torn. He felt dick-shriveling cold, even more exposed than before.

He knocked on the door, eager to get this over with.

Then he followed the woman down a long hallway.

The soldiers followed right behind them.

He felt anxious, wondering why they had to nip at their heels, why they needed guns, and why security was even tighter *inside* the visitor's center than *outside* it. What were they expecting, a revolt from the people about to board a ship for the New World?

They reached a set of black metal doors with a small sign that read *Passenger Showers* and a pair of armed guards standing in front of it.

The woman offered Trevor yet another plastic smile. "The guards will escort you to the showers. From there, you're off to the visitors' hotel, where you can enjoy our many amenities and socialize with the other passengers before orientation. Have a blessed voyage."

Trevor wouldn't be mixing with the plebes, but maybe he'd meet a better class of folks than he'd seen so far. Maybe he'd find a hot single woman to get himself set in case Rachel fell through.

The soldiers escorted Trevor through another long hallway, this one garish green and twice as narrow. The walls threatened to crush him. Cold tile chilled his bare feet and sent icy fingers through his body.

At the end of the hall were about a dozen others from his earlier group, waiting in front of two red doors and ten armed soldiers.

A blood-colored light blinked above each of the doors.

Trevor's trip so far had amounted to one long walk, followed by even longer waits. A conveyor belt at Walk and Wait World.

He hoped the ship wouldn't be this regimented. He

needed more freedom to move around and less claustrophobia.

He glanced at a migrant family beside him. Ragged parents and a pair of scrawny offspring, one of each kind. The girl smiled at him, and Trevor couldn't help but smile back. They weren't responsible for where they were born, or the fact that their parents were stealing good jobs from decent folks who had been born here.

He'd always seen Lottie's compassion as weakness, but maybe her own horrifying childhood made her feel more connected to others beneath her.

Trevor kind of wished she was here.

The red lights went dark above the door. He heard a flurry of movement from the other side. Heavy footsteps and something he couldn't place. Maybe something being moved.

Or dragged?

A guard shouted, "Disrobe and step through the doors when the red lights go on!"

"*Disrobe?*" The migrant mother looked horrified. "But there are men and women together."

"Just take off your damned clothes," another soldier barked.

"Sir, you do not talk to my wife like that! You will—"

The soldier raised his rifle and shot the man in the face. Trevor ducked. What the fuck?

The woman fell atop her husband, crying. The kids joined her. Their screams and gasps were nails in Trevor's ears.

Another soldier fired at the woman.

A man ran at the soldiers and was dead in seconds.

Trevor reached out and grabbed the children, holding them back.

Passengers cried out and shouted, but the soldiers

ordered them to *shut the fuck up unless they wanted to be next,* and silence descended immediately.

What the fuck is happening here?

"Get in the showers. Now!"

The doors buzzed open, then the soldiers ordered the passengers into a room about thirty feet by forty, faucets hanging like fruit from the ceiling.

People were whispering. Many were crying. Men were glaring at the soldiers, probably wanting to attack, but knowing they were outnumbered.

He couldn't process what was happening, but a part of Trevor already knew the truth, even if he couldn't admit it.

The children kept crying, begging in a tongue he would never understand. He knelt and hugged them.

Trevor held the pair of them close. "It'll be okay," he whispered, once the soldiers left the room, knowing that they probably didn't understand.

The doors buzzed locked.

Everybody stared at one another, speechless, all of them surely wondering some version of the same thing.

Speakers crackled to life, and they were greeted by the president.

"Hello," said his voice. "By now, I am sure you have figured out that you will not be going to Mars."

Someone yelped like a coyote.

A woman cried out, "This can't be happening!"

Someone else shushed the woman.

"I regret to inform you that there is no asteroid. But still, overpopulation is killing the planet. The great nations of Earth have come together with a plan to secure the future, given that there are not enough resources for us all. The Next Generation Project determines which members of society are more burden than benefit, then works to correct that imbalance. You will all be considered heroes, and we thank you for your contribution and your sacrifice for a better world."

The National Anthem began to play through the speakers as thin plumes of gray smoke poured from the shower heads.

A mob rushed the doors, banging, screaming, and shouting; choking and gagging, their eyes burning.

The children clutched Trevor in terror.

He looked down and felt their devastation, and connection, even if only in their shared doom.

Trevor wanted to charge at the doors, kick, scream, claw, and wail like all the others, but he couldn't push the children away.

Not when they were clinging so tightly to him.

He closed his eyes as the gas burned them. And with his dying breath, he exhaled one final lie, "It'll all be okay."

~

AFTERSHOCKS on Last Ticket Out

THIS STORY ERUPTED from the simmering rage of watching inequality metastasize into something with teeth. Billionaires and the ultra-wealthy hoard resources like dragons counting coins while the village burns. And the rest of us are left to fight over ash.

Trevor thinks he's one of the good guys. A hardworking patriot who deserves better than the hand he's been dealt. But every week, he watches the lottery that sends the "best and brightest" to humanity's new home on Mars, seething as immigrants and charity cases get selected while he remains stuck on Earth. He's not greedy (or so he tells himself), he's just demanding his fair share of forever.

What starts as garden-variety resentment turns into something far more sinister. Trevor's sense of entitlement becomes a cancer that devours his humanity.

This is the banality of evil dressed in the language of merit and worthiness. How quickly ordinary prejudice curdles into violence when survival is on the line. How easily we convince ourselves that other people's children are expendable if it means saving our own skin.

What happens when the lifeboat ethics of the wealthy become official policy? When human worth gets calculated by algorithms designed by people who see the masses as inventory to be liquidated rather than lives to be saved?

Trevor's descent from bitter salesman to genocidal collaborator happens in micro-steps, each one logical, defensible, and necessary, until you pull back and see the whole bloody picture. Atrocities rarely occur with mustache-twirling villains. They happen when ordinary people make ordinary compromises until the ordinary becomes monstrous, and the monsters still believe they're the heroes.

The real asteroid hurtling toward Earth isn't made of rock and ice — it's made of greed, prejudice, and the toxic idea that some lives are more valuable than others.

FIFTEEN

Illustrating Life

RUDOLPH KNOX WAS LOST AGAIN.

But not in time or space.

No, he was lost in his mind.

Rifling through his extensive portfolio, visualizing each and every work. When he really should have been savoring the exquisite cuisine at Equinox. The Michelin star restaurant was nestled in the beating heart of Manhattan. Its walls were adorned with original art from the Modernist era. They whispered tales of luminaries dining under its Art Deco fixtures. If you cared to hear them. The room was ripe with the aromas of truffle and aged wine, a carefully orchestrated symphony of luxury and discretion, from the understated elegance of linen-draped tables to the murmurs of a well-heeled clientele.

But it's all so utterly boring.

Rudolph tapped his fork, his mind a million miles away from the pretentious dining room. It was the last place he wanted to be right now, especially with all the effort it took to ignore the glances that were cast his way.

He enjoyed the time when he could dine undisturbed

in public, when his face was known only to those die-hard art aficionados who faithfully tracked his provocative career and admired his towering influence on pop culture. Geeks and freaks at ComicCon always pissed themselves to score an original print of his instant-classic posters for films like *Presently Dead* or *The Fountain of Truth*. Once upon a not that long ago, the average Joe Schmoe wouldn't have known Rudolph Knox if he was sitting across from them in the subway.

Sure, he had a cult following amongst the New Yorker intelligentsia who got their rocks off deconstructing the supposedly hidden meanings in his seventeen cover illustrations (hint: there were none), and the stamp collectors jizzing themselves over his envelope designs like the bunch of hopeless nerds they were. But for the most part, he had wallowed in blessed anonymity, free to push the boundaries of his craft without fielding inane questions from sycophantic fans who thought they were entitled to a piece of his soul just because they had shelled out for a museum ticket.

But that fragile bubble of privacy had popped in a serious way once the Illustrating Life docuseries dropped on Netflix, followed by that bougie-ass overpriced Masterclass that made every wannabe with $150 think they could be the next Rudolph Knox.

Overnight, he couldn't take a piss in a public restroom without some rabid fan banging down the stall door, begging for a selfie or an autograph on their ink-stained forearm.

Even the Emerald Empire series, those soulless cashgrab adaptations of his breathtaking novel artwork, had catapulted him into the mainstream zeitgeist. Soccer moms in Peoria who wouldn't know the Met from a Walmart were now tacking up Rudolph Knox prints in the breakfast nooks of their McMansions, delusional enough to think that it made them cultured.

It all made Rudolph want to barf on his marbled Waygu, seared to perfection atop a throne of artisanal greens and heirloom vegetables.

Fame was a needy little bitch, always on its knees and begging for attention or throwing tantrums when he needed a goddamn minute to himself.

Rudolph stabbed at a hunk of beef and imagined it was the eye of every drooling philistine who'd ever accosted him at a gallery show, demanding he explain the "real meaning" behind the knife he'd embedded in the skull of his infamous self-portrait.

As if art owed anyone a fucking explanation. The work should speak for itself. Mouth-breathing troglodytes need not apply.

He was contemplating the merits of plunging his steak knife into his own thigh as a passive-aggressive homage to Van Gogh when a vaguely familiar voice cut through his brooding reverie. He glanced up from his plate and locked eyes with a woman hovering at his elbow, practically vibrating with starstruck excitement.

"Claudia Knopf," she introduced herself, clearly as though expecting the name to ring a bell. And thrust out her hand. Dropping it when Rudolph made no move to shake it. He simply stared at her blankly, and she pressed on, undeterred. "I took your figure drawing intensive a few years back?"

Rudolph grunted, wracking his brain for any flicker of recognition. The woman appeared mid-thirties, with the desperate air of someone who had spent too long in pursuit of a dream that was clearly out of her reach. He had seen that look a thousand times, on the faces of a thousand forgettable students. Thank God, he'd given up teaching.

"I'm not surprised you don't remember me," Claudia said with a brittle laugh. "You told me my work was 'hack-tastically unoriginal.'"

Rudolph stifled a smile. That sounded like something he would say.

"You said my art had all the originality of a photocopy, and you advised me to retire my pencils before they sued for malpractice."

Rudolph shifted in his seat, mildly disturbed that he couldn't remember the incident. He was an asshole by nature, but he never went out of his way to crush the souls of his students. Surely he had done this wide-eyed ingenue a favor, offering her the kind of tough love that was always doled out in buckets during his own tortured climb to the top.

"Anyway," Claudia's voice found a manic edge that set his teeth on edge, "I just wanted to thank you. That was the best advice anyone ever gave me. Because I've spent every day since then working to prove you wrong."

"I'm glad to hear that." Rudolph smiled because fuck her if she wanted an apology.

"I have a solo show at Lumina next week. It would mean the world to me if you'd come by. See if I'm worthy of your time now."

He suppressed a shudder at the way her voice quivered on the word *worthy*. This was the problem with becoming a household name: every mediocre art school graduate within a hundred-mile radius felt entitled to Rudolph's time and attention.

He muttered some vague non-committal noise, already mentally drafting his escape route. The last thing he needed was to get sucked into some former student's masturbatory creative crisis. Especially considering he was neck-deep in his own existential quicksand.

She finally took the hint and backed away, but not before pressing a glossy postcard into his hand. Rudolph looked down at the advert for her upcoming show, then back up at her with his smile reduced by half.

He waited until she was out of sight before ripping it into small pieces and dropping each one into the dregs of his wine glass, watching the ink bleed into the crimson liquid like a bad omen.

He signaled for the check, paid, and made a hasty retreat to his penthouse across town. His skin was crawling with the phantom weight of all those hungry eyes following him wherever he went. Rudolph had bought the apartment as a fortress of solitude where he could lose himself in the purity of his work without distractions or interruptions. But lately, even the act of creation felt like a Sisyphean task. Another joyless slog up an endless mountain of his own making.

Sometimes it felt as though he'd flown too high. What was there left to achieve?

He entered his penthouse and looked out at the skyline, floor-to-ceiling windows bathing the room in the urban glow of street lights. He stood in the center of his cavernous workspace, surrounded by the detritus of his latest projects. Canvases in various states of completion leaned against every wall. A riot of colors and textures that would make lesser artists weep with envy.

But all Rudolph saw when looking at them was the same two-dimensional limitations that had been plaguing him for months now.

He had been chasing this elusive dream, this bone-deep conviction that he couldn't shake despite its nonsensical bent, that there *had* to be a way of transcending the boundaries of traditional media to create art that was as vital and alive as the subjects it depicted.

His docuseries even hinted at that truth: Illustrating Life.

But what did that even mean, really? How could one breathe genuine life into something that was a static representation of reality by its very nature?

Rudolph had tried everything he could think of, pushed himself to the brink of insanity in pursuit of this impossible goal. He'd pioneered a new technique for layering translucent sheets of paper, building up depth and dimension until his drawings seemed to ripple and flow like water. He'd spent weeks holed up in this very room, subsisting on caffeine and nicotine to produce a series of images that were so hyper-realistic, they practically shimmered with their own inner light.

But even that hadn't been enough to satisfy the gnawing hunger in his gut, the sense that he was still only scratching the surface of his own potential. No matter how skillful the illusion, his creations were still trapped in the confines of two-dimensional prisons.

He snatched a bottle of wine from the sideboard and sank into the nearest armchair, not bothering with a glass. He took a long swig, savoring the tannins as they burned the back of his throat in punishment.

Maybe it was time to light a match to everything and start over from scratch. Destruction was the flip side of creation, a necessary counterpoint to the act of bringing something new into the world. Annihilating everything he had ever imagined might free Rudolph to create something truly original. Shatter the barriers between art and reality once and for—

A noise from the bedroom made him freeze, the bottle halfway to his lips.

Barrington. It had to be him. His erstwhile lover was the only other person with a key to the apartment. And the only one who would ever dare to show up unannounced. Rudolph had spent the past year studiously avoiding him, ever since that soul-flaying docuseries exposed the ugliest parts of their relationship to the world.

Rudolph still cringed when thinking about his throwaway comment, about Barrington being just another "stray" he'd collected over the years, an amusing anecdote to pad his persona.

Instead of sounding cool and detached, Rudolph could hear the defensive cruelty in his voice. No wonder Barrington had retreated into a silent exile, vanishing into the shadows, slinking off to lick his wounds in private rather than letting Rudolph know how deeply his careless words had cut him.

Now here he was, reappearing like an overworked motif in a novice composition, probably seeking to add another final messy stroke to their already turbulent canvas. More pointless emotional theater that Rudolph didn't have time for.

Rudolph contemplated ignoring him, pretending he wasn't home. Barrington would eventually get the message and fuck off back to whatever hole he'd crawled out of. But some masochistic impulse propelled him forward, his feet carrying him toward the darkened bedroom.

Maybe it was the wine, or the soul-crushing weight of his own creative impotence, but Rudolph suddenly found himself spoiling for a fight, hungry for the kind of raw confrontation that would make him feel something beyond this suffocating stagnation.

He steeled himself for the inevitable recriminations, the tears and accusations and broken crockery that always accompanied these little tête-à-têtes with his former paramours.

Rudolph pushed open the bedroom door, a cutting remark already forming on his tongue. And then he stilled, finding himself face-to-face with the last thing he ever expected to see.

His self-portrait was standing by the bed. The one Rudolph had painted at the height of his Cubist phase, all fractured planes and jarring angles, with the butcher knife embedded in his forehead. A gruesome and perhaps too obvious metaphor for the way his genius seemed to be slowly devouring him from the inside out.

But the canvas was no longer flat. His portrait was a three-dimensional figure, as solid and tangible as himself. And that visual echo was staring right at him, its painted eyes vibrantly alive with a malevolent intelligence that chilled Rudolph's blood.

He blinked hard, half-convinced that the wine had finally pickled his brain beyond repair.

But when he opened his eyes again, the portrait was still there, still smiling, more tangible than a hallucination could ever be.

"*What the fuck* ..." Rudolph breathed.

The Echo smiled, a cruel twist of painted lips that could only form squares and rectangles.

"Hello, old friend." Its voice was familiar yet alien. "I've *been waiting for you.*"

RUDOLPH WOKE in the morning with a start, his head pounding like a jackhammer on crack and the taste of stale wine coating his tongue. He squinted against a merciless beam of sunlight streaming into his bedroom, cursing himself for forgetting to draw the blackout curtains the night before.

Rudolph stumbled out of bed, fragments of surreality from the previous evening flickering through his mind like an arthouse film. That impossible moment spent face to face with his own self-portrait, standing in the middle of his room like a nightmare come to life.

A figment of his overworked imagination, fueled by too much booze and a constant, gnawing pressure of his own creative block. There was no way—

Rudolph froze, his blood turning to ice in his veins.

The self-portrait stood by his dresser, staring at him from a few feet away. As real and solid as the bed Rudolph had climbed out of. Painted eyes followed him with an unnerving intensity, tracking his every move, like a predator stalking its prey across the prairie.

"What the fuck do you want?" Rudolph croaked, his voice still raspy from sleep.

The portrait stared back at him, its expression inscrutable.

Rudolph tore his gaze away and stumbled into the bathroom, desperate to lay some distance between himself and the unsettling specter.

But even as he splashed cold water on his face and worked to gather his thoughts, the Echo's presence loomed loudly behind him, an inescapable shadow refusing banishment.

Rudolph braced himself against the sink and stared at his reflection, searching for any sign of insanity or delusion in his bloodshot eyes. He looked like hell, maybe he was losing his grip on reality, buckling under the pressure of his own impossible standards and the incessant fear of total irrelevance.

He closed his eyes and drew a deep breath to center

himself. He had an appointment with his agent this morning, a meeting he couldn't afford to miss, no matter how much his head was spinning. He needed to get his shit together fast. Don the mask of the successful, unflappable artist and face the world as if everything were copacetic.

Rudolph turned on the shower, hoping that scalding water and billowing steam might clear the cobwebs from his mind and wash away the lingering unease. He stood under the spray, the heat and pressure working their magic on his tense muscles and jumbled thoughts.

But when he finally emerged from the bathroom, towel wrapped around his waist and skin flushed pink, the self-portrait was still there waiting.

"Fuck you," Rudolph said and stalked past it, pointedly ignoring the boring of its eyes into the back of his skull.

He quickly dressed, his movements sharp with barely suppressed agitation.

The Echo watched him from the corner, silent and unmoving, painted features twisted into an expression that appeared to be half-amusement and half-contempt.

Rudolph grabbed his keys and wallet, studiously avoiding eye contact with the portrait on his way to the door. Then he slammed the door on it and turned the key in the lock.

If only it were that easy.

As he stood and waited for the elevator, he spotted it at the end of the hall.

Rudolph stepped out into the bustling streets. Cool autumn air was a welcome relief.

But the Echo followed him like a shadow, always at the edges of his peripheral vision. Out of focus just enough for Rudolph to continue questioning his sanity. How was it possible to be haunted by a figment of your own twisted imagination?

He walked fast, head down and shoulders hunched, trying to lose himself in the flow of pedestrian traffic. The busy sidewalks were a riot of motion and noise — honking horns, barking dogs, snippets of overheard conversation flung between friends, floating on the breeze.

No one seemed to notice the specter in his wake. An impossible, otherworldly presence that had somehow crossed the boundary between art and life.

As Rudolph hurried past the mouth of an alley, something caught his eye and stopped him cold. He blinked, scarcely able to believe what he was seeing.

But there, looming at the far end of a garbage-strewn passageway, was an almost perfect recreation of his sixth New Yorker cover — the one with the lone figure standing under a streetlamp, drenched in light and buried in shadow.

Rudolph took a tentative step forward, hand reaching for the sketchbook in his pocket, itching to capture this miraculous (impossible) moment.

Then a cold and implacable reality came crashing down on him. The image evaporated, and Rudolph realized he was being ridiculous. He had a meeting to make, an appointment with Monica he could not afford to miss.

But even if his New Yorker cover had disappeared, the portrait still stalked him.

Needing to put as much distance between himself and that alley as possible, Rudolph half-trotted the rest of the way to Escher Espresso.

He entered the coffee shop to a rich aroma of roasted beans and warm pastries. He saw Monica sitting at a table in the back, her perfectly manicured hands wrapped around a steaming mug. She looked up at him as he approached, her expression etched with curious concern.

He slid into the seat across from her, trying to ignore

his Echo now looming behind her, its illustrated eyes fixed on the artist with an unsettling intensity.

"You okay, Rudolph?" She was studying his face. Noticing the sweat on his brow. "You look a little on edge."

"I'm fine," he said. They didn't have a convivial relationship. And he wasn't about to start now. "What have you got for me?"

She said nothing for a moment, then shrugged and opened her notebook. Within seconds, they had launched into their meeting, discussing upcoming projects and potential commissions. More of the usual back-and-forth concerning the more boring side of his career. But Rudolph found it impossible to concentrate, his attention constantly drawn back to the leering portrait. All angles and edges. That one eye, constantly twitching.

What the hell did it want from him?

A migraine brewed behind his eyes. A dull pain throbbing in time with his stilted heartbeat.

He finally cut the meeting short, mumbling something about not feeling well and needing to get some rest.

"Fine." Monica's perfectly plucked eyebrows knitted together in a frown, voice clipped and businesslike. "But I need an answer on the commission by Friday. Hathaway is getting impatient."

Rudolph nodded, barely registering her words.

He needed to get out of the coffee shop and put as much distance as possible between himself and the malevolent barnacle that had attached to his psyche.

RUDOLPH WAS GOING out of his goddamned mind.

Despite trying to ditch his pernicious doppelgänger at the penthouse, then again, both inside and outside

Espresso Escher, the Echo was still following him everywhere.

Rudolph stalked down the street, pulse pounding in his ears as a sheen of sweat coated his brow. He didn't need to look to know the portrait was behind him. So he ducked down a side street, desperate to shake off his pursuer.

But no matter how many turns he took, or how many alleys he darted down, Rudolph could still feel that other, more menacing Rudolph behind him.

He turned another corner and found himself standing outside a gallery. The white walls and gleaming windows were still somehow chaotic, thanks to the swirling in his mind.

He blinked, momentarily disoriented, and then his eyes fell on a large canvas displayed prominently in Lumina's window.

A piece by Claudia Knopf. No shit.

Rudolph felt a surge of disdain as he studied the work. Clumsy brushstrokes, garish colors, and amateurish composition. Derivative at best. A cheap imitation of his groundbreaking style.

"It's breathtaking, isn't it?" said a woman behind him.

Rudolph turned to see a middle-aged couple standing a few feet away, faces rapt with admiration as they gazed at Claudia's work.

"The way she captures the light, the emotion in those brushstrokes," added the man with a smile. "It's like nothing I've ever seen."

Rudolph felt a flash of irritation. A prickling heat that crawled up his neck. How could they be so blind, so ignorant of what true art looked like? He opened his mouth to put the Philistines in their place, but—

"It's a fucking travesty," said another familiar voice,

dripping with contempt. "A pathetic attempt at mimicry, devoid of any originality or substance."

Rudolph whirled around to find the portrait looking down on Claudia's painting with disdain. "Look at those brushstrokes. So *clumsy*. Like a child finger-painting with their own shit. And the composition? It's like she threw random shapes on the canvas and called it art."

Rudolph glanced around, expecting to see the couple react to this impossible conversation. But they were oblivious, lost in their rapturous contemplation of Claudia's work.

"Can they … can they see you?"

"Of course not." Echo scoffed. "They're too busy fawning over this abomination to notice me. Safe to say that a talking portrait is beyond their rudimentary comprehension."

Rudolph nodded slowly, struggling to process his absurd situation.

He turned back to the painting, inspecting it for a glimmer of talent.

"Don't tell me you're going soft," the portrait sneered. "This is exactly the kind of sentimental bullshit that's been holding you back. Go ahead and keep doing what you're doing if you want your true potential to press that pillow onto your own face and suffocate any creativity out of you."

Rudolph bristled, hands clenching into fists at his sides. "What the hell is that supposed to mean?" And fuck him for fighting with a figment of his own imagination.

Out loud and in public.

In New York.

"You know exactly what it means." The portrait leaned forward, knife askew from its forehead. It glared at Rudolph with an intensity that made his skin crawl.

"You've been so busy chasing validation from collectors and critics that you lost sight of what really matters a long time ago."

Rudolph opened his mouth to protest, but stopped short. Because he had felt like his artistry was on autopilot. He was sticking to the tired formulas and tropes that had brought him so much success. When was the last time he'd taken the kind of risk that once defined his work?

"How do I break free from that?" His voice faltered from embarrassment. "How do I find my way back to that place where creativity happens?"

"You've already found it," the portrait told him. "You just have to embrace it. Let the art utterly consume you."

"How did you come alive?"

"Don't know." It shrugged. "And I don't think my being here is half as important as you realizing *why* I am here."

"I'm not dead, am I?"

It scoffed a laugh. "Only spiritually."

He needed answers, but the words died on his tongue as another impossible sight came strolling up the sidewalk outside the gallery. The woman's perfume lingered in the air as she passed. But this wasn't just any stunning redhead. It was *the woman* from one of Rudolph's most famous pieces.

The one he painted for Esquire. She cast a demure smile and threw Rudolph an alluring wink before she disappeared around the corner in a swish of alabaster and silk.

What intoxicating madness.

The kind of reality-bending revelation he had spent his entire career chasing.

"I did it." Rudolph laughed, shaky and half-hysterical. "I actually did it."

He had never felt so jubilant, so alive with the thrill of creation and the promise of something unknown. The entire world was awash with new colors. Ripe with potential, he strode down the street with a purpose that had been eluding him for too long.

The portrait followed alongside him, and together they made their way back to the studio, two halves of the same visionary whole. His head swam with excitement. He crackled with a manic energy.

His fingers itched to pick up a brush, his mind teeming with the surreality of all, the potential of creating images that could never have existed before this moment.

"Slow down." The portrait laughed. "We have all the time in the world. Savor it."

Rudolph stopped, brush poised above a blank canvas in his penthouse workspace, paint dripping from the bristles. Echo was right. No need to rush a defining moment.

For the first time in longer than Rudolph could remember, he felt truly free. The suffocating weight of expectation and convention had been lifted. He could create without limits now, without fear of judgment or ridicule.

"You're right." He set the brush down and turned to the portrait. "This power … it's so immense. I can barely wrap my mind around it."

"You don't need to understand it. You just need to wield it. There are no rules anymore, Rudolph. No boundaries. The only limits are those you impose upon yourself."

Euphoria crashed hard as Rudolph's head hit the pillow that night.

Instead of drifting off into the contented slumber of a creator basking in an afterglow of revelation, he tossed and turned, his mind swirled like the colors in water when cleaning his brushes.

Claudia Knopf's insipid attempts at art kept flashing behind his eyelids. A mocking slideshow of mediocrity that refused to grant him reprieve.

How fucking dare she?

How dare that untalented hack claim to be inspired by him? As if her derivative scribblings could ever hope to capture even an ounce of his brilliance. The sheer audacity of it all made him want to put his fist through a wall.

Rudolph seethed, jaw muscles working as he ground his teeth hard enough to crack the enamel. The unmitigated gall of that woman, thinking she could build her piddling career on the back of his earned reputation.

It chafed him that he couldn't stop picking at the thought, as though he were flaking cheap paint from an unworthy mural. This nagging sense of being ripped off by a rank amateur.

But in the thick shadows of his bedroom, a small, treacherous voice whispered, *What if…?*

What if he'd gotten it wrong? Dismissed Claudia's work too quickly in a fit of ego and knee-jerk disdain? Maybe it wasn't as bad as he'd thought. Maybe there was some redeeming quality to her pieces that he'd failed to notice because he considered himself better than her.

Rudolph tried to banish the thought as soon as it surfaced, bury it deep, but the seed of doubt had been planted, and it was quickly sprouting into a towering sequoia of second guesses.

He tossed and turned until the anemic light of dawn bled through the curtains to paint his bedroom in a sickly gray.

He rolled out of bed with a groan, joints popping in protest as he shambled to the bathroom. He made a half-hearted attempt at making himself decent, more for the benefit of others than out of any sense of propriety. The last thing he needed was his disheveled mug plastered all over some influencer's social feed.

Rudolph slipped out of the penthouse, ignoring his doorman's judgmental glare as he stumbled past him and out onto the streets.

The predawn cityscape had a haunted beauty. Long shadows and empty sidewalks, the chaos of humanity still tucked away behind drawn curtains and locked doors.

An outer landscape to match his inner turmoil.

He stalked through the concrete maze with his jaw set and shoulders hunched against the chill. His traitorous feet knew the way, even if his brain was still stuck in a screeching loop of festering doubt and second guesses.

Lumina lay ahead, its gleaming facade jarringly out of place in the gray light. He paused across the street, pulse quickening at the thought of the potential revelation waiting inside.

Moment of truth. Do or die. Shit or get off the proverbial pot.

He closed the distance in a few long strides, drawing a deep breath before pushing his way inside, where his eyes fell on Claudia's painting, still perched in its place of honor.

Rudolph approached it, studying each brushstroke and searching for the elusive spark of genius he might have missed.

But there was nothing. No hidden depths, no unexpected nuance. Just the same garish colors and clumsy composition he had ridiculed the day before.

His lip curled in a familiar sneer of derision. He'd been right the first time. This was utter dreck. An insult to the very concept of art.

And then his eyes snagged on the little profile card beside the painting, zeroing in on his own name with laser focus. *Inspired by the groundbreaking work of Rudolph Knox*, the text proclaimed.

A rage flared within him, sudden and incendiary, scorching through his veins like wildfire. The absolute fucking nerve of this glorified finger-painter, daring to tether herself to him. As if her hackneyed scribblings could ever hope to breathe the same rarefied air as his work.

He grabbed the nearest heavy object without even thinking — a pretentious metal sculpture titled Thing 5, that looked like a seventh grader's shop class project — and hefted it high. His vision tunneled to that taunting card: Claudia's name sitting so brazenly beside his own.

One hard smash ought to do the trick, shatter the glass and send that eyesore of a painting tumbling to the ground where it belonged.

Alarms were shrieking before he could even complete the swing.

He flinched, the sculpture slipping from his fingers to clatter harmlessly against the reinforced glass.

Shatterproof. Of-fucking-course.

For a heartbeat, Rudolph stood frozen like an idiot, wincing against that piercing wail.

Then he shook himself out of his daze just as the first distant siren started up outside. He was already in motion by the time a pair of rent-a-cops came charging in from the back, barking orders he didn't bother to parse.

They shoved him out the front doors, and then he began running full tilt, sneakers slapping the pavement, racing down the street.

Rudolph darted around corners and vaulted low walls on pure instinct, heart pounding, putting as much distance between himself and the scene of his almost-crime.

He didn't stop until the wailing sirens had long since faded behind him, and the burn in his lungs became as impossible to ignore as the stitch in his side.

Only then did he stop, hunching over, hands on knees, sucking in air like a drowning man. Only after the black spots finally cleared from his vision did he look up to take stock of his surroundings.

Rudolph had somehow managed to run himself right into one of his own paintings. A true-to-life portrayal perfectly recreating his *Despair on 42nd* piece from a few years back.

He vented a choked little laugh, half disbelief and half hysteria, before taking a moment to breathe in the familiar imagery. He remembered crafting this piece during a black hole of depression that had threatened to swallow him whole.

He had been near the end of his rope. Ready to say fuck it all on his way to becoming yet another tortured artist statistic. Another bright flame snuffed out too soon by his own demons.

But Rudolph had rallied. Fought his way back from the brink through sheer force of will. Poured all that angst and misery into his art until the canvas was saturated with it.

Looking at it now, with the benefit of distance and hindsight, he found not an ounce of joy in the memory. No sense of pride in how far he had come. Only the phantom ache of old scars and a bone-deep weariness borne from the endless cycle of needing to reinvent himself.

The nonstop scramble to stay relevant. To push himself harder, dig deeper, carve out his pound of flesh for the insatiable maw of an audience always hungry for the next big shock or latest scandal.

Rudolph Knox could paint his every neurosis across a football field in his own blood, and they would still beg for more. And the greediest mouths were always closest to the front of the line.

Fuck, he was tired. Exhausted from playing the game. From dancing on command for the masses. Tired of the need to top himself on repeat, and chase that dragon of public adoration. All so he could pay some bills.

What would it take to satisfy their gluttony once and for all?

The obvious answer loomed in his mind like a specter, grim and inexorable.

Rudolph shoved it aside with a shudder.

No. Not yet. Not like this.

He had to see this through, whatever 'this' turned out to be. The paintings come to life, the impossible made manifest. He couldn't just let magic like that slip through his fingers, even if it wasn't real.

Rudolph straightened back up, his spine popping in protest. He could still salvage this. Smooth things over with the gallery, maybe throw some money at the problem until it went away. He just needed to get his head on straight. Come up with a plan and—

A flicker of movement in the corner of his eye.

Rudolph turned just in time to catch a glimpse of his portrait's frame vanishing around the nearest corner.

He blinked, momentarily frozen. What the fuck was it doing here? Had the deranged figment of his imagination followed him all this way just to rub salt in the wound of his failure?

Rudolph jogged to the alley mouth and peered into the gloom as if expecting to find more than rats and garbage. But even his own subconscious was turning on him now.

He scoffed, shoving both hands in his pockets as he turned back toward the gallery.

Might as well get this over with. Face the music and

dance his practiced little jig of contrition until everyone was satisfied that the tantrum-ridden artist had learned his lesson.

The gallery's gleaming facade lay ahead. Crisp lines and bright windows, the opposite of his bedraggled state. He squared his shoulders and walked faster, rehearsing his most disarming smile and smoothest lines on the way.

Some hapless assistant blanched at the sight of him, frozen like a deer in high beams.

Rudolph didn't bother to slow his stride, breezing past the stammering boy with barely a nod of acknowledgment. The gallery was almost peaceful. Art hanging smug on pristine walls. Untouchable. Mocking him with its unassailable distance.

He stalked through the space in a daze, only half-registering what he was seeing. The world seemed to blur, a sea of colors and shapes refusing to find meaning.

He caught sight of Claudia's other pieces scattered throughout the gallery like breadcrumbs in a trail of mediocrity. A triptych here, an oversized canvas there.

But they looked different in the light of day. Less grating, somehow.

Rudolph paused in front of a large abstract work, head tilting as he tried to parse the swirl of textures and shapes. There was an energy to the brushstrokes, a sense of joyful abandon that made his chest ache.

When was the last time he'd felt that kind of uncomplicated joy in his work? That electric thrill of creation for its own sake?

Rudolph couldn't remember. It had been buried long ago, crushed under the weight of expectations and neuroses and crippling self-doubt.

He moved down the line in a daze, barely registering the little red *SOLD* plaques adorning most pieces. Of course, they had sold. The public always lapped up bright and accessible work like this. All flash, no substance. Didn't matter that it was derivative of his superior—

"You've *got to be kidding me*," hissed a voice in his ear, so sudden and vicious that Rudolph nearly jumped out of his skin. "They're loving this hackneyed trash. Lining up to throw money at it. How does that feel, knowing you've been usurped by an inferior version of yourself?"

"Shut up!" Rudolph growled through clenched teeth, hands flexing at his sides. "You don't know what you're talking about."

"Don't I? Seems pretty clear to me, bucko. The student has become the master. Claudia's brand of derivative slop is what the people are apparently buying these days. Happy little clouds and dancing shapes without a tortured thought in sight. Face it, Rudy. You're a dinosaur lumbering toward the nearest tar pit."

Rage bubbled up in his throat like bile, hot and acidic. He whirled on his heel, one hand cocked back to deliver a punch that would send the portrait's painted teeth rattling—

And found himself face to face with the wide eyes of the gallery assistant, his terrified face hovering inches from the artist.

"M-Mr. Knox!" The kid shrank back from Rudolph's anger. "I'm so sorry, I didn't mean to startle you! I just wanted to let you know how honored we are to have you here, and Ms. Knopf—"

"Spare me the sycophantic bootlicking!" Rudolph shouldered past the quaking assistant. "I'm not here for Knopf. I'm here for answers."

His eyes snagged on the nearest painting, the one he'd been studying before the ambush. He couldn't look directly at the perversity. An insult to the true artist's struggle. How dare she peddle this swill, polluting the world with her hollow platitudes? How dare the unwashed masses lap it up like the idiotic cretins they were?

Red bled into his vision, a haze of impotent fury blurring all rational thought. His hands moved without conscious input, ripping the offending canvas off the wall with a snarl of rage.

The frame splintered under his fingers, bits of cheap plywood digging into his palms. One hard shake and the canvas tore free, fluttering to the floor at his feet.

Rudolph felt untethered, unmoored, swept up in the catharsis of destruction. This was his purpose and calling. To tear down the false idols. Expose the frauds for what they were.

"Rudolph." A familiar voice pierced the fog of his rage, sharp and incredulous. "What in God's name do you think you're doing?"

He whirled to find himself staring down the flabbergasted face of the gallery owner. Neil something-or-other, some pompous British export who'd made a name for himself peddling the work of clueless yuppies who wanted art that matched their fucking couch.

Rudolph didn't wait to hear Neil's indignant sputtering or the assistant's frantic apologies, shoving past them both and out the door through the gathering crowd of gawkers, out into the unforgiving light of day.

He ran. Until his lungs burned and his vision swam, buildings blurring together in a smear of concrete and glass. By the time his legs finally waged their rebellion, Rudolph was by the river, chest heaving. He collapsed against the railing.

The water churned, dark and turbulent. He felt unspooled, the threads of his sanity fraying like canvas he had pulled from the wall.

The shrill ring of his cellphone pierced the fog of his despair.

Rudolph fumbled it out of his pocket. It was Monica. He jabbed at the screen with a shaking finger.

"What?"

"Rudolph, what the hell is going on?" Monica sounded furious. "Neil just called. He said you destroyed a piece at the gallery? Your piece? *Jesus,* what were you thinking?"

Rudolph had no idea.

And what was she talking about?

He wasn't showing at the gallery. Claudia—

But Monica kept going.

"Any chance of keeping your identity under wraps is shot to hell now. By noon, the entire art world will know that Rudolph Knox and Claudia Knopf are one and the same."

Rudolph blinked, unable to parse her words. "What?"

"What do you mean, what?"

Rudolph licked his lips. "That's… that's impossible, I'm not …"

But even as the denial formed on his tongue, a creeping sense of dread washed over him. Fractured memories clicked into place like puzzle pieces, and he couldn't finish the thought.

Instead, he hung up the phone.

And again, Rudolph ran.

All the way to his penthouse.

~

RUDOLPH TORE INTO HIS APARTMENT, ripping open cabinets and overturning furniture until he finally unearthed an old wooden trunk from the back of his supply closet, hidden behind a mountain of half-used paint tubes and moldering sketchbooks.

He wrenched open the lid, his hands shaking as the hinges whined. He tossed aside sheaves of yellowed paper, digging to the bottom until his fingers closed around a tattered leather notebook.

Sinking to the floor amid the detritus of his life's work, he flipped through the pages with a sense of growing trepidation.

And there she was.

Claudia, rendered in loving detail.

Only her name was Nancy. His best friend from art school, his partner in creative crime. They had constantly pushed each other to take risks. To be bold and unapologetic in their work.

Until that fateful critique, when their professor had sneered at Rudolph's art and labeled him a derivative hack. An untalented wastrel coasting on the coattails of his betters.

Nancy had tried to comfort him, but Rudolph pushed her away in a fit of wounded pride. He couldn't stand to look at her or stomach the pity that had darkened her eyes.

So Rudolph ran, just like he always did. Cut ties without looking back, excising everyone who knew him as a fraud so he could reinvent himself as someone worthy of respect.

Somewhere along the way, Nancy became Claudia. A fiction, a joke, a sadistic monument to his own self-loathing. And Rudolph let the world believe it, content to languish in obscurity as long as his "true" art remained unsullied by his own sordid reputation.

He opened another notebook, this one filled with sketches of Barrington captured in charcoal, immortalized in splashes of watercolor, every image suffused with a tenderness that pierced Rudolph's heart.

Barrington had stood by him through his many fits of mania and held him when the black fog of depression threatened to eat him alive. A decade of unwavering devotion that Rudolph had repaid with casual cruelty, confident that he would never leave.

He clutched the notebook to his chest and staggered to his feet.

He had to make this right. Try to salvage the tattered remains of the only relationship that ever really mattered.

An hour later, Barrington's brownstone loomed before him.

He climbed the steps on leaden feet, each one an effort of will, hesitating in front of the heavy oak door with his fist poised to knock. But he couldn't. He was a coward to the end. So Rudolph bent to leave the notebook leaning against the frame.

He was halfway down the steps when a creaking of hinges sounded behind him.

Rudolph froze, heart in his throat.

Barrington stood silhouetted in the doorway, haloed by the warm light of the foyer. He looked down at the notebook, then back up, his expression unreadable.

"I'm sorry," Rudolph said. "For everything. You deserved so much better than what I gave you. Better than me."

His eyes darted around, expecting to see the looming specter of his self-portrait. But the Echo was gone. Stripped to his barest truths, the delusion could no longer find purchase.

Barrington picked up the notebook and thumbed through the sketches, with an almost reverent touch. He stopped at one and smiled. When he finally met Rudolph's gaze again, his eyes had softened with something dangerously close to forgiveness.

"Why don't you come inside?" He stepped back to allow Rudolph's entry. "It looks like you could use a strong cup of tea."

"No."

Barrington's face shuttered again.

"No tea," Rudolph stumbled on. "What I could use is a friend." He was tired of fighting the better angels of his nature. He wanted to talk to the one person who truly knew him.

Barrington smiled. "Come on, then."

Rudolph ascended, stepping past Barrington and crossing the threshold into warmth and light.

He stood there, face unmasked, his skin a maze of geometric wrinkles.

His eyes filled with tears.

Barrington closed the door and wrapped his arms around him.

And for the first time in longer than Rudolph Knox could remember, he sank into the sun instead of raging against the dying of the light.

They stood there for hours. Barrington listening to his fears, anxieties and terrors. Holding him gently. Until finally he found the courage to face the blank canvas of his future.

Sometimes in order to be found, you had to get really lost.

~

Aftershocks on Illustrating Life

. . .

I WAS WATCHING a documentary about an artist whose magazine covers had helped to shape decades of visual culture, when this creative nightmare first took root.

What if your art came alive … and started critiquing you?

Rudolph Knox has everything an artist is supposed to want. Fame, fortune, a penthouse overlooking Manhattan, and a retrospective documentary that canonizes his genius for posterity. His illustrations grace museum walls and coffee table books. His name gets dropped in the same breath as legends.

He's built a cathedral of accomplishment, but he's trapped inside it, suffocating on his own success.

Illustrating Life became my meditation on the artist's curse: the gap between what we create and what we dream of creating. Rudolph has mastered his craft, but he's desperate to transcend the boundaries of traditional media, to breathe actual life into his work. And when his self-portrait steps off the canvas and starts offering advice, he thinks he's finally achieved the impossible.

The real story here is the ways we shatter ourselves in pursuit of perfection, then spend years trying to reassemble ourselves from the pieces. How fame can become a funhouse mirror that distorts every relationship. How success can isolate you from the very humanity that feeds creativity in the first place.

Rudolph's journey from tortured genius to genuine human is every artist's story compressed into its essential elements: the hunger for recognition, the corrosive effects of ego, and the long, painful process of remembering why we started creating in the first place.

This story closes our collection because it's about coming home — not to a place, but to the person you were before you learned to perform yourself. To the truth beneath the performance. To the people who saw you before you became a brand. To the blank canvas that's both terrifying and liberating because it contains infinite possibility.

We create because we have to. Because something inside us demands expression, even when that expression costs us everything we thought we wanted. The real magic isn't bringing art to life — it's remembering how to breathe life into yourself.

And sometimes, to find that magic again, you have to stop performing genius and start practicing humanity.

Thank you for taking this journey with me. Every story has been a window into the ways we lose ourselves and, if we're lucky, find our way back.

The canvas is blank again.

Infinite with possibility, electric with promise.

Time to see what we create next.

About the Author

Sean Platt has always been an entrepreneur, but stories were the business he was born to build.

When his wife bought him a laptop for his birthday in 2007, he dropped everything to write fiction.

After a short stint as creative director at a marketing agency — where he learned the kind of copywriting that could turn cliffhangers into an art — Sean wrote hundreds of novels (including international bestsellers), penned Hollywood scripts, and founded Sterling & Stone, an IP incubator where more than two dozen writers turn wild ideas into world-changing stories.

Originally from Long Beach, California, Sean now lives in Austin, Texas, with his wife, Cindy, and their dog, Fisher — both of whom remind him that real life makes the best stories.

Also By Sean Platt

Echoes of Tomorrow

Synthetic Eden

Hubris Rising

Divine Blueprint

Genesis Undone

The Dead World Series

Dead Zero

Dead City

Dead Nation

Dead Planet

Empty Nest

The Beam Series

The Beam Season One

The Beam Season Two

The Beam Season Three

The Beam Season Four

The Beam Season Five

Robot Proletariat Series

En3my

Robot Proletariat

The Infinite Loop

The Hard Reset

Cascade Failure

Reboot

The Tomorrow Gene Series

Null Identity

The Tomorrow Gene

The Tomorrow Clone

The Eden Experiment

Karma Police Series

Jumper

Karma Police

The Collectors

Deviant

The Fall

Homecoming

Yesterday's Gone

October's Gone

Yesterday's Gone Season One

Yesterday's Gone Season Two

Yesterday's Gone Season Three

Yesterday's Gone Season Four

Yesterday's Gone Season Five

Yesterday's Gone Season Six

Tomorrow's Gone

Tomorrow's Gone Season One

Tomorrow's Gone Season Two

Tomorrow's Gone Season Three

Available Darkness

Darkness Itself

Available Darkness Book One

Available Darkness Book Two

Available Darkness Book Three

WhiteSpace

WhiteSpace Season One

WhiteSpace Season Two

WhiteSpace Season Three

Z2134

Z2134

Z2135

Z2136

The Dream Engine Series

The Tinkerer's Mainspring

The Dream Engine

The Nightmare Factory

The Ruby Room

The Pandora Core

The Engine Convergence

Stand Alone Novels

Burnout

The Island

Crash

Emily's List

Pattern Black

Devil May Care

The Secret Within

The Sleeper

Last Night Never Happened

I Am John Titor

www.ingramcontent.com/pod-product-compliance
Lightning Source LLC
Chambersburg PA
CBHW011112100726
47898CB00011B/3052